A KILLING CURE

"A real treat . . . Secret passageways, a coded ledger, a mysterious group known only as the Chamber, experimental drugs, blackmail, sexual assault, betrayal: all the ingredients of a good whodunit."

—*Lambda Book Report*

A SMALL SACRIFICE

"A smart and shocking thriller."
—*The Minnesota Daily*

FAINT PRAISE

"Packed with mystery and scheming characters, *Faint Praise* is one of the year's best. It's no wonder Ellen Hart is everyone's favorite author."

—R. D. ZIMMERMAN

By Ellen Hart
Published by Ballantine Books:

The Jane Lawless Mysteries:
HALLOWED MURDER
VITAL LIES
STAGE FRIGHT
A KILLING CURE
A SMALL SACRIFICE
FAINT PRAISE

The Sophie Greenway Mysteries:
THIS LITTLE PIGGY WENT TO MURDER
FOR EVERY EVIL
THE OLDEST SIN
MURDER IN THE AIR
SLICE AND DICE

Please turn to the back of the book
for a conversation between
Ellen Hart and Sophie Greenway

Praise for Ellen Hart and her Sophie Greenway mysteries

THIS LITTLE PIGGY WENT TO MURDER

"Strong characters and a rich Lake Superior setting make this solidly constructed mystery hard to put down. Another winner for Ellen Hart!"

—M. D. LAKE

"There are some good, nail-bitingly-tense scenes and lots of red herrings."

—*Publishers Weekly*

FOR EVERY EVIL

"A dilly . . . A fair-play plot and contemporary characters that leap off the page . . . Stir in Martha Grimes with P. D. James and add a dash of Christie and Amanda Cross and you begin to get the idea: a cozy with a brain."

—*Alfred Hitchcock Mystery Magazine*

"Another splendid specimen of the classical mystery story, nicely updated and full of interesting and believable characters."

—*The Purloined Letter*

Praise for Ellen Hart
and her Jane Lawless series

HALLOWED MURDER

"Hart's crisp, elegant writing and atmosphere [are] reminiscent of the British detective style, but she has a nicer sense of character, confrontation, and sparsely utilized violence. . . . Hallowed Murder is as valuable for its mainstream influences as for its sexual politics."

—*Mystery Scene*

VITAL LIES

"This compelling whodunit has the psychological maze of a Barbara Vine mystery and the feel of Agatha Christie. . . . Hart keeps even the most seasoned mystery buff baffled until the end."

—*Publishers Weekly*

STAGE FRIGHT

"Hart deftly turns the spotlight on the dusty secrets and shadowy souls of a prominent theater family. The resulting mystery is worthy of a standing ovation."

—*Alfred Hitchcock Mystery Magazine*

SLICE AND DICE

Ellen Hart

FAWCETT BOOKS • NEW YORK

A Ballantine Book
Published by The Ballantine Publishing Group
Copyright © 2000 by Ellen Hart

www.randomhouse.com/BB/

Library of Congress Catalog Card Number:

ISBN 0-345-42153-1

Manufactured in the United States of America

First Edition: September 2000

OPM   12   11   10   9   8   7   6   5   4   3

For Joe Blades, editor, mentor, dear friend—with
gratitude and much affection

Every great man nowadays has his disciples,
and it is always Judas who writes the biography.
—OSCAR WILDE
The Critic as Artist

Acknowledgments

Many thanks to Rick Nelson, food staff writer at the *Minneapolis Star Tribune*, for his insight into the inner workings of restaurant reviews and reviewers. Also, thanks to Dr. Tom Rumreich for his always fascinating forensic expertise. And finally, thanks beyond measure to Kathy Kruger and R.D. Zimmerman for reading the book in manuscript form and offering not only patient encouragement, but sound advice.

Cast of Characters

SOPHIE GREENWAY: Owner-manager of the Maxfield Plaza hotel in St. Paul. Restaurant critic. Wife of Bram Baldric. Mother of Rudy.

BRAM BALDRIC: Radio talk-show host for WTWN in the Twin Cities. Sophie's husband.

CONSTANCE BUCKRIDGE: Cookbook author. Founder of the Buckridge Culinary Academy in New Haven, Connecticut. Mother of Nathan and Emily. Stepmother of Paul. Wife of Wayne.

NATHAN BUCKRIDGE: Chef. Director of the Buckridge restaurant chain. Son of Constance. Sophie's old boyfriend.

PAUL BUCKRIDGE: Chancellor of the Buckridge Culinary Academy. Chef. Brother of Emily. Stepbrother of Nathan.

MARIE DAMONTRAVILLE: Writer-biographer.

LELA DEXTER: Guest at the Maxfield Plaza.

EMILY BUCKRIDGE-MERLIN: Photographer. Wife of Kenneth. Daughter of Constance. Half-sister of Nathan and Paul.

KENNETH (KENNY) MERLIN: Constance Buckridge's attorney. Husband of Emily.

DAVID POLCHOW: Chef at the Belmont.

HARRY HONGISTO: Owner of the Belmont. Old friend of Sophie's father.

GEORGE GILDEMEISTER: Restaurant critic at the *Times Register* in Minneapolis.

ARTHUR JADEK: Author. Professor. Clinical psychologist. Constance's brother.

WAYNE BUCKRIDGE: Paul and Emily's father. Owner of Buckridge Construction. Husband of Pepper. Later, husband of Constance.

PEPPER BUCKRIDGE: Mother of Paul. Wayne's first wife.

Prologue

Late October, 1963

It wasn't fair. Pepper had waited for years to have a child, and now that she had a beautiful little four-year-old boy, she was too sick even to play with him. She sat in a wooden lounge chair at the edge of the water, watching her son, Paul, dig in the sand next to the dock. He was such a sweet child. Wispy blond curls and a sunny smile. He had her husband's aqua-blue eyes and his intense scowl, but in every other way he was a miniature reflection of her. He even had her love of the outdoors. It didn't matter that the air was chilly and a dreary fog hugged the shoreline. Every afternoon after his nap, come rain or shine, little Paul had to have his time down by the dock.

When her husband, Wayne, had first started construction on their Lake Minnetonka house six years earlier, the forty-eight steps leading from the back porch down to the lake had seemed like nothing. Now it was a daily struggle. If her health didn't improve, it wouldn't be long before she couldn't make it at all.

Pepper had spent the last five months visiting one doctor after another, trying to find answers. She'd seen at least a dozen specialists, taken more than three dozen tests, and been prescribed a mountain of pills. And yet, except for the dizziness, the tiredness, the stomach pains, the eye problems, and her growing anxiety, nobody could agree on what was wrong with her. Her husband had tried to remain supportive and loving, but she could feel him losing patience.

"Mrs. Buckridge?" came a soothing voice.

"Yes?" she said, removing her eyes from her son and fixing them on the young, attractive, blonde-haired woman who was leaning over her chair. "Oh, Connie. It's you."

Connie Jadek had been a maid at the Buckridge home for almost two years. Last spring she'd taken over as the cook. Although she seemed competent enough, Pepper didn't like her. Her constant cheerfulness was enough to drive anyone to drink.

"I brought you another blanket," said Connie. "I thought you might be cold." She spread it over Pepper's legs.

"What about my rum and Coke?"

"It's on the table right next to you."

Pepper glanced to the side.

"Are you sure you wouldn't like something to eat?"

"No, nothing." Even the idea of food made her sick to her stomach.

"Can I get you anything else?"

Before she could respond, she heard Paul calling, "Nonnie! Nonnie!" He tossed his tin shovel in the sand and ran to show Connie what he'd found.

She bent down to look at the small feather in his hand. "Oh, that's beautiful, Paul. We'll have to put it with all the others."

Pepper was instantly furious. Why hadn't Paul shown *her* the feather first? He'd spent so much time with Connie lately that she'd almost replaced Pepper as a mother figure. She fed him all his meals. Played with him on and off during the day. Read him stories and then tucked him in bed at night. It was insidious, but because she was too weak to do anything else, Pepper had to sit by and watch it happen. She'd mentioned the situation to Wayne just last night, said it was becoming intolerable. But he wouldn't hear of any more staff changes. They'd already gone through three nannies. Nobody did anything well enough for Pepper's high standards. What the hell did she want, anyway?

She'd screamed at him that she wanted her life back. She wanted to be healthy, to take care of Paul herself, the way she had when he was a baby. She ached for the feel of him, for the smell of his hair. *She* was his mother, for God's sake—not these strangers! Couldn't Wayne understand how hard it was for her to watch her son transferring his affections to others?

"What's the solution?" Wayne demanded. "You're too sick to take care of him yourself. What am I supposed to do? Let him fend for himself while I'm away at work? Do you want him crawling around the house eating bug killer and stuffing marbles in his ears?"

She knew there was no good answer. Connie would stay, of course, as would the rest of the staff. Until Pepper felt better, she'd simply have to live with the consequences of her illness. But she'd be damned if she'd let anyone take her son away from her.

"Paul," she said softly, reaching out her hand. "Come sit with Mommy."

The little boy handed the feather to Connie, looking uncertain.

"Aren't you cold?" asked Pepper. "Come get under the covers with me and we'll watch the waves together. I'll tell you a story about when I was a little girl."

Hesitantly, the boy got up and stood next to the chair.

"That's all, Connie," said Pepper dismissively, taking several swallows of her rum and Coke—her third of the afternoon. "Come back in half an hour. We'll be ready to go in by then."

Connie nodded, looking hesitant herself. Finally, giving a tiny wave to Paul, she turned and walked back up the steps to the house.

Once Paul was bundled up next to her, Pepper stroked his hair and said, "You know Mommy loves you more than anything else in the whole wide world."

He made a movement that was part nod, part yawn.

Pepper had lived her whole life on Lake Minnetonka. As a child, she'd discovered a secret: The lake had a heartbeat. Sometimes it was wild and roaring, sometimes it was buried under layers of ice and snow, but it was always there, full of spirit, strong, and insistent. Now the sound of it gave her courage. "Mommy's been sick for a long time," she said, kissing the top of her son's head, "but she's going to get better."

"Can we play in the park tomorrow?"

"No, not tomorrow." She sighed, realizing she'd disappointed him once again. "But soon. Very soon. I promise."

He buried his face in her sweater. "Okay." His tiny arms hugged her tight. "I love you, Mommy."

Her heart nearly broke. "Don't ever forget this moment," she whispered, her arms wrapped around him. "And please, Paul, whatever happens, don't ever forget me."

PRESENT DAY

Journal Note

Friday, 3 P.M.

No sign of her yet. I've registered at the hotel under an assumed name. I'll go with my standard game plan this time and reserve using my real name until later. I shouldn't have any trouble passing as just an ordinary tourist.

Tomorrow I start planning the preliminary interviews. I've spent months reading everything I could get my hands on about Constance Buckridge, America's culinary sweetheart. Books, articles, old television programs—getting the facts and figures straight. But this is where it all began. Ground zero.

My own personal "Deep Throat" inside the Buckridge camp insists that the bodies are moldering beneath the floor-boards, just waiting for me to dig them up. He hasn't been specific, but he's promised me that my time will be well spent. I have a good feeling about this project. The hero with clay feet—my specialty.

More later.
M.

1

Sophie had hoped that after a couple of martinis and a plate of the Belmont's famous tiger shrimp on a bed of spicy couscous, Bram would be in a good enough mood for her to drop the bomb. She'd been preparing her speech all afternoon—ever since she'd talked to her son, Rudy. Rudy was currently biking and backpacking his way across Europe with his partner, John Jacoby. On the phone, they'd made an important decision, one she needed to tell Bram about right away. However, not only were the tiger shrimp no longer on the menu, but the usually prompt and friendly service at the restaurant was tonight a study in indifference. Any good mood the drinks might have engendered had been destroyed by the annoying boy-waiters buzzing about the dark, intimate dining room.

Neither Sophie nor Bram had eaten at the Belmont since last fall. Almost all the old wait staff was gone, replaced by a more youthful crew, lads who seemed to think having fun was the essence of their job description. They clumped together at the wait stations, chuckling at little in-jokes, and occasionally, when the mood struck, wandered off toward one of the gilt-edged mirrors to check their look. They were exceedingly adept at pouring water, but that was about the extent of their skills. Initially, Sophie and Bram were so amazed by the staff's bustling inactivity that they hardly noticed that their waiter had hardly noticed them.

Twenty minutes after their arrival, having received nothing more than two glasses of water and a couple of menus, Bram reached his limit. At first he tried some polite arm-waving, but when that was ignored, he stood, placed two fingers between his teeth, and gave a piercing whistle. Not only did that catch their waiter's attention, but every other eye in the place as well. Most of the other diners nodded their approval. Some even clapped.

According to local restaurant scuttlebutt, the Belmont, an institution in downtown Minneapolis, was currently having problems. This was clear not only from the lax service but also from the wilted rose on the table, as well as the pile of dry toast and a slice of bland pâté the waiter brought them when he finally sauntered over to take their order.

"What the hell's happened here?" muttered Bram as the young man strolled off toward the kitchen.

Sophie just shook her head.

Harry Hongisto, the owner of the Belmont since the early Fifties, was an old poker-playing buddy of her father's. They were both Finlanders from the Iron Range, both born and raised in Hibbing. During the past winter, Sophie had been sad to see a restaurant review in the *Times Register* trash the food at the Belmont. She couldn't believe the place had sunk that low, especially since she knew the bias of the reviewer, a man with whom she rarely agreed. And yet, perhaps in this one instance, the review had foundation. For the first time, Sophie felt as if she was sitting in the faded glory of what had once been a premier restaurant in the Twin Cities.

That wasn't to say that Harry hadn't done his best in the last few months to stem the tide of decline. First, he'd hired David Polchow as the new head chef. Arriving with the highest of recommendations, David was a graduate of the New Orleans Cooking Institute and had studied under some of the best chefs in Europe. He'd worked at Sur la Mer in Boston before coming to Minnesota. His attempts to improve the food service at the Belmont, however, didn't seem to be working. Sophie couldn't understand how a chef of his caliber could have produced such an insipid pâté, though perhaps it was an off night. Or, more likely, the rest of the kitchen staff wasn't working at his level. He could do his best to educate and make demands, but he couldn't do all the work himself.

Harry had also begun to modernize the interior, though interior decorating seemed to be the least of the restaurant's problems. It was true, of course, that the wine-colored leather booths, once the height of elegance, had begun to look a bit tired. So had the pool-table-green walls and the heavy-handed gold accents. In an earnest attempt at modernity, Harry had replaced the carpeting, a bold playing-card design of clubs, hearts, diamonds, and spades, with a dreary putty color, all wrong for the more aggressive Las Vegas–style ambience. And plants, totally unnecessary greenery, seemed to be starving for light in every corner of the room. The Belmont had history and tradition going for it. It had a flavor, a style. All it needed was some retouching—not a whole new look. Ferns and minimal furnishings belonged in a more self-conscious Uptown bistro. A less self-conscious, more overt Fifties take on opulence was the name of the game here. Why not appreciate it for what it was?

"A piece of rancid pâté for your thoughts," said Bram, gazing at Sophie over the rim of his martini glass.

Her smile was wistful. "Oh, I was just thinking about what this place used to be like."

"You came here with your parents a lot when you were a kid, right?"

"In those pre-cholesterol-conscious days of yore." She sighed.

"Well, at least there's one upside to the evening. We're not here so that you can review the place. That headache is finally behind us."

Sophie did her best to hide her startled look. "You never told me you hated my reviewing."

"I didn't *hate* it, but on those rare occasions when you convinced me I had to come with you, you insisted I wear one of those silly disguises, too. It made me feel like a freak—not, I might add, the best way to enjoy an evening out with one's wife."

"Come on," she said, smiling and chucking him on the

arm. "Restaurants today are theatre. You simply have to think of yourself as one of the cast."

He grunted. "I never understood how you could enjoy eating a meal dressed like a biker's moll."

"I had other costumes."

"Right. The professor with the beard and pipe. Very sexy."

She was beginning to believe that he really had hated her reviewing. "But, honey, I needed to keep my identity a secret. When you came with me, you did, too. Otherwise we'd get the royal treatment. I wouldn't be able to report accurately on the food or the service."

"Well, now you don't have to report on it at all." It was Bram's turn to chuck her on the arm. "We also won't have to put up with irate restaurant owners and chefs calling you in the middle of the night to rant about how you slandered their béchamel sauce—or whatever."

She had to admit that she'd never much liked that part either.

Last fall, Sophie's parents announced their intention to retire and spend some time traveling around the world. In a matter of days, Sophie found herself the surprised and somewhat bewildered new owner of the Maxfield Plaza in downtown St. Paul. She'd been playing catch-up all winter, trying to get a handle on the day-to-day running of a large metropolitan hotel. Bram had grumbled every now and then about how much time she was spending in her office and how little time she was spending with him. His job as a talk-show host for a local radio station didn't consume him in quite the same way Sophie's new position consumed her.

Sophie was a perfectionist. She also couldn't stand the thought that she might fail her father, a man who had total confidence that his only daughter could take over the reins of the hotel and run it profitably and well. During the winter, she'd let every nonessential part of her life slide, including her occasional restaurant reviews for the *Times Register*. She simply couldn't do everything. Her editor at the paper hadn't wanted to lose the column. Since she'd begun writing it five years earlier, Sophie had developed quite a loyal following, and that kind of interest sold newspapers. But she had to put the hotel first.

Once she had everything in order at the Maxfield, she'd promised Bram, she wouldn't put in such long hours. She'd already begun to ease up on some of her duties. For the most part, Bram had been a good sport about the extra workload, because he expected their lives would get back to normal sooner or later. And that was Sophie's dilemma now. How could she tell him about the phone call she'd received yesterday?

"You seem kind of preoccupied tonight, honey." Bram gave her hand a reassuring squeeze.

She tried a smile but knew it was a weak attempt.

"You know, Soph, when you get that look on your face—"

"What look?"

"The one where your eyes get all big and round and . . . well, you start to look like some tragic Dickensian waif. Sometimes I get the irresistible urge to find you a bowl of gruel."

"Cute."

Unfortunately, Sophie knew Bram's description was accurate. She'd looked like a waif ever since she was a small child. The fact that, barefoot, she was just over five feet tall only added to the image. Actually, her Tiny Tim face, as she thought of it, was why she favored tailored "power" clothes, spike heels, and a sophisticated and short cut for her strawberry-blonde hair. "How nice that you see me as such a strong, independent woman."

"But I do," he protested. "You're beautiful. Sexy. Everything a guy could want. I just see other sides of you as well. Sometimes, when you get upset, flustered that maybe you're not doing the right thing, that's when Oliver Twist appears."

"Tiny Tim," she muttered, correcting him.

"Whatever."

"And what side of me do you see tonight?"

"The one that wants to tell me something but is afraid I won't like what I'm about to hear."

It galled her that she was so transparent.

"So, tell me, Tim, what's the big secret? Once it's out in the open, we can have our argument, and then, when I've won, you can enjoy your sea scallops in lobster sauce and I can enjoy my steak."

Sophie knew the humor and the smirk were intended to lighten the mood, make it easier for her to say what she had to say. Bram was essentially a kind man, though he hid it well on his radio show, where raucous opinion was the name of the game. "First you've got to promise you won't get mad. That you'll think about what I'm going to say before you respond."

He touched his fingers lightly to the knot in his silk tie. "I am the picture of rationality, as always."

"Finish your drink."

He eyed her a moment, then downed the martini in two quick gulps.

"Good. Now . . ." She took a deep breath, then began. "Yesterday afternoon I got a call from Yale McGraw."

"Managing editor at the *Times Register*?"

She nodded. "It seems George Gildemeister announced last week that he was going to retire." George had been the food editor and primary restaurant reviewer at the paper since the mid-Seventies. He also happened to be the man who'd written the negative review of the Belmont.

"And?" said Bram, elongating the word.

Another deep breath. "They've offered me his position—if I want it."

Bram cocked his head. "Am I missing something here? You have a job, running one of the most prestigious hotels in downtown St. Paul. It already takes all of your waking hours just to handle that. Or is the operative word here 'waking'? Are you planning to give up sleeping?"

She ignored his sarcasm. "The position at the paper wouldn't need to be a full-time one. Besides, I'm in the process of cutting down on my hours at the hotel. Things are humming along pretty smoothly now. I feel like I can ease back on some of the reins."

He gave her a disgusted look. "You're kidding me, right? You're not really serious about this. I already have to make a date weeks in advance if I want to have a five-minute conversation with you. I'd never see you if you took a second job."

"That's not true," she said, twisting the wedding ring on her finger.

"Maybe it's not literally true, but it's the way I feel."

"But . . . just give me a chance to explain how it would work." When he didn't object, she continued. "I told Yale that I'd think about it, but only on one condition. I want to hire a full-time assistant, someone I can train to do some of the reviewing as well as answer mail, E-mail, and phone calls and take care of the website. And someone who could organize all the menus we'll be receiving. George stopped keeping them on file years ago. If you ask me, he's been coasting for a long time, waiting for his magic sixty-fifth birthday. I know I could do a much better job. I adore food, Bram. I always have. I remember my whole life in terms of the food I've eaten. And I've got the absolutely perfect candidate for the assistant position."

Bram had all but tuned out. "Who?"

"Rudy."

His head popped up. "You're going to ask them to hire your son?"

"He'd be perfect for the job. He's responsible, intelligent, and he's been cooking part-time in the Maxfield's kitchen for the last year. Now that he's graduated from the university, I think it would be good for him to work nine to five for a while. Get his feet under him before he decides what to do next. He's got three major interests—food, theatre, and theology. I don't have a crystal ball, so I don't know where he'll ultimately end up, but I know he's currently unemployed. And I'd dearly love to work with him, teach him what I know about the restaurant world, pass on my love of food."

"Doesn't Rudy have something to say about this? He might hate the idea."

"He doesn't," said Sophie, leaning back as their meals arrived. "I caught up with him at the youth hostel in Venice this afternoon. Explained the entire situation." Her eyes took on an excited glow. "He *wants* to do it, honey. He's agreed to work with me!"

Bram cut into his steak, mulling the idea over. "I get it now. This isn't so much about becoming the food editor as it is wrangling a chance to work with Rudy."

"Do you blame me? I've lost so much time with him, honey. Since he's willing, how can I turn it down?"

Sophie had been separated from her son for most of his life. The reason why was a long, convoluted, and ugly story. He'd only come back into her life a few years earlier. Working together would give her a chance to get to know him in a way she'd only dreamed about.

"I can see that any protests I might make would fall on deaf ears."

That hurt. "Bram, listen to me. You have my solemn promise that I won't let this new position interfere with our lives any more than absolutely necessary. You've been nothing but patient with me while I've been learning the ropes at the Maxfield."

"Damn straight I have."

"As soon as I get Rudy trained, we'll take a long vacation. Anywhere you want. Just as long as we're together—and alone."

"I want that in writing."

She could tell he'd relented. That he wouldn't fight her. "I'll start collecting travel brochures first thing in the morning, right after I have a meeting at the paper with Yale and George."

"And when does Rudy return from his European adventure?"

"A week from this Sunday."

Bram was about to make another comment when the sound of a loud crash and angry shouts burst from the kitchen.

"What the hell is that?" he demanded, turning around.

The shouting didn't let up. If anything, it grew even more hysterical.

"Maybe we better check it out," said Sophie. She'd recognized one of the voices as Harry Hongisto's. From the tone of the commotion, she was concerned that he might be in danger.

There was another loud bang.

"Come on," said Bram, pushing his chair away from the table. "At times like this, I wish I looked more like our honorable governor, Jesse the Body."

"Worry about your pecs later, darling."

"That's the problem, *dear.* I never worry about my pecs."

2

"A gun! Somebody just get me a gun."

When Sophie and Bram entered the kitchen, they found a man in a white chef's uniform waving a newspaper under Harry Hongisto's nose. Harry looked shaken, his ruddy complexion even ruddier than normal. His black tuxedo and immaculate white shirt—Harry always dressed formally to meet and greet customers—had been splashed with something red, most likely tomato sauce, and the halo of white hair that surrounded his balding crown, usually perfectly combed, stuck out at odd angles, making him look as if he'd been electrocuted.

"What's going on?" demanded Bram.

The chef whirled around. "This," he said, his eyes flashing. He pointed to the paper, then ripped it to shreds and threw it on the floor. "Who the hell does that guy think he is? Auguste Escoffier?"

Sophie eased up next to Harry, laying a hand on his arm. "Are you all right?" she asked, sotto voce.

He grimaced, then whispered back, "No."

"Of course he's not all right," snapped the chef. "Tell them what was in the paper, Harry. Tell them!"

Harry cleared his throat. "We got another bad review today."

"I'm so sorry," said Sophie. "Who from?"

"Gildemeister."

"Again?"

"Yes, *again*," bellowed the chef. He was a small man with a long, narrow face, thin sharp nose, and fierce eyes. "He said our food was so bad the last time he was here that he wanted to return to the scene of the crime to see if we'd actually killed anyone with our beurre blanc!"

"Did he really say that?" asked Sophie.

Harry shook his head. "He came back to give us a second chance."

"Some second chance," roared the chef. "It was butchery from start to finish!"

Harry—always the gentleman, even in the worst situations—said, "Bram, Sophie, I'd like you to meet Chef David Polchow. David's been with me now for almost four months."

"Four grand and glorious months," repeated David, eyeing the rest of the kitchen crew with disdain. Unlike the waiters, they were standing apart from one another, in different sections of the room, but each as far away as he or she could possibly get from the chef. "I've worked at some of the top restaurants in the world and this is the first time anyone's ever called my vegetables mushy. Mushy!"

Sophie could see the fury in his eyes. He obviously wasn't the kind of man who let criticism roll off his back.

"I'm so sick of this bloody expression 'al dente,' " he continued, picking up a boning knife and pointing it menacingly at Harry. "The rule is, vegetables should be cooked. Not overcooked. Al dente is the excuse people use for undercooked vegetables. 'Oh, why, they're *supposed* to be that way, they're al dente,' " he simpered. "Yeah, right." He paused, nailing everyone with his eyes. "You know what they are? They're salad. Raw vegetables are *salad*!"

Harry nodded weakly.

The chef continued to glare until he'd assured himself that everyone understood his point. "When will people learn that it's not against God's immutable laws to cook a vegetable? That reviewer flaunts his ignorance. He doesn't know a damn thing about food or service or dining. Reviews are just a pissing contest, anyway. *Mushy* vegetables. Give me five minutes alone with that guy and I'll show him a mushy vegetable!"

"Come on, David," said Harry, trying to sound as soothing as his deep, gravelly voice would allow. "Let's just get back to work. We've got customers out there."

"How can you bear to have me cook for you? According to the grand George Gildemeister, I'm the cause of this restaurant's demise. You should fire me! String me up by my thumbs and flog me till the blood spurts."

The head chef's personality inevitably sets the kitchen's zeitgeist. Sophie couldn't imagine what it would be like to work for someone with such a hot temper.

"Of course I'm not going to fire you."

"No?" David's eyes shot flames. "Then I quit." He pulled off his paper chef's hat and threw it on the floor next to the review. "Mark my words, Harry. One of these days somebody's going to see that one of those ignorant idiots meets with a small accident. In a just universe, they'd be skewered on a spit until they were roasted clear through—and I don't mean *al dente*."

Gathering up his knives, Chef Polchow took one last look at the empty line, then left through the back door, slamming it on his way out.

Once he was gone, everyone in the room heaved a collective sigh of relief.

"Back to work," ordered Harry, clapping his hands. "Matthew, for the time being, you're the head chef. Get everyone back to their stations."

The sous chef nodded. A few seconds later the kitchen once again bustled with activity.

"I need a drink," said Harry, squeezing the back of his neck.

"Sit with us at our table," suggested Sophie.

After Sophie and Bram resumed their seats, Harry arrived carrying a snifter of brandy. He looked worn out, his eyes bloodshot. For the first time, Sophie could see the result of the stress he'd been under. She felt more than a little guilty for being part of the crowd David Polchow wanted to fricassee. She didn't agree with him about critics, but she felt terribly sorry for Harry. First thing on her agenda when she got back to their apartment at the Maxfield tonight would be to find a copy of today's *Times Register* and read Gildemeister's review. Perhaps he had crossed the line. If so, Sophie would do everything in her power to remedy it. The problem was, most of the damage had already been done.

"I've about had it," said Harry, tipping the snifter back and taking several swallows.

"Maybe you should take the rest of the night off," said Sophie. "Go home and watch a movie. You'll feel better in the morning."

"No," said Harry, his wide blue eyes clouding with emotion. "You miss my point. I mean I've about had it with this restaurant. Being a restaurateur has to be the hardest way in the world to make a living. What am I? Some sort of masochist? We got problems all the time. First we don't get deliveries on time. Or we get them but the produce is wilted or the fish isn't fresh. Then it's an argument with the deliveryman and a fight with the vendor. And finally it's a mad scramble to find what we need to replace what we didn't get. I don't have the energy I used to. I'm tired and I'm sick of dealing with arrogant assholes like Gildemeister."

"He's retiring," said Bram, pushing his cold steak away.

"So? Another jerk will take his place."

Sophie didn't say a word. This was a good example of why most restaurant reviewers didn't develop close friendships with chefs and restaurateurs. It was too painful. And yet, in this case, she didn't have a choice. She'd known Harry since she was a child.

"You know what it's like?" continued Harry. "You get a bad review and it hurts business. Customers stay away. So you end up with too much inventory and eventually serve food that isn't quite up to your normal freshness standards. If you don't use the food, your profit margin takes a nosedive. But you end up losing money anyway because some of the produce inevitably spoils before it's sold and you have to dump it. So then you reevaluate your ordering. But because you put out substandard food for a few days, or a few weeks, you lose more customers and the cycle continues. You don't know how to plan anymore. None of this is David's fault. He's a talented chef, one of the best I've ever worked with. It's just that that first review hurt us. And unless you believe in miracles, today's installment will probably kill us. I can't fight it any longer, but it makes me so damn mad I could spit nails." He downed more of the brandy, then went on. "I go home at night and I write letters to the editor at that damn paper. To date, I've written seventeen, all of them unprintable. To think that one man could wield such power."

Sophie might have pointed out that Harry's current problems were a combination of many factors, though she had to admit that it was probably the review that had tipped the scales.

Harry finished his drink, his anger building.

"Hey, buddy," said Bram. "You'd better go easy on that stuff."

"Why?" Harry asked. "It's not every day you see your life's work crumble before your eyes."

Sophie and Bram sat with Harry for another hour, listening to his tale of woe. He covered the same ground over and over again. Since the death of his wife four years earlier, Harry made it clear that he'd lost his best friend and sounding board. The restaurant had become his whole life, and now it was about to be taken away from him. The conversation occasionally veered into surprisingly venomous tirades. Neither Bram nor Sophie could offer much other than a sympathetic ear.

When they finally parted, shortly before ten, Sophie still hadn't told Harry that she would be replacing George Gildemeister at the *Times Register*. The truth was, she didn't have the nerve.

Journal Note

Friday, 9 P.M.

She's arrived. Finally. I'm sitting in the lobby, watching her entourage swirl around the bell captain and the front desk like a bunch of sleek, well-dressed ocelots. I expected to see Constance and her lawyer, Kenneth Merlin—apparently, she never travels without him—but I was surprised to find the rest of the family in attendance, too. Something big must be in the works, something other than a simple stop on a promotional tour for Constance's newest cookbook. How a woman who has morphed into the living embodiment of Betty Crocker could have produced such a strikingly handsome set of children is beyond me. They're all adults now and will surely play a role in her story.

This is so delicious—food fit for the gods. What's so special about gourmet cuisine when you can serve up good, old-fashioned scandal?
M.

3

Not being terribly interested in spending the shank of the evening alone, Bram decided to make a small detour into Scotties, the Maxfield's first-floor bar, to have that second martini he'd never ordered at the Belmont. Sophie had some hotel business she needed to attend to before she could join him upstairs in their apartment.

Because it was such a beautiful springtime evening, Scotties wasn't particularly crowded. Bram nodded to a few regulars, then slipped onto one of the chrome bar stools and ordered his drink. Pulling a basket of peanuts in front of him, he eyed the photographs of various theatrical stars hanging on the wall behind the counter.

A few minutes later, as he was being served, an attractive woman sat down two stools away. She placed her order—a Tequila Rose on the rocks—then removed some pamphlets from her purse.

Bram glanced at her and smiled.

She smiled back.

After a few awkward moments, the woman said, "Of all the gin joints in all the world, I've got to sit down next to a guy who looks like—"

He held up his hand. "Don't say it."

"You object to looking like an old-time movie star?"

"No, but after a good night's sleep, I look much more like Tom Cruise."

She laughed.

He knew he was flirting, but it was fun. And meaningless. "You'd be amazed what eight good hours can do to wash away the years."

"Would I?"

"I'd never lie to a beautiful woman."

She smiled again. This time she turned to face him. "Lela Dexter." She held out her hand.

"Bram Baldric." For some reason, she looked vaguely familiar, though he couldn't say why.

"Are you a guest at the hotel?" she asked as her drink was set in front of her. She signed the receipt, charging the drink to her room.

Bram noticed that her shiny black hair was pulled up in a pearl-studded net. Very classic. Next to the dark hair, her skin was a fine white porcelain. The red lipstick and bluish eye makeup suggested a French figurine—flawless, touched with just the right amount of color, yet essentially cold. "Not exactly."

"A man of mystery."

"Would that bother you?"

Her eyes dropped to his wedding band. "It might bother your wife."

He held up his drink, saluting her, tacitly suggesting she was undoubtedly right.

She glanced over her shoulder for a moment and surveyed the room, then shrugged and turned back to him.

Bram figured she'd decided he was the best bet in town. She might as well stay put.

"I'm here on vacation," she said, removing a cigarette from her purse. Before she could find her lighter, the bartender appeared with a lit match. He was a new employee, a kid in his midtwenties, and Bram assumed his hormones were on overdrive. "Thank you," she said, rewarding the bartender with an amused nod. Turning back to Bram, she continued. "I flew in this afternoon from New York."

"Where you live?"

"Now and then."

She obviously wanted to project her own sense of mystery. "Do you have family here?" he asked, popping a couple of peanuts in his mouth.

She shook her head.

"You're traveling alone then?"

This time her smile was more openly seductive. "Why, sir, where I come from, all these questions would seem extremely forward."

Under the hard New York inflection, he noticed a hint of softness. A drawl, if he wasn't mistaken. "If I had to guess, I'd say you grew up in the South."

"You have a good ear, Mr. Baldric. I'm originally from Savannah."

"Midnight in the Garden of Good and Evil."

She shuddered. "Horrible book. It made the entire town look like a freak show. Have you ever been to Savannah?"

"Years ago. I was a DJ at a local radio station there for about six months. That was back in the Seventies, during my wild, impetuous youth."

"You're no longer impetuous?"

He wasn't going to touch that. The gleam in her eyes told

him they were getting awfully close to a line he wouldn't cross. "You know, I loved everything about Savannah. In so many ways, it doesn't even feel like it's part of the same country as Minnesota."

She studied him through the smoke from her cigarette. "And your career in radio. What happened to that?"

"Actually, I have a talk show here in the Twin Cities now. It's just recently been syndicated to nine states, but not as far away as New York. I doubt you've heard of it."

When she turned to him this time, Bram could see a question in her eyes. "A talk show. How . . . fascinating."

Something had just happened, though he couldn't say what it was. "You know, this may sound crazy, but you seem familiar to me. Could we have met somewhere before?"

"I'm sure I'd remember if we had."

"What do you do in New York?"

Drawing on her cigarette, she said, "I work at the UN. I'm senior attaché to Steven Bell."

"Our new ambassador?" He laughed, then shook his head. "And what does a woman used to living in the fast lane do for a vacation? She comes to the Maxfield Plaza in sunny St. Paul, Minnesota."

"Don't put your town down. It's lovely. Charming even. And this hotel, it's like stepping back into the Thirties. It must have been the height of luxury back then." Her eyes took on a faraway look. "Gangsters with guns under their double-breasted suits and handsome men in tuxedos. Women in fur, crepe de chine, and pearls, sipping champagne while they danced the night away. Fated love and illicit desire. Hatred, passion, lies, and lust . . . maybe even murder."

Tugging his collar away from his neck, Bram said, "You have quite an imagination, Ms. Dexter."

"Lela."

"Maybe you should have been a writer, not an attaché."

She just smiled at him.

"I take it Art Deco buildings really speak to you."

"Don't tell me you can't feel it. This hotel reeks of adventure."

His smile turned to a grin. "You came to Minnesota

seeking adventure? Maybe you saw *Fargo* one too many times."

She ground out her cigarette, a faint smile pulling at the corners of her mouth.

"Well," said Bram, holding up his drink. "Here's hoping you find it."

She touched her glass to his. "I think I already have."

4

When Sophie entered George Gildemeister's office on Saturday morning, she found him sitting in his chair, feet up on his desk, reading a seed catalog. In his jeans and red plaid shirt, he was the picture of a burned-out food critic. His office, while almost neat to a fault, reflected far more interest in his current passion: horticulture.

Plants were everywhere—draped off cabinets, crowded onto his desk and on the window ledge behind him. There were even seed pots resting under a grow lamp on top of a filing cabinet. On the floor to Sophie's right was a circle of nasty-looking cactus plants. To her left was a table filled with orchids. This greenhouse-away-from-home might have made sense if George wrote the gardening column, but he didn't. He would talk endlessly about his hobby farm, the weather, the new corn hybrid he'd just planted, but rarely would he ever mention the wonderful sea bass Provençale or espresso fudge soufflé he'd been served at a local restaurant. When Sophie spied the Jell-O snack carton on his desk, it was the last straw. She marched into the room and said, "Jell-O, George? *Jell-O?*"

He glanced up at her. "Oh, morning, Soph. Have a seat.

Yale will be here any second." He returned his attention to the catalog.

People had known for years that George was coasting on the reputation he'd made during the Eighties. Five years earlier, after buying the hobby farm up near Fergus Falls, he'd become the farmer in the dell. Colleagues at the paper even called him silly names behind his back. It seemed that his passion for food was totally gone. He still kept an apartment in the city, but every moment he could spare away from his job at the paper was spent on "the land," as he referred to it, with his wife, his two golden retrievers, and his garden.

Well, Sophie thought, glaring at the Jell-O carton, the corn plants could have him.

She was just about to sit down when there was a knock on the door. A second later Yale McGraw entered. He looked his usual harried self, the stub of an unlit cigar clenched between his teeth. Yale, like George, was in his early sixties, but whereas George could easily have passed for middle-aged with his dark hair and healthy tan, Yale looked every minute of his sixty-two years. He was tall and lanky—well over six foot five—and when stressed, his arms and legs flew out at odd angles, much like a marionette manipulated by a novice puppeteer. He combed his white hair straight back from his forehead, allowing the world an unencumbered view of his classic Roman profile. Put a laurel wreath on his head and he'd be the spitting image of Julius Caesar—Caesar with a stogie. It was an image he nurtured, though everyone knew McGraw was a notorious softie. It didn't always make him the best managing editor, but it did make him a valued friend. He was well loved at the *Times Register*.

Dumping a pile of papers onto George's desk, Yale fell into a chair. "Lord," he said, biting down hard on the cigar. "What a day." He glanced at George, then at Sophie. "I'm glad you could make it," he said, giving her his trademark scowl. "I hope you brought a decision with you."

"Me, too," said George, tossing the seed catalog into a side drawer. "I've given two weeks' notice, but I'd like to be out of here as fast as possible." He sniffed the air, then glared at Yale. "You smell like an ashtray."

"I've been down in the smoking lounge. Don't worry, George, I won't light my stogie around your precious plants. We wouldn't want them to have a collective asthma attack. The noise would be deafening."

"Damn right you won't," muttered George. Switching his glare to Sophie, he continued. "You already know the drill. You should be able to step in without any hand holding."

"So what's it gonna be?" asked Yale, turning to her with his formidable gaze.

The moment had come. She hadn't realized she'd be this excited. "Yes, I'd like the job, providing you can meet two conditions."

Yale shifted in his chair, removing the cigar from his mouth. "You said one condition yesterday, Sophie. You wanted us to hire you a full-time assistant—in this instance, your son. I'll have to look at his résumé, of course, but I think I can guarantee it won't be a problem."

Now she was even more excited. "Rudy will be home from his trip next Sunday. I'll make sure he sets up an appointment with you right away."

"Fine," said Yale. "Now about this other condition . . ."

Sophie knew her second point might be a harder sell. Even so, she felt so strongly about it that in her mind it was a potential deal breaker. Taking a deep breath, she plunged ahead. "I don't want to use a star system for rating restaurants."

"What?" George sat up in his chair. "We've always used a star system. I instituted it twenty-three years ago."

"And now that I'm on board, I want to do away with it." She'd prepared her arguments ahead of time, so she started right in. "Star systems might work in Europe, but they don't here. In France, for instance, stars represent levels of refinement, so you know you need to achieve certain standards to qualify for certain star levels. But in the United States, there are no clear standards. When the restaurants being reviewed range from multimillion-dollar enterprises to simple storefront eateries, the system breaks down. It becomes meaningless."

"No, it doesn't," insisted George, his round face growing flushed. "Yale, tell her she's wrong."

Yale folded his arms over his chest. "I'd like to hear a little more on the subject—from both of you. A little healthy debate."

George shot him an exasperated look. "Look, the use of stars forces a reviewer to be honest. You can't be wishy-washy. You have to make a clear statement and then you use the force of the stars to back it up. Even Sophie has to admit that the market today demands stars. It adds weight and significance to a review. All the big boys do it, so we should, too. And then . . . well, there's a more pragmatic reason."

"What's that?" asked Yale.

"Time. It's a quick way for our readers to decide where to spend their hard-earned money. As far as I'm concerned, the case is closed."

"But that's just my point," said Sophie. "People look at the stars and don't read the review—and they should."

"It'll never work," said George, shaking his head. "People who read this newspaper expect our restaurant reviews to include ratings. Even the restaurants themselves expect it."

"The luxury restaurants perhaps. But is a luxury context always better than, say, an ethnic restaurant that operates on a shoestring?"

"You're muddying the point."

"That is the point," said Sophie. "Not all the restaurants in this town fall along the same continuum. Even you have to admit you don't have a clue how to rate some places."

George grunted.

"And even with the luxury restaurants, you could have meals there during a two- or three-week period, write your review, and then two weeks later the chef quits. But the rating stays until you get around to reviewing the restaurant again, which could be years later. It's not fair."

"Oh, I get it. You're going to be a bleeding-heart-liberal food critic. Fairness above standard business practice. Good luck," George said, spitting the words at her. "In my mind, fairness should remain secondary to truth."

"But, George," said Sophie, exaggerating her patient expression, "restaurant reviews aren't about truth, they're about *opinion*. Educated opinion, certainly, but opinion nonetheless."

"She's just throwing dust in the air," George blurted out, pointing a finger at her but looking at Yale. "That's what happens when you give a tough job to a woman. Criticism isn't for the faint of heart."

"You mean people like Ruth Reichl? Phyllis Richman? Gael Greene?"

In a slow, reasoned tone, Yale asked, "So what's your reviewing philosophy, Sophie?"

She'd thought about that a lot over the years. "Well, I'd say that the quality of the food always comes first. Next would be service. Third, atmosphere. It's an entire package, but again, just because you're sitting in the midst of luxury doesn't mean you're going to have the best dining experience. I want the review itself to be entertaining, fun, but I prefer to write my critique from the standpoint of an average diner. Since I know a great deal about different cuisines, where I can educate, I will."

"I educate all the time," muttered George.

"You mean, like your review of the Belmont?"

George flicked his eyes toward Yale. Pulling some dead leaves off a small schefflera, he said, "No, that was more on the order of a funeral notice."

"It was a hatchet job."

"And completely deserved."

"A review like that is never deserved."

"That's where you and I disagree. It was a tough call, but I made the only honest one I could."

"To destroy a restaurant?"

"I don't have that much power, Sophie. All I did was report on the demise, which, I might add, was a fait accompli before I ever walked in the door."

"Thanks to your earlier review."

"I call 'em as I see 'em. That's all any critic can do."

Yale stopped the argument by holding up his hand. "George,

I agree with Sophie. I think you did go overboard on that last review of the Belmont."

"Well, then," smirked George, "I guess you'll just have to fire me."

Yale gave him a pained look. A second later there was another knock at the door. One of Yale's editorial assistants poked his head in the room. "Sorry to interrupt, but I think you better take a look at this." The young man entered and handed an envelope to Yale.

As he pulled the letter out, Sophie could see that it was handwritten. She waited while Yale read through it.

Cupping a hand to his forehead, Yale finally said, "We better notify the police about this."

"Yes, sir," said the assistant.

"What is it?" asked George.

Yale sighed. "It's a letter from Harry Hongisto, the owner of the Belmont. It's addressed to you."

"Me?"

"Well, it's addressed to 'that piece of slime restaurant critic.' I assume he means you."

Sophie would have laughed out loud if the look on Yale's face hadn't been so grim.

"Let me see that," demanded George. He got up from his chair, walked around the desk, and yanked the paper out of Yale's hand. Adjusting his glasses, he read through it, then handed it back, looking more than annoyed. "The guy's a nutcase."

Sophie couldn't let that one pass. "I've known Harry Hongisto for many years. He's hardly that." She wanted to read the letter, but Yale had already given it back to the assistant, who had left immediately. "Since I'll be taking over George's position, I'd like to know what it said."

"It was a death threat," said Yale. "Hongisto said that any man who could take away another man's livelihood just to show the reading public what a clever wit he had didn't deserve to live."

Still standing, George folded his arms and rested them on his protruding stomach. "Just what I'd expect from someone like Hongisto. Sending a poison-pen letter shows what a coward he is."

"Harry's no coward," said Sophie.

Yale looked at her pointedly. "You think he intends to carry out his threat?"

"Absolutely not," she said quickly. "That's not what I meant. Besides, I'm not even sure you could call it a real threat. After what's happened, I think the man is justifiably frustrated. Angry. Hurt. Writing a letter is certainly preferable to coming over here and punching George out."

"If he can't stand the fire, he should get out of the kitchen."

Sophie groaned. "Gee, George, what happened to your 'clever wit'? If you wrote like you spoke, you would have been out of a job years ago."

He stared at her for a second, then reached down and grabbed his briefcase. "You know what, folks? I quit. No two weeks' notice necessary for that."

Yale stood to block his path. "George, wait." He flung his arms out awkwardly. "You don't want to leave on such a sour note. At least write your swan-song column for next weekend."

"Have her write it," George said, pointing his thumb at Sophie. "Oh, and since she's the new girl around here, she can cover Buckridge's event this afternoon at Kitchen Central. I intend to spend the rest of the day at the Como Conservatory communing with nature. "

"George, please."

"Get out of my way, Yale."

Looking defeated, Yale stepped aside and let him go.

Journal Note

Saturday, 1 P.M.

Got another E-mail message last night from Pluto, my "Deep Throat." He says he's in town, too. (Perhaps staying at the Maxfield?) He promised he'd be around to help me with my search, and he appears to be a man of his word. Not that he wants me to know who he is. Ever since his first contact five months ago, he's been using a pseudonym as well as an anonymous remailer. I suppose I could contact his E-mail server to try to find out his real name, but from what I've heard, some of these Internet remail groups are so private, it would take a court order to get the information I want. Pluto has his agenda and I have mine. But I do wonder why his privacy is so important.

Since he signs his messages with a male name, I guess I'm just assuming it's a man. Sloppy thinking like that won't get me anywhere. But I've been calling him "him" so long, it would feel awkward to change now. I just need to remember that Pluto may be a woman.

NOTE: Do some study into the origin of the name Pluto. It might help to figure out who s/he is.

Of course I have to find out. I can't stand not knowing— it's what makes me such a good "biographer to the stars." Ask Elton John or Liza Minnelli. I don't leave any stone unturned.

Last night's missive simply said: "Find a man called Oscar Boland. He lives somewhere in the Twin Cities. Ask him what he knows about Wayne and Pepper Buckridge. Press him hard. Don't let him brush you off. Next, get ahold of Eleanor Simpson. Last I heard, she was still working at the ABC affiliate in town. Ask her about the Constance Buckridge Show. *To find the gold, you'll have to dig deep. I want to know what you learn, so type up your interview notes and send them to me. Remember, no notes—no more help. Good luck. Pluto."*

Pluto has me convinced that there's a dark, deeply twisted story here. But I've been warned to tread softly. So I spent the morning chasing down leads. I finally found Boland. He lives in a condo in Edina. He agreed to meet me for a drink at eight this evening. Simpson was a little harder to find. She retired from the ABC affiliate two years ago. I finally located her, living with her daughter in Lake Elmo. I'm going to drive out to talk to her tomorrow—after she gets back from church. I can't help thinking I've somehow landed in Lake Wobegon

*and this woman will want to feed me Powder Milk Biscuits
after playing me a few Lutheran hymns on the piano in the
parlor.*
M.

5

Sophie returned to the Maxfield shortly after one. Before
leaving the paper, she and Yale had talked over her idea of
ending the paper's star system. He eventually gave her his
tacit agreement, though he didn't seem sold on the idea.
Changing a long-established custom was going to take some
getting used to, but Sophie hoped that in a year, Yale's attitude
would be far more positive.

After spending a few minutes going through George's
files, looking for a folder, a memo, anything that might tell
her which restaurants were slated to be reviewed in the next
month or two, she gave up in frustration and left for home.
She made a mental note to contact him tomorrow and ask
where his schedule was. Surely he had some record, some
system. In the past, when she'd done her guest reviews for
the paper, George had simply given her an assignment and a
deadline and she'd taken it from there. She'd never been involved in the day-to-day operations. Now that she was in
charge, she had a ton of questions and lots of important decisions to make. She'd hoped that George's research would
help ease her into the transition, but for the moment she was
on her own.

Once she'd returned to her office at the Maxfield and sat
down behind her desk, she placed a call to Harry Hongisto.
She wanted to warn him about Yale's reaction to his letter. He

needed to know that, whatever his intent had been, Yale viewed it as a real threat. She was positive Harry had only been expressing his frustration, but sending even a potential death threat through the U.S. mail was probably some sort of crime. Sophie wouldn't be a friend if she didn't tell him that he might be in hot water. The wisest course of action would be to send an apology right away—as much as it might stick in his throat. It was best to diffuse a potential explosion before someone got hurt.

After several rings, someone finally answered the phone. When Sophie asked to talk to Harry, she was told that he wouldn't be in until dinnertime. Since she knew he rarely missed a day at work, she found his absence strange, but she shrugged it off, thinking that he probably needed a break after the previous night's events. Retrieving her personal address book from the bottom desk drawer, she tried his house next but once again was thwarted when his machine answered. She'd simply have to call later.

The next order of business was to check the newspaper's website for George Gildemeister's recent reviews. Normally, she read all the restaurant reviews that were published in the Twin Cities during any given month, but she'd been too busy lately.

After spending a good hour playing catch-up, she felt the need for a short break. She hadn't had much of a breakfast, so lunch seemed like a good idea. Passing by the reception desk on her way up to the café, she checked to see that everything was running smoothly. For a Saturday, the hotel seemed unusually quiet. Most people were probably outside taking advantage of the beautiful spring afternoon. That's what I should be doing, she thought sourly to herself, instead of being my usual, overachieving self. Bram had the right idea. He'd gone golfing. His tee time was so early that he'd invited her along, suggesting that she get in a round before her meeting at the paper. Maybe next weekend, she thought, sighing. She spoke briefly with Hildegard O'Malley, the hotel's general manager, then headed up the central stairs to the mezzanine level, where the Fountain Grill was located.

Standing outside the double glass doors, she checked the daily specials. They were posted in brightly colored chalk on a blackboard sitting on an old-fashioned wooden easel. It was going to be a long afternoon if she had to cover Constance Buckridge's appearance at Kitchen Central. She was about to succumb to the shrimp jambalaya when she felt a presence behind her. She turned and looked up into the face of a man she hadn't seen in more than twenty-five years. "Nathan?" she said tentatively.

"Sophie?"

The voice told her she was right. "What on earth are you doing here?"

He stared at her for a moment, almost too stunned to speak. "I'm here with the family. Mom's on a book tour. God, Sophie, you look wonderful."

The sound of his voice caused her to shiver slightly. It was the faint breath of memory. Seeing him again plunged her instantly back to her youth—to the last time they'd spoken.

It was the early Seventies. Against her wishes, Nathan had followed her to California, to the Bible college in Altadena where she was a freshman. She'd been adamant about not wanting to see him again. God had called her to a different life, a higher purpose. But he'd refused to understand, wouldn't let her go. She was the woman he loved, the woman he wanted to marry. She'd told him they were too young, that it was just infatuation, though she'd known in her heart that she was deeply in love. Giving him up, convincing him to return to Minnesota without her, had been the hardest thing she'd ever done in her young life. She'd actually seen it as the sacrifice God demanded of her to prove her devotion. She'd been eighteen, Nathan twenty. Colors had been brighter back then, emotions stronger. Urgency had been attached to every feeling, every thought. As she looked at him now, it surprised her to find those feelings still stirring. The passion might be gone, but the remembrance of that passion vibrated deep inside her. Nathan had been her first love.

"The . . . reservation," she stammered. "It said only 'Buckridge, three suites.' "

He cocked his head. "Did your parents tell you my mother was coming? They still own the hotel, right?"

"No," she said, continuing to stare at him. "I own it now. I saw the reservation the same day it was made. But I never expected you to show up."

"You own—" He stepped back, but his eyes remained fixed on hers. "But, Sophie, last I heard, you were living in Montana with your preacher husband."

"God, that was a lifetime ago. I guess we haven't . . . kept in touch."

"No," he said, his brown eyes softening. "So . . . are you telling me you're no longer part of that church?"

Even after all these years, his voice still held bitterness. "I haven't been for a long time."

"And your husband? The minister?"

"We're divorced."

He gave a slow nod.

Sophie's mind flooded with questions of her own.

"Look, I've got to head over to a book signing this afternoon. Mom's written something new and it's kind of a command performance. But"—he glanced at his watch—"what do you say we have lunch first? Catch up a little. Please don't say no, Sophie."

The truth was, she was eager to talk to him.

Once they were seated and had placed their orders, Nathan just stared at her, making her feel awkward, scrutinized much too carefully. She wasn't eighteen any longer and didn't figure she'd come out on top if he was making mental comparisons. Thinking she had to say something to break the ice, she nodded toward his face. "You don't have your beard anymore."

He touched a hand to his jaw. "No. When I began apprenticing as a chef, it was just too much trouble. Besides, I only grew it because I knew you wanted me to."

She smiled and shook her head. "I guess I always did like beards on men." She could still remember the soft, silky feel of it against her skin. "Probably my hippie leanings."

"Your radical period, right before your religious period. What period are you in now?"

She could read the humor in his eyes. "My boringly stable middle-aged period."

"Somehow I doubt that."

She hesitated. "Nathan, you're remembering someone who doesn't exist anymore. We knew each other a long time ago. A lot has happened since then."

"Do you remember where we met?"

"Of course I do," she said indignantly.

"Where?"

"A Greenpeace rally at the Unitarian Society on Mount Curve."

"Very good. What were you wearing?"

She groaned. "I can't be expected to remember that sort of thing."

"You were wearing tight-fitting bell-bottomed jeans and an equally tight-fitting fuzzy yellow sweater. I thought you were the most beautiful girl I'd ever seen."

"You were handing out leaflets at the entrance to the sanctuary."

"And I stopped you on the way out the door and asked if you needed a ride home."

"I thought you were pretty full of yourself—and more than a little dangerous. Seriously counterculture in your frayed jeans, work boots, and chambray shirt. You seemed so much older than me. I guess I was flattered that you'd even talk to me, but I was also more than a little scared."

"But you let me walk you through the park to your girl-friend's car. And you gave me your phone number."

"A moment of youthful insanity."

"Was it?"

She hesitated again, then said, "I thought you were the most gorgeous man I'd ever seen."

"I fell in love with you that night, Sophie. I went home and told my brother that I'd met the girl I was going to marry. Funny how things that seem so right can go so wrong."

She didn't know what to say, so she was glad when the

waiter arrived with their drinks. After taking a sip of her iced tea, she said, "That was a long time ago, Nathan."

"You keep saying that, but, to me, seeing you like this again . . . time has no meaning. How often have we eaten together in this very restaurant, Sophie? We'd head up here after a movie or a lecture and order cheese fondue for two and those huge Caesar salads. We'd talk until the waiters threw us out. And then, remember when we used to sit up on the roof, watch the stars come out? We'd bring a blanket. I'd smuggle a bottle of wine from my mom's wine cellar. It's where we first made love."

She felt the heat in the room zoom up a good sixty degrees. "Nathan—"

"You haven't forgotten. I can see it in your face. You could never hide what you were thinking from me."

"I don't want to hide anything." She pulled her iced tea in front of her. Thinking that she needed to cool the conversation down, she said, "Why don't you start by telling me what you've been doing for the last twenty-five years."

They both laughed at the absurdity of her request.

"I don't know where to begin," he said, pouring some cream into his coffee.

"Are you married?" Probably not the best question to ask right off, but she had to know.

He stirred the coffee for a moment, then said, "Well, I suppose it would be more romantic to say that since I couldn't have you, I've lived a life of total celibacy. Joined a monastic order. Eschewed all earthly pleasures. The truth is, I did try marriage once. It lasted two years—your basic disaster."

"Children?"

He shook his head.

"You said you'd become a chef."

"Must be in the genes."

The waiter arrived with their food.

Taking a bite of his grilled chicken sandwich, Nathan chewed for a moment, then pushed it away. "After you booted me out of your life, I hitchhiked back to Minnesota. It was a pretty rough time for me. I moped around the house for a while, but Mom finally put her foot down, said I had to get either a degree or a job. I toyed with the idea of working in a restaurant, but eventually I started at the U. I got sidetracked by anthropology for a while. It's really a very poetic science." He paused, collecting his thoughts. "Anyway, during the summer between my sophomore and junior years, I flew to Paris for an internship. That's where I had the experience that changed my life. It was a twelve-course meal, Soph. When I was done, I realized God had spoken through the chef. I knew then and there that I had to learn what he knew."

She could see the same old fire in his eyes. It was one of the qualities that had first drawn her to him. When Nathan got excited about a subject, he became totally absorbed and was capable of learning at a furious rate.

"That was a long time before Mom started her culinary academy, but her TV show was really catching on. The idea that her oldest son wanted to study cooking in Paris must have appealed to her. She offered to pay to send me to the Cordon Bleu. After I graduated, I worked in France for a while, then in Italy for almost ten years. In '86 I returned to the U.S. and worked at a bunch of exclusive country clubs and resorts."

"Like where?"

"Well, the Trump Taj Mahal Casino Resort in Atlantic City for one. We might do as many as twenty thousand meals a day. The last place I worked was a cattlemen's club in Houston. I was hired to be the garde-manger. One day I filled a ten-foot-long ice corral with twelve thousand shrimp and totally blew out my sciatic nerve. I was in bed for a month."

Sophie winced.

"Cooking is hard physical work. When I was young, I loved it. Loved the chaos. Sauté was the biggest challenge. It's where the action is. Fire this! Fire that! I could be jiggling eight or ten pans all at once, flames leaping, making things happen. I loved the hot seat in any kitchen. I met some pretty incredible people, too. I've worked for chefs that I knew were completely mad, but behind the line, they were geniuses. One guy, I never knew if he was laughing or screaming. It didn't matter. He was brilliant. The pace in a kitchen is fierce—everything's in motion. I guess I must love that kind of intensity. I couldn't imagine anything more creative, more sensual than working with food. I mean, when you cook, it's like making love. You're using your eyes, your mouth, your ears, every sense you have. And if you're really good, you're cooking with your soul, too. I couldn't get enough of it." He leaned back in his seat and took another sip of coffee. "But by the early Nineties, I was getting tired. Too many nights I'd end up in a bathtub with a woman I barely knew and a bottle of Johnnie Walker Red, just trying to survive the day. I'd been cooking professionally for fifteen years by then. Mom had started her school many years before. My brother had graduated from the Culinary Institute of America and was pretty much running the academy."

"Your brother, Paul?"

"You seem surprised."

She laughed. "All I remember is him looking like Ted Nugent and jumping out at me when I went over to your house."

"He still looks like Nugent, but he had to cut his hair to get into the institute, and now it's all falling out."

"Is he married?" she asked, her spoon midway to her mouth.

"No, he's too busy being Mr. Big Shot Administrator. He eats, sleeps, and breathes that cooking school." He shook his head. "I suppose Emily's the only one with a remotely normal life. She's got twin boys and a lawyer husband. My mother's already grooming the grandkids to take over the reins of her culinary empire. She cooks with them every Sunday—well, every Sunday she's in town."

"Your mom's really done well for herself. She's a huge name in the culinary world. Right up there with Julia Child and James Beard."

"Yeah, she's made history all right. And she's made money hand over fist with her books and TV shows. It really is an empire now. Six years ago, when I decided I was sick of beating myself up, she asked me to oversee a new project. She and Paul wanted to open a series of restaurants all over the country and use them as training grounds for young chefs coming out of the B.C.A."

Sophie shot him a questioning look.

"Buckridge Culinary Academy. Sorry, I'm used to our shorthand. Anyway, I'm no dummy. I jumped at the chance. Since I came on board, we've opened nine of the finest restaurants in the United States. As director of operations, it's my job to oversee them. We offer our top graduates a chance for some on-the-job training at a good salary, including benefits. Best of all, I'm not killing myself any longer and the pay is ten times better." Taking a sip of coffee, he added, "That's my life story in a nutshell. It's your turn."

Since he'd done most of the talking, she'd nearly finished her jambalaya. Tapping a napkin to her lips, she said, "I don't know where to start."

"I'll interview you. Do you have any kids?"

"One son."

"The preacher man's the father?"

She nodded. "His name is Rudy and he just graduated from the U of M with a degree in theatre arts."

"He wants to be an actor?"

"He has a lot of interests. Right now he's in Italy traveling with his partner, John."

Nathan looked confused. "Business partner?"

"His lover. Rudy's gay. Before they left, he and John had a commitment ceremony. We had the reception here at the hotel."

"Gay," repeated Nathan, giving her a hard look. "How do you feel about that?"

"I was surprised, I suppose, but I've got no problem with it. It's been a very hard road for Rudy, though. His father is still a minister and thinks Rudy is committing a terrible sin."

"Lucky for your son he's got one parent with sense. I look forward to meeting him someday soon. You know, Sophie, you always were a liberal at heart. That's why I could never understand how you could get involved with such a narrow-minded, conservative, even reactionary religion. How you escaped that group with your old self intact is beyond me." He reached for her hand. "I'm just glad you did."

Feeling more uncomfortable with each passing second, Sophie blurted out, "I married for a second time about seven years ago. His name is Bram. I know you'll like him. Everyone does."

Nathan sat up a bit straighter, withdrawing his hand. "You're . . . married?"

"I should have said something right away, but—"

"I didn't realize," he said, looking stricken. "God, you must think I'm some sort of sleazy creep to go on like this about our past."

"No, of course I don't."

He pushed his sandwich even farther away, then raked a hand through his hair. "I feel so stupid." He thought for a moment, then looked up at her defiantly. "Hell, no, I don't. I wouldn't take one word back. I'm just sorry . . . well, I mean, I'm happy that you're happily married. You are happy, aren't you?"

"Very."

"Umm." He tapped his fingers on the table. "Damn," he said, shooting her an amused smile. "I'm glad but I'm not glad. I mean, here I find you again after all these years, discover you've rejected the theological crap that kept us apart—something I thought would never happen—and you're *still* unavailable. It's a lot to assimilate, Soph. You're going to have to give me some time."

Which reminded her of one of her questions. "How long are you going to be in town?"

"That kind of depends." He glanced at his watch. "Look, it's getting late. I've got to get to my mother's book signing. You wouldn't want to tag along, would you? I know she'd be happy to see you again. So would Paul and Emily."

"Your brother and sister are here, too?"

"The whole clan. Even my uncle Arthur. Wolves travel in packs, remember?" This time his smile was less convincing.

She made a quick decision. Bram would probably be out with his buddies for another couple of hours. She'd already made a commitment to cover the event for the paper. It just made sense for her to go with Nathan. "I'd love to," she said, smiling broadly.

"Great." He took out his wallet.

She quickly laid her hand over his. "The meal's on me. Put your money away."

He grinned. "Just like old times, huh? We could always eat here for free." He turned his hand over and held hers for a moment. "God, I wish the rest of the world would just go away and leave us alone for a day, a month, the rest of our lives."

She gazed at him sadly. "Not possible."

"No, I guess not. But at least I've got you for the afternoon. That's a start."

It wasn't exactly the sentiment she wanted to hear, but she allowed him to hold her hand as she eased out of her chair. It felt so strange to be near him again, walking out the door with his hand pressed to her back. At the same time, she noticed a lightness inside her body she hadn't felt in years.

6

Bram returned from his golf game a little before two. After checking Sophie's office to see if she was around and finding it empty, he decided to take Ethel, their much-adored mutt, for a short walk down by the river.

Ethel's transition from living in a house in south Minneapolis to becoming a hotel dog had been rocky. Bram and Sophie had tried hard to ease her into her new digs, but Ethel was an old girl, set in her ways, and not terribly interested in new people, new surroundings, or even new tennis balls. The fact was, Ethel had never been a ball of fire. She walked slowly, ate slowly, slept soundly, and dragged through every day in third gear. She'd spent most of the winter moping around the apartment on the sixteenth floor, primarily because it didn't have an attached porch where she could sit and watch the garbage trucks lumber down the alley. Elevators were a brief curiosity, but she lost interest in them after a couple of weeks.

Down by the Mississippi, Ethel had rediscovered bug watching, a favorite activity now denied her because she had no patio to guard. *Activity* wasn't usually a word Bram associated with Ethel. Bug watching was about as athletic as she ever got. Knowing they had to do something to get her out of her funk, Sophie had finally come up with a plan.

One afternoon she went over to Manderbach's department store and bought a large, overstuffed pillow. That night she placed it next to their bed and encouraged Ethel to sleep on it. Ethel loved anything soft, so it wasn't a tough sell. She snoozed on top of it for several weeks before Sophie finally moved it to the hotel lobby. When Ethel saw the pillow in its new location, she immediately dragged her old bones over to it and slumped down. If she could have jumped for joy, she would have. Instead, she just morosely raised her eyes. Both Bram and Sophie recognized it as a good sign.

Now she reclined in comfort for most of the day, glowering at the guests. They might not be as entertaining as bugs or garbage trucks, but hotel dogs had to make certain sacrifices. The bellmen took her out regularly for her daily ablutions, while the rest of the staff fawned over her with comments like "The poor thing. She needs some cheering up." They all thought she was such a pathetic little pooch. Ethel was good at *pathetic*—she'd been working the image for years.

"Well, old girl," said Bram, giving her leash a gentle tug, "I think we better head back to the hotel. Your pillow's probably getting cold. And I've got some research I need to do for one of next week's shows."

Ethel smacked her jaws a couple of times, then looked up, giving him her most pitiful stare.

Back at the hotel, Bram stood for a few moments at the

reception desk, checking the day's mail. It was mostly bills, with one postcard from Rudy and John "somewhere in the Black Forest." Bram had grown close to Rudy and John during the past winter. They'd made a number of plans to get together for dinner, movies, theatre, and musical events, only to have Sophie back out at the last minute because of some crisis at the hotel. That left the three of them to trudge along without her. Eventually, they all became so annoyed with her continual excuses that they started referring to themselves as "the Stood-Up Club"—Rudy's term. Bram laughed at it now, wondering when Sophie would return from her meeting at the paper.

As he was about to lead Ethel back to her throne, she dropped like a ten-pound sack of potatoes on top of his loafers. He looked down at her, amazed at her lethargy. She couldn't even sit down and wait like a normal dog; she had to fall over. "Come on, old girl. You have to get your afternoon nap, especially if you're planning to have your usual rock 'n' roll evening lying on your pillow under the dining room table." He slipped the mail into the pocket of his jacket, then glanced up, surprised to find Sophie leaving through the front entrance. She was with a man Bram had never seen before. From their laughter and the intimate way the man maneuvered her through the doors, Bram wondered who he was. He would have shouted for Sophie to stop but didn't want to make a scene. The guy was probably just some bozo she'd met on the elevator. Nothing to get excited about. But where was she going?

Dragging Ethel over to the concierge desk, where Hildegard O'Malley was seated, he asked if Sophie had left him a message.

"None that I know of," she replied in her schoolmarmish, rounded tones.

He thanked her and was about to walk away when he heard a voice behind him say, "Does *that* belong to you?"

Bram turned to find the woman he'd met in the bar last night peering curiously at Ethel. She was dressed in gray slacks and a gray silk blouse. Both items of clothing accentuated her slim figure. Bram eyed her briefly, noticing she looked like a million bucks.

"Lela, hi. I didn't see you there."

"I was just using the hotel fax." She glanced down at the puddle of black fur covering his shoes.

"This is . . . ah, Ethel." He wiggled one of his feet, trying to get her to stand. "Ethel, say hi to Lela Dexter."

Ethel opened one eye.

"Actually, that was a rather warm hello for her."

"Is she yours?"

"Afraid so."

"But that's the dog that sits on that blue pillow between the club chairs in the lobby. I was told she belonged to the owners of the hotel."

"She does."

"*You* own this place?"

"Well, technically, my wife owns it. But it's a community-property state." He gave her a mischievous grin.

"You're full of surprises, Mr. Baldric."

"All good ones, I hope."

Placing a hand on her hip, she glanced up at the clock over the reception desk. "Do you have any plans for the afternoon?"

You had to give it to this woman. She wasn't shy, and that made Bram all the more intrigued. "That depends on what you've got in mind."

"A visit to Kitchen Central. It's somewhere in St. Paul. The streets in this town are a maze of confusion even to my New York sensibilities. There's a book signing I'd like to attend. I thought it might be nice to have some company. If you like, we could have coffee afterward. My treat."

It sounded much more fun than reading through a stack of boring newspaper clippings in an empty apartment. He could always do the preliminary research for next week's radio interviews later. "Sure. Why not? I'll even drive."

"I guess I picked the right escort."

"I guess you did." He grinned.

* * *

Half an hour later they entered the Har Mar Mall. Since Sophie had dragged Bram to this particular shop more than once during the past few years, he knew right where to find it. A good two hundred yards away from Kitchen Central's entrance, they could see a line forming.

"Who's the celebrity *du jour*?" he asked, observing several people carrying the same book.

"Constance Buckridge."

"Oh, sure. I watch her TV show every now and then. I think she's originally from Minnesota. Lives somewhere out east now."

Lela picked up the pace. "She's also staying at your hotel."

It was news to him. "Do you know her?"

"Not well. We met once, socially."

"But you're a fan of her show?"

"In a manner of speaking. Come on." She pushed through the crowd at the front of the store and made her way slowly to the back, where a table had been set up with stacks of books, a water pitcher, and a glass.

Everybody knew what Constance Buckridge looked like, so Bram spotted her with no trouble. She was in her early sixties, attractive in a Kim Novak sort of way. She favored neutral tones, creams and tans, colors that highlighted her still flawless skin and dyed-blond hair. She usually wore her hair in a bun or twist—Bram wasn't sure of the word—and today was no exception. He'd never noticed it on TV, but in person she had an infectious energy that radiated throughout the room. He'd heard that she was well liked in the cooking world.

Scanning the crowd to see if he recognized anyone else, he was surprised to find the same man he'd seen leaving the Maxfield earlier with Sophie. "Who is that guy?" he asked Lela, pointing him out.

She turned to look. "That's Constance Buckridge's oldest son, Nathan. The New York gossip mills consider him a real catch, sort of a creative hunk with a huge bankroll. He's divorced. Never remarried. And that man over there"—she nodded to the opposite side of the room—"the shorter, balding one wearing the chef's uniform? He's standing behind his mother. Sort of clean-cut and preppie, wire-rimmed glasses. He's Paul Buckridge, Constance's younger son. He's talking to two women. The one with the long hair is his sister, Emily. The other one—the woman Paul has his arm around—I don't think I've ever seen her before."

But Bram had. It was Sophie.

"They sure seem glad to see her," said Lela, looking puzzled. "Especially Nathan. He's hardly taken his eyes off her. Maybe she's his new squeeze."

"No, she's not," said Bram.

Lela stopped and looked up at him. "You sound pretty sure of that."

"I am."

"And that would be because . . ."

"She's my wife."

She glanced back at Sophie. "I see."

"I don't," muttered Bram, though he planned to find out.

Cocking her head, Lela added, "But she's so short. And you're so tall."

"Works for me."

Moving behind the table, Constance called out, "May I have everyone's attention for a few seconds?" She waited until all the talking died down. "I want to thank everyone at Kitchen Central, especially Jean Lundstrom, for inviting me here this afternoon. I intend to sign books until my hand falls off, but before I begin, I want to introduce you to some special people who've accompanied me here today. First my two handsome sons, Chef Nathan Buckridge . . ." She held out her right hand to him.

Nathan smiled as the crowd clapped.

"And Chef Paul Buckridge."

He moved closer to his mother and gave a polite nod.

"My daughter, Emily," continued Constance, putting her arm around the younger woman's waist.

With her long, straight blond hair and large, soft eyes, Bram found her very attractive. He wondered if Constance had resembled her daughter in her youth.

"By the way, Emily did all the photography for the latest book, *Cuisine America*."

Again, applause burst from every corner of the room.

"Next, I'd like to introduce my son-in-law, Kenneth Merlin. Kenneth is our senior legal counsel."

More applause as a thin man in a dark suit stood in the back.

"And since we have a local luminary here with us today, I'd like to introduce you all to Sophie Greenway, who has just taken over the restaurant-critic position at the *Minneapolis Times Register*. Sophie is an old friend of the family's."

Sophie waved as everyone clapped.

"There's one last person I need to include in my introduction." Constance stepped over to a small, professorial-looking white-haired man standing at the front of the crowd. Slipping her arm through his, she continued. "This is my brother, the eminent clinical psychologist, Dr. Arthur Jadek. Since his retirement four years ago, he's become my right arm. I don't know what I'd do without him."

The man smiled somewhat shyly as people applauded. Bram thought he looked ill at ease and wondered if perhaps he didn't much care for the spotlight.

"And now I'll be happy to sign your books." Constance kissed Arthur on the cheek, then sat down behind the table. In an instant, the knot in the room formed itself into a line.

"She's going to be here for hours," said Lela disgustedly, folding her arms over her chest.

"You better squeeze in somewhere if you want her signature," said Bram.

"Oh, I'm not interested in that."

"Then why are we here?"

She shrugged. "I'm fascinated by celebrity?"

That couldn't be her entire reason, thought Bram, but he didn't have the interest to pursue it.

"Do you want to go talk to your wife?"

"I would, but she's gone," he said, feeling miffed. As soon as Constance Buckridge had begun signing, Nathan and Sophie had exited through the back door.

"Are you sure?" Lela stood on her tiptoes to look around.

"I saw her leave."

"Do you want to get back to the hotel?"

"Correct me if I'm wrong, Ms. Dexter, but I thought we had a date for a cup of coffee."

"A date?"

"As in an appointment. A social engagement."

"You're sure your wife won't mind?"

She was trying to match his light tone, but her words stung. Something about the look in Nathan Buckridge's eyes told Bram he wasn't just an old friend. "As a matter of fact"—he checked his watch—"it's almost happy hour in our fair town. I don't suppose you like hot New Orleans jazz?"

"You have to ask?"

"Then I know just the place for a couple of cool draft beers. What do you say?"

"Lead the way."

7

Several hours later Sophie surveyed the Belmont's dark interior looking for Harry Hongisto. For a Saturday night, the dinner crowd was pretty thin. Okay, so it was just after six, but in a town noted for early dining, it didn't bode well. Sophie had been wanting to talk to Harry all day and finally decided that having a face-to-face conversation with him was better than doing it over the phone.

She and Nathan had returned to the hotel immediately after leaving Kitchen Central. In the car on the way back, she'd tried to keep the conversation neutral and impersonal. She told him about Harry Hongisto's restaurant and the bad reviews he'd received from the former restaurant critic at the *Times Register*. Nathan seemed sympathetic, asking her how much power the reviewers had in this town. In New York, he said, a bad review could sink a restaurant. Did she think that was the case here?

She described the slow decline of the Belmont during the past few years, adding that she felt the two reviews had really hurt business. In the end, if Harry had to shut down, it would be hard to say whether the reviews themselves had pushed the restaurant over the edge. Nathan asked a couple more questions: Where is it located? What sort of food does it serve? But before she knew it, he'd brought the subject back to their past again.

Sophie had grown increasingly ill at ease in his company, especially after he made it clear that he'd never gotten over her. As a way of ending their afternoon together, she'd agreed to meet him for lunch on Monday. He was so insistent, and in her heart she had to admit that she was just a little bit flattered. Still, she made sure he knew that she was very much in love with her husband and that all they could ever hope to be now was friends. Nathan said he understood, and that, for their lunch, he had something special in mind. She didn't exactly know what to make of his enthusiasm, but they'd parted by the elevators on a friendly note, Sophie heading up to her apartment in the north wing, Nathan returning to his suite in the south.

Relieved to finally be away from him, Sophie sailed into her front foyer, hoping to debrief with Bram. For years he'd pushed his pet theory about old flames: Old boyfriends—and girlfriends—never die. They always pop up again sooner or later, sometimes with expectations, sometimes just out of curiosity. Sophie thought he'd be happy to hear another story that proved his theory. Unfortunately, he wasn't back yet. His golf game couldn't have lasted this long, but since she knew he had to prepare for next week's shows, she figured he was off doing research.

Normally, if either of them had to be somewhere other than home in the evening, they would call or leave a note. This morning, however, before she'd left for her meeting at the paper, they'd made plans to drive to the Mall of America for an eight o'clock movie, so she knew he'd be back by seven at the latest. Since she had some time to spare, she grabbed her purse and returned to the lobby. Next stop, the Belmont.

Sophie found Harry in the bar. He was seated at the counter, head in his hands, staring morosely into a glass of Scotch. She knew it was Scotch because the bottle was right next to him.

Slipping onto a stool, she could see that he was completely lost in thought.

"Harry?" she said softly, touching his arm.

When he looked over at her, it took him a moment to focus. "Sophie," he said finally. "What are you doing here?" His voice was gravelly even on good days, but tonight it was mixed with alcohol and aimless despair. His eyes were bloodshot, and the black bow tie he always knotted perfectly was untied and hanging down limply over his tux jacket.

"I was hoping we could talk for a few minutes."

He picked up his glass, gesturing to the empty room. "Talk away. I've got nothing but time. My usual audience seems to have failed me."

She knew he wasn't in the best shape, but she'd come to warn him that he was in potentially serious trouble. She had to make him listen.

"You look pretty as a picture tonight, Sophie Tahtinen. Your father would be so proud."

He'd used her maiden name. Not a good sign.

"Harry, listen. I didn't tell you this last night because I thought it would upset you, but you're going to find out sooner or later." She paused, screwing up her courage. "I'm taking over George Gildemeister's job at the *Times Register*. I'm the new restaurant critic."

He narrowed his eyes. "You?" was all he could squeak out.

"You know I've done guest reviews for the paper for years."

"But to *become* George Gildemeister."

"No, no, Harry. I'm not becoming him, I'm just taking his job."

He gave the traditional Finnish sigh of resignation. "Hoi, hoi." After shaking his head a few more times, he said, "This is a sad, sad day, Sophie. It's such a loathsome profession you've chosen. Your father—maybe I should tell him. Break the news to him gently." He was about to pour himself more Scotch when Sophie grabbed the bottle out of his hand.

"Hey."

"I'll give it back to you in a minute. Right now you've got to concentrate. Can you do that?"

He glowered but grunted affirmatively.

"Good, because this is important. When I was at the paper this morning, Gildemeister received a letter from you."

His glower turned to a grin. "I know. I hand-delivered it. Made sure they took it right up to his office."

At least that was good news. The U.S. mail hadn't been involved. "You threatened him, Harry."

"Huh?" He passed a hand over his face.

"You said a guy like him didn't deserve to live."

A vague smile returned. "I worked on that letter all night last night. It was my pièce de résistance."

He murdered the French pronunciation, but Sophie got the point. "The letter's been turned over to the police. Yale McGraw, the managing editor, took your words seriously."

"He should! That Gildemeister is a menace. He's single-handedly responsible for ruining my business!"

Sophie could have argued the point, but now wasn't the time. "Harry, the police are probably going to want to talk to you."

"Yeah, yeah, yeah," he said, downing the last of his drink. "They were already here. I was out. I guess I'm supposed to call some sergeant ASAP."

"Did you?"

"If they want to talk to me, they can come back. I'm not hiding from anyone. I'm a businessman and I've got rights."

"Harry, this is serious!"

"It's a crock of you-know-what. I'm not gonna hurt that bastard, though I have dreamed of stuffing him in our convection oven and cranking the heat up to broil. Sophie, don't look so shocked. I just wanted to blow off some steam."

"The police don't know that." The problem was, if she encouraged him to call the officer back now, in his present state, who knew what he'd say?

"Don't worry, *pikku* Sophia. I've got everything under control. As a matter of fact, before long I'm going to be a very rich man."

He was slurring his words, mixing Finnish with English, so she wasn't sure she'd heard him right. "You're going to be rich?"

He glanced at her sideways. "I've got options. Plans. I always land on my feet. Gildemeister may hate my guts, but this is one guy who's got tons of *sisu*."

Another Finnish word meaning determination. Not that knowing the definition helped her understand what he meant.

He yanked the bottle away from her and poured himself another drink. "There's more than one way to skin a cat—in this case, a Gildemeister." His laugh was more of a cackle.

"Harry, you need to be careful. You've got to stay away from George Gildemeister. Promise me you won't go near him."

"Hell, sure. You're so pretty tonight I'd promise you anything."

He might be old and drunk, but he still knew how to flirt. He was laughing so hard now that he spilled half the Scotch lifting the glass to his mouth.

"I think someone should take you home."

"Nah, I gotta stay here until it's finished."

She was losing her patience. "Until what's finished?"

"My business," he grunted, turning morose again.

For a moment, she thought he might be planning to do something drastic, like burn the building down.

Setting his glass on the counter, he added, "You shouldn't be sitting here talking to an old man. Go home to that handsome husband of yours. Thank the good Lord every day that you've got him, *pikku* Sophia. I'd give anything to have my Lempi back with me."

"Are you sure you're going to be okay?"

"Fine." He waved her away.

He was a sad man, in a sad situation, but she'd done what she'd come to do. And he was right, she had to get home now. She hoped Bram would be waiting.

Journal Note

Saturday, 11 P.M.

While it's still fresh in my mind, I want to type up my taped interview with Oscar Boland. But first a few general comments:

We met at the Lyme House, a restaurant on Lake Harriet in south Minneapolis. It was his choice. The dining room looked inviting, but he wanted to sit in the downstairs pub. Apparently, he goes there quite often. It was too noisy for my taste, but we found a back room that was less congested than the main one, and I set up the tape recorder between us.

Boland looked like a retired marine. Gray crew cut. Ramrod-straight posture. An expression that was pure concrete. Initially, I felt his suspicion quite keenly. He made it clear that he'd been a friend to all the Buckridges and wasn't going to participate in any character assassinations. I knew it wasn't going to be easy getting the information I wanted. If nothing else, I hoped Boland would provide me with a framework on which to place the rest of my research. In actuality, he gave me much more than that. I now feel I've narrowed down the areas that will yield the most potent results.

Boland started the discussion by asking me about my background. I knew he wanted to check me out, make sure I was on the level about being a published author and biographer. I told him I'd been writing since I was twenty-three. Seven biographies to date, all still in print. I mentioned that I had earned a great deal of money during the last fifteen years but that I did the work because I loved it.

He wanted more. I told him that as a child growing up in a large southern household, I tripped over lots of nasty secrets. I spent a great part of my youth trying to untie the Gordian knot that was my family. It turned out to be good practice for my future profession. I explained that I despised secrets and that I didn't believe in heroes. Heroes were unreal, deeply dangerous constructs, mainly because they allowed us a false concept of what it was to be human. I don't know whether he understood any of what I said, but he sat politely and listened.

After I gave him a copy of my last book—a biography of Gore Vidal—and he checked out my photo on the back cover, he seemed impressed. I told him he could keep the book, so he asked me to sign it. I wrote: "To my friend Oscar Boland. Thanks for the highly informative interview. Best wishes, Marie Damontraville." I thought the "highly informative interview" part might spur some cooperation. His reaction was far more positive than I could have imagined. There was a sudden sea change in his demeanor. He seemed both flustered and flattered—well, as flustered and flattered as an ex-marine type with a stone face can get. We ordered drinks, I turned on the recorder, and we were off.

INTERVIEW: OSCAR BOLAND, THE LYME HOUSE, MINNEAPOLIS, MAY 8

M: *How did you first meet Wayne Buckridge?*
Boland: *I never talked about this to anyone before, but I guess it's okay to tell you. I mean, you want the truth, right? That's what you're telling me is important, and I agree that it is. I just don't want to hurt anybody. I want to make that perfectly clear up front. Okay, so I've been thinking about all this since you called, trying to get it straight in my mind. It must have been about '52, the year before Wayne married Pepper. He was probably thirty-four or so. I was twenty-two. I'd taken my*

parents' speedboat out on the lake one afternoon. *What lake?* Oh, Minnetonka, where we had a summer home. It was a beautiful day, so I thought I'd just stop somewhere out in the middle and catch some sun. It was a weekday, pretty quiet on the water. I cruised around for a while, looking for just the right spot, when I spied this guy in a rowboat. He was standing up, holding what looked like a gun. I watched him for a few seconds. He was just staring at the waves. Before I realized what was happening, he pointed the thing at his head, I heard a blast, and he fell headfirst into the water. I throttled up and shot across the water, then cut the motor and dove in. I was a pretty strong swimmer in those days. I found him all right. About twenty feet down and sinking fast. The bullet had barely grazed his temple, but he was out cold, probably from shock. He would have drowned for sure if I hadn't come along.

M: *It was a suicide attempt?*

Boland: *He never actually admitted it, but yeah, I think so. From what I could piece together later, I figured it had something to do with the war. WW II. He spent most of his tour in France. It changed him, he always said that. I remember him telling me once that he'd gone into the army an innocent young boy and come out a corrupt old man. Between you and me, I don't think Wayne Buckridge liked himself very much after the war. But as far as I know, he never tried to hurt himself again. He'd been drinking that day. And he'd lost his job the week before. A man can only take so much.*

M: *When did he meet his wife?*

Boland: *You mean his first wife, Pepper? I'd known her since I was a kid. Her real name is Leona, but no one ever called her that. Pepper just fit her personality better. Her parents had a beautiful summer home just down the road. By the time I introduced her to Wayne, he and I had become great pals. I don't know why. We were total strangers before the accident happened, but for some reason it sort of drew us together. Life can be strange like that. Hell, the guy didn't have many friends, and he needed someone to talk to. You know—about life, the crap that happens, how to deal with stuff. Wayne's*

*family was all gone, except for an unmarried aunt he rarely
saw. I had a big family. We all just sort of adopted him—well,
mainly me, I guess, but my mom and dad were happy to have
him around. He was a swell guy. Husky. Good-looking. Athletic. Great personality. But he had this dark side to him. I'd
seen it, though I doubt very many other people had. Back in
the early days, he was always the life of the party. You'd never
know he had a care in the world. But I knew. He hated what
had happened in France, all the men he'd had to kill. He
thought of it as murder, kids murdering kids. I suppose that's
why he drank too much sometimes. I even saw him cry once.
Funny, it was the night before he married Pepper.*

M: *What was he crying about?*

Boland: *Beats the hell out of me. He should have been on top
of the world. I know he loved her, so that wasn't it. I think,
though, deep down inside, he thought she was too good for
him. I mean, he really got lucky when he met Pepper Skeffington. Not only did he get himself a rich young wife but his future career as well. His father-in-law thought the sun rose
and set on him. As soon as the happy couple got back from
their honeymoon, Skeffington started grooming Wayne to
take over the company—when he was gone, of course. Which
was many years later.*

M: *What sort of company was it?*

Boland: *You've never heard of Skeffington Construction?
Jesus, lady, they built half the homes in this town. After the
war, the economy boomed. Alan Skeffington was a multimil-
lionaire by the time his only daughter was seventeen years
old. She even dated my older brother a few times, but you
know how it is. No sparks. But when she met Wayne at one of
our summer lake parties, it was love—or at least lust—at first
sight. They were married ten months later.*

M: *Was she pregnant?*

Boland: *Nah. It wasn't like that.*

M: *Was the marriage a happy one?*

Boland: *Sure. As happy as marriages go. Pepper wanted kids
badly, but they didn't have much luck for a while. Finally,
when she was around thirty, they had Paul.*

M: *So Paul isn't Constance Buckridge's natural son.*

Boland: *No. I believe Connie formally adopted him, though. Anyway, after he was born, I sensed that Wayne had pulled away from Pepper, or maybe it was the other way around. Whatever the case, Wayne started working longer hours and Pepper spent all her time with her kid. She didn't seem all that unhappy, though from what I observed, Wayne did. I was good friends with both of them, you understand, but I was closer to Wayne. By then I'd gotten married myself. Had a good job at an insurance company. We all got together at least once every week or two for drinks and cards. Pepper was a real bridge player. She even organized a bridge club. Wayne was always at work, so she needed the company. When Paul was two, they moved into a new house, a mansion really. Wayne built it for them. It was on the other side of the lake from my parents' summer home. Very ritzy. They hired a maid and a cook and a guy to keep the grounds. Wayne was vice president of Skeffington Construction by then. He'd helped the company branch off into some highly lucrative product development. I don't remember now what it all was, but Wayne was a natural at business. When Paul was three, Alan Skeffington died, leaving the company to Wayne and Pepper. Wayne immediately renamed it Buckridge Construction. I guess I understood, although Pepper didn't. She would have preferred him to keep her father's name on the business.*

M: *Wayne must have been thrilled.*

Boland: *Yeah, I guess so. But it was hard to tell by then. He was drinking too much. I guess you could say his unhappiness was beginning to show. What made it worse was that Pepper had become a full-fledged hypochondriac. I figured it was her way of getting his attention, but actually she always was a hypochondriac, even when we were kids. She'd get a cold and have to go to bed for two weeks. But by her midthirties, she was sure she had cancer, diabetes, a bad heart, walking pneumonia, and just about every other malady known to modern man.*

M: *Was she really sick?*

Boland: *If you'd asked me then, I would have told you it*

was all an act. But, in the end, it turned out she wasn't making it up. Something was wrong with her, all right. She went to dozens of different doctors to find out why her body didn't feel right. I mean, the tests that woman had—it was enough to curl your socks. And the money it cost. But nobody could help.

M: *Maybe it was psychosomatic.*

Boland: *You mean, it was all in her head?*

M: *No, it was real, but it was caused by her emotions. It sounds like her husband wasn't around much. She couldn't have felt very loved or supported.*

Boland: *(Shrugs) Yeah, I guess you're right. It's too bad, really. They started out with so much going for them. But I'm not sure Wayne knew how to be happy. Maybe that's why he was crying the night before he got married. Maybe he knew he was going to make Pepper miserable, ruin both their lives.*

M: *If he was that prescient, he was an unusual man.*

Boland: *Pardon me?*

M: *Tell me, Mr. Boland, how did Pepper Buckridge die?*

Boland: *Well, I was on the road at the time, so I heard about it later from Wayne. He was pretty torn up. Seems she got real sick one night. She'd been bedridden off and on for many months, but the last week was the worst. That night she had some sort of crisis. Stomach pains. Vomiting. I don't know what else. Wayne rushed her to the emergency room and the doctors did what they could, but she died in his arms. I arranged most of the funeral. Wayne was too upset. He said he blamed himself for her death. He should have been more sympathetic, should have helped her find a specialist who could really get to the bottom of her medical problems. It was just that he was so tired out by her continuous complaints. I think, after a while, he just tuned her out.*

M: *What happened to Paul while all this was happening?*

Boland: *He was pretty small. When Pepper was no longer able to care for him, she hired a nanny. The woman didn't last a month. She hired a couple more, but nobody worked out. So I guess between the cook, the maid, and the groundsman, little Paul was looked after. Every time I was there he always seemed happy enough.*

M: *How did Wayne meet his second wife?*

Boland: *Connie? She was one of the housemaids and then, later, the cook. She came to work for the family in '61, right after they moved into the new house. I doubt she was more than twenty-two or twenty-three at the time, although she had a son who was around seven. If I'm not mistaken, Nathan was five years older than Paul.*

M: *So Nathan was Constance's natural son but not by Wayne Buckridge.*

Boland: *Right. You know, if you do the math, you realize that she must have gotten pregnant when she was fifteen. I don't think I'm telling tales out of school. I'm sure someone's figured that out by now, although when I've seen articles printed in newspapers about her and the kids, they often make Paul and Nathan the same age, and several years younger than they really are. It's probably a source of some shame on her part. I mean, she never talked much about Nathan's father. Wayne told me some guy got her pregnant and then took off, though you can't quote me, because I don't recall the details, if I ever heard any. But I don't think she was ever married. And a problem like that carried a real stigma back then. From what she told me later, she came to Minneapolis to live with her brother because her parents threw her out. Bad situation all around. Connie was a nice-enough young woman but not very well educated. She was extraordinarily pretty. A natural platinum blonde. Great body. But terribly shy. She was what you might call sweet. She was from somewhere in Wisconsin, I think. That's all I know about her background.*

M: *How did she become romantically involved with Wayne?*

Boland: *Well, now, I don't have all the details on that either. I know she worked in the house for at least a year before she took over the cook's position. It was lots more money than the maid position, but I don't think that's what got her interested in it. She and the cook got along famously. Connie would always ask her if she needed any help. Even then, Connie—we never called her Constance—had an affinity for cooking. She*

*learned everything the woman could teach her and then she
started taking out books from the library. I remember Wayne
saying once that the dinner we were having that evening was
one of "Connie's many learning experiences." To be honest, it
was a superb meal. When the cook decided to accept another
position, Connie applied for her job and got it. By then,
Wayne was in his midforties and was starting to put on
weight. Funny. As I think about it now, while Pepper was
wasting away up in her room, Wayne was stuffing himself with
Connie's fabulous food in the dining room. One of life's crazy
ironies, I guess. I suppose it was only natural that Wayne and
Connie struck up a friendship. For all practical purposes,
they were alone in the house most evenings. See, during the
last six months of Pepper's life, she was always in bed by
seven. Wayne rarely got home before then, and he wanted his
dinner right away.*

M: *So, as far as you know, it was just an innocent relationship
that turned romantic because Wayne's wife was essentially
absent from his life.*

Boland: *I guess that about covers it.*

M: *Constance didn't lay a trap for Wayne? Seduce him? Ply
him with food and wine to get him in the sack?*

Boland: *(Shrugs) Maybe. But he never would have married
her unless he loved her. And I really believe that was the case.
Connie had been taking care of baby Paul for almost two
years by then. They'd become inseparable. When Pepper died,
I think it was normal for Wayne to turn to the one person he'd
become close to during that awful time.*

M: *In other words, this young, penniless woman just got
lucky. She was at the right place at the right time.*

Boland: *I suppose you could put it that way.*

M: *Sounds like a fairy tale to me.*

Boland: *Yes, it does. (Smiles pleasantly.)*

M: *I don't believe in fairy tales, Mr. Boland. Let's move on to
their marriage.*

Boland: *Here's where my information gets even more spotty.
My wife and the kids and I moved to Chicago in '65. It was a*

year after Wayne and Connie were married. Little Emily didn't come along until '66.

M: *So Emily is the only natural child of Wayne and Constance.*

Boland: *Right. Paul was seven by then and Nathan was practically a teenager. Our families still saw each other once or twice a year, but it wasn't like it was back in the old days. All I remember is, Wayne finally seemed to be content. The kids were thriving and he and Connie traveled a lot together. Wayne had a bunch of overseas accounts to visit, and Connie always went along. Little by little, she got the education she'd missed earlier in her life. If you ask me, the only thing she was really interested in was food. She couldn't learn about it fast enough. Really, she'd become this incredible hostess, throwing dinner party after dinner party for Wayne and his current and potential business associates. Getting invited to one of her soirees was a sign that you'd made it socially.*

M: *Did the Buckridges still employ a cook?*

Boland: *Yes, but the dinner parties were special. Connie did it all. By then, she'd kicked out the staff and made the third floor, where the staff quarters had been, into a playroom for the kids. They still had a maid, a gardener, and a cook, but none of them lived in. Connie limited when they could be at the house because she didn't like nonfamily members around in the evenings or on weekends. Just a different approach, I guess.*

M: *And everybody seemed happy?*

Boland: *As far as I could tell. As I said, I wasn't around as much. Wayne and I drifted apart during those years. Too bad, but then I suppose it couldn't be helped.*

M: *Tell me about his death.*

Boland: *Again, I wasn't there when it happened, so this is secondhand information from Connie. Let me back up a minute so that I can put this into some sort of context. In '71 or '72—you'd have to check with Connie to get the exact dates—she was asked to do a couple guest spots on a local TV show. They wanted her to talk about appetizers or some such thing—what she served at her famous dinner parties. In a matter of weeks, she'd become a household name in the Cities. She was offered more spots, then a weekly segment on the show. Eventually, she was offered her own show. And from there anybody could see there was no stopping her. That was around '73. Wayne was in his fifties by then and was totally out of shape. He was a good hundred pounds overweight, his blood pressure was through the roof, and he'd had one small heart attack. His doctors were telling him to slow down and lose weight. He did neither. Nobody told Wayne Buckridge what to do. I think Connie's brother, Arthur, had come to live with them that same year. He'd applied to graduate school at the U of M and had been accepted. Kind of an odd man, if I recall correctly. I know Wayne didn't like him, but he put up with him because Connie wanted him around. Then early in January of '74, I got a call from her. Wayne had suffered another heart attack. She was in the house when it happened, but she was busy down in her study. The TV or the radio was on and she never heard him call for help. I guess when she went upstairs later, she found him on the floor in the bathroom. She called the paramedics, but it was too late.*

M: *I suppose she was devastated by his death.*

Boland: *Yes, she was. It was a very hard time for her. Her career was taking off, but when her husband died so unexpectedly, her world was thrown into chaos. I think she almost had a nervous breakdown.*

M: *But she didn't.*

Boland: *No, she pulled it together. Connie is a very strong woman. I really admire her.*

M: *Thanks for your time, Mr. Boland. If I have further questions, would you mind talking to me again?*

Boland: *Not at all. Say, give my best to Connie. I haven't seen or talked to her in years. I assume you've already interviewed her.*

M: *Not yet.*

Boland: *Well, just tell her Oscar says hi. She's a peach of a woman. Tops in my book. You can quote me on that.*

* * *

Journal Note:

I E-mailed this interview to Pluto shortly after midnight. Can't help but wonder what response I'll get from him, if any.

8

Constance rose early on Sunday morning. In the living room of her suite, she sat behind a desk in her robe and slippers, drinking a cup of strong black coffee, absorbed by the notes she'd made last night for this afternoon's speech at the Women's Club in downtown Minneapolis. She wanted to talk about *Cuisine America*, the theme of her latest cookbook. There would be lots of reporters in attendance this afternoon, all eager to take down her words and print them in local newspaper and magazine articles. It seemed that people couldn't get enough discussion these days about food.

She planned to quote Brillat-Savarin today: "Tell me what you eat and I will tell you what you are." In Constance's opinion, food was a highly personal, emotionally charged issue. In the nearly thirty years she'd been working in the food industry, she'd seen the country's interest in wine and fine cuisine move from mild curiosity to national obsession. The Television Food Network, which she helped to start in 1993, had become the third-fastest-growing cable network in the land. Constance still couldn't believe her luck. She'd actually caught a star as it was rising.

Not that her life had started out with much promise.

Abusive, alcoholic parents. Pregnant at fifteen. Even so, she'd felt certain that Nathan's birth was the first of many blessings. She'd wanted so much to make her life work, to have a family that made sense. She'd loved Nathan's father, and she'd thought that love would be enough to get her through any problem. But she'd been naïve. The fact was, she'd had no money and no skills. Her past wasn't something she was proud of, and therefore she wasn't eager to talk about it. She and Nathan had survived, but at a terrible cost.

After she married Wayne Buckridge and her life took a public turn, the requests for interviews made her feel deeply threatened. But as time went on, she realized her fears were only a paper tiger. She caught on eventually that interviews were nothing but shallow little dances. The interviewers were all looking for quick soundbites or a quote or two that would translate well on the printed page. Constance had become a master at giving them just what they wanted: a little content, a little sizzle. When the questions waxed too personal, they were easily deflected. She learned from politicians that you never needed to answer a question you didn't want to; you simply talked about something else.

It was odd being a celebrity. Since Constance had moved into that netherworld, everyone assumed they knew her. She was available. On TV. On the covers of national magazines. On talk shows. She appeared on the *Today Show* regularly and had even been coaxed into doing a couple of commercials. Since she was familiar, she was known, almost an old friend. And that assumption was very easy to hide behind. She'd refused offers by several prominent writers to authorize a biography. Other requests for background information were easily handled by a standard bio sheet she and Arthur had put together years ago. No one had ever really pressed the issue—until now.

Looking up, Constance saw Arthur pad out of the far bedroom, stretching his arms high above his head. He was wearing a striped robe over his silk pajamas, his white hair tousled in a boyish way.

"Morning, Connie. You're up early." When he finally focused his eyes on her, his expression sobered. "Something wrong?"

There was a knock at the door.

"Get that, will you?" she asked, a tight edge to her voice.

"It should be Kenny." Kenneth Merlin, her daughter's husband, was her legal muscle. This morning she hoped he could work a small miracle.

In the seven years Kenny had been married to Emily, Constance couldn't think of a time when he hadn't been wearing a suit. This morning was no different. She half suspected he slept in one. Kenny was fourteen years older than her daughter, an obvious father figure replacing the one she'd lost. Emily had been hurt the most by Wayne's death, something Constance regretted. She and her daughter had been close before he died, but afterward Emily had grown distant. It was almost as if she blamed Constance for her father's heart attack. Unlike Paul, Emily wanted no part in the growing family fame. She had little interest in food, and as soon as she graduated from Macalester, she'd headed east to New York, mainly to get away from "Mother."

Emily had somehow wrangled herself a job on one of the ABC soap operas. The Buckridge name probably hadn't hurt. Constance assumed the job paid pretty well because Emily never wrote home for money. Backstage, she took care of the actors' costumes, ensuring that everyone's dress or sweater or suit was available when needed, clean and in perfect condition. She also signed up to take photography classes at night. Cameras and lenses and darkrooms interested Emily. She wrote her brother Paul that if she was going to be the black sheep of the family, she might as well shoot a photo-documentary of her demise.

Emily's life had been running along pretty smoothly when one of the resident divas on the soap accused her of stealing a black sequined evening gown. Constance heard about Emily's arrest only after the fact, but it didn't really come as a surprise. That old adage about falling apples and trees seemed appropriate. Constance knew she was capable of doing almost anything to get what she wanted and suspected Emily had inherited that same ruthless determination.

It came out later that Emily had been stealing clothes all along and selling them to a small boutique in the Village for a nice profit. Constance assumed that her only daughter wasn't used to scraping by on crummy wages, and since she was too pigheaded to ask her mother for help, she found her own way to fund her lifestyle in the Big Apple. And that's how fate brought Emily and Kenny together.

Up until then Kenneth Merlin—tall, dark, and not very good looking—was just a name in her little black book. They'd met at a bar one night, had a couple of drinks together, and exchanged phone numbers. When the bartender mentioned to Kenny weeks later that the pretty blue-eyed blonde with the Minnesoo-ta accent was in legal trouble, he roared in on his white horse—a red BMW—and offered to help. Thanks to his knowledge of the New York City legal system and the fact that it was Emily's first offense, she got off with paying a fine and doing some community service. She lost her job, of course, but she got Kenny in the bargain, a reasonably well-to-do New York attorney. From then on, they were inseparable.

Constance recognized Kenny for what he was the first time they met. He registered dollar signs in his eyes every time he smiled at her, but since he apparently made Emily happy, Constance didn't interfere. They were married less than a year later.

Once Kenny was an official member of the family, he started doing little favors for Constance. Checking out a contract here, writing a letter there. Emily made it clear that she didn't like it one bit. Her mother's culinary biz was strictly off limits, but as time went on she mellowed. It was hard work staying mad at everyone, especially since she loved her brothers and hated being estranged from them.

In time, Emily even seemed to melt a little toward Constance, mostly due to the birth of her twin boys. Emily doted on them and so did Constance. It was a passion they could finally share, and in a way it facilitated a certain rapprochement. Emily had even consented to take the photographs for Constance's last cookbook, something she would never have considered during her photojournalism period. So, as much as Constance saw Kenny for what he was—a hustler in an expensive suit—she put up with him because he seemed to be good for Emily. And somehow, over the years, he'd become invaluable to Constance as well. As he so often pointed out, "Everyone needs a Kenneth Merlin in their life."

"Come in and pour yourself some coffee," said Constance, waving him inside.

Kenny nodded to Arthur but declined the offer, saying that he and Emily had just had breakfast.

"What's going on?" asked Arthur, shooting Constance a hard look. He shut the door and then took a seat on the couch. "How come you look so . . . so dour?"

Kenny unbuttoned his suit coat and sat down in one of the club chairs. He folded one leg carefully over the other to avoid crushing the crease in his pants, then straightened his tie. "My question, too, Constance. You sounded upset on the phone."

As she watched her son-in-law primp, she thought again how distinctly reptilian he was. When he was deep in thought, his eyes would narrow to slits, and when he was pleased, his red lips would spread thinly across his flat, pallid face. Even though he was an unusually clever lawyer, the emphasis he placed on his appearance—the cologne, the heavy gold jewelry, the thin, always perfectly clipped mustache—repulsed her. His vanity suggested that he saw himself as nothing less than a Casanova, which was absurd. Funny how some people could deceive themselves about their sex appeal. Did he live in a world with no mirrors?

"Constance?" Arthur sat forward, trying to get her attention. "Where are you? You seem so far away."

She turned to look at him. More and more these days, she was getting lost in her own thoughts. Perhaps it was her age, but reverie at a time like this could spell trouble. Coming back to Minnesota had only intensified these minor trances. She was feeling uncharacteristically fragile and sentimental, and that wouldn't do. Switching her attention back to Kenny, she said, "I received a phone call last night. Someone—I don't know who—has been given a very large advance to do a tell-all biography. Unauthorized."

"On you?" said Kenny, examining his nails.

"Don't be an ass. Of course on me. I want you to find out who it is."

"That could take some time. And money."

"The money's no problem; the time is. Whoever's doing it is here in town right now digging into my past. From what I was told, he or she might even be staying at this hotel." She paused, glancing at Arthur. "I want it stopped, Kenny. And I want it stopped immediately."

"That might be difficult."

"Damn it! Do something to earn your keep."

He flicked his eyes toward her, then continued examining his nails. After a few seconds, he removed a silver cigarette case from his inner pocket. "Would anyone care for a smoke?"

Arthur shook his head.

"No," said Constance curtly. The ashtray in front of her was already filled.

Patiently, Kenny plucked one from the case. "Why don't you tell me who your informer is? I can start there."

She hesitated, then said, "Milton Culbertson at Random House. He edited one of my cookbooks a few years back. But be discreet, Kenny. That's important."

"I'm always discreet."

"I've got some friends in publishing," said Arthur, scowling at a spot in the rug. "Maybe I could shake something loose."

"I don't care how we do it," she said, rising from her chair. "We've got to stop this person."

Kenny touched a match to the tip of his cigarette, then shook it out. "Would you care to tell me why you're so concerned?"

"Oh, come on," said Arthur, not even trying to hide his indignation. "Everyone's got moments in their past they'd rather not share with the world."

"Moments?"

Constance could almost hear his tail rattle. "Just do your job."

"And what am I supposed to do when I find this man or woman?"

"Buy him or her off."

"And if I can't?"

"Then threaten to tie the book up in court. You're good at that."

His thin lips spread. "Information has a way of leaking, Constance."

"Just find the person before they can do any damage."

"You make this sound serious."

"It is." She adjusted her robe, giving herself a moment to calm down. She didn't want to lose her temper because, knowing Kenny, he'd read too much into it. "I refuse to allow my good name to be smeared by a lot of cheap gossip."

"Is that all it would be? Cheap gossip?"

She glared at him. "Yes." She said the word coldly. "I don't need to explain myself to you. If you want, I can find someone else to do the job. You've made a lot of money working for me, Kenneth, but there are other lawyers out there."

He leaned forward and tapped some ash into an ashtray. "Don't get all huffy on me, Constance. I have your best interests at heart."

"Because they coincide with your own."

He acknowledged her comment with a slight shift of his eyebrows. "I'm just trying to understand what's going on here. If you want my help, any information you can give me will only make my task easier." He paused. "Is there anything else I'm *allowed* to know?"

Constance walked to the window that overlooked the river. "Milton only passed on one other fact. The tentative title of the book."

"And that would be?"

"It's a stupid play on words."

"But it could be helpful."

She turned to face him. Squaring her shoulders, she replied, *"Slice and Dice."*

She couldn't quite decipher the look on his face, but since he loved innuendo, she figured he got the point.

9

Sophie set the breakfast tray on the bed, crawled under the covers, then pulled the tray closer. "You don't mind sharing, do you?" she asked, kissing Bram on his nose.

"I like sharing," he said, glancing at Ethel on her pillow next to the bed. "As long as it's just you and me."

Sophie peered down at Ethel, too. Poor dog. She'd been so devastated when her pillow had been moved to the lobby that Sophie had to buy another pillow to replace the one in the bedroom. And then another for the living room so that Ethel would have someplace soft to sit while she lazed in the morning sun. And then one more so that she'd have a comfortable perch from which to guard her tennis balls under the dining room table. Sophie wasn't sure where it all would end. They were already tripping over the damn things, and Ethel seemed to be lobbying for a new one. She wanted it in the kitchen, next to the refrigerator, so that she could be close to whomever was cooking just in case a potential food opportunity arose. It was really pretty funny, watching her drag herself, with all the drama of an aging Norma Desmond, from pillow to pillow. The furniture no longer got the workout it used to, but the apartment was beginning to look like a Turkish harem.

"So did you enjoy the movie last night?" asked Bram, chewing on a piece of bacon.

"Moderately."

"We didn't talk about it much on the way home. We usually do."

"I was tired, I guess."

"You were preoccupied."

She snuggled closer to him. "I suppose I was."

"About the new job at the *Times Register*?"

"Yes, that, and Harry Hongisto."

"Ah, the poison-pen letter."

She nodded.

"Anything else?"

Chewing the tip of her toast, she said, "Hmm?"

"I asked you if you were preoccupied about anything else."

"No, not really."

Taking a sip of orange juice, Bram continued. "Who was that man I saw you with yesterday afternoon?"

She moved away from him and studied his face. Was he psychic or what? "What man?"

"The tall guy with the mangy brown hair. Widow's peak, if I'm not mistaken. Dark eyes. Didn't catch the color. Too far away. Sensitive mouth. More or less our age, I think. Reasonably well dressed. Too L.L. Bean for my taste. Confident type. Handsome, I suppose, if you like your looks rugged. Or should I say craggy? He won't age well. His hair's probably got, oh, another year or so before it starts falling out. And I detected the beginnings of a potbelly under his suit. My guess—too much beer. Of course, the sensitive mouth won't change, but if he doesn't take care of his teeth, he could be looking at a false set before you know it. Oh, and I believe his name is Nathan Buckridge."

She banged him on the arm. "What's going on? You're having me followed by some sleazy private eye?"

"The only sleazy eyes that were following you were Nathan's. What the hell is that guy to you?"

She was caught. Yesterday she'd wanted to tell him that his theory about old boyfriends never dying had once again proved accurate. And yet this morning she would have preferred to drop the entire subject. She needed more time to think about how to tell him she'd bumped into her first love. Not that Bram was the kind of man to feel threatened by an old boyfriend. Still, she wanted to break it to him gently, just in case.

"I'm waiting," he said, chewing his bacon.

"He's a guy—"

"A guy. Good. Keep going."

"I knew him a long time ago. When I was in high school. He was a couple of years older than me. We dated. And, well, he followed me out to California."

"Was he part of your church?"

"No." She sighed. "He hated the church. If it hadn't been for that . . ." She stopped, looking down at the toast in her hand.

"You seem to be having a hard time telling this story, Soph. I wonder why. I'm a big boy, you know. I realize you had a life before you met me."

Brushing a lock of hair away from his forehead, she said, "He wanted to marry me."

"And how did you feel about him?"

"I loved him. Very much. But we couldn't be together. I'd made a commitment to a different kind of life."

"The Church of the Firstborn."

She nodded.

"He must have been pretty angry."

"He was."

"And what about you?"

Again she hesitated. "Giving him up was . . . difficult."

Bram tossed the half-eaten bacon back on the plate. "So what we have here is a case of unrequited love—on both your parts. A fairly combustible situation. Is he married?"

She shook her head.

"I don't suppose, in the interim between the time you last saw him and now, he's discovered he's gay."

She smiled. "No such luck. But look, Bram, I don't have any feelings for him anymore. I was just a girl the last time I saw him. More important, I'm happy with my life now, and I happen to be very much in love with my husband."

"That's good to hear."

"It's the truth."

He drew her to him, kissing the top of her head. "Well, if

it's not, all I can say is, you were pretty convincing last night in bed."

"It wasn't a performance."

He stroked her arm. "How long is this Buckridge character going to be in town?"

"No idea."

"Are you planning to see him again?"

She knew he wasn't going to like her answer. "Actually, I agreed to meet him for lunch on Monday."

"Ah. Love in the afternoon."

"Bram!"

He held up his hand. "I know, I know. But you'd tell me if . . . if anything changed for you, right?"

"Nothing's going to change." She hoped with all her might that she was telling the truth. "Nothing's changed for you, has it? I mean, I'm still your one and only."

"Forever and ever, Sophie."

She smiled, laying her head back against his shoulder. Unfortunately, she'd lived long enough to know that sometimes forever had a way of dissolving into nevermore. But she was determined that it wasn't going to be that way for them. Bram was the man she wanted to spend the rest of her life with. Nathan Buckridge was just a memory.

"So what's on our agenda for this evening?" asked Sophie, nibbling her toast.

"Would you believe I've got tickets for a Twins game?"

She groaned.

"You're not delighted?"

"I love you madly, dear, but not madly enough to sit through one of those interminable ballgames."

He retrieved his piece of bacon. "Well, I guess I'll just have to call one of my old girlfriends."

She rolled her eyes. "Try your cop buddy, Al Lundquist."

"You know, his knuckle cracking has been getting on my nerves lately."

"I had no idea you'd ever noticed."

"You think I'm some sort of insensitive gorilla type, right? Some Darwinian primate?"

"You're much too suave to be a gorilla."

"Thank you." He narrowed one eye. "I can tell you're about to compare me to something else. An orangutan, perhaps?"

"Actually, I was thinking of a penguin. They wear tuxedos and they're awfully cute."

"Cute?" Disgusted, he pushed himself out of bed.

"Where are you going?"

"To my tailor's. From now on, I will wear nothing but loud Hawaiian shirts and cheap drawstring pants. Nobody calls me a penguin and gets away with it."

While Bram barricaded himself in his study to go over the research for next week's shows, Sophie spent the afternoon in her office, writing a short feature about yesterday's event at Kitchen Central. She tried contacting George Gildemeister several times but had no luck. Around four, however, she finally found him at his apartment.

"George, hi. I don't mean to interrupt your Sunday, but I'm kind of under the gun here. Do you have any files at home, any of your old reviews? Also, I dug through the filing cabinets at your office yesterday and couldn't locate anything that resembled a list of new restaurants in the metro area—or those that will be opening soon."

"Yeah," he said, letting out his breath slowly. "I've probably got some of that stuff around here. When do you want it?"

She was annoyed not only by his disorganization but also by his total disinterest. "Can I come by this evening?"

"I suppose. Look, Soph, I'm not feeling very well. Probably the flu or something. Buzz me when you get here and I'll let you up, but if I don't feel like being sociable, I'll put a box outside in the hall. If you need to talk to me about anything else, I'll be here through Wednesday night. On Thursday morning I'm driving up north to my farm."

"I'll stop by around eight."

"Whatever."

Before heading off in different directions, Bram and Sophie grabbed a quick bite of dinner together at the Fountain

Grill. Al Lundquist had consented to go to the Twins game, which got Sophie off the hook. They could have a "guys' night" and she could get some work done. Driving over to George's apartment wouldn't take long and then she could spend the rest of the evening concentrating on hotel business.

Sophie hopped on I-94 at about ten to eight and made it to Hennepin Avenue in Minneapolis in record time. As she pulled up to the curb halfway down the block from George's building, she hoped that he would be in a more sociable mood than he'd been earlier in the day, mainly because she'd thought of several more questions she needed to ask. Cutting the motor, she sat for a moment going through her purse, looking for a piece of paper and a pen. If nothing else, she'd slip a note under his door asking him to call her first thing tomorrow. No more talking to answering machines.

She scribbled a few lines on the back of a business card, then started to get out but stopped when she saw a man emerging from the front door. It was getting dark and she was a fair distance away, but something about him seemed vaguely familiar. Before she could get a good look at his face, he hurried off in the opposite direction.

10

The Lakeland Terrace was located on the edge of Uptown, a ritzy inner-city area between Lake Calhoun and Lake of the Isles. It was a five-story security building, redbrick facade, probably built in the Forties. Sophie had been there twice before, both times to drop off a restaurant review. Since George spent only half-days at the paper three times a week, it shouldn't have come as a complete surprise to her that he kept some of his files at home.

Once inside the front foyer, she searched her purse for the scrap of paper on which she'd written his apartment number. She'd noticed that her memory wasn't what it used to be, so she was forced to write herself notes. Just as she found the paper, a young couple came out of the locked door. Assuming that she must be searching for her key, they held the door open. She smiled and thanked them. It was a bad security risk, but then, in her cotton cardigan and khaki trousers, she hardly looked like an ax murderer.

When the elevator reached the fifth floor, she got out and immediately spotted the box outside George's door. Damn. She was hoping to talk to him in person if only for a few minutes.

Then again if he *was* sick . . .

In a moment of angry resolve, she tossed her Midwestern manners to the wind and knocked on the door. She could always leave him the note, but he had to take some responsibility for helping her make sense of the mess he'd once called his job.

She waited a good minute. When nobody answered, she knocked again. "George, it's me. Sophie Greenway. I have to talk to you."

Trying the handle, she found that the lock hadn't caught, that the door was open. Now she was in an even bigger quandary. She couldn't just walk in on him. What if he was asleep or . . . ? The possibilities were endless. And yet she couldn't leave with her tail between her legs, begging him on the phone tomorrow for some crumbs of help. This was business. He had to deal with it. Cracking the door several inches, she called, "George? I'm not going away until we talk."

No answer.

Moving hesitantly into the front foyer, she could smell something wonderful cooking in the oven, probably a pot roast. How sick could a guy be if he was about to eat a pot roast?

"George?" Rounding the entryway into the living room, she found it deserted but saw that someone had been sitting on the couch drinking wine. One wineglass sat on the coffee table in front of the couch and one was on an end table next to an armchair. Had he been entertaining?

Following the scent of roasting meat through the dining room, Sophie entered the kitchen, growing angrier with each passing second. The man didn't have the flu; he had *other plans*. She couldn't believe his apparent lack of obligation toward helping her settle in her new position.

Marching past the kitchen table, she was prepared to give him a piece of her mind when she saw him sprawled face-down on the white-and-black-checked linoleum in the pantry.

"George!" she shouted, rushing to him. Both of his arms were flung outward and blood oozed from several wounds in his back. Pressing her fingers to the side of his neck, she could feel that he was still warm. But as she pressed harder, searching for even the faintest sign of life, she realized it was futile.

For a moment, all she could do was stare. How could this have happened? There was no sign of a fight, not in the living room and not in the kitchen, and no weapon had been left behind. She wasn't a master of human physiology, but from the position of the wounds, she guessed his heart had been involved. No wonder there hadn't been a struggle. It had probably been all over in a matter of seconds.

Glancing up at the kitchen counter, she could see a knife block set to the right of the sink. The slot where the chef's knife should have been was empty. Perhaps she was jumping to conclusions, but it appeared that George might have been murdered with his own knife. She knew there was a certain irony in that, but she couldn't think about it now. She had to call someone. The police.

Backing out of the pantry, she decided not to use the phone in the apartment. She didn't want to touch anything. That left her cell phone, which was in the glove compartment of her car. As she passed the box on her way to the elevator, she hesitated. Surely this couldn't be considered part of the crime scene. Besides, if the police decided to take it into custody just because it had belonged to the deceased, there was no telling when she'd see it again. Making a quick decision, she scooped it into her arms and hurried to the elevator. She supposed there was no real reason to rush. George wasn't going anywhere, and he was surely beyond anyone's help now.

After placing the 911 call, she sat in her car and watched the light fade over the city. The police had asked her to wait at the scene until they arrived. No matter how hard she tried, she couldn't get the image of George lying dead on his pantry floor out of her mind. He might have been a lousy food critic, but he certainly hadn't deserved this.

Journal Note

Sunday, Midnight

A profitable day. I spent a good part of the morning doing research on the Internet. The more I think about it, the more convinced I am that the name of my Deep Throat, Pluto, must have a larger meaning. I feel that if I could just understand the clues, or which clues are significant, I could figure out who started this whole process. That's important to me because, the truth is, I would never have considered doing a biography of Constance Buckridge if I hadn't been fed some tantalizing leads. Bottom line: I'd like to know who I'm corresponding with.

Here's what I've put together so far.

1. *Pluto, also called Hades in Greek mythology, was the god of a dark, gloomy place called the Underworld.*
2. *In Roman mythology, Pluto was considered the judge of the dead.*
3. *Since the ground is where he lives, and all wealth comes out of the ground, Pluto was also thought of as the god of wealth.*

4. *He had two siblings.*
5. *Black sheep were offered to him as sacrifices.*
6. *Agamemnon said: "Hades is not to be soothed, neither overcome, wherefore he is most hated of all the gods."*
7. *Pluto (Hades) wore a helmet that made him invisible. Specifically, he wore the helmet when he went to kill Medusa, a female monster with snakes for hair and a gaze that turned people to stone.*
8. *Pluto sat on a throne holding a two-pronged fork. (Food image?)*
9. *Astronomy: Pluto is the farthest planet from the sun.*

Pluto led me to believe that the eminent Ms. Buckridge wasn't the generous, down-to-earth, levelheaded culinary guru everyone felt they knew and loved but instead was a duplicitous fraud. Oh, she can wield a saucepan, but my inside source insisted that she had secrets buried deep in her past, secrets that if fully brought to light would produce a scandal that would sell millions of books. Needless to say, Pluto had gotten my attention.

My feeling is that Pluto can't prove what he thinks he knows, and that's why he brought me in. He not only wants answers, he wants clear-cut confirmation of his theories. The other, more obvious reason, of course, is revenge. In each of the E-mails he's sent me, I can detect an undercurrent of hate. I've had a lot of experience reading between the lines and I know for a fact that something dark is at work here. But then I'm happy—no, not just happy, I'm eager—to be used if it will produce the kind of in-depth investigative biography that has become my trademark.

After my interview with Oscar Boland yesterday, I believe I can narrow my field of inquiry. I'm mainly concerned with four areas of Constance's past life. First, her relationship to Wayne Buckridge while she was still an employee in his house. Second, the death of Pepper Buckridge. Third, I want to know why Constance insisted that her brother come to live with them and, perhaps more important, why Wayne didn't like him. Wayne died less than a year after Arthur Jadek arrived. I need to know if there's a connection. And fourth, I need all the information I can find on her family of origin. So far I've come up with very little, and that confirms my own feelings that there's a real story here. Anybody who is so closemouthed about her past must have something to hide.

No comment from Pluto today on the Boland interview.

It's getting late. I was hoping to type up my interview with Eleanor Simpson, a secretary at WTWN-TV, when Constance had her show there, but I'm beat. I visited with her this afternoon in Lake Elmo. I will say that she gave me a fascinating piece of information. I don't know where it fits, but I intend to find out. I'll leave the transcription until tomorrow.
M.

11

"Remember I told you I had something special in mind for our lunch today?" Nathan held the car door open as Sophie got out.

"Where are we?" She gazed up at a wooden sign affixed to a stone arch above an iron gate. " 'New Fonteney'," she read, her eyes moving past the sign to a graveled path that led, as far as she could tell, deeper into the woods.

As they'd sped along I-94 heading east, Nathan had kept their destination a secret. All she knew was that he seemed as excited as a kid with a new toy. He'd arrived at her office at the Maxfield on the stroke of one but frowned when he saw what she was wearing.

"Don't you have something more casual you could put on? Jeans? An old sweatshirt?"

"We're having Happy Meals at McDonald's?"

He smirked. "Would a Cordon Bleu–trained chef do that to you?"

"I don't know. Would he?" Since she'd assumed they'd be eating lunch at one of the Twin Cities' more tony locations, she'd dressed up, not down. "What's with your face? Your electric shaver break?"

He rubbed his chin. "I thought I'd try growing a beard again. Just for old times' sake."

She shook her head but smiled. "Is that why we're lunching at the Golden Arches? You don't want to be seen around town looking like an aging derelict."

"Hey, I thought I looked sort of trendy."

The truth was, in his jeans, heavy leather belt, and denim shirt, he looked rough and handsome, the way she remembered him.

It took Sophie only ten minutes to change. Since the day was warm and humid, she decided to wear a cotton shirt. As she was putting on her hiking boots—she'd noticed that Nathan was wearing a pair, so she thought it might be smart to follow suit—she wondered what it would feel like to spend the day with him again after all these years. Her imagination clicked into overdrive. If she was going to back out, make up some excuse, it was now or never.

But once she stepped off the elevator and saw him waiting for her in the lobby, all his energy and anticipation focused completely on her, she knew that she couldn't disappoint him. Maybe she was being selfish, but she just wanted a few hours to enjoy the company of a man she'd once cared about very deeply.

On their way north through Stillwater, a small, historic town on the St. Croix River, all Nathan would say was that she'd better stop bugging him and be patient. In a few minutes, she'd find out where they were going.

Well, now they were there and she still didn't know where they were. "What's New Fonteney?"

"A Cistercian monestary built in the 1920s. Or, I should say, it was up until six months ago. That's when the monks packed up and left."

"Where'd they go?"

"The order merged with a similar one in West Virginia. That left this place looking for a new owner."

"You?"

"No, not exactly. I'll explain everything, but let's go take a look first."

The iron gate screeched as she pushed it open. "How atmospheric. A deserted monastery. You always were good at finding new places to explore. Remember when we discovered the ruins of that old mansion on Mount Curve, the one that used to sit on that amazing bluff overlooking downtown Minneapolis?"

"Sure I remember," he said, locking up the car. "We'd sit on the grass and try to figure out which room had been where. And if we rebuilt it someday, how we'd do it."

"Funny," she said, laughing at her own näiveté. "I always thought of that place as ours. In case you didn't know, they finally cut down the lilacs and built a bunch of condos." She turned just in time to see him hoist a picnic basket and a blanket out of the trunk. "Fried chicken and deli potato salad?" she asked.

"Have a little more faith, woman." Nathan grinned, slamming the trunk shut and then joining her. "Have I ever cooked you a bad meal?"

"You've never cooked me *any* meal."

"Well, we'll have to rectify that." Grabbing her hand, he led her through the gate, then turned off the path almost immediately and headed into the woods.

"I take it this is the back door?"

"More or less. There's a main entrance, but the approach isn't nearly as pretty."

As they came to a clearing, Sophie caught her first sight of New Fonteney, just as he'd wanted her to see it. It was . . . She couldn't quite find the word. "It's idyllic," she said finally. "Like a Constable painting." Huge puffy clouds rose up over the soft, undulating green hills. Next to her, she could feel Nathan breathing it all in. He was so different from Bram. An outdoorsman. Less polished.

"I love it here," he said, setting the picnic basket down.

They stood at the top of a grassy hill. Flowering apple trees dotted the landscape as the ground sloped gently away from them down to the St. Croix River. Sophie was transfixed by the beauty of it. After a few silent moments, they began their search for a suitable picnic site. As they walked along, she could see several low buildings in the distance emerging in the bright afternoon sunlight.

"Wait until you get inside the main hall. All the wood timbering—you couldn't afford to build a place like this today. Really, Sophie, it's amazing. And perfect."

"For what?"

He switched the picnic basket to his other hand. "I want Mom to buy New Fonteney. She's been talking for years about opening another campus for the cooking school. This place is ideal. It's secluded, with sublime views, but near a main highway and a small funky town. It has separate rooms for ninety students, which would be just about right. There's already a great garden, an apple orchard, a grape arbor that the brothers nurtured for years. I'm told they even made a little wine, just for themselves. There's a small guesthouse for visitors. A barn. A large kitchen. We'd have to add to it, but there's plenty of space. It wouldn't be a problem. The main hall is straight out of a Brother Cadfael novel. Ever read any of those?"

Sophie shook her head.

"The first time I was here, I thought I was in some kind of medieval time warp. The monks were all walking around in those dark brown cowls. I even got to sit in on one of their evening complines. It was almost unearthly, it was so peaceful."

"What would you do with the sanctuary?"

He shrugged. "I suppose we could use it for a study hall. Maybe a library. It's an impressive space, but not as churchy as you might think. Everything here is simply constructed, no stained glass, no obvious ornamentation, and yet it's so powerful. I'm sure we won't have any trouble putting every building to good use."

As they strolled toward the main hall, they continued to talk. Nathan explained what he'd learned from his first visit to New Fonteney. "The monks valued solitude, chose to live away from large towns. They wanted time to work, pray, study, to live a balanced life dedicated to God. I was impressed, although it's not the kind of life I'd want. And yet I don't know." Once again he breathed the air in deeply. "I always feel so relaxed when I come here. It's a special place. I'd hate to see that change."

"Do you think it will?"

"I think the peacefulness at New Fonteney is part of the karma, to borrow a term from our past. I'd like to see some of that being passed on to the students." He set the picnic basket down again, then spread the blanket on the grass.

The sweet, delicate scent from the apple blossoms was almost unbearably lovely. As Sophie watched Nathan smooth the wrinkles out of the blanket, time melted away.

"What are you thinking?" he asked, sitting down and pulling her down beside him.

"Oh, nothing very important."

His brown eyes seemed so sad. "You mean, nothing we can do anything about."

She looked away.

"Sophie, listen. I don't want this day to be a bummer for either of us. I just thought we could spend a few hours together. But if we can't, if it's too hard . . ."

"No," she said softly. "Of course not. I'm fine. Are . . . you fine?"

"I think so."

After a long moment, she began rubbing her hands together, hoping a change in subject would help. "What kind of grub did you bring?"

He laughed, dragging the picnic basket in front of him. "That's something I always loved about you, Soph. You never had a lot of pretensions."

"That's because to be a good card-carrying Minnesotan, you must never get *the big head*."

"God, where did all that crap come from? I've lived all over the world, and I can tell you from firsthand experience, the Midwest is a weird place."

"That's our Scandinavian heritage you're defaming, Mr. Buckridge. You're making light of the only place where true, God-given values are left in this world." Hearing a low rumbling in the distance, she looked up at the sky. Dark clouds were gathering along the western horizon. "You know, unless you brought something pretty minimal for us to eat, our picnic plans may have to be put on hold."

"Nonsense." He eyed the heavens with perfect serenity. "I checked the weather forecast before we left. We've got hours before any storm hits." He opened the basket and took out two champagne flutes and a bottle of 1990 Veuve Clicquot. "I was lucky enough to find this in a local wine shop."

She was impressed. It was one of the world's great luxury bottlings of champagne.

"And this way," he said, still grinning, "I didn't have to remember to bring along a corkscrew." He quickly unsealed the wrapping and popped the cork, pouring Sophie's glass first and then his. "Shall we make a toast?"

"Sure." She had to think fast. She didn't want him to propose something uncomfortable. "Why don't we drink to New Fonteney and the new cooking school."

"All right," he said, adding, "and to our time here this afternoon. May it be something we always remember."

They clicked their glasses.

After taking a sip, Nathan set his glass down. "This is wonderful, isn't it? A peaceful setting, fabulous food, and a beautiful woman to enjoy it with."

Sophie blushed. Hoping he hadn't noticed, she said, "I haven't seen any of that fabulous food yet."

"Well," he said, lifting out a series of packages wrapped in white paper, "it's not fried chicken and potato salad—not that I've got anything against that great American fare—but this seemed like more fun."

Watching him unwrap each item, Sophie was treated to an array of soft cheeses, some thinly sliced prosciutto, a wedge of duck terrine, and a special German wunderwurst—braunschweiger studded with pistachios. Next appeared thick, fragrant onion rolls and several varieties of French and German mustards. Then an assortment of fresh fruit, all cut and ready to eat: peaches, a honeydew melon, strawberries, and kiwis. And finally a cold Provençal ragout of vegetables.

"No dessert?" she asked, looking disappointed.

By the gleam in his eyes, she could tell he'd saved the best for last.

"As I recall, you like chocolate."

"You know I do."

He lifted a small covered dish out of the bottom. Removing the cover, he presented it to her. "A simple but elegant gâteau au chocolat. It has a brandy butter filling and a bittersweet glacé frosting. You like?"

Sophie's mouth watered. "Why don't we start with dessert first?"

He laughed. "You haven't changed a bit, you know that?"

For the next hour, they sipped their champagne and ate their food, all the while reminiscing about the past. Occasionally, Sophie would hear the rumble of distant thunder, but Nathan ignored it completely. Nothing was going to ruin the day for him.

Although the glow she felt was partly the wine, Sophie knew that most of it came from being with Nathan again. She couldn't exactly ignore the sensations churning inside her. The more they talked, the more she realized she still had some disturbingly intense feelings for him. And yet she loved Bram, too. She'd allowed herself to be coaxed into an untenable situation. Glancing at Nathan, she saw that he'd grown quiet, and wondered if he felt as unsettled as she did.

"Are you happy?" she asked finally. She had to know.

He picked up her hand and brought it to his lips. "At this moment, completely. Just don't wake me, okay?"

She smiled. "No, Nathan. I mean, are you happy with your life?"

"Sure."

"You don't sound all that convinced."

He shrugged, then wiggled his eyebrows. "It's nothing a fast car and a beautiful blonde couldn't cure."

"Come on, don't flirt. Answer me. Truthfully."

The light seemed to drain from his eyes. "I love my job."

"Your job isn't your life."

"Funny, for years I thought it was." He poured the last of the champagne into their glasses. After a moment he asked, "Do you know what a frustrated system is, Sophie?"

"I've never heard the term."

"Well, it's a matrix of sorts, a mathematical system in which the elements or the relationships, or both, are defined in such a way that all of the conditions for harmonious existence can never be met."

"Ah, okay. You want to explain that a little more clearly?"

He lifted his glass and studied the champagne's color. "My life is a frustrated system, Soph. I need three specific elements in it to feel whole, but at any one time I can only have two."

She nibbled a piece of cake. "You're going to have to be more specific. I don't really get it."

"All right." His eyes narrowed. "I can't be close to my family, be happy, and have a conscience all at the same time. I can have any two, but not all three."

Sophie frowned in thought. "So which one have you given up?"

A crack of thunder followed by a bright flash of lightning interrupted his answer.

Looking up at the sky, Nathan said, "I think I may have been wrong about that storm." He scrambled to his feet, dumping the dregs of their food into the basket.

A sudden gust of wind picked up the blanket and tossed it down the grassy slope.

"I'll get it," called Sophie, reaching it just as the first rain began to fall.

"Come on," he shouted as another bolt of lightning split the sky. "Let's head for the main hall."

Grabbing her backpack, Sophie followed him. It was a good half-mile to the vine-covered building. They traveled as fast as they could, hopping over rocks and thrashing their way through sections of tall grass. The storm was bad and getting worse. In the distance, Sophie saw a flash of light. An instant later the trunk of a tree exploded, the main part toppling over. By the time they reached the side door, they were both soaked to the skin. Nathan felt around in his pocket for the keys, and after pressing one into the lock, they were inside.

"Do I look as ridiculous as you do?" laughed Sophie, shaking the water from her clothes and hair like a wet dog.

Just as they'd entered the building, the rain poured down in sheets. Daylight faded into darkness. Every few seconds lightning flashed and thunder wasn't far behind. The storm was almost on top of them now.

"I wish we had a radio," said Nathan, rushing to one of the many windows that overlooked a graveled courtyard.

It was warm outside, but the air inside the hall was cold. "This could easily turn into a tornado." Sophie looked around, observing that the place was completely shut up. Nathan had been right about the timbering. It made the long, narrow, two-story room feel both solemn and grand, like a cathedral in miniature.

"We're going to be fine." He moved toward her. "I just wish we had something to help us dry off. We could freeze to death in here."

Another crack of thunder caused Sophie to jump.

Nathan put his arms around her. "Don't worry, Soph. I won't let anything hurt you . . . ever."

As she turned her face up to his, a curious thing occurred. She'd been talking nonstop all afternoon, but now she couldn't think of a thing to say.

"I love you," he said softly. "I never stopped."

"I know," she whispered. "God, I know."

"What are we going to do?"

When he kissed her, she felt helpless to resist. To be in his arms again seemed so right. And yet she pulled back. "Nathan, we can't."

"I know." He turned away, the palm of his hand pressed hard against his forehead. Walking back to the window, he said, "We can't get out of here until the storm lets up. This hall is connected to the living quarters. If I'm not mistaken, the brothers left a couple boxes behind. Maybe I can find a towel, a napkin. Anything we can dry ourselves off with." He glanced at the stone fireplace in the corner. "I'll get that going as soon as I come back. Will you be okay for a couple minutes?"

"I'm fine."

He turned and looked at her, then disappeared through a door at the back.

Sophie gazed down at her dripping clothes, feeling miserable. Utterly loathsome. How could she have let him kiss her? She should never have come. She had to get her bearings. Sitting down on a bare wood bench, she tried to shake off the feel of his mouth against hers.

Nathan came back a few minutes later looking triumphant. "I found some tablecloths and a couple of the brothers' cowls. We've got to get out of our wet clothes or we'll catch pneumonia. Here," he said, handing half of what he was carrying to her. "I'll go back and get dressed in the living quarters. You can dry off here. Okay?"

She nodded, hoping this wasn't another mistake.

"Get cracking. I want to start that fire ASAP."

Sophie waited until she was alone, then quickly peeled off her wet clothes, dried herself, and slipped the cowl over her head, tying the braided belt around her waist. It was a soft wool, a little scratchy but warm. The only problem was her feet. The fieldstone floor was like walking on ice.

"Are you decent?" called Nathan a little while later, some of the natural humor back in his voice.

Sophie thought it would be idiotic to make a joke out of her answer, considering the situation they were in. "I'm dressed, but my toes have turned to icicles."

"I've got just the answer to that." He breezed into the room carrying a pair of thick white socks. "I found some for myself, too."

Sophie tried them on. "Hmm. About five sizes too big. But

who's counting?" The cotton felt warm and soft against her tingling feet.

"Now," said Nathan, opening a wooden box next to the fireplace. "Hey, we're in luck. They left some logs and even some kindling." In just a few short minutes, the fire blazed. Nathan spread a blanket he'd found in the living quarters on the floor in front of the open hearth and they both sat down to dry their hair. "Thunderstorms don't last long. This one should be over soon."

She nodded, feeling chilled to the bone. Glancing sideways at him, she said, "The fire feels good."

"It smells good, too. I think it's applewood. I love smoking ribs over an applewood fire."

"Makes we wish we had some ribs."

He laughed. "You could eat again so soon after our picnic?"

"It might help us warm up."

He gave her a concerned look. "Not to worry. I've got just the thing." He jumped up to find the picnic basket. After removing a bottle Sophie hadn't seen before, he came back and sat down. "Cognac," he said, pulling out the cork. "Sorry, I don't have a clean glass. You'll just have to drink from the bottle. It'll give you that special 'wino' feeling we all know and love."

She shot him a nasty look. She felt as if the champagne she'd drunk earlier had left her system during their mad dash to the main hall, so the cognac did sound appealing.

Nathan held the bottle out to her. "Come on, it will warm you clear to your toes. Since I'm the designated driver, it's all yours."

Gingerly, she took a sip. And then another. It did feel good going down. Relaxing. Calming. She hadn't realized how tense she'd become.

"One more," said Nathan.

She didn't feel like arguing, so she took another swallow.

"Good. That should do it." He pushed the cork back into the bottle, then set it aside. "Better?"

"Yes, I think so."

He took hold of her hands. "Sophie, you're shivering."

When she looked into his eyes, she saw that he'd guessed the truth. She wasn't shivering from the cold but from being so close to him again. She could control her intellect but not her emotions. Her body simply wasn't cooperating.

Nathan gently put his arm around her, tipping her head back and kissing her again, this time with less urgency and far more tenderness. The kiss seemed to last forever. They lay back against the blanket, lost to everything but themselves.

"Sophie," he whispered finally, his lips close to her ear, "I know you love your husband. I don't want to interfere with that, but can't we have today? Aren't we due something after all these years?"

She had no answer.

"I just want to forget about everyone and everything and—" His mouth found hers again, this time more passionate, more searching.

Even though an important part of her didn't want this to happen, she could feel her body responding. He'd already unzipped her cowl and slipped his hand inside, caressing her breasts, her bare skin. She moaned softly in his arms. "Nathan, we can't."

"I want you, Sophie. So badly." His lips traveled down her neck, nibbling, biting, exploring.

It was like a dream. The fire. The strange building. The feel of him against her again. It seemed like they'd never been apart.

Suddenly, without warning, Nathan stopped and rolled away from her. "No" was all he said.

Sophie looked up at the wood timbers, feeling flushed and confused, her body still trembling from his touch. Closing her eyes, she knew he was right. She was glad he'd stopped because she wasn't sure she would have stopped him. But even so, she still didn't understand. "What's wrong, Nathan?"

He sat up, hugging his knees to his chest. "If we do this, you'll hate me. Not today maybe. But later. You won't be able to look me in the eye ever again."

"That's not true. I wouldn't hate you. But I might hate myself."

"It's all the same. I don't want any of those feelings between us because I've made a decision."

The ominousness of this pronouncement made her sit up. "What?"

"I want you, Sophie. Not just for a few hours but forever." He held up his hand. "I know you're married, but you didn't know I was free when you married the guy. Now that we've found each other again, I'm not leaving. I'm staying in your life until you realize you love me more than you love what's-his-name."

"Bram."

"Right." He stared at her. "Well? Say something."

"Do I have any choice in the matter?"

"Of course you do. You have the ultimate decision."

"If I asked you to leave me alone—now, today—would you?"

He dropped his head against his knees. After a long moment he said, "Yes." Looking up at her again, he added, "Is that what you're asking?"

She felt as if her emotions were being torn into a million pieces. She was a middle-aged woman, for God's sake. Her life should be stable. She shouldn't have to make decisions like this. She couldn't make a decision, not here, not now.

"Well?"

"I don't know, Nathan. I don't know what I want." And that scared her, more than she could say.

"You're telling me I have a chance then?"

"I'm telling you that I don't know."

"That's enough. For now."

Maybe he was happy with her response, but she wasn't. Glancing at the windows, she realized she'd barely looked outside since they'd come in from the storm.

"It's stopped raining," said Nathan, following her gaze to the courtyard.

"We can go."

He nodded.

She didn't get up. "It's like . . . you've just turned my life upside down, like you've dumped all my precious treasures out on the ground and then stomped on them."

"You're saying you'd rather have my memory than me?"

"I don't know. Maybe I would."

"I'm sorry," he said, covering her hand with his. "You've complicated my life, too. But I don't think either of us can turn our back on what just happened. We have to find a way through this, whatever happens."

She knew he was right, but she wasn't any less confused.

As she rose to find her clothes and stuff them in her backpack, her cell phone rang. "What time is it?" She'd taken off her watch when she was drying off.

"Ten after five."

"My God. I had no idea it was that late." Stepping over to her backpack, she retrieved the phone and clicked it on. "This is Sophie."

"Where the h . . . are . . ."

"Bram? Is that you?"

"You're break . . . up . . . can't under . . . aying . . ."

Damn. With everything that had happened last night, she'd forgotten to recharge the battery. She checked the warning light. Sure enough, it was low. "The battery's going," she said slowly, hoping he'd catch some of it.

Static. Then, " . . . get home right . . ."

"I should come home?"

More static. "Harry Hon . . . for Gil . . . murder."

"What? Say that again?"

"Arrested! Harry . . ." The rest was unintelligible. "Where are you . . . waiting since fo . . . ids ben . . . night."

"I'm not picking you up. Harry was arrested?"

" . . . es. This . . . diculous . . . Are . . . with Natha . . ."

"Yes, Nathan's here. We're fine."

" . . . home!"

"I got that. I'll be back in forty-five minutes." She shut it off.

"Sounds like we'd better get going," said Nathan, tying the shoelaces on his still soggy hiking boots. "If you want to pick up in here, I'll go get the car. It's a good mile and a half, but I'm a pretty fast runner, especially if I don't have to carry anything. I'll drive around to the main gate. Go out the side door and around the front of the building. You'll see it about fifty yards in front of you." He got up, straightening his cowl. "I guess we're going to make a real fashion statement when we get back to the hotel."

How was she going to explain *that* to Bram?

"You gonna be okay while I'm gone?"

"Just hurry, Nathan."

12

Bram checked his reflection in the mirrored elevator just before the doors opened and he stepped off. For the last few hours, his impatience had been fighting with his concern and anger. Sophie had promised she'd be home by six. At least that's what he thought he'd heard. The phone connection had been horrible. It was six-thirty now and she still wasn't back. If she was forty-five minutes away, where had the two of them gone? It was supposed to be a lunch date, right? Not an all-day marathon.

Against his better judgment, Bram pictured a secluded cabin in the woods, where Nathan Buckridge kept his back issues of *Playboy*, his king-size waterbed, and his sex toys. Shaking off the image, he felt a wave of disgust overwhelm him. Why hadn't Sophie kept him better informed? He shouldn't have to wait around while his wife was out on the town with her ex-squeeze.

Entering the crowded lobby, his eyes swept the room. Still no sign of them. Bram had stuck around Sophie's office until six—playing computer solitaire—then gone upstairs to get dressed for the AIDS benefit they were supposed to attend tonight. He hadn't forgotten about it. He wondered if she had.

Noticing Lela Dexter sitting in a club chair reading a magazine, he eased behind one of the marble pillars and watched her for a few seconds. She looked exceptionally serious and beautiful tonight in her black dress and gold jewelry. At the same time, Bram knew that if he didn't already know her, her remoteness would put him off. It was as if she wanted to be at the center of the action, but at the same time invisible. She also appeared nervous. She kept crossing and uncrossing her legs and every now and then would shoot a furtive glance around the lobby. It was almost as if she were trying to hide in plain sight, which made no sense at all. Snaking his way through the crowd waiting to be seated in the atrium—a string quartet was playing tonight—Bram stood over her, clearing his throat.

She turned a page, then looked up. "Well, if it isn't my favorite matinee idol." With a slow grin, she eyed his tux. "Going somewhere?"

"That was the plan."

"Don't tell me you've been stood up."

"Remains to be seen."

She gazed at him admiringly. "You know, men who look like you were born to wear a tux. If you were mine, Mr. Baldric, I'd make you wear one all the time, even to bed."

"Would you now?"

"I'm not kidding." Her voice grew decidedly seductive. "And I'd have a great time removing it, pearl stud by pearl stud."

He glanced up at the front entrance as a young couple entered through the glass doors.

"Looking for your wife?"

He checked his watch. Quarter to seven. Where *was* she? "Listen," he said, slipping his hands into his pockets, "if you're not busy, why don't I buy you a drink? You can fill me in on your vacation adventures."

She considered it for a few seconds, then closed the

magazine. "Sure, why not? The man I'm supposed to meet won't be here for another half hour."

His eyes still fixed on the glass doors, he said, "Great. Let me just tell the front desk where I'll be."

"I'll wait for you in the bar."

After conferring with Hildegard and learning that she had expected Sophie back by four at the very latest, Bram's worry grew exponentially. Had the bad weather caused them to be in a traffic accident? Was his wife lying in a ditch somewhere, calling his name?

All right, he told himself. Sophie always said he had a little too much melodrama in his soul. Maybe he shouldn't hit the panic button just yet. He'd give her another half hour. If she wasn't back by then, he would not only hit the panic button, he'd stomp on it with both feet.

Striding across the lobby to Scotties bar, he noticed Paul Buckridge, Nathan's younger brother, standing near the bank of courtesy phones. He was totally absorbed in the contents of a manila folder. On impulse, Bram walked toward him, his hand thrust out.

"Mr. Buckridge, hello. I'm Roger Thornhill . . . the, ah . . . food and beverage manager here at the Maxfield." He wasn't prepared to let Nathan's brother know that he was worried about his wife. Better to hide behind an alias.

Paul stood up straight and shook his hand. "I thought I'd already met the food and beverage manager, a Mr.—"

"He's my assistant. I trust everything has been to your liking during your stay with us?"

Paul adjusted his wire-rimmed glasses. "Yes, everything's been fine."

"Good, good. Your entire family feels happy and satisfied?"

"Yes, I'm sorry, Mr. . . ."

"Thornhill. Roger Thornhill. An old New England name."

"Right." Paul cocked his head. "Did anyone ever tell you you look a lot like—"

"No, no one ever has." Bram took him by the arm and guided him away from the phones.

"In *North by Northwest*, wasn't Cary Grant's character's name—"

"I'm absolutely no good at movie trivia, Mr. Buckridge. Say, I don't suppose you know where your brother is. I'd hoped to get back to him about a small matter today, but I haven't been able to locate him."

"I haven't seen him since this morning. He had a date with an old girlfriend."

"Really?"

"Yeah, funny thing, he ran into her by accident. I haven't seen him so excited in years. Who knows?" He grinned, elbowing Bram in the ribs. "Maybe he got lucky."

"Was he hoping to get lucky?"

"God, yes. She's an old flame from way back. His first true love. As far as I'm concerned, you can wake me when it's over."

"You don't believe in true love?"

"No, and I don't believe in the tooth fairy either. Now, if you'll excuse me . . ."

"Certainly." Bram let go of his arm. "But one last thing. I don't suppose you know where they were having lunch?"

"Did I say they were having lunch?"

"Yes, I think you did."

"Funny, I don't remember it."

Bram's voice grew less friendly. "Call me psychic."

Paul Buckridge stood back and really looked at him for the first time. "Why are you so interested in my brother?"

"As I said, I have a private matter I need to discuss with him."

Paul tucked the folder under his arm and said, "Good evening, Mr. Thornhill." Turning abruptly, he walked away.

Well, thought Bram, yanking on his French cuffs as he headed into the bar, that was a fruitless interaction.

"You look like you just lost your best friend," said Lela as he slid into the other side of the booth.

"I wouldn't go that far—yet." He saw that she'd already ordered.

"The waiter said he'd bring you a martini as soon as you

arrived. They must know your likes and dislikes around here.
Pretty soft."

"I'm a lucky man."

"You don't sound like you mean it."

He smoothed his graying temples. "My luck, or lack
thereof, isn't a very interesting topic. Why don't we talk about
something else?"

"All right. How about some local color?" She drew her
finger around the edge of her glass. "I understand there was a
homicide in Minneapolis last night, a food critic."

"Ah, another relaxing topic."

"Yes, I suppose it kind of hits close to home, since your
wife found the body and is taking over his position at the
Times Register."

"If you're wondering if I'm happy about Sophie's choice of
second careers, I'm not."

"I don't suppose you've got any inside information on why
he died."

Bram shrugged. "They've arrested a fellow named Hongisto.
He owns a restaurant that Gildemeister basically killed with two
negative reviews."

"You're saying it was revenge?"

"I assume so. And I can't tell you how pleased I am to think
that Sophie's about to dangle the culinary sword of Damocles
over the heads of the other restaurateurs in this town."

"You know, Bram, I've been around the block more than
once in my—shall we say—youngish life. I've never known a
food critic to be murdered before, not that some of them don't
deserve it. Trust me, you don't need to worry. Your wife isn't
in any danger."

The waiter finally arrived with his martini. Hoisting it in a
mock toast, Bram downed several swallows as if it had just
arrived in the nick of time.

"You really are upset, aren't you?" All her normal playful-
ness dropped away.

In its place Bram could see real concern in her eyes. For
some reason, it surprised him that she would care. "I'm okay.
Or at least I will be when my wife gets back."

"You know, guys like you don't grow on trees. I hope Sophie knows what a lucky woman she is."

"I hope so, too." Taking another sip, he continued. "So what have you been up to since I saw you Saturday?"

Her serious expression returned.

"Hey, what's up?"

"It's good to have a friend. You are my friend, aren't you?"

"Sure."

She glanced down at her drink. "I was hoping you'd say that. I don't know you very well, but I feel that you're an honest man. I'm a good judge of character. It comes in handy in my line of work."

"The UN."

She looked up at him. After a long moment she said, "Friends trust each other, right?"

"That's what I've heard."

"What if I told you I didn't work at the UN? That it's just a cover story I sometimes use?"

"Why?"

She gazed at him pointedly, then looked down again. "For anonymity's sake. Sometimes it comes in handy in my profession."

"You're a spy?"

She had a surprisingly wicked laugh.

Bram was delighted that he'd said something funny, though he didn't know what. Even so, he enjoyed watching her. Her laughter made her seem more touchable somehow.

"I'm a writer," she said finally.

"Ah, I get it. If you construct a particularly bad sentence, you don't want anyone to know who did it."

She shook her head and smiled. "I like you, Bram. You're good for me. You don't take life as seriously as I do. I need that kind of perspective sometimes."

"You can always count on me for perspective." He finished his drink and then held up the glass, motioning for the waiter to bring him another.

"You can't tell anyone what I'm about to tell you, okay? That's essential."

He crossed his chest and held up his hand. "Deal."

"This really is serious."

"My lips are sealed. But why take the chance of confiding in me, basically a total stranger?"

She hesitated before answering. "Sometimes I need a solid physical presence to bounce ideas off of. I do a lot of traveling in my line of work. My life can get pretty lonely at times."

"What exactly is your line of work?"

Again she hesitated. "I started out as an investigative reporter. For the past ten years I've been writing unauthorized biographies."

"Any published?"

"Yes, seven."

"So you write the kind of books that elevate gossip to art?"

She lifted her head and met his eyes directly. "My books are carefully documented. I hold myself to the very highest standards. That's why I'm so good at what I do and why publishers salivate when they hear I've found a new project. I find what my subjects want to bury—the lies, the hypocrisy, and the sizzle. I entertain, but at the same time I enlighten. In this country, we make celebrities into minigods. In my books, I bring them back down to earth. I feel as if I'm performing a public service, showing how insidious the notion of celebrity really is. We're all alike underneath."

"No saints, no heroes?" The waiter arrived with Bram's second martini.

"Would it surprise you to learn that, once upon a time, I actually thought I might be a saint? I came from a very devout Catholic family, raised on the stories of the saints. When I was ten, it occurred to me one day that I really was a superior being. And my family, well, they were pillars of the community. It seemed only right that they would produce someone special. I knew I might have to suffer, even be martyred, but once the idea was fixed in my mind, it took some pretty hard knocks to push it out."

"Like what?"

She sipped her drink. "Oh, things like discovering my mother was the town whore. And my father, well, he wasn't really my father. My real father was the parish priest who baptized me, the one I made my confession to every week. I was fifteen when I discovered the truth. You can imagine that it came as quite a shock. So I started digging deeper into my family's background. Turns out the man I thought was my father liked little boys. That's probably what drove my mother into the arms of other men, not that she wasn't predisposed that way to begin with. Believe me, you don't want to hear the rest."

"It gets worse?"

She nodded. "So you can see why there are no saints in my world. I've been searching for years to find a true hero, but they don't exist. They're all just people—fallible, corrupt, sinners all."

"You must believe there's one out there, otherwise you'd stop looking."

Her features slowly tightened. "No, I lost my faith in humankind's essential goodness a long time ago."

For some reason, Bram didn't believe her.

"I'm researching something right now that may turn out to be the biggest book of my career."

"Anyone I know?"

She paused to light a cigarette. Lowering her voice, she said, "Constance Buckridge."

"So that's why you're staying at the hotel, why you wanted to go to Kitchen Central the other day."

She nodded, exhaling smoke high into the air.

"You're after an all-American culinary icon. But what could be interesting about her life? It's sort of Ozzie and Harriet, with Ozzie dying just as Harriet wins the lottery."

"I'm sifting through the essentials right now. It could be as simple as infidelity, but I'll bet my bottom dollar it goes much deeper. Perhaps," she added, lowering her voice again, "as deep as murder."

He wasn't shocked by much these days, but he was shocked by that. "Do you have proof?"

"Not yet. I'm just beginning my research."

Bram tried to rub the tension from the back of his neck. "Okay, but if you're so well known in the publishing world, how come I've never heard of you?"

"Lela Dexter isn't my real name."

He should have guessed as much. "What is?"

"Marie Damontraville."

Of course. Now he remembered. That's why she'd seemed so familiar the first time they'd met. He'd interviewed her once many years ago. "You were on my show. The book was about—"

"Mickey Mantle."

"Right!" He stared at her a moment, then cocked his head and crossed his arms over his chest. "But why do I get the feeling there's still something you're not telling me?"

"There's a lot I'm not telling you."

"No, I mean, you've got another motive for confiding in me." He hesitated. "Something's frightened you. That's why you looked so nervous sitting in the lobby."

She blinked. "God, am I that transparent? I pride myself on having such a poker face." She finished her drink, then set the glass down and pushed it away. Retrieving her cigarette from the ashtray, she continued. "It happened earlier in the day. I've never felt quite this shaken up before. I really believe my life is in danger."

"Any particular reason?"

"I received a threatening note."

"Which said?" Before she could answer, he glanced over her shoulder and saw that Sophie had entered the bar. "Hey, Soph!" He stood, waving her over. Looking down at Marie, he apologized. "I'm sorry. I've interrupted your story. I really am concerned."

"It's okay. We can finish this another time."

"Are you sure? Will you be all right?"

"As soon as the bodyguard I hired gets here, I'll be fine." She turned to look as Sophie rushed toward them. "Lord. Does she always dress like that?"

Bram couldn't quite imagine why his wife was wearing a

monk's cowl. And she wasn't alone. Nathan Buckridge, dressed in the same ludicrous way, followed closely.

"Sweetheart," said Sophie, hurrying up to the table and giving him a kiss. "I'm so sorry. We got caught in the storm and ended up inside a deserted monastery. Then, on the way home, we had a flat tire."

"Really," said Bram, his voice suggesting that he was less than impressed with her explanation. He turned to Nathan, glad that he was a good three inches taller. "You must be the *ex*-boyfriend."

Nathan nodded. "I'll leave you two alone now, but I just wanted to tell you that I'd hoped to have Sophie back here by four. I never counted on the storm or the crappy tires on my rental car. I take all the blame. I hope you won't be angry with her."

Now Bram was furious. "Look, *Bozo,* you don't need to protect my wife from *me*."

"I didn't mean—"

"Nathan," said Sophie, "why don't you go. I've had a really nice time. The picnic was wonderful."

"Sure. Okay." It was hard to look dignified in a monk's cowl, especially when everyone in the room was staring, but he made a valiant stab at it as he turned and stalked out of the bar.

"You had me worried sick!" said Bram, taking hold of Sophie by her shoulders.

"I know, honey. Really, I couldn't help it. But I'm back now. And everything's fine."

She sounded way too tittery, thought Bram. Something was up.

"Why are you wearing a tux?" she asked.

"We were supposed to attend that AIDS fund-raiser tonight, remember?"

"Oh, no." She touched her hair, then smiled weakly. "We got caught in the rain."

"Why don't we go upstairs? You can fill me in on all the details up there. That is, unless you plan to go to the St. Paul Club dressed like Friar Tuck."

She glanced at Marie. "Sophie Greenway," she said, holding out her hand.

"Lela Dexter."

"Nice to meet you. You know my husband . . . how?"

"He interviewed me on his show once. Many years ago. We bumped into each other in the lobby and just got to talking."

"Right," said Sophie, looking a little unsure. "My huband's very sociable. It was nice of you to keep him company."

"My pleasure."

Sophie studied her for several more seconds before turning to Bram. "Come on, honey."

He was torn. He wanted to make sure Marie was okay, but since she had help on the way, he decided that clearing the air with Sophie was more important. "I hope I see you again, Ms. Dexter."

"Oh, I'm sure we'll run into each other. I'm staying at the hotel through the end of next week."

Bram noticed Sophie sneaking peeks at Lela over her shoulder as he tugged her through the room and out the door.

Journal Note

Monday, 9 P.M.

I've switched rooms. I'm now in a two-bedroom suite on the eleventh floor. My new bodyguard, a man named Rafferty—his first name is Sean, but he prefers to be called by his last—is ensconced in his own bedroom. He isn't the talkative type, and that's just fine with me. He's huge, sufficiently menacing, trained in the martial arts, and carries a Glock neatly tucked under his suit coat. What more could a girl want?

I've finally calmed down, but after what happened earlier today, I still feel uneasy. Someone in the Buckridge clan has discovered not only that I'm here but that I'm digging into their past. I have to be more careful, although I don't like living this way. Then again, it was a quick means of discov-

ering that I'm on the right track. And that makes me more determined than ever to continue my search.

No word from Pluto. He's already got Oscar Boland's interview, and as soon as I'm done transcribing Eleanor Simpson's interview tonight, it will be sent off as well, winging its way in cyberspace to his anonymous remailer. If he has any more help to give, I wish he'd give it. This biography's got to take shape fast. Not that my leads aren't growing. This morning I put two of my best field researchers on the trail of the Jadek family. Supposedly, Arthur and Constance are from Wisconsin. I want to know more about their background. Were there other brothers or sisters? Are the parents still alive? None of this has ever been written about. Hopefully, I'll have the answers soon.

The short interview with Eleanor Simpson took place yesterday afternoon at her daughter's house in Lake Elmo. Eleanor is in her seventies now, but still vigorous. She said she walks a mile every day, if not outside, then on her daughter's treadmill. We sat on a screened back porch. Her daughter asked if she could stay and listen, and I agreed.

Eleanor wore matching pink sweats and smiled excessively. She was delighted that she might be quoted in a book and was very willing to answer all my questions. I didn't think I'd get much out of her, other than general background and a confirmation of various dates, and my sense proved to be true until the very last minute. Feeling frustrated that my time had been wasted, I tossed out a final question. I never expected the answer I received, and though I don't know where it will lead, I think it may turn out to be significant.

INTERVIEW: ELEANOR SIMPSON, LAKE ELMO, MINNESOTA, SUNDAY, MAY 9

M: *You worked for WTWN-TV in the Seventies, is that correct?*
Simpson: *(Nods) I was there for seventeen years. Started as a*

*file clerk and worked my way up to associate producer. Loved
every minute of it.*

M: *When did you first meet Constance Buckridge?*

Simpson: *After you called, I took out my old station records.
I've got them all right here. (Nods to a stack of folders and
notebooks) I guess you could say I never throw anything out.
I figure it will come in handy one day. (Checks in notebook) I
met Connie in September of '72. At the time I was a produc-
tion assistant on the* Daytime with Jerry & Emmeline *show.
About three months before, we'd started producing a cooking
segment. Jerry was hopeless. All he could do was stir things
and smile stupidly at the camera. Emmeline wasn't much
better. I think what sparked their interest was that in early
June that year they'd been invited to the Buckridge home for
one of Connie's special soirees. I mean, these parties were
the talk of the town. Everyone said how classy the house was,
how the food was like nothing they'd ever tasted before.
Connie Buckridge had a reputation as a fabulous cook. Her
husband, Wayne, built houses for a living. They were very
well off. They lived in a beautiful home on Lake Minnetonka. I
think* House & Garden *even featured it once. The interior design was very chic, lots of Oriental touches. Outside, the
place looked sort of Sixties modern, with a terraced front
yard, a patio in the back, lots of old trees and shrubs, a
boathouse, a pool, speedboats, a gazebo close to the beach—
everything you'd ever want. I suppose you could say the
Buckridges were the cream of the Twin Cities social scene.
Anyway, one morning I was informed that, for the afternoon
show, Connie Buckridge would be coming in to do the
cooking segment. I liked her immediately. She was funny,
quick, even a little bit theatrical, a natural in front of the cameras. She was also attractive in a wholesome sort of way.
After the first couple shows, she started coming in once a
week. A neighbor of hers helped her do the setups.*

M: *Do you remember the neighbor's name?*

Simpson: *I wouldn't have recalled, but I just read it in my
notes. Her name was Wells. Vashti Wells. She was very dark
and beautiful, born in India but raised in America. Her hus-*

band was a banker, I believe. Anyway, she and Connie were quite close. Vashti would come in early to prep the set and then Connie would arrive just before showtime and whip up something wonderful. We all got to eat whatever she made that day. It wasn't long before she became a regular. People just seemed to love her.

M: *After working with Constance for a while, what did you think of her, personally?*

Simpson: *Well, she could be demanding at times, but it was because she wanted everything perfect. I respected that. It was hard not to like her. She was warm, a wonderful mother. Her two sons would come to the set with her sometimes. Both handsome boys, although the younger one was kind of scruffy-looking. I think she was having some problems with him. His hair was awfully long. But then it was the early Seventies. Connie was down-to-earth. That quality came through on the shows. I mean, she'd done a lot of traveling, been taught by some of the finest chefs all over the world, but she was just a regular person. When she got her own show—*

M: *When was that?*

Simpson: *In April of '73. It ran for about five months on WTWN and then it was canceled. It had a horrible time slot. Seven o'clock, Sunday mornings. Connie was devastated, of course, but it wasn't long before the local PBS station offered her a contract. She was billed as Minnesota's answer to Julia Child, who was very big at the time. And from there Connie went nationwide and became the celebrity she is today. She's a real homegrown success story.*

M: *What year did she start at the PBS station?*

Simpson: *(Pages through her notes) October of '73. Several months later her husband died. He had a heart attack. Very sad.*

M: *Did Constance miss any shows because of it?*

Simpson: *I don't know. I didn't see her much after she left WTWN. But since I know they were taped, she probably had a few in the can and was able to work around it. I know it was a very hard time for her and the children.*

M: *I assume she and her husband had a close relationship.*

Simpson: *(Hesitates) I'd only seen them together a couple of times. Mr. Buckridge had put on a lot of weight after they'd gotten married. Connie was forever worrying about the way he ate. She tried everything she could think of to get him to eat more sensibly. But Wayne Buckridge was a bullheaded man. Anybody who'd spent five minutes in the same room with him knew that. I'm sure it was hard for Connie to watch his health deteriorate. Did you know she was one of the first TV chefs to talk about low-cal eating? It's funny, and please don't quote me, but I don't think Mr. Buckridge was a very happy man. I'm sure he loved his wife and his family, but in a way I believe he was eating himself to death. People can commit suicide in a lot of different ways. He may have been attractive once, but at the end, he was a sight. Way over three hundred pounds.*

M: *You really believe he was trying to kill himself?*

Simpson: *(Shrugs) Maybe that wasn't his intent. But with his doctors all telling him he had to change his lifestyle, otherwise he was a dead man, what conclusion would you draw?*

M: *Is there anything that really stands out in your memory about Constance? Anything unusual that might have happened?*

Simpson: *Like what?*

M: *You tell me. I'm not asking for things like how Connie might have burned the onions one day or fought with the director over the lighting or the menu. But perhaps you remember something that had to do with her children? Or her brother? Even her husband? Something she said or did that seemed odd.*

Simpson: *(Taps a finger to her chin) Well, now that you bring it up . . . (Shakes her head) No, you wouldn't be interested in that.*

M: *Please let me decide.*

Simpson: *(Hesitates) Well, there was this one time. I don't know if it's exactly what you're looking for. It happened when we were taping one of her morning shows. One of the first ones, late April or early May of '73. I believe the subject that day included fruit ices—or homemade ice cream. Whatever. The tape*

*began rolling and Connie started some things chilling, talking
all the while about the differences between sorbets, gelatos,
sherbets. A few minutes into the show, this rather frightening
man walked into the studio.*

M: *Why frightening?*

Simpson: *It was the way he looked. Furtive. And filthy.*

M: *Did the station have a tight security system?*

Simpson: *Not really. If the woman at the front desk was busy,
he could have slipped in through the side door without
anyone seeing him. The guys in the booth wouldn't have noticed. During a taping, they were totally focused on their tech
stuff.*

M: *Can you describe the man?*

Simpson: *I'll never forget him. He was thin and tall, probably
over six feet. And he had long black hair and a long scraggly
beard, matted and smelly and dirty. His jeans and army
jacket were ripped and torn, badly soiled, and his sandals
were falling apart. I can still remember how filthy his feet
looked, how long the toenails were, like he hadn't had a bath
in years. He wasn't just a hippie, he looked like someone
who'd been living on the street most of his life.*

M: *Was he old? Young?*

Simpson: *Young. Twenties, I'd say, although under all that
hair and dirt, it was hard to tell. But he moved like a young
man. Talked like one. Anyway, the minute Connie saw him,
she stopped what she was doing and rushed off the platform.
The producer was furious. Everything on the set was about
to melt under the hot lights, but Connie didn't seem to care.
That was very unlike her. All she said was "This is important.
Give me a minute, please." She pushed the man farther into
the darkness, closer to where I was standing, and they talked
quietly.*

M: *Could you hear what they were saying?*

Simpson: *(Hesitates) Well, first he said something like "Did
you bring the bread?" I assumed he was talking about
money. Connie nodded that she had and told him to lower his
voice.*

M: *Did you hear anything else?*

Simpson: *Just some snippets of conversation. At one point the man said the words "very ill" and then "crazy talk." But that was it. Whatever they were discussing, however, was serious. At one point, Connie started to cry.*

M: *Go on.*

Simpson: *Well, she never said where she was going or why. She never even said goodbye. She and the young man just rushed out. She also didn't come back that day or try to call to explain her odd behavior. I know the producer was ready to fire her.*

M: *Had she ever done anything like that before?*

Simpson: *Never. She was always totally professional. Anyway, her producer tried to reach her at home that night, but nobody answered. She finally reappeared three days later, full of apologies. She explained that the man was a friend of her younger son's, and he was in some terrible legal trouble. He was also penniless. If the police found him before he got some much-needed legal advice, he could have gone to prison. Connie said she found him a lawyer and now everything was okay.*

M: *Did you believe her story?*

Simpson: *I wanted to, but—(Shakes her head) It didn't square with what I'd heard.*

M: *And what do you think they were talking about?*

Simpson: *I figured that somebody was sick, someone Connie loved. So sick, possibly feverish, that he or she wasn't making any sense.*

M: *Did she ever mention this man again in any way?*

Simpson: *Never. Thankfully, the producer bought her story. He was still angry but said he'd give her another chance. The taping was rescheduled.*

M: *You have absolutely no idea who the guy was?*

Simpson: *No.*

M: *And you never saw him again?*

Simpson: *Never.*

M: *Thank you for your time, Eleanor. You've been a big help.*

* * *

Final note:

When I sent this interview to Pluto tonight, I included a request: "Please, if you have any idea who this man is, let me know right away. Since I assume you're a family member, or a close friend of the family, you may be my only way to get to the bottom of this. I believe it to be highly significant. Also, I need to find Vashti Wells. Do you have any idea if she's still alive, and if so, where she's living? One last point. My life was threatened today. I assume it was by someone in the Buckridge family. Do you have any knowledge of this? I've hired a bodyguard, but I feel a much greater sense of urgency now. You started all this in motion, Pluto. You've got to help me finish it before someone gets hurt!"
M.

13

Late Tuesday morning Sophie was ushered into a small, nondescript waiting room on the second floor of City Hall, where she would finally meet with Harry Hongisto. After attending his arraignment earlier in the morning, she had agreed to write the bail bondsman a check so that Harry wouldn't have to remain in jail until the trial. Harry was strapped. Every last bit of his savings had gone into keeping his restaurant afloat. He'd even taken out a second mortgage on his house. She didn't know all the details, but from what everyone said, the evidence against him was damning. Still, she wanted to hear it from his own lips, especially since he claimed that he was innocent and that someone—he didn't know who—was trying to frame him.

Before leaving the hotel, Sophie had invited Bram to come along to the arraignment, but he'd declined, saying he had to get to the radio station for a staff meeting. She wasn't sure she believed him, which depressed her more than she could say. She sensed that he wanted to get away from her. He was still acting somewhat cool after yesterday's fiasco, and in many ways she didn't blame him.

Bram couldn't understand why she hadn't called if she knew she was going to be late. After all, common courtesy would dictate that, in order to prevent her poor husband from worrying, she'd pick up the phone and let him know she was okay and when she'd be back. She tried to frame an answer that made sense but couldn't be entirely truthful, and somehow he seemed to know. How could she tell him she'd been sitting in front of a roaring fire with her old boyfriend, caught up in his embrace? Caught up also by feelings she thought had died more than twenty-five years ago? She couldn't exactly paint a picture of what had gone on, why her mind had been elsewhere. She knew Bram trusted her, but she also knew he was confused. Sophie had tried her best to prove to him last night how much she loved him, but this morning she wondered if she'd done nothing more than behave like a guilty spouse.

When it came right down to it, she was angry at herself for the way she'd behaved with Nathan. She loved her husband. What had she been thinking yesterday? She wanted a life with Bram, not with Nathan Buckridge. She didn't even know Nathan anymore. Sure, maybe she continued to be flattered that an old flame was still interested after all these years—interested in a slowly crumbling, middle-aged woman, to be exact—but she had to back away before matters got out of hand.

Then again it was much easier to be clearheaded and resolute when she wasn't staring into Nathan's eyes. She couldn't deny the power he still exerted over her. After all these years, the electricity hadn't dimmed one bit. But to Sophie's mind, the worst part was that she'd hurt Nathan badly all those years ago and now she was about to hurt him again. She saw no use in debating whether life was fair or not. The fact was, no matter how hard it might be, she had to tell him the truth. There could be nothing between them now, not even friendship.

A few minutes later the door opened and Harry, still dressed in orange coveralls, entered. When he joined Sophie at the table, he lowered himself into the chair like a weary old man who'd accepted his defeat.

"Are you all right?" she asked tentatively.

"No."

"No one's hurt you, have they?"

He shook his head. "Sophie, I appreciate that you came down to the arraignment and put up the money to get me out. If there's ever any way I can repay you, I will, because staying another day in that hellhole . . ." He looked away.

"You're going home, Harry. As soon as they process you out of here."

"I don't belong in a place like this," he said, slamming his fist hard into the tabletop. "I'm an innocent man. I've always lived an honest life. I'm not a criminal, for chrissake. You believe me, don't you? I may have wanted to see Gildemeister squirm, but I never would have hurt him. Never!" A dark red color rose in his cheeks.

Sophie was concerned for his blood pressure. The stress couldn't be doing his aging heart any good.

"The D.A. seems to think my case is a slam dunk. That's what my lawyer called it. They've got enough evidence on me to put me away for the rest of my life."

"But I don't understand. Nobody saw you murder George, right?"

"Doesn't matter."

"Sure it does. It means the case against you is circumstantial."

He gripped his hands together in his lap. "I just wish to God I'd never heard the name George Gildemeister. Think of it, Sophie. What's your father going to say when he finds out what's happened?" He nodded to his clothing. "*This* is the crime. But your father's going to think he's got a murderer for a buddy."

"Harry?" She hesitated. "What exactly do the police have on you?"

He huffed. "Just about everything but a signed statement admitting my guilt."

"Can you be more specific?"

He tapped his fingers impatiently on the tabletop. "First, they've got my prints on a glass at Gildemeister's apartment."

Sophie remembered now. When she'd entered the living room, it looked as if George had been entertaining someone. "A wineglass?"

He nodded.

"You mean you were actually in his apartment the night he was murdered?"

"Sure. I never denied it. I had to go, Sophie. I had to give that bastard a piece of my mind."

"And did you?"

"Oh, you know George. He was all smiles. Invited me in, poured the wine before he even asked if I wanted any. He was going to be the reasonable one, take the high road. I tried to keep my temper from boiling over, tried to have a reasonable discussion with the man, but it was impossible. We ended up arguing, screaming at each other. I'm not proud of that, Sophie, but I think I had a right to let off some steam."

"So what happened?"

"What do you mean what happened? You're asking me if I went into the kitchen, removed a knife from his knife block set, and stabbed him in the back?"

"Did you?"

"No!" He raked a hand over his two-day stubble. "At exactly five to seven, he looked at his watch and then hustled me out of there. Our conversation was over, he said. From the way he acted, I assumed he was expecting someone."

"Do you know who?"

"If I did, I wouldn't be in jail. I should have stuck around, but it never occurred to me that I'd need to know who his murderer was."

Sophie thought of the man she'd seen leaving the building that night just as she'd arrived. He'd seemed familiar somehow, but it hadn't been Harry. She was sure of that. "What else do they have on you?"

He groaned. "The murder weapon. The police found it in my neighbor's garbage can. The knife was wiped clean of fingerprints and wrapped in some old newspapers. They assume, incorrectly, that I put it there after I killed him. There's a residue of blood on the blade, I guess. They've matched it to George's blood type. Now they're doing some DNA tests to prove beyond the shadow of a doubt that it was his."

"But if you didn't put it there, that means the murderer planted it. How would he know to do that? You could have had an airtight alibi, could have been at your restaurant with dozens of people to confirm that fact."

"But I wasn't. And that means he had to have seen me coming out of Gildemeister's apartment. Maybe he also knew about the reviews Gildemeister had written and figured the police would assume I had a grudge against him, which I did. I was the perfect patsy." Harry's body seemed to sag under the weight of the evidence against him. "I had to close the restaurant today, Sophie. My lawyer called the assistant manager this morning and told everyone to go home. I can't deal with any of that right now, not when I'm fighting for my life."

"Do the police have other evidence against you?"

He ran a hand over his balding crown, then through the halo of white hair surrounding it. "Plenty. For starters, they've got that note I dropped off at the paper last weekend. My lawyer thinks it might be inadmissible, but I'm not holding my breath because, well, after they found the murder weapon a few feet from my back door, they had probable cause to search the house." Dropping his head in his hands, he added, "God, I never thought anyone would read all the other letters I wrote. I mean, I was half in the bag when I wrote most of them. I know they were full of rage. Maybe they even made me seem a little crazy. But it was just fantasy, Sophie, playing with what I would do to that bastard if I could. But, I mean, I *wouldn't*. I didn't!"

Sophie winced at the realization that Harry's chances of

beating this charge were pretty slim. "I don't suppose you've got any idea why someone would want Gildemeister dead?"

Lifting his eyes and giving her a defeated look, he said, "Maybe you'd better check the rest of his reviews. He no doubt stepped on other toes."

She nodded, though she didn't want to believe that was possible. If critics thought retaliation against them for a bad review included murder, nobody would want the job.

"And hey, come to think of it, if you'd put a gun in the hand of my head chef the other night—"

"You mean David Polchow?"

"That's the guy. He was breathing fire when he stormed out the door."

Perhaps it was worth checking out. But as it was, the entire subject was starting to make Sophie uneasy. Surely there had to be another reason why George had been murdered. "Do you have Polchow's address?"

"He lives in the Willow Square Apartments, near Riverplace."

She took a pen and a piece of paper out of her purse and wrote it down. "Okay, any other thoughts?"

Harry shook his head. "The problem is, I didn't know Gildemeister personally. Who knows? Maybe his wife hated his guts. Or his kids. But it's all moot now. The police believe they've got their man. They aren't going to do any further investigating, unless it's to nail me. The worst part is, I hammered the final nail in my own coffin with those letters."

Sophie tried to look encouraging. "Don't give up, Harry. Please. I'll do everything I can to help."

"Maybe you think the real killer's going to come down to the courthouse and turn himself in? As far as I can see, that's the only way I'm not going to prison."

She didn't want to promise him too much, but she couldn't just let him swing in the wind, with no one on his side. She really did believe he was innocent. For his sake, and for the sake of the lifelong friendship he'd shared with her father, she had to do something to find out what had really happened to George Gildemeister last Sunday night.

14

"Is everybody here?" asked Constance, glancing quickly around Paul and Nathan's suite.

"Paul's still in the shower," answered Arthur. He was sitting alone on the love seat, smoking a cigarette and tapping the ash carefully into an ashtray. "He's been out playing tennis and wanted to clean up before the meeting."

Constance moved farther into the room. Sitting down on one of the brown mohair club chairs, she crossed her legs and adjusted her gray linen skirt over her knee. Although she loved her family, at this moment she felt a pang of anxiety so intense, it made her stomach clench.

Emily sat on the sofa, hugging her knees to her chest, the phone pressed between her ear and shoulder. A lock of straight blonde hair fell across her forehead, making her look more like a teenager than a well-respected professional photographer and the mother of two small boys. Kenny sat next to her, absorbed in a magazine. "Who's Emily talking to?" mouthed Constance, looking back at Arthur.

"The twins," he whispered, giving her a wink.

Constance would have loved to talk to her two grandchildren at home back in New Haven, but she had more pressing matters on her mind right now. She smiled at Nathan, who was standing by the windows, also smoking. When the family was nervous—they always were before a family powwow—almost everyone relied on nicotine to calm down. She supposed it was better than Valium or marijuana, but she still wished more of them would try to quit. So far, Paul had been the only one to kick the habit completely. She had to give him credit. He had more willpower than anyone else in the family, including her.

"No, Eric," said Emily patiently, "you each get to pick one program to watch. That's the way it works. You have to share." She listened a moment. "Eric, tell Brandon to give the remote to Nanna Bailey. What?" She looked at Kenny, shaking her head. "No, not to you, to Nanna. Just because you're one minute older than your brother doesn't mean you get to control the TV. Now, has Brandon given the remote to Nanna? Good. Tell him Mama says he's a good boy." She waited. "Eric, I've got to say goodbye. No, Daddy's already talked to both of you. We'll be home soon, pumpkin. You do what Nanna Bailey tells you to do. And don't forget to brush your teeth before bed." More silence. "You know the rule, sweetie. One treat after dinner, unless you want all your teeth to fall out. Do you want that, Eric? Your smile would look kinda funny." She grinned at Kenny. "Good boy. Mommy and Daddy love you. Give Brandon a big hug from us. What? Say that more slowly. No, pumpkin, your brother can't read. Well, I don't care what he says. He can't. Neither can you. I have to go now. I love you. Goodbye, Eric. See you soon."

"Jeez," said Paul, emerging from his bedroom wearing a light blue terry-cloth robe and rubbing his wet hair with a towel. "You don't know how glad I am that I've always used birth control."

"Paul!" said Constance, her tone scolding.

"He's just jealous," said Emily, smirking at her brother.

Paul sat down on the love seat next to his uncle. "So," he said, tossing the towel over his shoulder, "we're all here. But we already know the big secret." Glancing sideways, he added, "Uncle Arthur let the cat out of the bag yesterday."

"I know," said Constance, shooting Arthur a withering look. "But we still have to talk about it. It's important that we're all on the same page here. I don't want any member of this family talking to Marie Damontraville. Is that understood? Kenny is searching for a legal way to stop the book before it ever gets written."

"I don't get all the urgency," said Paul. "I mean, what do we have to be so afraid of?"

"We're not afraid of anything," said Constance, knowing she sounded a little too defensive. "We're just protecting our privacy."

Emily took hold of her husband's hand. "We've all got things in our past we don't want the entire world to read about."

Constance knew her daughter was referring to her arrest in New York City. Even though it was many years ago, the memory still stung.

"Not me," said Nathan. "I'm clean as a whistle."

"Right," grunted Paul, puckering up and blowing him a kiss. "Seems to me you got this family into some big-time hot water a few years back during your, shall we say, Greenpeace days. Hey, speaking of Vashti Wells—"

"Stop it!" ordered Constance. This was too much. Paul had always been the one to push everyone's patience to the limit, but lately he was even more contentious than usual. "I told you I never wanted to hear that woman's name again."

"She's still in town, you know," continued Paul, ignoring his mother's outburst. "I checked. Same house."

"Zip it," ordered Emily. She shot her brother a cautionary look. "How long do we have to stay in this town, Mom? It's getting to all of us."

"Until we've come to a decision on New Fonteney," she replied, her voice firm.

"I think we should buy it," said Kenny, speaking up for the first time. "Just as a piece of real estate, it's a good investment."

"I have no idea whether or not it's a good investment," said Paul, "but as a site for a cooking school, it leaves a lot to be desired."

"You're just saying that because I found it," said Nathan.

"And you want us to buy the property just so you can be close to your old girlfriend."

"That's not true!"

"No? You mean the romantic reverie you've been wandering around in since Saturday has nothing to do with Sophie?

Maybe I'm mistaken, but I thought I overheard you telling Emily last night that you intended to marry her."

"It's none of your damn business."

"But it is mine," said Constance, wondering if there was any truth to it. She'd seen them together at Kitchen Central, but she had had no idea her son still had feelings for Sophie. "She's married, Nathan."

"So? She's still in love with me."

"She told you that?" asked Arthur, looking up at him.

"She didn't need to," said Paul. "She just did her usual swoon." He mimicked a swoon, falling across his uncle's lap. "Romeo and Juliet, right? Or, maybe, given the time period, Sonny and Cher?"

"Just stuff it," said Nathan. "And don't use my love life to change the subject. New Fonteney is a perfect spot for a second campus."

"Boys," said Constance in exasperation, holding up her hand.

"Don't ever expect them to agree on anything," said Emily, her voice full of disgust. "I think you should ignore them and follow Kenny's advice."

"Why?" demanded Paul. "He's just a lawyer. He doesn't know a damn thing about the needs of a culinary academy. And besides, he's not even a Buckridge."

"For that matter, neither is Nathan," said Emily.

"You're all my children," said Constance, attempting to put a stop to this ridiculous argument.

"Even Kenny?" asked Emily.

Gritting her teeth, Constance replied, "He's the father of my two grandsons, isn't he? And they're our future."

Arthur finished his cigarette, stubbing it out in the ashtray. "I suggest we get back to the main reason for this meeting. Marie Damontraville."

"Why don't we hire someone to bump her off," suggested Paul, crossing his legs and leaning back against the couch cushions.

"Not funny," replied Constance.

"I didn't mean it to be. Come on, folks. It would be the simplest and quickest way to get rid of her."

"You know, Paul, you add so *much* to our family meetings." Nathan's voice dripped sarcasm. "Maybe you should go watch a game show on TV. I'm sure we can muddle along without you."

"I plan to offer Ms. Damontraville a sizable amount of money later today," Kenny said in a bored tone. "That will no doubt get her attention."

"You think she'll back off that easily?" asked Nathan. He walked away from the windows and sat down on the arm of a chair. "I don't. I think she's after blood. All our blood." He held his mother's eyes.

"I say we forget about her," said Paul. "Let her do her job. If she finds some dirt, so what? Given the current climate in this country, it will only make Mother more popular, especially if that woman finds actual pictures of you hopping in and out of bed with someone, preferably someone famous." Eyeing his mother, he added, "I do hope you showed some taste in your choice of paramours."

"Shut up," said Arthur. "Your mother deserves more respect than that. She's worked hard to give you all a good life."

"Spoken like a true-blue brother," said Kenny, tapping a cigarette against his gold cigarette case. "But then Arthur's not a Buckridge either. That seems to be a very strong undercurrent in this room today. My guess is, it always has been."

Paul's expression sobered. "My father was a fine man. I'm proud to be his son."

"Don't burst a blood vessel," muttered Kenny, flipping his lighter open. "We aren't the royal family. Lineage is hardly a significant issue."

Constance felt suddenly weary. She was sick of her life, sick of all the pressure to look and talk and act a certain way. If only she could disappear, live the rest of her days simply, away from the TV cameras and the ever-present media. The problem was, she'd made her bed a long time ago, before she'd understood the total immutability of all her actions and decisions. If she checked out now, especially with this gossipmonger snapping at her heels, her children would suffer for all her failures. She couldn't allow that to happen. She had to protect them, no matter what the cost. She prayed Kenny would be able to buy this Damontraville woman off. If that didn't work, she'd be forced to use stronger methods. But whatever happened, she was determined to keep her past buried, where it belonged.

Journal Note

Tuesday, 4:30 P.M.

I finally got an E-mail from Pluto early this morning. No specific comments about the transcriptions I've sent him, but he encouraged me to keep going. He gave me another lead. He told me about Phillip Rapson, the man who worked for years as the handyman-gardener at the Buckridges' home and lived above the garage. He also included an address and a phone number for Vashti Wells. I called her and set up an appointment for one o'clock this afternoon. Pluto had no idea who the strange visitor to the set of Constance's cooking show was, but he agreed it might be important.

The bulky Mr. Rafferty drove me to Ms. Wells's house on Lake Minnetonka. After doing a low-key check of the premises, he took a chair by the front door and we got down to business in the living room. I led Ms. Wells to believe that a bodyguard was a precaution I always took due to the sensitivity of my investigations. She seemed amused.

Vashti Wells is now in her late fifties—five years younger than Constance, she pointed out with obvious pleasure. Initially, she had a quiet, almost proper manner. I thought I might have some problems getting her to open up, but as soon as we started talking, my fears faded. She had an edge to her personality—and a frankness—I appreciated. Her parents had emigrated from New Delhi when she was a small child, so she was raised in California. She had no trace of an accent.

Her black hair was streaked with gray and wound tightly

into a knot at the back of her neck. Her suit was classic Chanel—probably not new, but she wore it with the air of a woman who'd seen the world and appreciated the best. Still a strikingly beautiful woman, she must have been even more so back in the late Sixties and early Seventies when she and Constance were close. It was immediately clear, however, that there was no love lost between them now. I was curious to learn why their relationship had deteriorated but also glad that it had since she might be more forthcoming, less interested in protecting a friend. She turned out to be a wealth of information, and for some of the questions, I just let her ramble.

INTERVIEW: VASHTI WELLS, MINNETONKA, MINNESOTA, TUESDAY, MAY 11

M: *When did you first meet Constance Buckridge?*

Wells: *Before we get to that, do I understand correctly that what I say here may be quoted in your book?*

M: *This interview will be used as source information, and if I decide to quote you directly, I'll need your signature on some legal documents. But we can handle all that later.*

Wells: *I see. (Amused smile) All right. I agree to your terms. (Delicately clears her throat) I first met Connie Buckridge in 1969, right after my husband and I bought this house. Connie came over during the first week and welcomed us to the lake community. I thought it was kind of her. I think she brought some homemade jam or chutney, something she'd made. Our backyard bordered theirs, so I'd already seen Connie and Wayne and the kids out on the patio grilling steaks. Initially, Wayne was less friendly. After a few months, the four of us— my husband, Gary, me, and then Wayne and Connie—started getting together for dinner every few weeks. One week I'd prepare something, the next time Connie would. Connie's energy matched my own, though with the exception of food and dinner parties, we had different interests. I thought she was a lot of fun. I guess you could say that, as a group, we just fell in together. Before I knew it, Connie and I had become best friends.*

M: *So you never knew Pepper Buckridge, Wayne's first wife.*

Wells: *No. Connie married Wayne in '64, I think, the year after his first wife died. If you're asking me whether or not I know that Connie was his maid and then later his cook, yes, she told me. I thought it was a beautiful love story. From what Connie said, Pepper was a sickly woman and Wayne was quite lonely. I'm sure they were in love—possibly even sleeping together—before Pepper died, but Connie never confirmed that.*

M: *Did the Buckridge family seem happy?*

Wells: *Yes, I think so. Connie was doing a lot of traveling with Wayne during the late Sixties and early Seventies, when we became friends. She really loved seeing the world. I don't think she'd ever been out of the country before. And the kids . . . well, Emily was pretty small. I've never been very interested in children myself, but she was fun to have around. She was bright and playful but was always getting into things—smearing hand cream on the mirrors, pouring her mother's expensive perfume down the sink, eating dirt in the backyard. Paul and Nathan were older. (Hesitates) Nathan was a quiet young man. He must have been about fifteen when we first met. Very serious. Very shy. From what I could see, he did a lot of reading and kept mostly to himself. I don't think there was much love lost between Wayne and Nathan. Nathan wasn't his natural son, you know. Wayne always favored Paul, and I'm sure that must have hurt Nathan a great deal.*

M: *Did Paul and Nathan get along?*

Wells: *Well, Paul was a few years younger, so they really didn't play together, but it was clear that Paul already thought of himself as the cock of the walk. He and Nathan had very different personalities. Paul was outgoing, aggressive, opinionated, very much like his father, but he didn't have the mitigating— shall we say, charming vulnerability—that Wayne had. Wayne was an odd mixture. On the one hand, he was an incredibly successful businessman, always very sure of himself, very confident and upbeat. But in his private life, I think he was a lost soul. He seemed so self-deprecating at times, to a degree I found almost painful. I didn't understand it, because, I mean, the man had everything, a beautiful wife, a wonderful family, a successful business. But, deep down, I don't think he thought very much of himself. I'm sure that made him hard to live with. I know he had very black moods. He never talked about his past, so I have no idea what experiences created Wayne Buckridge. I guess you could say, even with everything he had, I felt sorry for him. (Pauses) But back to Nathan and Paul. Yes, they got along all right—no overt fights—but I don't think they were close. It was a fairly typical family, lots of tensions but mixed with love.*

M: *Was there a rivalry for Wayne's attention or affection?*

Wells: *If there was, by the time I came on the scene, Nathan had abdicated in favor of his brother. Nathan rarely spoke to Wayne, and Wayne mostly issued orders when he said anything to Nathan. I know Connie felt terrible about it. The way it set up was, Paul claimed Wayne as the parent he loved most and Nathan claimed Connie. And then little Emily . . . well, everybody loved her. She was the only one who really got a fair shake in the family, and I really believe she always felt left out because she wasn't a boy. She thought nobody took her seriously. I think, as she got older, she acted out just to prove she was as tough as her brothers.*

M: *And was that the case? Was she taken less seriously?*

Wells: *(Shrugs) Not that I ever noticed. The whole family adored her. If anything, she was spoiled because everything she wanted was taken too seriously. Let's just say, she usually got her way. The only one who didn't seem to buy her act was Connie's brother, Arthur. I think he thought Emily was a little too manipulative for her own good. He didn't seem to get along with her as well as he did the boys.*

M: *I'd like to talk more about Arthur in a minute, but first, I understand you helped Connie do her cooking shows. You prepped the set for her.*

Wells: *That's right. It just seemed natural for me to help. We both loved to cook, though by '72 when Connie was asked to do the* Daytime with Jerry & Emmeline *show, she'd been taught by some of the finest chefs all over the world. When it came to food, she soaked up everything in sight. Wayne seemed to love it. After a while, they even planned his business trips around her growing chef and restaurant connections. Sometimes they'd stay an extra month somewhere just so she could get some intense instruction. When she returned home, she was bursting to tell me everything she'd learned. In many ways I felt as if I was learning along with her. That's why she gave those elaborate dinner parties. I know they helped Wayne's career, but mostly she just had to have an outlet, a forum in which to show off her new skills. She'd decide on a theme and then make these elaborate buffets. I might still have some of the menus around here if you're interested.*

M: *I'd love to see them. I'm curious. What happened to the kids while Wayne and Connie were away?*

Wells: *They had a live-in nanny who always came to stay when they were out of town. Can't recall her name, but she was old. I doubt she'd still be alive. It was mostly for little Emily's sake. Nathan and Paul were getting older and could take care of themselves, not that they didn't need supervision. Especially Paul. By the time he hit junior high, he was a terror. I think it was about the eighth grade when he discovered rock music and did his thirteen-year-old version of tuning in, turning on, and dropping out.*

M: *Did he use drugs?*

Wells: *Not then, but later, in high school. I don't know whatall he used, but Connie was constantly worried about him. Thank God Nathan was never any trouble. He was a good student and reasonably popular. By the time he was sixteen, he was actively involved in the peace movement. Later, he got interested in Greenpeace. He was very socially aware, wanted to participate in the world, not drop out like his brother had. But then Paul was pretty angry at his father during that time. Wayne had put on a lot of weight. He'd come home after work, pour himself a double Scotch on the rocks, and spend the rest of the night eating in front of the TV. Paul* was disgusted with his behavior and let him know it. It just pushed Wayne further into his shell. Connie was the only functional parent by that time, and she was busy with her TV shows. It wasn't a particularly healthy family situation, I suppose, but then how many are?

M: *Did Paul ever get in trouble with the law?*

Wells: *Not to my knowledge. Nathan was arrested once at a sit-in at the university, but since he was a minor, they just let him go.*

M: *Getting back to Connie's TV appearances. Did you also help prep the sets for the Saturday morning show on WTWN?*

Wells: *Yes, and by then I was actually getting paid. Not that I needed the money, but it felt good to be professionally involved in something I loved. I hoped that, one day, Connie would have me on, let me show some of what I could do. But then the show got canceled. She was very upset. So was I.*

M: *I'm told that while Connie was doing one of her first tapings, a strange man appeared on the set. He was possibly a street person or a hippie—tall, long beard, long hair, very dirty. Connie seemed to know who he was. As a matter of fact, she left with him in the middle of the taping. The producer was furious. Do you know anything about this guy? What he was doing there? Who he was?*

Wells: *(Pauses) Sure, I know all about it, but (Grins) I'm not supposed to tell. It was a big secret back then, and I suppose it still is.*

M: *If you'd feel comfortable talking about it . . .*

Wells: *After what Connie did to me, I'm thrilled to be asked. Anything I can do to repay her in kind makes my heart soar. (Laughs)*

M: *What did she do to you?*

Wells: *That's for later. (Winks) I always think it's good to end on a high note. (Laughs again) Okay, the mystery man. Well, his nickname was Zippo, I believe. Like the lighter. It probably had something to do with how much marijuana he smoked. If he had a real name, I never heard it. (Pauses) How much do you know about Connie's brother, Arthur?*

M: *Just that he was a psychologist. He's retired now. I think he's even written a couple of books. I haven't read them, but I will. I know he moved in with the Buckridges in July of '73, right around the time he began some graduate work at the University of Minnesota.*

Wells: *He went on to get his doctorate in clinical psychology at UCLA.*

M: *I didn't know that. He's what, four years older than Constance?*

Wells: *Yes, that's about right. (Folds her hands in her lap) Okay, back to Zippo. Connie had always been very close to her brother. From what she told me, their home life growing up was a horror. When she became pregnant by some local idiot, her parents threw her out. That's when she came to Minneapolis and moved in with her brother. Arthur was nineteen or twenty. After he'd graduated from the U of M with a degree in philosophy, he began having some . . . problems.*

M: *Can you be more specific?*

Wells: *Mental problems. He'd always been a high-energy person, like Connie, but for Arthur it turned into something else. Out of the blue one day he told her that the papier-mâché globe in their apartment had begun talking to him. At first it was just a comment on his clothes or his eating habits, but the more receptive he appeared, the more it said. Sometimes he'd ignore it, wouldn't even look at it, and then it would pout. He'd end up feeling sorry for it and go sit next to it until it said something. He told her he knew the whole situation sounded farfetched, but it had been going on for several months and he was convinced that what the globe was telling him was not only true but a matter of life and death for the planet.*

M: *Which was?*

Wells: *The globe wanted him to write an article for the local newspaper warning the world of an impending invasion from a race that lived at the center of the earth. They were called Nimwaths, or Nimwroths, or something like that, and they looked like dogs, but they were superintelligent. Connie was nonplussed. She knew right away that he was delusional, but he'd always been her rock. She was also young and penniless*

*and didn't have a clue as to how to help. She urged him to go
see a doctor, but that only made him angry. He wasn't sick.
He just had to write that damn letter. The fate of the world de-
pended on it, more or less. It wasn't long before he lost his
job. In an effort to keep body and soul together, he did things
like pump gas, load trucks, move furniture, anything that
would give him time to think and to write. His mind moved a
million miles a minute. I can still hear Connie explaining it
all to me. She said that talking to her brother was like having
an intimate conversation with a jet engine. At times he was
more rational than others. Once he said that he knew he
was screwed up, but the mystery was, given the state of the
world, why wasn't everybody as screwed up as he was? He'd
rant about various things—government secrecy, the idiocy of
Immanuel Kant's theory of empirical knowledge, the ridiculous taste of the candy bar he'd just bought. He started
drinking more, sleeping less, but there was so much to be
upset about he couldn't be bothered with things like food and
sleep. Life was coming at him fast and furiously. He told
Connie that because we all operated on such limited notions
of logic, we missed things, relationships, signs. For a while,
he decided he wanted to be her teacher. He'd sit in the kitchen
while she fed Nathan and talk to her about the deeper mean-
ings of existence, all the secrets the globe had passed on to
him. Connie would listen, but she'd get confused. In the
middle of one sentence, he'd start another. Subjects changed
so fast that she finally realized there was no subject. Then
(Pauses) the crying started. First Arthur would cry in front of
her, but then he'd have to get away so he could be alone. Anything could set him off. Once she asked him if he wanted a
sandwich and all he did was break into tears. He said he
needed to get his "mind off his mind." I've always remembered that line. But the problem was, nothing felt or seemed
or reacted like it used to. The world was an entirely new place
and not a safe one. He was obsessed with writing that letter,
but not one of his four thousand drafts was good enough. He
was weighed down by the sense that he was responsible for
the fate of the world, and his failure to carry out the mission*

the globe had given him made him even more anxious and depressed. Something was happening to him, and while at times he seemed to revel in his newfound power, at other times he was desperate. Not sleeping and not eating eventually took a toll. There would be days, weeks, when Connie wouldn't hear from him. When the weeks stretched into months, she became frightened. She assumed he was living on the street. They had a joint savings account, so she was okay financially for a while. When he did come home, she'd try to get him to stay. He loved little Nathan. He'd play with him for hours. I assume that Nathan may remember him from that time, but it would be a pretty dim memory. Arthur couldn't stay anywhere for very long. He was getting worse. After about a year of this, all of his rationality seemed to fade away. In its place was a man Connie barely recognized. He'd lost weight, had dark circles around his eyes, and sometimes he didn't even recognize her. That's when he stopped coming home for good. She was beside herself with worry. She'd take Nathan and wander around downtown trying to find him, but she never had any luck. She wasn't even sure he was in town any longer. It was a terrible time.

M: *My assumption is that Arthur was suffering from some form of schizophrenia, or possibly manic depression.*

Wells: *(Nods)*

M: *So, what happened to him?*

Wells: *He was lost for many years. I don't know where he was or what he did, but I'm sure it was quite an odyssey. After Connie married Wayne, she had the money to hire private investigators, and that's just what she did. It took many years, but finally one of them located this Zippo. He was living under the Tenth Avenue bridge at the time. He said he knew a man named Jadek, and that for a certain amount of money—I think around a thousand dollars—he would take Connie to where Jadek was living. He said the man was pretty sick, so if she wanted to see him before he died, she'd better hurry. For some reason, he refused to deal with anyone but Connie. That's why he showed up on her set that day. She left with him immediately because she thought her* brother was on his deathbed. Turns out he was sick, but it was just the flu. He was living in a flophouse on Washington Avenue, if you want to call it living. He didn't recognize her, but she wasn't a penniless young woman any longer. She knew what needed to be done and she had the money to finance it. She had him admitted to the best psychiatric hospital in the state. Once he got on some antipsychotic drugs, his memory started to come back to him. It took many months, but amazing as it sounds, he did recover. This was all very hush-hush, you understand. Connie didn't tell her husband or kids the truth. I think she was afraid they'd ostracize him or be afraid of him. Back then, and maybe even now, mental illness carries a terrible stigma. She didn't want the kids to know there were any mental problems in the family gene pool, because there was some thinking that there might be a genetic component.

M: *Why did she confide in you? It seems strange that she'd chance it.*

Wells: *We were having drinks together one night and she got really weepy. I think she felt guilty that she was spending so much time fussing over her brother and not enough time worrying about her husband's health.*

M: *Was that true? Did she?*

Wells: *(Shrugs) I know she did everything she could to get Wayne to exercise and eat less, but she was awfully focused on Arthur.*

M: *When you first met Arthur Jadek, what did you think of him?*

Wells: *I found him to be a delightful, intelligent, charming man. Later, after I found out the truth about his history, it was hard for me to believe he had ever been the man Connie described. When he moved into the Buckridges' house, Connie told her family that he'd been working out of the country for years, governmental secrecy stuff. A CIA operative. Whatever. That's why she never mentioned him. He couldn't talk about what he'd been doing, and nobody was supposed to ask. I think because James Bond was so big at the time, everyone bought the story. Paul and Nathan thought he was utterly fascinating. To this day, I don't believe any of them know the truth.*

M: *So Arthur went back to school.*

Wells: *From what Connie said, he wanted to study his disease, find out what really happened to him. He also wanted to help others with the same problem. I mean, he understood it from the inside out. I can only believe that insight made him a highly gifted clinician.*

M: *I was told that Wayne Buckridge didn't like Arthur Jadek.*

Wells: *Yes, I think that's true, although he didn't put up much of an argument when Connie wanted Arthur to move in. And believe me, Wayne could have. There was just a coldness between them. Most of it came from Wayne, I'm sure. The first few weeks after Arthur was let out of the hospital, he was feeling quite tenuous. At the time I didn't really know why, but he was thin and drawn, looked almost as if he'd been in some kind of concentration camp. That was all part of the CIA security stuff nobody could ask him about. But as time went on, and his physical health returned, he really bloomed. I'm sure that irked Wayne, because his own health was on the decline. Arthur was a good ten years younger than Wayne, and for some reason Wayne seemed jealous of that fact. He didn't want any man close to Connie, not even her brother. I'd never seen that part of Wayne before, and it took me by complete surprise. Again, I think he felt Connie was too concerned about Arthur and not concerned enough about him. Typical male selfishness. They don't just want a wife, they want a mother.*

M: *I understand that Wayne suffered a heart attack about six months after Arthur came to stay with them.*

Wells: *That's correct.*

M: *Can you tell me what you know about it?*

Wells: *Well, the night it happened, Connie was in her study preparing the menu for the following week's show. Arthur wasn't home. He was at the library. Wayne never got home before seven, so Connie wasn't expecting him. I guess she had some music on, so she didn't hear him come in. She found him*

*shortly after seven in the upstairs bathroom. He'd been trying
to get to his medication but died before he could reach it.*
M: *It was a heart attack?*
Wells: *Yes, a massive one. Everybody saw it coming. It wasn't
a surprise.*
M: *The police didn't find anything suspicious about his
death?*
Wells: *Heavens, no. What are you suggesting?*
M: *Just asking.*
Wells: *No, there was never a question that his death wasn't
entirely natural. I may not think very highly of Connie, but I
don't for a minute believe she's capable of murder.*
M: *You mentioned a falling-out. When did that happen?
And why?*
Wells: *(Takes a moment, seems to relish this part of her story)
It all started when Connie got her PBS show. I was once
again asked to do the setups and I said I would on the condition that she'd have me on her show at least once a month.
The first month came and went. I wasn't included. The second
month came. Nothing again. This went on for a good four
months before I exploded. I told Connie that she was afraid to
share the limelight with me, afraid that I might steal her
show. She responded that I was just being a prima donna. She
intended to include me in her broadcasts, but she had to get
her feet on the ground first. I said fine. Give me a date. She
thought about it for a moment and then said in two weeks I
could prepare something, a ten-minute segment. The date
came and went and I still wasn't allowed in front of the cameras. So I quit. I told her she was selfish and a liar, and I'd had
enough. She was furious, of course, mainly because I hadn't
started my prep work yet for the next day's taping. I told her
I couldn't believe she'd treat a friend with so little respect, especially since I'd been with her from the very beginning. She
said I was ungrateful. She was the star and I was just a helper.
I tossed my apron on her desk and walked out. I hoped I'd
never see her again. That night she came over to my house.
My husband was out of town and she knew it. To this day
I don't know if she came to apologize or to tell me where*

I could pick up my final check. I guess it's moot because when she knocked and didn't get an answer, she let herself in with her key. She found me in the living room, naked on the sofa. I wasn't alone.

M: *(Wants to be prodded) Who were you with?*

Wells: *(Smiles) Her son Nathan. (Another smile, this one of triumph) You can imagine how upset she was. Nathan grabbed his clothes and ran home. He was twenty years old at the time, and a beautiful young man. Between you and me, I taught him everything he knows about the female body. He was an eager student and I was a willing teacher. Nathan had a natural sensuality I've rarely seen in a man. He was very tender but also very strong. It's an explosive mixture. We didn't love each other, of course. There was never any talk of that. But we were bound together by our desire for each other's bodies.*

M: *Did you ever sleep with Paul?*

Wells: *(Shudders) Never. He wasn't my type. Too arrogant. And too dirty.*

M: *How long had you been sleeping with Nathan?*

Wells: *Since he was fifteen. Connie knew nothing about it. Neither did my husband, although at the time, I didn't think it would have mattered much. Over the period of our marriage, he'd had dozens of affairs. I just had one. At the beginning, Nathan was simply a sweet boy, a diversion. He was willing and full of youthful lust, but untrained. By the time he met his special young woman, he really knew how to make love to a woman.*

M: *Special young woman?*

Wells: *Her name was Sophie, I believe. Poor Nathan. The night Connie caught us together, he finally told me about his trip to California in September. He'd followed Sophie there hoping to change her mind about marrying him. Three months later he was still depressed. I'd never seen him so down. He needed me that night. I was glad he'd come. And when Connie charged into the room like an angry bull, shouting and breaking things, I thought she finally got a little of what she had coming. I was sorry for the embarrassment it caused Nathan but glad that Connie had to face the truth. She couldn't control the whole world, even though, by that time in her life, she thought she was entitled to try. I doubt she learned her lesson that night, but it was a start in the right direction.*

M: *What did she do?*

Wells: *Oh, she blustered and fussed for a couple of days. She forbade Nathan to ever see me again. And then when my husband returned from his business trip, she told him what I'd been up to. Needless to say, I could have killed her with my bare hands. It never occurred to me that she'd have so little class. I didn't think it was any of her business in the first place, but to go behind my back and inform my husband, well, that was the very last straw. Connie was too embarrassed to tell him how long her son and I had been sleeping together, but Gary got horribly huffy about it, anyway. He filed for divorce the next week. I had so many of his mistresses' names and addresses that it was a standoff. I got the house and a nice monthly allowance, and he got his freedom. I guess, in the end, we both got what we wanted. In a way, Connie did me a favor, but I never spoke to her again. And I never will.*

M: *And did Nathan stay away from you?*

Wells: *(A smile pregnant with meaning) Why, Ms. Damontraville. A woman never answers a question like that.*

15

"Make it something really memorable," said Yale McGraw, clasping his hands behind his neck. He leaned back in his leather chair and gazed at Sophie with an expression of wistful sadness. "That's the least we can do. Gildemeister was an institution around here for two decades."

"But are you sure I'm the best person to write the feature?" Sophie had found a memo on George's desk, her desk now, summoning her to Yale's office as soon as she got in. She'd arrived at the paper shortly after three, hoping to complete some organizational chores before Rudy arrived home.

"You'll do a fine job," said Yale. "Doesn't have to be too long. Just hit the highlights of his career. Assign a researcher to help if you need it. Don't forget to include some photos. The researcher can check the photo archives, come up with something suitable. I want the full piece on the feature editor's desk by Friday afternoon."

"The paper's still working four days out, right?"

He nodded. "I plan to run it next Wednesday. Oh, and don't include anything on the murder investigation. I've got the crime beat covering that."

With all the other work facing her, writing a glorified obit for George was hardly a welcome task, but she could hardly say no to her new boss. It was a onetime job, and if she could just find some quiet time after someone else gathered the significant details, she could hammer out the story in a few hours. "Okay, I'll get right on it."

"Good. And, Soph, there's a staff meeting tomorrow afternoon that I'd like you to attend. Three o'clock in the sixth-floor conference room. Shouldn't take more than an hour."

Her mind raced. She was pretty sure there was nothing on her schedule at the hotel tomorrow afternoon. She might as well face it. From now on, she couldn't go anywhere without her daily appointment calendar. "Sure. I'll be there."

As she left the office, hurrying through the newsroom, she prayed that nothing would prevent Rudy's plane from landing at Twin Cities International on Sunday morning. This was her first real day at the paper and already she felt the need for an assistant. She could hear Bram's voice inside her head. *I'd never see you if you took on a second job. I already have to make a date weeks in advance if I want to have a five-minute conversation with you.* Well, it wasn't true. Her life simply took a little juggling right now.

Once back upstairs in George's office, she punched in Bram's private extension at the radio station. He should be done with his afternoon show, which meant he was sitting behind his desk, eating some sweet but empty calories and reading the *New York Times*, his daily reward for a job well done.

He picked up the phone after the second ring. "Bram Baldric."

"Put that chocolate doughnut down!"

"What . . . who . . . Sophie?"

"Does someone else know about your current chocolate doughnut addiction?"

He laughed. "Only you, babe. When I have guests, I always bring out those horrible gourmet biscotti, the kind of cookie that seems refined, European, and maybe even satisfying—if you've been living on lettuce leaves and Evian water for a few months. I have to maintain my image, you know. I am a man of the finest tastes."

"Admit it. Al Lundquist got you hooked on those grease bombs."

"Are you suggesting that police officers spend their days eating doughnuts? That's a professional slur. It might even be a felony."

"Al looks like he's eaten a few in his day."

"He's thin as a rail."

"With a potbelly."

"It's a vitamin deficiency."

She snorted. "A bad case of bachelor malnutrition. But don't worry, sweetheart. The secret of your true culinary leanings is safe with me." She hoped the fact that he was being playful meant he'd forgiven her for yesterday. "What are you doing for dinner tonight?"

"Let's see." He rustled some papers. "I have to check my engagement calendar. My dance card is usually filled." He paused. "Say! You're in luck. The governor canceled on me, so I'm free. Shall I pencil you in?"

"Do that."

"The name again?"

"Finchley. Martha Finchley."

"Ah, yes, Ms. Finchley. I believe your address and phone number are already recorded in my little black book."

"You burned your little black book on our wedding night."

"No, I think that was my Franklin Planner."

She rolled her eyes. "I'll be back from the paper by seven or so. I need about half an hour to take care of a few matters at the hotel and then I'll meet you at the Zephyr Club for a night of dinner and dancing." The Zephyr Club was the hotel's fine dining restaurant on the top floor of the south wing. As the place where Bram had proposed, it always had a special meaning for both of them.

"I'll polish my tennis shoes, scrub the ketchup stains off my T-shirt, and meet you at eight. Oh, should I call for reservations?"

"I'll take care of that."

"Good. Then I can go back to eating my snack without further interruption. *Ciao bella,* baby. God, I'm so sophisticated. How can you resist me?"

"I can't. See you tonight."

Sophie spent the next few hours working in George's office. She watered all his plants, thinking that perhaps his wife or one of his kids would want to come and clean out his personal belongings. It wouldn't really feel like her space until all of the tomato seedlings were gone.

After arranging with a staff researcher to pull together the information she needed for the feature on George's life, she spent a few minutes just sitting and looking out the window. As soon as her mind wasn't occupied by the growing list of restaurants she wanted to review, or the local industry news she had to catch up on, her thoughts turned to Nathan. How was she going to tell him that she couldn't see him again—ever? In many ways, it wasn't even something she wanted. She wished they could be friends, but the chemistry between them was too volatile. It wasn't just hard; it was deeply embarrassing to admit that she couldn't trust herself around him, but the fact was, she couldn't.

As she was switching off the computer, getting ready to leave, her thoughts returned to the moonlight walks she and Nathan used to take around Lake Harriet. Winter or summer, it didn't matter, it was their special place.

Nathan knew a great deal about the natural world. Learning about trees and flowers from him was far more fun than learning about it in school. Sometimes they'd sit on a bench by the lake, holding hands and watching a muskrat play in the water or a bunch of baby ducks trail lazily behind their mama. In the summer there were sailboat regattas and band concerts at the Lake Harriet Bandshell. And in the fall, the coots, one of Sophie's favorite birds, would return for a few weeks before heading south. She had so many memories of that time, all of them good. If her life had taken a different turn, perhaps she and Nathan would have gotten married. Had children together. Built a good life. She couldn't help but wonder if his unresolved feelings for her hadn't played some part in his life-long inability to find the right person to love. Even though she knew she had no reason to feel guilty, she nevertheless did.

Outwardly, Nathan appeared to be successful and happy, a man on the go, but yesterday she'd detected in him a sense of resignation. He'd called his life a "frustrated system," not that she entirely understood. If she cut off all ties with him now, she'd never understand.

Realizing she wasn't getting anywhere with this trip down memory lane, she made a quick decision. It was a quarter to six. All day she'd been wanting to drive back to George's apartment. If the police believed they had their man, it stood to reason that they'd called off any further investigation. And that meant they might have missed something important that could clear Harry. Sophie believed he was innocent. She knew her confidence might be misguided, but she couldn't let the matter drop until she'd talked to George's neighbors. One of them might have seen or heard something that didn't fit the police theory.

Before leaving the Times Register Tower for the day, Sophie

stuffed a copy of the day's paper into her briefcase. She wanted to take a closer look at the article she'd written on Constance Buckridge's visit to Kitchen Central last Saturday.

The rush-hour traffic was typically chaotic, but Sophie made it to the Lakeland Terrace in good time. She got lucky again, finding a parking spot directly across the street. Walking up the steps, she realized she faced the same problem she'd had on Sunday night. How was she supposed to get into a security building without a key? Thinking she had nothing to lose, she stood in the foyer pawing through the contents of her briefcase. She hoped someone would think she was looking for her key and simply let her in, just like the other night.

During the next few minutes, several people emerged, but no one held the door open for her. She silently berated herself for lacking the guts to grab the damn door and walk in. The next time someone came out, that's just what she was going to do. But nobody did for another ten minutes. She was getting sick of waiting when a young man suddenly came sailing through the front door juggling two overstuffed sacks of groceries. "You going in?" he asked, puffing to a stop.

"Yes, but—"

"Here, use my key. I've already got it out." It was dangling from his right hand. Without Sophie's help, he wouldn't be able to negotiate the lock unless he set everything down.

Once the door was open, the young man said, "Thanks. God, my wife's going to kill me. We've got guests coming for dinner and I was supposed to be home with the food two hours ago. Wish me luck," he shouted over his shoulder as he steamed up the half-flight of stairs to the elevators.

"Good luck," said Sophie, giving a small wave.

She waited until he was gone, then made a mental note to suggest to Yale that he put someone on a story about security buildings—how secure are they really? Checking the time, she realized she had less than an hour before she was due back at the Maxfield, all dolled up and ready to dance the night away.

The fifth floor of the Lakewood Terrace was filled with

the rich aroma of dinners cooking. Sophie thought she could detect a meat loaf, something decidedly Oriental, and a meal that required lots of garlic—perhaps lasagna. It was a poor time to interrupt George's neighbors, but at least they were home.

She approached one of the adjacent apartments and knocked a couple of times. It didn't take long before a man wearing a bathrobe and slippers drew back the door. He looked as if he'd just gotten out of the shower.

"I'm sorry to bother you," Sophie began, "but I'd like to ask a couple of questions about George Gildemeister, your neighbor."

"You with the police?" The guy seemed curious but also a bit suspicious.

"No, I'm working for Harry Hongisto, the man who's been accused of his murder."

"I see." He nodded, sizing her up. "You a P.I.?"

"Men aren't the only P.I.'s in the world, you know."

He held up his hand. "Fine. Whatever."

"Have the police talked to you?"

"Yeah, they came by on Sunday night. Asked a couple of questions. Nothing very extensive. They said they might want to talk to me again, but nobody's called." He paused, re-tying the belt on his robe. "What do you wanna know?"

He clearly had no intention of inviting her in, and that was fine with her. "On the night George died, last Sunday, were you home?"

"All evening. My girlfriend came over and we watched a movie, ordered a pizza."

"Did you hear any shouting coming from George's apartment?"

"Everyone on the floor heard it, lady, unless they were deaf. It got pretty loud a couple of times."

"Do you remember any specific words or sentences?"

"Sorry. I didn't pay that much attention."

"What time did the argument take place?"

"Oh, about a quarter to seven, I guess. It was before my

girlfriend arrived. I was watching a game show, so I just turned the volume up. I think I may have banged on the wall once—no, that was later. During the next round."

"There was another round?"

"Yeah, it was about seven-thirty. I remember because that's when my girlfriend got here."

"Did you notice anyone out in the hallway?"

"Nope, it was empty."

"Did you tell the police about the second argument?"

"Yeah, I think I mentioned it. They figured your friend Hongisto stayed longer than he let on." He scratched his chest through his bathrobe. "Course, I couldn't say for sure that George was arguing with the same man. Then again . . . eh, I don't know. Maybe it was Hongisto again. But there was something about the voice. It wasn't quite as deep. That Hongisto sounds like Henry Kissinger with a bad head cold."

Sophie couldn't help but smile. It was an accurate description. "So you think there's a possibility it could have been a different person? Someone else visited George that night?"

He shrugged. "It's possible, although I wouldn't swear to it. If I'd thought George was about to get snuffed, I would have paid more attention."

"You never looked out in the hall again?"

"Just when my girlfriend came. Like I said, nobody was around. Carol didn't leave until the next morning."

She nodded. "Thanks. You've been a big help."

"No problem," he said, wasting no time in shutting the door.

Next Sophie tried George's neighbor on the other side. She knocked several times, glancing briefly at George's door while she waited. Police tape stretched across it, designating it a crime scene. After another minute or so, she knocked again but finally gave up. It was only then that she noticed one of the doors across the hall was cracked open several inches. She was positive it hadn't been like that a few minutes ago.

It hardly seemed like an invitation to talk, but someone was at least interested in what a stranger might be doing in the hallway. "Hello?" she said gently. "I wonder if I could talk to you for a minute."

The door closed, but not all the way. "What do you want?" came an elderly voice. "Are you with the police?"

"No—"

"Good. Because if you were, I'd slam this door in your face. Those men put my nephew in jail for no reason."

"I'm sorry to hear that."

"You think you'd be able to trust them, but you can't."

"I understand. My name's Sophie Greenway."

"Ada Pearson." The door opened another inch.

"I'm working for Harry Hongisto. He's the man who's been accused of the murder of your neighbor, George Gildemeister."

"I know who my neighbors are. I'm not senile."

Her tone was more ornery than unfriendly.

"Of course you're not. Do you often stand by your door and watch what happens in the hall?"

"Sometimes." The door opened another couple of inches.

Sophie could now see a frail old woman leaning on a cane. Unlike her neighbor across the hall, however, she was completely dressed: pearl earrings, pearl necklace, a light blue cotton dress, and a jaunty red scarf tied at her neck. Her white hair looked as if it had been styled recently at a beauty parlor. Also, it was her apartment that smelled so strongly and deliciously of meat loaf.

"Were you looking out in the hall the night George died?"

"Maybe."

Sophie's pulse quickened. "Did you hear the fight in George's apartment?"

"I'm not deaf."

"Do you remember what it was about?"

"I just heard shouting. No words."

Sophie hesitated. "Did you see anyone enter or leave George's apartment that night?"

"I might have."

Sophie wished she'd bag the terse act. "Harry Hongisto is an older man. Balding, with wisps of white hair—"

Ada cut her off. "Yeah, I saw him."

"Did you see him leave the apartment?"

She shook her head. "I saw him come. It was about six-thirty, quarter to seven. Then I heard the fight. Then I ate dinner. I heard more fighting while I was finishing dessert. It was quiet for about half an hour, so I looked outside again."

"And?"

"And what?"

Sophie tried to curb her growing irritation. "Did you see anyone else?"

"Sure. You. You came right after the other man left."

Sophie could feel a jolt of adrenaline hit her system. "What other man?"

"Middle-aged fellow."

"What was he wearing?"

"Can't remember."

"Can you remember anything about him?"

"He looked scared." The woman switched the cane to her other hand. "You think this Harry Hongisto is innocent?"

"I do." Now more than ever.

"It's just like my nephew. The police got the wrong man."

"I hope you're right."

After several seconds had elapsed, the woman said, "Since you're so interested, I'll show you something."

Sophie watched as Ada shuffled into her living room. She picked through some papers on the couch, then returned to the door. "That's the guy," she said, pointing to a picture in the Leisure section of the *Times Register*.

Sophie's eyes opened wide in surprise. It was the photo of the Buckridge family the paper had included next to her article. "Which one are you pointing to?" she asked, almost afraid to learn the answer.

"This one," said Ada, tapping the picture of Nathan impatiently.

Sophie closed her eyes, recalling the man she'd seen coming out of the building that night. He'd seemed so familiar. Something about his walk. The way he moved. Now she knew why.

The old woman continued: "He took off out of George's apartment so fast that he left the door unlatched. You have to pull that door shut if you're going to close it properly, but he didn't even try. That's how you got in."

Sophie was almost too stunned to speak. But she had to ask, had to make sure. "Are you positive that was the man you saw?"

The woman lowered the paper to her side. "First you treat me like I'm senile. Now you accuse me of not being able to see."

"No, no. I didn't mean to suggest—"

"I've got to go turn off the oven. My dinner's done."

Before Sophie could say another word, the door shut in her face.

16

Bram eyed the muscle man at the other end of the bar. "So you bought yourself a bodyguard. When he gets hungry, I suppose you just toss him a T-bone."

Marie smiled like a mother about to comment on a favored son. "He does eat a lot. He's Irish, but he prefers Italian food. Linguine. Manicotti."

"Submachine guns in violin cases."

"He's thorough, and he keeps to himself. After what happened yesterday"—there was a quiver in her voice—"I wouldn't feel safe going anywhere without him. I've moved into a suite now, so we each have our own bedroom."

"I'm sure he wouldn't mind changing that arrangement." Bram shot the guy a dirty look.

"Why, Mr. Baldric. If I didn't know better, I'd think you were jealous."

"Me? Absolutely not. I'm just worried about your ... your—"

"Safety? That's what he's there for, remember? He's licensed, bonded. He understands what the boundaries are."

"Yes, but he's a man and you're a very beautiful woman."

She picked up her wineglass and gazed at him over the rim. "If you're worried about my virtue, don't give it another thought. I'm a big girl. I can take care of myself."

"Yes," he said, clearing his throat. "I'm sure you can."

Bram had arrived back at the hotel around six. After showering and changing into something more suitable for the coming evening, he'd rung Marie's room and invited her downstairs for a drink. He had some time to kill, and he also didn't want to leave her with the impression that he wasn't concerned about the threat she'd received yesterday. Beyond that, he had to admit that he was intrigued by her comments about the Buckridge family. Since Sophie seemed to be having some difficulty getting rid of Nathan Buckridge, perhaps Bram could move the ball along by dropping a few unflattering tidbits from Nathan's past, tidbits to be supplied by Marie Damontraville. If there were no unflattering tidbits, he'd simply have to make some up.

"You never did tell me what caused you to be so frightened yesterday."

Marie turned her wineglass around in her hand. "Well," she said, pausing to collect her thoughts, "when I got back from an afternoon interview, there was a note pushed under my door. It was inside a plain white envelope—sweet and to the point. Here," she said, removing it from her evening bag. "I brought it down so you could read it yourself."

Slipping on his glasses, he pulled one of the bar candles closer.

Consider this your only warning. Stop your research NOW. Have you ever seen someone with both their knees shattered, Marie? It's horribly painful. You can count on being crippled for years—possibly for the rest of your life. Don't

*play with fire. I guarantee you will be burned. Just leave
quietly and move on to your next victim.*

The note was typed and left unsigned.

As he handed it back to her, he said, "I assume you've gone
to the police. The person who sent it may have been sloppy.
There could be fingerprints."

She took a sip of wine. "I considered it, but for reasons of
privacy, I don't want my name talked about on the evening
news. And believe me, that's what would happen. I've got to
keep this to myself for now. Rely on my bodyguard to do his
job."

Bram didn't think that was enough, but it wasn't his call. "I
suppose you know best."

"I do. But to make my situation work, I need something
else. Two things, really. Both involve you."

"Me?"

She handed him back the note. "If anything happens to me,
I want you to take this to the police."

He didn't like the sound of that. "Sure, but—"

"I've received threats before, but never one so graphic. I
think that's why I was so shaken up. Then again, nobody's
ever followed through on a threat, so I feel pretty confident
I'll be okay, especially now that Rafferty's with me."

Bram wanted to believe she was right. "Maybe this was
just some idiot trying to call your bluff."

"Exactly."

"If they're able to scare you off with a note, they haven't
risked a thing."

"And I don't scare easily."

He studied her a moment. "You'll be fine, Marie. I'm sure
of it."

She reached over and covered his hand with hers. "Thank
you for that."

Bram felt the room grow suddenly warmer. "You don't
have to thank me."

"But I do. In more ways than you could ever understand. I

just hope I'm not getting you involved in something dangerous. If anything happened to you . . ."

"What could happen to me?" Then it hit him. "What's the second part of your request?"

She removed her hand. "When I'm working on a new book, I always keep journal notes, and I make transcriptions from the taped interviews. I want you to look at the transcriptions, Bram. I want you to tell me if I'm crazy, if I'm reading something into the research that isn't there. I need an unbiased opinion, someone to help me see if I've made a wrong turn in my analysis. I'll tell you quite honestly, I don't think my conclusions are faulty. I believe I may be on the verge of uncovering a forty-year-old murder. And if I'm right, my life could very well be in danger. I can't mail my notes to my editor. I'm not sure I could count on him to keep them confidential, and I don't want any leaks that might threaten my investigation. This is too hot." She lowered her dark eyes, then raised them again, meeting his with even greater urgency. "I need someone I can trust. Someone I can rely on. Will you be that person for me? I know it's a lot to ask. You've got no reason to want to get involved in this."

He was not only flattered, he was mesmerized, not just by her request but also by the woman herself. "Of course I'll help you."

"We'll have to stop meeting publicly. I don't want anyone in the Buckridge camp to get the idea that we're anything more than casual acquaintances."

"All right. But how do we pass the research? And when?"

"Tomorrow. I'll need to make a copy of it for you first. I have an interview in the morning, then I'll want to get that transcription done before I give you the packet. Can I call you sometime in the afternoon? Do you have a work number?"

He removed a card from his wallet.

While he was writing his private number down, she continued. "I had an unexpected visitor this afternoon."

"Oh?" He handed her the card. "Who?"

"Kenneth Merlin, the Buckridge family attorney."

"Did he look like the knee-breaking sort?"

She smiled. "Not really. He's their mouthpiece. But given the word, I'm sure he'd be delighted to hire the muscle to do the necessary dirty work."

"Too smart to get his own hands messy, huh?"

She nodded, finishing her glass of wine. "But he came with a very interesting offer. He said that he'd learned, through certain unnamed channels, what I'd received as an advance for the Buckridge biography."

"Was the figure accurate?"

"To the penny. Without blinking an eye, he informed me that he'd double it if I stopped my research and gave up any thought of writing the book. He said he'd also pay for any legal fees I might incur in getting out of my contract."

"I assume we're talking lots of money here?"

"*Lots* of money."

"And how did you respond?"

"I turned him down."

Bram grinned. He liked her style.

"That's when he made a second offer. He said he knew there were such things as foreign sales, book club rights, even TV and movie rights, which he conceded might make me a very wealthy woman. So he offered to double the advance again—on the spot. He took out a checkbook. I thought, Hell, if I just sit tight a while longer, he'd up the ante again."

"Did he?"

She shook her head. "He told me to think about it. He was only authorized to offer so much, and he'd reached the limit."

"Which means he isn't calling the shots."

"I'm sure Constance is behind everything, but how much power he has within the organization remains to be seen. He said that he'd get back to me in a couple of days, but that I should think long and hard about it before I turned him down."

"Another threat."

"This one was far more genteel, but I got the message. He promised me that if I didn't cooperate, he'd tie the book up in the courts for years. I'd be an old woman before I ever saw a dime of the money coming to me. But then, as he was leaving,

I pointed out the sad state of tabloid journalism today. Constance would have to continually worry about leaks. He countered that I was probably right, but that the tabloids could never pay me what he'd just offered. Why settle for macaroni and cheese when I could have champagne and caviar?"

"But you said you didn't want any leaks."

"It's a chess game, Bram. They threaten. I threaten."

"But if you do find evidence of a murder, you'll have to turn it over to the police."

Now she was indignant. "Are you crazy? Not before my book hits the stands. The dead aren't going anywhere. What I need is for the living to stay out of my way long enough for me to write the damn story. But that means I'll have to conduct my investigation very carefully from here on out. If my theory's correct, and even one of the Buckridges gets wind of what I've got, they'll do anything to stop me. And I mean *anything*."

Sophie dropped her car off at the Maxfield's front entrance, requesting one of the bellmen to park it for her in the hotel's lot across the street. She didn't want to waste a second. She only had fifteen minutes between now and seven-thirty, and she had to talk to Nathan first, otherwise she wouldn't be able to concentrate on anything else during dinner.

Entering the lobby, she wondered briefly if Bram was upstairs in the apartment getting ready. Sometimes he came down to have a drink at Scotties before dinner. Deciding to peek inside and take a look around, she immediately spotted him at the bar. He was sitting with that Lela Dexter again. They seemed to be deep in conversation, which irked Sophie more than she cared to admit. She assumed that men found Dexter attractive, but to Sophie, all that dark hair combined with those pointy features made her look like the Wicked Witch of the West. Saying a silent prayer that she'd get flattened by a flying house, Sophie headed to her office.

On the way there, a woman at the concierge desk stopped her. "Ms. Greenway, the information you ordered from Grandview Travel arrived this afternoon." She handed her a thick manila envelope. "Are you and your husband planning a vacation?"

God, she'd completely forgotten about that. "As soon as we can make the time." She thanked the woman, then hurried across the lobby to the reservation desk. Glancing briefly at the entrance to the atrium, she noticed Paul Buckridge standing with a wineglass in his hand, talking to another man. When she looked closer, she realized that the other man was David Polchow, the chef who left the Belmont the night George's second review came out. She wondered how he and Paul knew each other.

"Where have you been all day?" came a familiar voice from behind her.

Sophie turned to find Nathan smiling at her. He was dressed in jeans and a short-sleeved striped polo shirt. His beard had grown out even more since yesterday. "It's gray," she said, reaching her hand to touch it but stopping herself at the last moment.

He looked a little sheepish. "My hair's still dark, so who would've thought my beard would betray me? It's not all gray, just in spots. I suppose you think it makes me look like an old man."

"You're hardly that." How someone could eat as much as he probably had to on a daily basis and still look *that* buff— well, the only answer was that he probably killed himself at the gym several days a week. "And what do you mean, where have I been? I've been working."

"Not here you haven't."

"I spent the morning with a friend and the afternoon at the paper."

"Ah." The smile cranked up another couple of notches. "You look wonderful, Soph. As usual." He fixed her with an excited look.

"What? You look like you're about to burst."

"Sophie, I'm going to cook for you."

"What?"

"I've got it all set up. A buddy of mine has an apartment a few blocks from here. There's so much I want you to taste. I spent part of the afternoon just picking out the wines. This meal will have a heavy Italian influence. That's my personal preference. But there's so much else—"

"Nathan, we have to talk."

"I know. God, I know."

"No, you don't know. It's not about us or about food."

He took her by the arm and led her over to the floral arrangement near the front door. The Maxfield always kept fresh flowers on display in the lobby to greet the guests as they entered the hotel. Yesterday the florist had arrived with an inspired spring creation: yellow daffodils, pink daisies, and white tulips.

"I wanted to get you some flowers," said Nathan, walking her around behind the arrangement, "but I thought it might create problems for you with your husband. I mean, you'd have to explain it somehow."

She was grateful that he'd shown *some* sense.

"If I'd had my way, I would have filled your office with lilacs. I know how much you love them."

"Nathan, you mustn't—"

He pressed a finger to her lips. "Just give me a second, okay? See, I had to bring you some piece of beauty. A reminder of what happened between us yesterday. But I knew I had to be sneaky about it." He nodded to a single red rose hiding amid a spray of white tulips. "Every time you look at it, remember how much I love you."

She couldn't help herself. She was touched.

"It's a special rose, too. I went to seven florists this afternoon before I found just the right one. It's not only beautiful, it has the most heavenly fragrance. Go ahead," he prodded. "Smell it."

"Nathan, I can't—"

"Please? For me? The scent reminds me of all the summer nights we spent walking through the rose gardens, just relaxing, holding hands, talking about our lives, what we wanted to accomplish, how we'd always be together. This flower has the perfume of memory in it, Sophie. It's a magic rose."

"Nathan, that's very sweet of you, but I'm not the same person I was twenty-five years ago. And I don't believe in magic."

"Sure you do. You have to. Otherwise you'd be swallowed up by the mundane, like the rest of the world. You're not like that, Soph. I know you. Come on. Just put your nose right up next to it. Good. Now close your eyes. I want you to stand there like that for one minute. I'll tell you when the time is up. See if you can feel the memories in the flower, Soph. I'm not kidding, it's really all there."

Feeling as if she had no other choice, she closed her eyes and breathed in the fragrance. It was lovely. Fresh, sweet, just a hint of spice. She remembered those nights as vividly as he did. The light fading over the lake in the distance. The sounds of dogs barking and children playing. A soft breeze blowing through the trees. Her hand would slip into his back pocket as they walked along. She couldn't imagine anything more wonderful than being close to him.

"Taking time to smell the roses?" asked another familiar voice.

When Sophie looked up, she saw Bram standing next to her. She turned around, but Nathan was gone. He must have seen Bram coming out of the bar and taken off. "Yes, I guess . . . I am," she stammered. She plastered on a smile.

"How can you look guilty for taking a moment to sniff a flower? Have those lousy Puritans over at that right-wing rag been beating on you all afternoon?"

"No, I'm still me."

"Good." He kissed the top of her head. "Because I sort of like you."

She continued to smile.

"Well, are you ready for our night of romance?"

She hadn't even made it upstairs to change, but she supposed she could get by with what she was wearing. "All set."

He reached around her and plucked the rose, threading the stem through his buttonhole. "There. That's a proper finishing touch." He sniffed it. "Kind of cloying, but then roses are like that."

She nodded, the same stiff smile plastered on her face.

"Is something wrong, sweetheart? You look funny."

"No, everything's just fine." If she had to sit and stare at the rose for the rest of the night, she was going to throw up.

He offered her his arm. "I hope you have your dancing shoes on."

She was exhausted by the world in general and he wanted to dance. This day had turned into a ghastly marathon. She had to have a long talk with Nathan first thing in the morning. She couldn't put it off any longer.

Journal Note

Wednesday, noon

Busy morning. Rafferty and I walked two and a half blocks to an old brick warehouse that had been turned into artists' lofts about five years ago. Normally, I would have gone by myself, but I can't take any chances for the duration of my stay here in Minnesota. I met with Phillip Rapson, the Buckridges' onetime handyman-gardener. He has a loft on the sixth floor. It wasn't a terribly long interview, but I learned some interesting details that may prove to be important.

It was immediately clear to me that Mr. Rapson took a rather Pollyanna-ish view of Constance Buckridge. They were friends, so he saw none of the red flags I did. Thankfully, I'm good at reading between the lines. If what I'm thinking now turns out to be true, Nathan Buckridge may have had a hand in the death of Pepper. Perhaps he was entirely responsible, though I lean toward the idea that it was a joint effort between mother and son. Somehow, I've got to get my hands on the hospital records. I need to know the official cause of death. I assume there was no autopsy performed, but some document must exist with the information I need. Since I have a couple of field researchers on the payroll at the moment—both in Wisconsin looking into the Jadek family history—I think I may have to put another researcher on this angle. But more on that later.

No more E-mails from Pluto. All along I've been suspicious about his real motivation for starting me down this road. After my conversation with Phillip Rapson, I'm now wondering if he might not be using me to see how much information can actually be unearthed about Pepper Buckridge's death. Perhaps he's already employed several P.I.'s to see what was out there but had no luck. By dangling an extraordinarily appealing carrot in front of my nose, and knowing it would be backed up by a sizable advance from a well-known publisher as well as by my own desire to uncover a nearly forty-year-old mystery that would turn a simple biography into a national bestseller, he assured himself that this time, if there was evidence to be found, I'd uncover it.

Whoever Pluto turns out to be, someone in the Buckridge household clearly wants me to stop my search and someone else wants me to continue it, and that makes me feel as if I'm walking on a tightrope. At one end is Pluto. At the other, Constance. Neither is my friend. And both are willing to push, perhaps violently, to get what they want.

I keep asking myself, Is any book worth this kind of risk? Why don't I just take the money Kenneth Merlin offered me and run? The fact is, I'm exactly the kind of person Pluto wants for his investigator. It seems I always get to a point in my research where I become obsessed to one degree or another by my subject. That's my reputation, and it's accurate. If I flew back to New York now, resumed my everyday life, I'd be a basket case inside a month. I'd go to bed at night thinking about Constance Buckridge, Wayne, Pepper, Arthur, Nathan, Paul, Emily. I'd drive myself crazy with all the unanswered questions. My personality is my cross, I guess, and I'm stuck with it. I have to go on.

So, to Phillip Rapson. Mr. Rapson was originally hired by Pepper Buckridge in 1961 and lived in a small apartment above the garage until he quit in 1974, a few months after Wayne's death. When he started as their handyman-gardener, he was in his early twenties, approximately the same age as Constance. The job allowed him a reasonable income, a place to live, and time to paint—both his hobby and passion.

Today Mr. Rapson is an internationally known artist, although he prefers to live simply. He explained that he has a small house in Bayport, Minnesota, but that he drives in every day to work at his loft. He's in his midsixties, stocky, bearded, and balding, although he assured me that when he was younger, he had a full head of thick red hair. He's never been married, a fact that he put down to luck and an inability to allow hope to triumph over experience. He was more than willing to talk about his days with the Buckridges, most of which he remembers quite fondly.

INTERVIEW: PHILLIP RAPSON, ST. PAUL, MINNESOTA, WEDNESDAY, MAY 12

M: *When did you first meet Constance Buckridge?*

Rapson: *In 1961. Wayne and Pepper Buckridge had just moved into the house on Lake Minnetonka and were hiring staff. I wanted a job that would allow me time to paint. I felt their position would be perfect for my needs, and was delighted when I was hired. Mrs. Buckridge—*

M: *You mean Pepper?*

Rapson: *Yes, Pepper. We hit it off right away. She was a funny, intelligent, lively woman. I thought Wayne Buckridge was a very lucky man. I believe their son, Paul, was two at the time. Connie was hired a few months after me to be one of the maids. She was shy, very pretty in a girl-next-door way, and she also had a son, Nathan. Seems to me he was about seven. A real nice, well-behaved kid. The kind you didn't know was in the room until you tripped over him. Connie said his dad had taken off before he was born, so I felt sorry for him. Actually, Nathan and Connie and I became good friends. We went on picnics together. Took in an occasional movie.*

M: *Did you date Connie?*

Rapson: *I suppose you could call it that. She was a very level-*

headed sort of young woman. Not intellectual in any sense of the word, but she had practical smarts, if you know what I mean. She'd had a rough life and didn't like to talk about the past. I respected her privacy and didn't pry.

M: *If you don't want to answer the next question, just say so. Were you and Connie lovers?*

Rapson: *No, but it wasn't for lack of trying on my part. She just wasn't interested. She was totally centered on getting ahead in the world. You might even call her an early feminist. Nathan's father was a deadbeat and a jerk, so she had to come up with a way to put food on the table and a roof over their heads. She said she was never going to make the same mistake again.*

M: *What mistake was that?*

Rapson: *Thinking that a man was going to take care of her. She was in charge now. Nathan was going to have the best of everything because she was going to get it for him. She just hadn't figured out how to do it yet. But if it meant she had to sacrifice for their future by cleaning toilets and scrubbing floors, she was willing to do it. I had every faith that she'd make a real success of her life in the end, and she proved me right. Connie had a lot of spunk, and I admired her for it. She was going after what she wanted, and in a way it gave me the courage to do the same.*

M: *Sounds like she had awfully big ideas for someone taking a job as a maid.*

Rapson: *Maybe she did, but you gotta start somewhere. Why not think big?*

M: *Are you still in contact with her?*

Rapson: *No. Last time I saw Connie was in 1974.*

M: *What were the living arrangements like for the staff?*

Rapson: *Well, like I said, I lived above the garage. The two maids and the cook had rooms on the third floor. Nothing very fancy.*

M: *Did Nathan have his own room?*

Rapson: *No, there were no provisions for that. There were only three bedrooms up on third, and one bath. It was pretty tight quarters, but I think Connie was grateful to have a place*

*to live. She got room and board and a salary. Compared to
what she'd been doing before—*

M: *What was that?*

Rapson: *She'd been sharing a tiny apartment with her best
friend, her best friend's husband, and their little girl. It
wasn't a good situation. Connie had done just about everything you could think of to make money. She worked as a
maid in a hotel, a waitress at a café on Lyndale. She took care
of other people's kids. Worked at a dry cleaner's, a drugstore.
She was even a receptionist at a beauty shop for a while. Most
of the positions ended because of child-care problems. She
didn't have any relatives in the city, and when her friend
couldn't baby-sit, she'd have to stay at home with Nathan.
When that happened too often, she'd get canned.*

M: *What was the best friend's name?*

Rapson: *Let me think. (Scratches his beard) Beverly. Beverly
and Tom . . . Custerson. I remember because I dated Peggy
Custerson shortly before I met Connie. Turns out, Peggy and
Tom were cousins.*

M: *Are you still in touch with this Peggy?*

Rapson: *As a matter of fact, I am.*

M: *Would you mind asking her where her cousin and his wife
are living now? I'd like to talk to Beverly if at all possible.*

Rapson: *Sure, no problem. Peggy's a real family person. If
anyone would know, she would.*

M: *Back to Nathan. Did he find it hard living in one bedroom
with his mother?*

Rapson: *I suppose so. He never said anything, though. He
wasn't the kind of kid who complained.*

M: *Did the Buckridges allow him the run of the house?*

Rapson: *Well, he was in school most of the day. Summers
were the biggest problem. Things started out okay. He and
Paul even played together. But Nathan was bigger, older. Paul
would get pushed over or knocked down and he'd start to cry.
Eventually Pepper laid down the law and said she didn't want
them playing together any longer. Like I said, I liked Pepper,
but I will say she was kind of a snob. She thought of Connie
and Nathan as low class, uneducated and basically dumb.*

I'm sure she viewed all the help that way. That kind of thinking has always seemed silly to me. On the other hand, anyone who says we don't have a class system in this country isn't living in the real world. Anyway, I was able to ignore it, but it hurt Connie. And I know it upset Nathan terribly. All of a sudden, one day he was no longer allowed in the pool or the gazebo or on the swing set or the beach. And the dock, where he loved to feed the sunfish, was off limits, too. There was a park about three blocks away and that's where he was supposed to play when he wanted to be outdoors. Indoors, he was pretty much confined to the bedroom.

M: *That seems rather draconian.*

Rapson: *It was.*

M: *Did he have a TV to watch?*

Rapson: *Connie couldn't afford one. I think she had a radio. He listened to that a lot. And he read. I've never seen a kid read as much as he did. When he first came, he was a lot more happy-go-lucky. As time went on, he withdrew. But then when Pepper started having all those physical problems—*

M: *When was that?*

Rapson: *The summer of '63, I think. Yes, I remember because Connie had just taken over as the new cook. The old one got another job or something. I don't really know all the details of what was wrong with Pepper, I just know she started seeing a lot of doctors. I used to drive her into the city when she didn't feel up to driving herself. By fall, she rarely ever drove herself anymore.*

M: *Do you think she was feigning illness just to get her husband's attention?*

Rapson: *(Looks puzzled) That never occurred to me. He did work long hours, but no, I think the woman was ill. Not that the doctors were much help.*

M: *You were about to make a comment about Nathan.*

Rapson: *Yes, well, when Pepper wasn't around to keep an eagle eye on the house, Nathan did use the pool a few times. I even found him sitting in the family room one afternoon watching TV. Pepper was having one of her spells that day and was in bed upstairs. After it became apparent that she couldn't take care of Paul, she hired a series of nannies, but none of them lasted more than a month. That meant his daily care fell to the staff. Connie took the most interest in him. He'd sit in the kitchen and play while she prepared the meals. I think she really liked the little guy. Since Pepper was in bed upstairs most of the day, Nathan began to play with Paul again—mainly, I think, as a way to entertain him and get him out of the staff's hair so that they could do their jobs. And that meant, of course, that Nathan once again had the run of the house.*

M: *I get the impression that Wayne didn't have much to say about the home situation.*

Rapson: *No, he left that up to Pepper. And as Pepper had more bad days, Connie sort of took over as head of the household. It wasn't official or anything, but someone had to make the decisions. Actually, I remember a couple of occasions when I came back from town in the evening and saw Connie and Wayne sitting in the living room together having a glass of wine. Everyone else was in bed.*

M: *Are you suggesting that she and her employer had something other than a business relationship?*

Rapson: *No, because I don't know it for a fact. Then again I couldn't exactly ignore the way Wayne looked at her. I mean, I knew what was in his mind. But you can't fault a guy for looking. Wayne was really at loose ends right around that time. He didn't have much of a marriage because Pepper was always sick in bed. A man has needs, you know.*

M: *And Connie was only too willing to supply those needs.*

Rapson: *You've got the wrong idea about Connie, Ms. Damontraville. She wasn't after Wayne Buckridge. She wasn't after any guy, especially one who was old enough to be her father.*

M: *But she might have been after his money.*

Rapson: *(Shakes his head) I don't believe it. She wasn't that kind of woman. I grant you, she did marry him eventually.*

M: *Fairly soon after Pepper's death.*

Rapson: *It was almost a year, but you've made your point. Perhaps their friendship had turned into something more, though I don't fault either of them for it. It probably just happened. It's just . . . I never once had the sense that Connie was in love with Wayne.*

M: *Not even when they were about to be married?*

Rapson: *(Hesitates) I'm getting in way over my head here.*

M: *The question is still on the table.*

Rapson: *No, I don't think she loved him. But I also don't think she married him for his money.*

M: *Then what reason would she have?*

Rapson: *Very simple. Nathan. I think he'd settled into his life there. Once Pepper was out of the picture, he was a lot more comfortable. I think Connie wanted him to have a father, a normal family life. She thought marrying Buckridge would give him that.*

M: *And did it?*

Rapson: *I suppose so.*

M: *You don't sound sure.*

Rapson: *Well, Wayne wasn't the warmest man I'd ever met. As a father figure to any of his kids, he left a lot to be desired. But you have to understand something. Until Pepper became too ill to control what was happening in the house, Nathan lived like a second-class citizen. That lasted for nearly two years. I know it really took a toll on the boy. I have to say, I felt sorry for him. He used to come up to my apartment in the evenings and we'd play checkers. I know he loved his mom, but he needed a man to talk to.*

M: *Before their marriage, did Wayne ever pay any attention to him?*

Rapson: *Not much, but then he was never overtly mean to the kid either, like Pepper had been. I think Nathan liked Wayne. I know he always tried to be helpful. He'd look for ways to do things for him. Like, when the morning paper got tossed in the bushes, Nathan would always go out and get it for him. (Laughs) One night, I remember, I caught him in the garage. He'd taken a gallon jug of antifreeze down from the shelf and was about to leave. He hadn't turned on a light, so I figured he was up to no good. When I flipped the light on, the look on his face told me I was right. He looked guilty as hell. But then*

*he explained that Wayne had asked him to get the antifreeze
for him so he could put it in his trunk. Apparently he had a radiator leak and hadn't had a chance to get it fixed. Every
morning he'd just top off the liquid and head off to work.*

M: *Sounds like a careless way to take care of a car.*

Rapson: *Yeah, I agree. And it was a Jag, too. Come to think of
it, I asked Wayne about it a few weeks later. He was in a bad
mood that day. I don't know if I mentioned it before, but he
was kind of a moody guy. He said he didn't know what I was
talking about. If he had a leaky radiator he'd have it fixed.
End of story.*

M: *So what do you think Nathan was doing with the antifreeze?*

Rapson: *He was probably telling me the truth. Wayne was
terrible about maintaining cars, and he was probably embarrassed. He'd use and abuse it, then get rid of it and buy
another. I'm not sure he ever remembered to have the oil
changed. I had to remind him about it all the time. Sometimes I just did it myself.*

M: *So you stayed on as the handyman-gardener until 1974.*

Rapson: *Right. I'd saved quite a bit of money over the years
and had started to sell some of my paintings, so I figured it
was time. It was hard to say goodbye. Nathan was twenty by
then. Even with all the strikes against him, he'd grown up to
be a fine young man. Paul was in his late teens, kind of a
handful, but basically a good kid. And Emily was about the
same age Nathan had been when he'd first come to live in the
house. Wayne was gone. He'd had a massive heart attack in
late January. Time moves on, I guess. Nothing stays the same.*

M: *Just a couple more questions. I assume you knew Arthur
Jadek, Connie's brother.*

Rapson: *Sure did. I don't think this is common knowledge, but
he was a CIA operative for a while. I assume it had something
to do with east Asia. Vietnam. The war effort over there. Very
hush-hush stuff. The boys idolized him.*

M: *What did you think of him?*

Rapson: *He was ill when he first came to live at the house.
Well, maybe not ill exactly, but certainly malnourished. But
his health improved almost right away. I liked the guy. He had*

an undergraduate degree in philosophy, so we used to talk about that some.

M: *Were you home the night Wayne had his heart attack?*

Rapson: *No, I left to have dinner with friends about a quarter to six. Funny, Wayne rarely ever got home before seven. But that night he arrived early, just as I was leaving.*

M: *Connie was home?*

Rapson: *Yes, but she was in her study with some music on. Wayne apparently went upstairs without saying anything to her. She found him in the bathroom later that night. Connie felt he was trying to get to his heart medication. He must have called out to her, but she wouldn't have heard him. It was a real tragedy.*

M: *I understand Arthur was also away at the time. At the library.*

Rapson: *(Hesitates) No, I don't think so. At least, his car was in the drive when I left. I'm sure he was inside.*

M: *I've been told by others that he wasn't around.*

Rapson: *(Thinks for a moment) No, he was there. As a matter of fact, I saw him go in the back door around five-fifteen.*

M: *But none of the kids were home?*

Rapson: *No, I'm positive of that. Nathan was out of town. Paul was playing in a football game. And Emily was staying at a friend's house for the night. The only other person who could possibly have been there was the housekeeper, and she usually left by five.*

M: *If she was still around, would you have seen her car?*

Rapson: *She didn't have one. She'd walk out to the main road and take a bus home at night.*

M: *Do you remember her name?*

Rapson: *Sure. Laurie Lippert. She owns her own business now, the House Cleaning Company. Very successful. Probably has a couple dozen employees. Actually, I use one of her people to take care of the loft. The woman comes in once a week and does a bang-up job.*

M: *So it's a local company.*

Rapson: *Right here in St. Paul. Just look in the phone book.*

M: *I guess that's about it, Mr. Rapson. Thanks for your time.*

Rapson: *My pleasure.*
M: *Oh, and don't forget. If you can call me with an address for Beverly Custerson, Constance's best friend, I'd be very grateful. You've still got my number at the Maxfield?*
Rapson: *I do. And I promise, I'll get on it right away.*

17

Sophie spent Wednesday morning in her office at the Maxfield, handling tasks she should have addressed yesterday. She needed to read a report about a new idea that one of the staff had generated concerning the hotel's deluxe amenities for guests. Sophie had seen refillable dispensers at other hotels—dispensers that hung on the bathroom walls and were used for shampoo, hair conditioner, body lotion, body shampoo, etc.—but she wasn't sure she wanted to make such a radical change at the Maxfield. The report was intended to convince her that it was not only wise ecologically but also that it would save tons of money.

As she stared at the words on the page, she willed herself to concentrate, but the meaning wouldn't penetrate. She would read a paragraph over and over, and each time she had only the vaguest recollection of what it had said. She hadn't slept well since Saturday night, and her increasing tiredness was taking a toll. No matter how hard she tried to stay on point, her thoughts kept drifting back to Nathan.

She'd called his room at least a dozen times during the morning, left several messages, but still hadn't heard from him. The words that George Gildemeister's elderly neighbor had said to her yesterday evening kept swirling around in her mind. Nathan had been in George's apartment the night he died. Sophie needed answers, but Nathan wasn't around to explain. What worried her most was her fear that, when they finally did talk, he wouldn't tell her the truth.

After a short meeting with the housekeeping supervisor, Sophie worked the front desk until two. She was dead on her feet, making silly mistakes that frustrated the guests checking in and out. She wanted to take a nap but couldn't. She had an appointment at the Times Register Tower and knew that missing her first staff meeting would be unacceptable.

Thinking that she might as well change into something more comfortable—nobody dressed particularly formally at the paper—she stopped by Hildegard's office to let her know where she'd be for the next few hours. After a brief conversation, she walked briskly to the elevators. The briskness was an effort to convince herself that she wouldn't fall asleep midstride.

As she got off on her floor, an idea struck her. Perhaps Nathan was in his mother's room, or someone there knew where he was. She got right back on the elevator and descended to the tenth floor.

Standing in front of the door to Constance's suite, she lifted her hand to knock, then stopped. Anxiety rose in her chest. She wanted to talk to Nathan, wanted to clear the air, and yet she could feel a heavy tension coiling itself around her shoulders. She'd already decided to phrase her questions in such a way so that if he was going to lie, she'd know immediately. Should she then go to the police with what she knew, or should she give him a second chance to explain? Could she really implicate Nathan in a murder? This wasn't about the titillating advances of an old boyfriend any longer. It was about life and death.

Summoning her courage, she knocked on the door. A moment later Arthur opened it. "Sophie, what a nice surprise. Come in."

She glanced into the room and saw that he'd been sitting at the desk working on a laptop computer. A cigarette rested in an ashtray, a trail of smoke rising into the air. A jumble of books and papers clustered around the base of the chair. "If I'm interrupting something—"

"No, not at all. I assume you came to find Nathan."

"Actually—"

"Please." He gestured to the living room. "I'm afraid nobody's here but me, but I'd like to talk to you if you've got a couple of minutes."

"Well, sure."

"How about some coffee? I just made a fresh pot."

Even dressed casually in soft corduroy pants and a blue oxford cloth shirt turned up at the sleeves, Nathan's uncle appeared formal. Sophie remembered now that he'd always been fastidious about his appearance.

Once upon a time she'd counted Arthur Jadek as a good friend. She'd always been at ease in his presence. With his gentle, inquiring gaze, she felt like a favored child when he talked to her. He liked to talk, but he was also a good listener, and that was rare. "No thanks. I've got to be at a meeting at three."

"Then we'll make this short." He picked up his cigarette before he sat down and tapped off the ash. "Everyone except me drove out to New Fonteney this morning. I didn't go along because I wanted to get some work done, although I hear it's a lovely spot. I probably should have gone just for the fresh air."

"It is lovely," she agreed. "Nathan and I took a drive out there on Monday."

He nodded, giving her an appraising look. "I suppose I should preface what I want to say by telling you that I feel very protective of my nephew, Sophie. You undoubtedly know that. Nathan is a fine man. I don't want to see him get hurt. To be honest, I've never seen him as happy as he's been the last few days. He tells me it has a lot to do with you."

She looked down at the wedding ring on her left hand.

"You're married, aren't you?"

"Yes, I am. And I love my husband very much. I think Nathan's got the wrong idea about us. I tried talking to him last night, but we didn't have much time, and he wouldn't let me get a word in edgewise."

Arthur smiled. "He's like that when he's excited. Still a boy." The smile faded slightly. "What you're telling me is, there's no chance for the two of you."

"I'm sorry."

"I am, too. I know you've always represented a huge unresolved issue in his life."

"I was hoping to talk to him about all that today."

"He's going to be terribly disappointed." Arthur sat back in his chair and gave a heavy sigh. "Bad timing," he mumbled.

"Why do you say that?"

"Oh, well, Nathan's been somewhat depressed these last couple of years. Seeing you pulled him right out of it, but now I'm afraid he'll be even more down."

"I didn't know. Is there some specific reason why he's been depressed?"

Arthur lifted the cigarette to his lips, inhaled deeply, then blew the smoke out slowly through his nose. "I don't know," he replied. "We've always been close, but it's something he won't talk about. I'll admit I'm worried. Has he said anything to you?" He watched her carefully.

She wasn't going to betray Nathan's confidence, not that he'd been all that forthcoming about his problems. "Nothing specific. Look, Arthur, tell me the truth. How worried are you?"

"I suggested an antidepressant, but like most people Nathan has an instinctive distrust of pills, and the idea that he has a condition that could be considered psychological, emotional, or, worse, *mental,* scares him to death. He'd rather tough it out than get help."

"I see."

"Do you? Depression can be treated, Sophie. It's often just a chemical imbalance. If you had asthma or diabetes, would you be embarrassed to go to a doctor, or tell your friends about your condition? But mental problems—anxiety, depression, bipolar disorder, even schizophrenia—all of these can be helped, both through talk and drug therapy, but there's a stigma attached when your brain chemicals get out of whack. It's what keeps people from seeking treatment and, often, from getting the help they need to keep themselves alive."

"You think Nathan is that depressed?"

"I don't know. Maybe. I just wish I knew if there was some precipitating event in his life, some personal issue that's causing it."

"And you think if I tell him there's no chance for us, it will make his condition worse?"

Arthur ground out his cigarette. "I'm certainly not telling you to lie. He can't hold on to a pipe dream as a way of keeping his head above water. I'm here for him, Sophie. I have a great deal of experience in these matters. I promise, I won't let anything happen to him."

Sophie was relieved to hear it. "He's lucky he has such a supportive family."

Arthur flicked his eyes to her and then away. "Yes, he is."

"I've hardly seen Paul and Emily since they've been here. They seem in good spirits."

"Oh, Paul's his usual swaggering self. He's only happy when he's got something to complain about. But there's always plenty of that to keep him occupied."

She smiled. "I remember."

"He's very concerned right now about New Fonteney. He doesn't want his mother to buy it. He thinks it's a bad investment and the wrong place for a new campus. But he's fiercely loyal to Constance and to what she's created. He's not saying it just to annoy Nathan, although I'm not sure Nathan sees it that way. I respect Paul for his integrity."

"What about Emily?"

He smiled warmly. "She has two beautiful children, you know. Twins. But it's funny. She's been so quiet on this trip. Perhaps she's tired. She worked very hard on the photographs for Connie's newest book. This was supposed to be a vacation of sorts for her, but I'm not sure it's turning out that way."

Sophie decided to do a little fishing. It couldn't hurt. "I'm curious. Have you ever heard Nathan speak of a man named George Gildemeister?"

He shook his head. "No. Why?"

"He's an old friend of mine. It's not important. I'll talk to Nathan about it later."

"I know he's hoping to have dinner with you tonight. Has he talked to you about it?"

"He mentioned wanting to prepare a meal, but we never discussed a date or a time."

"If you do get together this evening, it might be a good opportunity for you to break the news to him . . . gently."

"I'm not sure that's such a good idea. I think it might be better just to sit down and talk when there's no other agenda. No wine and roses and soft music. You understand."

He leaned forward, clasping his hands between his knees. "Please, Sophie, tell me if I'm becoming too personal, but I sense some ambivalence in you. Are you sure that you've really examined your feelings on the matter, that you're not just reacting out of a sense of obligation to your husband?"

She tugged at her blazer and shifted in her chair. "Of course I have an obligation, one I take seriously. It's called marriage. But I also love my husband. There's no doubt in my mind about that."

"And there's no doubt that you don't love Nathan?"

How was she supposed to answer? "I loved him once, a long time ago. But I haven't seen him in so long. How can I say I love the man he's become?"

"But he hasn't changed, Sophie. Surely you've discovered that by now."

She shook her head. "Okay, so sometimes it's like we've never been apart. We banter just like we used to. There's still an easy rapport. And, of course, there's still a physical attraction. But I won't turn my back on my marriage and the life I've built with my husband just for that."

Arthur seemed so dismayed by her response that Sophie thought she should say something more. "Maybe Nathan hasn't changed, but I have. We can't turn back time."

He gave her a long, hard look. "It's sad. I suppose I'm a hopeless romantic, but I always thought the two of you were fated to be together. Then again I understand. You and Nathan are in very different places in your lives right now. Most important, you aren't free. But give me this much, Sophie. If you were free, would you still believe you'd changed too much to love my nephew?"

For old times' sake, she supposed he deserved an honest answer. "I don't know, Arthur. But as you said, I'm not free, so the point is moot." She had to get going, but she didn't want to leave on such a negative note. She decided to introduce a new subject—briefly. "What are you working on?" She nodded at all the books and papers.

"Oh." His eyes shifted slowly from Sophie back to the computer. "It's a pet theory of mine. One day it may be a book, or it may end up in the trash heap."

"What's it about?"

"You're sure you want to know?"

"I was always fascinated by your ideas."

Again his smile was gentle. "It's about the concept of free will, the cornerstone of Christian theology. I'm afraid I no longer believe it exists, at least not the way we usually think about it. I've been playing with this notion for years. I'm building my theory brick by scientific brick. When I'm done, perhaps I'll have a house. Or perhaps I'll have a structure I can blow over with one breath."

Sophie was captured instantly. "Explain a bit more."

"Well, to put it simply, if man doesn't have free will, if his fate is already determined by factors beyond his control, then he cannot sin. If there's no such thing as sin, man needs no redemption. The whole system of Christian thought is based on free will. It's a rather large issue."

"You were always good at understatement."

He grinned. "I'm not saying that humans don't need morals and ethics. We do. Society must have order. But isn't it interesting that with all the dos and don'ts out there, we're all still making terrible choices, both personally and as a society. Why do you think that is?"

She shrugged. "Disinterest. Stupidity. Arrogance. Confusion. Simple rebellion."

"Possibly. But when it comes to the larger issues of life, I think it's more basic. You've heard the old argument about nature versus nurture?"

She nodded.

"Are we born who we are or did our experience create us? Most psychologists and philosophers have come down somewhere in the middle. We're a mixture of nature and nurture. It's a safe position. Hard to refute. Theologians maintain that our nature is evil, but that we must fight against it. Choose to be good."

"You're saying that's not possible?"

"In the larger sense, no, I don't believe choice is possible. At least not according to the theory I'm positing."

"What decides for us? God?"

"Heavens, no. It's simply our chemical makeup. The more scientific evidence that becomes available, the more studies that are done, the clearer it becomes that we're simply small chemical factories. Hormones. Neurotransmitters. Put simply, our genetic code rules. We've already discovered that there is a genetic component to sexuality, also to the way men's and women's brains function. Some people think an additional Y chromosome may designate a criminal, though it's never that simple, never just one thing. There's a genetic component to genius, madness, shyness, aggression. People are genetically predisposed to be happy, cheerful. And the reverse is also true. The more we understand, the more we see that our very natures are defined by our DNA—and our unique and changing chemical makeup. Anyone who has ever had a chemical imbalance knows what a precarious existence we all live."

"Okay, so if one person murdered another, there's nothing wrong with it because sin doesn't really exist? Just chemical reactions?"

"No, no. Of course it's wrong. And we have to punish people who commit such acts. But one can determine ethics and morals without a theological basis. Society has to have a way to regulate its members. But the murderer himself, he's not a sinner condemned to lower hell. He's a result of his genetic predispositions and the choices those predispositions engender."

"His chemicals made him do it."

"More or less, yes. If you could change his genetics, you'd have a very different kind of man. His brain chemistry could probably be altered once we know more about what we're dealing with."

"I'm not sure I'd want to live in that world."

This time his smile was sheepish. "I'm not either. As I said, it's just a theory, but one I'm very drawn to. I give up on it for years at a time, but then some study comes out and it brings it all back. I'll probably die before I come to any firm conclusions."

"Maybe the conclusion would be nothing more than a chemical reaction."

He laughed. "You're too smart for your own good, young woman. I wish you well, Sophie. I also hope you'll give the situation with Nathan a little more thought before you dump him again."

"If there's no right or wrong, Arthur, then you can't guilt-trip me."

He laughed again, shaking his head. "God, you'd be a great addition to this family. Think about it, Soph. A little more time couldn't hurt."

18

After her meeting at the newspaper, Sophie took a quick trip up to George's office to retrieve the names of several local restaurateurs from his Rolodex. When she entered the room, she was surprised to find that all of his personal items—including the picture of his wife and kids, the cacti, the orchids, and the grow lights—had been removed. His son had left a note on the desk asking her to give him a call if she found anything else that had belonged to his father.

Looking around, she realized that this was what she'd wanted. The office no longer felt as if it belonged to George, but it also seemed painfully empty. She was struck momentarily with intense guilt for being annoyed by his tomato seedlings. She hoped his son would care for them, see that they had a good life on the hobby farm George had loved so much. At the same instant, the horror, shock, and regret she'd experienced the night she'd found his body all rushed back to her, more forcefully than at any time since that awful night. She'd been insensitive about the office, too eager to erase a man's life. Feeling ashamed of herself, and totally exhausted in general, she left without checking the Rolodex. What she needed was to go home.

On her way out of the building, she nearly bumped into Nathan.

"Hey, are we simpatico or what? You're just the woman I came to see."

When he smiled at her, she found herself smiling back. "How did you know I was here?"

"I spoke to a woman at the concierge desk back at the hotel. Come on, Soph. It's after five. Time to stop working and relax a little. Let's walk over to Orchestra Hall and sit by the fountain. It's a beautiful spring day. We should be enjoying it." He studied her face for a moment, paying particular attention to her eyes. "You look tired. Dr. Buckridge suggests a strong cup of coffee."

Sophie had an overwhelming urge to just chuck all her fears and concerns and go play with him. Why did everything have to be so hard? Here was the opportunity she'd been waiting for, and yet now that Nathan was standing in front of her, not only were her feet cold, they'd turned to ice. She considered making an excuse. She needed to get back to the Maxfield because her dog missed her. Or she had to clean her refrigerator.

By the time she realized it was hopeless, they were already across the street heading for Peavey Plaza. She was joking with him and he was laughing. How she was able to carry on two conversations at once, one with herself and one with him, was beyond her.

"You sit here and I'll go get us some coffee. What would you like? Espresso? Cappucino? A latte?"

"Surprise me."

He grinned, then took off across the Nicollet Mall and disappeared into a coffeehouse.

She was grateful for the moment alone. She knew she should be formulating her questions about his presence in George's apartment. Instead, she could focus only on her own anxiety. At the same time, the birds twittered, the sun warmed her face, and a soft breeze ruffled the short wisps of hair around her ears. How could the day be so perfect when she was feeling so miserable?

Before she knew it, Nathan was back.

"I got you a double Turkish. In ten minutes, you'll have more energy than you thought humanly possible."

"Either that or I'll be so nervous I'll twitch uncontrollably until midnight."

"Yeah, I suppose that's possible. But it's a risk we caffeine addicts gotta take." He handed her the small cup, then sat down next to her, leaving several feet of space between them.

She was glad for even a little distance. She supposed that there were lots of women who wouldn't find Nathan attractive. Unfortunately, she wasn't among their number. "Thanks."

"Anyone ever tell you you work too hard?"

She took a sip. "Frequently."

"You should slow down. Take time to smell the roses."

She thought of what Bram had said last night. "Is that what you do?"

He looked away. "No, not really. But I'd like to change. I'd like to change a lot of things."

"Are you okay, Nathan? Really okay?"

He looked over at her and smiled. "Sure, especially now that I'm with you."

He had no idea how hard he was making this for her.

He glanced back at the Times Register Tower. "What were you doing in there?"

"I had a meeting. My editor's asked me to write a feature on George Gildemeister, sort of a long obituary. Did you know him?"

Again he looked away. "Yes, I'd met him once or twice." He sipped his coffee.

She closed her eyes and took the plunge. "Did you know I was the one who discovered his body?"

"Yes, you told me."

"Did I?" She remembered now that she had. They'd been driving home from New Fonteney. "I suppose it's kind of a funny coincidence," she continued, smoothing the crease in her slacks, "but when I pulled up to his apartment that night, I saw you coming out of the building."

He didn't respond for several seconds. "Yes," he said finally, "I was there." He fixed his gaze on a bus rumbling down the mall. "Believe it or not, I still have a lot of friends in this town."

"Anybody I know?" She finished her coffee, then crushed the cup, waiting.

Nathan finished his as well. "An old high school buddy. No one you'd remember."

So there it was. The lie. She should be angry, probably even scared, but all she could feel was a terrible sense of desperation. "Nathan, look at me."

He turned toward her, his face a tight scowl.

"Tell me the truth."

"What do you mean?"

She waited. When he said nothing more, she exploded. "You may have visited an old friend, but you saw George, too!"

He stared at her. "You're actually accusing me of lying?"

"I know you were in George's apartment that night."

Now he looked shocked. "That's ridiculous."

"Is it? A neighbor saw you leave. An old woman across the hall. I spoke to her last night."

He closed his eyes. "God, I don't believe this."

"Did you murder him, Nathan?"

"No! How could you even think that? I found him on the pantry floor, just like you did. I knew I should call the police, but I was afraid I'd become the number one suspect. I mean, I was there. There were no witnesses. How could I prove I *hadn't* done it? I panicked, Sophie."

His explanation seemed thin.

Raking a nervous hand through his hair, he continued. "Look, it wasn't just the fact that it would cause problems for me. I had to protect my mother and the rest of the family. I'd stumbled on to a murder scene, but I knew the local and national media would make more of it than that—just an innocent fact. They'd jump on the story because of my last name. And right now it's the worst possible timing because—" He stopped himself.

"Because of what?"

He shook his head, looking up at the sky. "God, this is such a mess."

"Nathan, please. I want to believe you, but you have to help me understand. You say you're innocent, that you didn't call the police because it was bad timing. What does that mean?"

He took Sophie's hands in his, squeezing them gently. "Listen to me. Nobody knows about this except my family, so you've got to promise to keep it to yourself."

She wasn't sure what sort of bargain she was making, but she needed him to finish his story. "All right. I promise."

He appeared terribly uneasy, but he went on. "There's a woman, a writer. Her name is Marie Damontraville. She's writing an unauthorized biography of my mother and the Buckridge family. She's trying to dig up as much dirt as she can. All families have secrets, Sophie, things they don't want the rest of the world to know about. My mother's no different. She hasn't done anything evil or illegal, but she wants to keep her private life private. If I were to become a suspect in a murder investigation, the entire family would be put under a microscope. I can't allow that, especially with a piranha out there looking to make a buck on whatever cheap gossip she can dream up."

Sophie let his words sink in. "I guess I can understand your reasons," she said finally. "But why did you go to see George in the first place?"

"It was nothing, really. I'd called him Sunday morning wanting to talk about New Fonteney. He said he knew the spot and thought it would make a great place for a culinary school. He told me to come by his apartment that evening around eight. I was a little early, but I didn't think it would be a problem. See, I felt his input might be important. He knows the metro area far better than I do. I figured he could help me sell the idea of developing a second campus in Minnesota to my mother. I also thought he might have some ideas on marketing. Our primary campus right now is in New Haven. Having a good local and regional base is very important. The Midwest has never been known for culinary excellence, so it's an area that's just waiting to be developed. I see it as a real positive. Paul sees it as a negative. I thought that if I could get George excited about it, I might be able to convince him to talk to my mother, get her to see all the reasons why it was such a good idea. George's opinion would have carried a great deal of weight. At least I figured it was worth a try."

"So walk me through this. You buzzed his apartment and he let you in?"

"No. I buzzed, but there was no response. I waited a few minutes and buzzed again, but when he still didn't answer, I figured he was in the shower or something. That's when a woman came out and I charged past her before she could stop me. When I got upstairs, the door was ajar. I found George in the pantry. Once I saw the blood and realized he was dead, I shot out of there as fast as I could."

"And you didn't see anybody else?"

"The only person I saw in the entire building was the woman leaving by the front door when I first arrived. I have no idea who she was. I'm not even sure I could describe her." He squeezed her hands again. "Sophie, you've got to believe me. I had nothing to do with his murder. I'd never lie to you about something so important. I should have trusted you and told you the truth right away. I hope you

can understand why I didn't. And, well, after they arrested
Hongisto, I guess it seemed even less important for me to
come clean—to anyone—about what I'd seen. I figured the
police had their man."

She acknowledged his comment with a slight nod.

"If he's innocent, Sophie, I hope he gets off."

"I do, too. Because something doesn't add up. The neighbors I talked to said they heard George arguing with some un-
known person on two different occasions on Sunday night.
Harry was gone by seven. The neighbor who saw you come
out of his place said she heard a second argument around
seven-thirty. Harry was gone. You said you didn't get there
until close to eight. Who was he talking to?"

Nathan gazed at her thoughtfully. "If Harry really was
gone, like you say, then the person George was arguing with
at seven-thirty probably murdered him. All I know is, it
wasn't me. I'm telling you the truth. Please, *please,* believe
me." He looked at her with pleading eyes.

Maybe she was a fool. Maybe she should have her head examined, but she did believe him. Her sense of relief was so
great, she felt almost giddy. "God, I'm so glad you finally
trusted me enough to tell me the truth." She threw her arms
around him and hugged him tight.

They stayed that way until Sophie's cell phone beeped.

"I'd better answer that," she said, drawing away from him.
She was embarrassed now. She knew her reaction had sent
him the wrong message again. Digging in her purse, she found
the phone and pressed the on button. "Hi, this is Sophie."

"Hey, beautiful. It's your equally beautiful husband."

"Bram. What's up?"

"I have to work late tonight. Someone just dropped a ton of
research on my desk. Life-and-death stuff. You know the
drill."

"Intimately."

"I think I'll grab a quick dinner with my producer and then
spend the rest of the evening in my office. Oh, except for part
of the time I'll probably be over at McDougals'Bar. Jerry
Mulzak just got engaged. I told him I'd help him celebrate.

But if you need to reach me, I should be here most of the evening."

"Thanks for letting me know. Don't be too late."

"I'm sure you'll find something to occupy your time. You usually do."

"Are you being snide?"

"Look, you're probably relieved to have me out of your hair for a night. You can bury your nose in your office computer with complete abandon."

"That's an interesting image, *dear*."

"I'm just doing the poor soul routine, *darling,* so you'll take pity on me and give me a back rub when I get home. Should be around ten. No later than eleven. I love you."

"I love you, too." As she clicked the phone off, Nathan gave her a questioning look.

"Bram has to work late?" he asked.

"Afraid so."

His smile returned. "Well, that's perfect timing because I was hoping to make dinner for you this evening."

"Nathan, I . . . don't know."

"Oh, come on, Soph. A little good food. A little Italian wine. No big deal."

"We need to talk first."

"I thought that's what we were doing."

She could see the humor return to his eyes, and that didn't help. She hoped the right words would come when she needed them. "I know you think there's a chance for us. But honestly, Nathan, there isn't. I love my husband. Friendship is all I can offer you." She couldn't cut him off totally, refuse to see him again, especially after what Arthur had said to her earlier in the day. She had to get a better handle on this depression business of his before she condemned him to even more gloom.

"Okay, Sophie. Message received. But I do cook for my *friends*, and that means I'd still like to cook for you."

The gleam in his eyes hadn't diminished one bit. For a second she wondered if he'd even heard her. But when she looked at him, his expression so open and eager, she couldn't say no. "Where and when?"

"My old college buddy, David Kingston, is a pilot for Northwest Airlines. He's got this great condo in downtown St. Paul, just a couple blocks from the Maxfield. Since he's winging his way to Japan as we speak, and I happen to have a key, I can prepare the meal there." He took out a pen and a piece of paper and wrote down the address. "Say, seven o'clock?"

"What are you making?"

His grin was pregnant with meaning. "That's a surprise. Except—I suppose I should ask. Are there foods you don't particularly like?"

"Okra."

"Spoken like a true northerner. Okay, I'll nix the okra bruschetta, the okra *coi gamberetti*, and the *zuppa di* okra."

"Yuck."

He smiled. "And I'll see you at seven."

Journal Note

Wednesday, 6:20 P.M.

Just finished dinner. Before I resume my pacing, I thought I'd write a few lines.

I messengered copies of the transcripted interviews to Bram Baldric at WTWN radio this afternoon. I didn't include my journal notes—they're nobody's business but my own. He called me a little while ago and said he'd just gotten back from dinner and was going to sit down and read through the information now. It shouldn't take him more than an hour or two. He's supposed to go have a drink with some buddy of his around eight, but I still hope he'll stop by my suite later. I've been cooped up in here all afternoon and I'm going a little stir-crazy. Rafferty seems to find endless enjoyment in TV wrestling and various shopping channels, but I'm too preoc-

cupied by my own thoughts and worries to do anything other than wear a groove in my bedroom rug.

Oh, I received a fax about an hour ago. I'll copy it here so that it will go into my personal record.

FAX TRANSMISSION
DATE: May 12
FROM: Timothy Suskind, Appleton, Wisconsin
TO: Lela Dexter, Maxfield Plaza, St. Paul, Minnesota
SUBJECT: Slice and Dice *research*
Page 1 of 1

Lela: I confirmed today that Constance and Arthur Jadek were indeed born in Goshen, Wisconsin, Constance in 1936, Arthur in 1932. Their parents are now deceased. The father, Leo, was the town librarian. The mother, Harriet, was a housewife. Leo apparently had a reputation for being a helpful, exceptionally kind, well-loved man. That conflicts with Constance's comments about her family life, I believe, but then families can look very different from the outside. The Jadeks moved when Constance was five. It may be just a coincidence, but it was the same year the U.S. entered WWII. I haven't determined yet if that was the reason for the move or where the move took them. I'll keep working on it.
Best wishes,
Tim

I haven't heard anything more from Kenneth Merlin, although I'm sure he'll be dropping by again soon to find out whether or not I've decided to accept his bribe. Also, I haven't received any more anonymous written threats. If this wasn't such a serious and potentially dangerous situation, a girl could get to feel unloved.

Ingrid Nelson, the field researcher I assigned to dig up the medical files on Pepper Buckridge's death, called me today and said that the file we need can only be accessed by a relative. Pepper died at Hennepin County General, now Hennepin

*County Medical Center. Those records have been transferred
to microfilm. If Pluto is a relative, as I suspect he may be, he's
our only hope of getting them released. When I E-mailed him
this afternoon with the interview of Phillip Rapson, I also let
him know the situation. The ball is in his court. Time will tell
whether or not I get a chance to look at the records. It still may
not prove conclusively that Pepper was poisoned by ingesting
antifreeze, as I now suspect, but it should point us in that
direction.*

More later.

M.

19

Bram leaned against the doorjamb, smiling at Rafferty.
"Evening."

"Evening," he grunted.

"I'd like to see Marie."

"Who is it?" a voice called from inside.

"Baldric," replied Bram, still smiling at the bodyguard.
"Eventful day?"

"Boring," he muttered, chewing on a toothpick. "Just the
way I like it."

Marie bustled into the living room, tugging on a sweater.
"God, I was hoping you'd stop by."

As Rafferty moved out of the way, Bram stepped inside.
"We need to talk." He'd read through all the interviews she'd
sent him, and he had to agree with her assessment. Something did smell rotten in the Buckridge family history.

"Fine. But let's go out. Anywhere other than the hotel. I've
been trapped in here too long."

Bram glanced at Rafferty. "Will you be joining us?"

The bodyguard picked up his suit coat and grabbed his keys. "I'll go get the car. I'm parked on the street a couple blocks away, so it may take a few minutes."

"We'll meet you at the front entrance," said Marie.

"Not a good idea. There's an alley behind the building. It's right next to—"

"I know where it is," said Bram, saving Rafferty the explanation. "We'll meet you there. Ten minutes."

"Take the service elevator down and leave by the rear door."

"Is all this absolutely necessary?" asked Marie, apparently irritated by Rafferty's rules.

"Yes." He said the word forcefully, then slipped on his coat, buttoning it so that the shoulder holster was no longer visible. "Ten minutes," he repeated as he left.

Once they were alone, Bram watched Marie light a cigarette. She seemed unusually tense as she walked over to the wet bar to find an ashtray. At least tonight he had no trouble understanding why. "Let's head over to the St. Paul Hotel. It's not far and they've got a decent bar. I think we could all use a drink."

A faint smile crossed her lips. "Rafferty orders root beer when he's on duty. It's his favorite nonalcoholic beverage."

Bram could have lived the rest of his life a happy man without knowing that fascinating tidbit. He assumed she was trying to dissipate her uneasiness with a stab, albeit lame, at normal conversation.

"Before we go," said Marie, finding her purse and making sure her billfold and key were inside, "just tell me what you think, in a nutshell. Am I crazy? Am I seeing a potential scandal where none exists? You read the interviews. You saw what Pluto said about Constance. He thinks she's a vile woman. He couldn't cite chapter and verse, but he promised me a story, a powerful one. He's got to be a member of Constance's inner circle. Possibly even a family member."

Bram nodded. "Judas, perhaps? Selling his master for thirty pieces of silver?"

"Or for something less tangible but far more compelling."

"Such as?"

"Maybe he wants to know the exact sort of monster his mother really is." She was smoking in quick jabs now, moving about the room restlessly.

"So you think Pluto is one of Constance's children?"

"Yes, I think I do."

"Who?"

"Emily or Paul."

"Not Nathan? From what I read, I think he may prove to be every bit as dangerous as Constance."

She stopped for a moment, then turned and studied his face through the smoke from her cigarette. "Tell me the truth. Do you think your judgment is affected because you know he's your wife's old boyfriend and he's still interested in her?"

He was indignant. "Who told you that?"

She grimaced. "Nobody needed to tell me. I've got eyes, Baldric. And I know how to use them. If it comes as a news flash to you, I'm sorry."

Feeling uncomfortable with the sudden turn in the conversation, Bram checked his watch. "Come on. We'd better get downstairs."

Marie crushed out her cigarette, then followed him to the door. They rode down to the main floor in silence, mainly due to the presence of a waiter returning dirty trays to the kitchen. Once they were finally out on St. Peter, Bram looked around but couldn't see anyone waiting for them. "What kind of car does Rafferty drive?"

"A Buick Park Avenue. Green."

"Do you know where he parked it?"

"It's just up the street a little ways. He said it wasn't smart to use the hotel lot."

Bram didn't feel like waiting. Ever since she'd made the comment about Sophie and Nathan, he'd felt itchy—like he needed to run, lift weights, jump rope, put on a pair of boxing gloves and slam his fists into a heavy bag, anything to drive the unwanted feelings out of his chest. Sitting in a bar sipping a pleasant martini with the lovely and intriguing Marie Damontraville might have appealed to him a few minutes ago, but it didn't now. He was angry and he wasn't sure he could keep from taking his anger out on her. "Do you feel like walking?"

"I thought we were supposed to wait."

"Let's live dangerously." He grabbed her hand and they started off.

"I suppose Rafferty could have stopped to buy himself some candy. He eats more garbage than any man I've ever known."

"Probably gives him energy."

She struggled to keep up. "Do you always walk like such a maniac?"

"Always."

She puffed along beside him. "You know, Baldric, your mood could use a little readjustment. I didn't say your wife was *having* an affair with Nathan Buckridge, just that—"

"Let's table that topic, okay?"

Coming to the intersection of Fifth and Sibley, Marie looked to her left. "There's the car. It's about halfway up the block."

They turned the corner.

Before Bram knew what hit him, an explosion slammed him hard into a brick wall. He struck the back of his head and was momentarily disoriented, but the sounds of screaming and breaking glass quickly revived him. Pushing away from the wall, he saw that Rafferty's car was on fire. Flames shot high into the air. People were running away from it, some calling for help, some just yelling. When he looked down, he saw that Marie had crumpled to the ground. She was clutching her arm, a look of horror on her face. "Are you okay?" he asked, dropping to his knees. Only then did he notice the blood oozing from between her fingers.

An instant later the night sky began pelting them with chunks of debris. Bram ripped open his coat and dove down over her. He could feel her shaking beneath him. Or maybe he was doing the shaking. He couldn't tell anymore.

When the raining debris stopped, he shook his coat and sat

up. In that short period, the quiet side street had turned into a madhouse. Cars were zooming by, leaving the scene as fast as they could. Curious onlookers were rushing in to view the carnage firsthand. People were leaning out of windows. Traffic on Sibley had ground to a halt.

"How deep is the cut?"

"It's not too bad," said Marie. "But it's still bleeding."

"Hold your hand over it hard. Will you be all right here for a minute?"

"Where are you going?"

"Up there." He nodded to the burning car. Everything had happened so fast, the enormity of the situation was just starting to sink in. "I promise I'll be right back."

She looked up at him with frightened eyes. "It was Rafferty. I know it was."

"I'll see what I can find out." Scrambling to his feet, Bram took off through the crowd. Just before he reached a solid wall of gawkers, he slowed his pace. The burning car was throwing off so much heat that nobody could get very close. Not that it mattered. No one could have survived such an inferno.

Bram dashed back to Marie. "Can you walk?" he asked, helping her up. "We have to get out of here." He was afraid that whoever had planted the bomb might still be around.

"Where are we going?"

"Not back to the Maxfield, that's for damn sure." He put his arm around her waist and led her across to Wacouta. They passed quickly through Mears Park. "How's the bleeding now?"

"Better, I think. I hit my head when I fell. I guess I'm kind of dizzy."

"Can you make it a couple more blocks?"

"Of course I can. I'm not an invalid. I'm just a little shook up."

He had to give her credit. She had a lot of spunk.

"Was it Rafferty's car?"

"I'm afraid so." Spunk or not, he felt her sag against him.

"It was meant for me. I'm the one they're after. I should have been with him. I would have been, except for you."

"Don't think about that now."

"How can I not think about it? I should be dead!" Her voice trembled and she began to shake. "What am I going to do?"

Bram could sense the hysteria building inside her. She was stumbling, losing her balance. He had to do something.

Stopping dead in his tracks, he turned and grabbed her by the shoulders. "You're fine, Marie."

"No, I'm not!"

"Yes, you are! Look at me!" He waited until her eyes finally settled on his. "Rafferty's dead. We can't change that. But we're alive."

"What if someone's following us?"

He looked around. "Nobody's following us."

"How do you know?"

He looked her straight in the eyes. "Do you trust me?"

"Yes," she replied tentatively.

"I wouldn't lie to you. We're going to be fine. But you have to get a grip, help me out. I can't carry you. You've got to walk. Can you do that?"

Her eyes flew wildly in every direction.

"Marie!" He squeezed her shoulders.

"Yes," she whispered finally. "I can walk."

"Good." He held her tight as they moved slowly down the sidewalk, heading for the Ardmore Suites. In the distance, he could hear sirens blasting their way toward the river. The paramedics would find out soon enough that they weren't needed, at least by the owner of the car. The police had a tough job ahead of them trying to figure out why a man in a Park Avenue had been the target of such a vicious attack. Bram might be able to point his old buddy, Al Lundquist, in the right direction, but for now his first priority had to be Marie. Once the fire burned itself out, only one body would be found. The bomb job had been botched. It seemed pretty obvious that Marie wasn't safe as long as her whereabouts were known.

"Where are we going?" she asked. She seemed more dazed than terrified now.

"We're checking into a hotel."

She looked up at him. "We?"

"Mr. and Mrs. Smith. Nobody's going to be looking for a married couple."

They entered the lobby a few minutes later. Glancing at his watch, Bram saw that it was just after eleven. He helped Marie find a seat, then approached the front desk. The clerk looked amused when Bram said they had no luggage and he wanted to pay for the night in cash. In a matter of minutes he had two room keys and a promise from the bell captain that he'd bring up a bottle of Courvoisier, some disinfectant, and several gauze bandages on the double.

Marie's eyes were closed when he returned, and her face was pale. He'd never seen her look so vulnerable, and it touched something deep inside him. Leaning down, he whispered, "Your suite awaits."

She opened her eyes and nodded. "I think you just saved my life."

"Damsels in distress are my specialty."

She tried to smile, but the tension in her face made it look more like a grimace.

Half an hour later Marie's arm was bandaged and she was resting comfortably on the sofa. She'd showered and slipped into one of the white terry-cloth robes the hotel provided for its guests. She sat with her feet up on the coffee table, a glass of cognac—her second double—in her hand. The color had finally returned to her cheeks.

Bram sat next to her, sipping his own drink. Marie seemed far more relaxed now, though he sensed that it was just a superficial calm, one undoubtedly brought on by the alcohol. He didn't think she should be alone tonight, but he could hardly stay.

"What am I going to do?" she asked, tipping her head back against a couch pillow. She rubbed one side of her face. "Do I run back to New York with my tail between my legs? Accept Constance Buckridge's bribe? Or do I stay and press on?"

He could tell by the way she'd phrased the questions that her mind was already made up. "Are you asking for my opinion?"

"You're the only one who knows the full story. If you were me, what would you do?"

Bram didn't hesitate. "A book is hardly worth your life, Marie. I'd cut my losses and leave. Life is far too fragile and too precious." He didn't add, but could have, that he'd never come as close to dying as he had tonight.

"You mean, just admit that Constance whipped me?"

"No. Admit that the stakes are too high. You want to live to fight another day."

"It's a fight, all right," she muttered, taking another swallow of cognac. "Sometimes I wonder why I don't just quit this writing business. I've got plenty of money. I could do anything I wanted. I'm not getting any younger, you know."

"What's age got to do with it?"

She darted her eyes toward him, then away. "You don't really have a concept of what my life is like. It's not your fault. How could you? You've got a wife. A stable job. All your todays are pretty much like your yesterdays." She paused. "For me, it's constant change and constant challenge. I'm never home for more than a few weeks at a time. I do a lot of traveling. Most of my writing is done on the road. It can be exciting at times, but it's a lonely life, Bram. I've formed some friendships over the years, but by my old standards they all seem pretty shallow."

"I'm sorry to hear that."

"I'm not asking for your pity. But I would like you to understand. Let's say I meet an attractive man, a man such as yourself. A one-night stand, or a short affair, is about all I've got to offer."

"I assume you get more than a few takers. With your looks, you probably have to beat guys off with a stick."

She finished her second double, then reached for the bottle on the end table and poured herself a third. "Sure, I won't deny I've had my share of affairs. But what's missing is the relationship part. The conversations, like we're having now." She sipped her drink in silence for a few moments. "I'm starting to realize that I envy that old idyllic scene, the vine-covered cottage with the picket fence outside. Ever since I turned my back on my family, left Savannah, and divested myself of all their wretched turmoil, I've prided myself on my independence. I left home and never looked back. I didn't want any personal entanglements. I knew from firsthand experience that the price was too high and that a relationship with a man would only slow me down. I had places to go, a career to build. But something's missing in my life, Bram. I'm finally willing to admit that it might be love. It's kind of pathetic, really. I'm thirty-seven years old and I don't have the faintest clue as to what it would feel like to be loved, truly loved, and to love someone in return. I want . . ." She looked away, raising a shaky hand to her forehead. "How do I make you understand?"

"Just tell me. I'm following you so far."

Her eyes dropped to the glass in her hand. "I feel like a child who's been led to the door of a candy store, but not allowed to go in. I . . . I need someone to be strong when I'm not. Like right now."

Bram could see her lower lip beginning to tremble. He moved over and put his arm around her. "You're alive, Marie. It's horrible what happened tonight. We're probably both still in shock. But you're fine. And you're going to stay that way if I've got anything to say about it."

She looked back at him, her eyes sparkling with tears. "That's not what I'm crying about." She sniffed a couple of times, then scraped at her cheeks with the back of her hand.

He was confused. "Then what—"

"I'm upset because what I want I can't have." She touched his face, tracing the deep cleft in his chin. "I want *you*, Bram. I think maybe I'm falling in love with you. Would that be so ridiculous? So appalling? So . . . pitifully predictable?"

He didn't know what to say.

"Don't go. Stay with me tonight." She stopped, then gazed up into his eyes. "Please?" She looked down again, the expression on her face turning rueful. "Look at me. You've reduced me to begging."

"Don't do this, Marie. I can't stay. You know why."

"Sure." She sniffed a couple of times. "You're married to a woman who's got all the time in the world to flirt with an old boyfriend, but when it comes to her husband, she's too busy to appreciate what she's got." Her fingers trailed around to the back of his neck. "I don't believe you aren't attracted to me."

He couldn't exactly argue the point.

Bringing her lips close to his, she whispered, "If you were mine, I'd never let you forget you were the most important person in my life."

Her breath felt hot and hungry against his face. "You may think you're made of steel, Marie, but this is simple fear talking. You just don't want to be alone tonight."

"I'm not made of steel," she said, taking his hand and easing it gently under the top of her robe. "And yes, maybe I am still scared, more than I'm willing to admit, but it doesn't change how I feel. I want you in my life, not just tonight. I want to wake up with you, Bram. Have breakfast with you. In the morning we can talk more, maybe come to some conclusions about what I should do next. What we should both do."

His hand caressed her skin until she closed her eyes and gave a soft moan.

"I don't want to think any more tonight."

Touching the belt of her robe, he whispered, "I can't do this." At the same time, he realized that the urge to untie it was almost irresistible.

"I know," she whispered back. "But a man is dead, and we need to feel alive. Make me feel alive, Bram. Drive the shadows away . . . just for a little while."

20

Sophie stood at the living room window while Nathan prepared a dessert tray in the kitchen. "I think they've finally got that car fire out." During dinner, they'd heard an explosion that was so loud it shook the building and rattled the windows. Once the worst of the rumbling was over, they'd rushed to look outside.

Halfway down the block on the other side of the street, a car was burning out of control. Nathan seemed alternately fascinated and repelled. Sophie felt pretty much the same way, although she had no interest in taking the elevator down to view the fire close up, as Nathan suggested. They argued about it briefly. Sophie insisted it was too dangerous. Eventually, her better judgment won out.

Nathan's friend lived in the Tate Building, a 1920s apartment complex that had recently been turned into condos. It was pure luck that the location had given them such an intimate view of the scene. Resigned to remaining four stories above the action, Nathan wondered out loud if it hadn't been a gas-tank leak. Sophie thought it might have been a bomb.

Shortly after the car had gone up in flames, the police blocked off both ends of the street. All the curious onlookers had been rounded up and ordered out of the area. The presence of a paramedic van and at least five squad cars was an ominous but necessary sight under the circumstances. Someone had been hurt, all right, possibly killed. Knowing they'd learn the details soon enough on the local news, they eventually returned to the dining room.

Nathan had set a lovely table. Not only had he created a

magnificent centerpiece of lilacs and white roses, but the table linens were exquisite. In the candlelight, the crystal and china sparkled. Unfortunately, after the explosion, all they could do was pick at their food. Neither wanted to admit that it had cast a pall on the evening, but the idea that some poor soul had just been incinerated on the street below took a toll.

Sophie drank more wine than she should have. The sight of the burning car got mixed up in her mind with finding George Gildemeister dead on his pantry floor. She tried to cover her jittery mood by talking animatedly about the dinner.

For the first course, Nathan had served a simple dish of the freshest oysters broiled on the half shell, *huitres gratinées en coquilles,* his one sop to his Cordon Bleu training. It was accompanied by a chilled Riesling. A salad of cucumber, tomato, romaine, and fried croutons in an anchovy and garlic dressing came next. A delicate *tortelloni de biete*, tortelloni filled with Swiss chard, was served as the pasta course. And the main course featured a delicious pan-roasted chicken with garlic, rosemary, and white wine—*pollo arrosto in tegame*. Fresh asparagus cooked in a small amount of heavy cream and finished with a bit of freshly grated Parmesan cheese accompanied it, as did a crisp Pinot Grigio. Sophie wished she could have given the food and wine more attention, but the truth was, her mind was everywhere but on the food.

As she stood at the window, looking down on the scene of the explosion, all that remained of the intense orange and yellow flames was a reddish glow where the engine used to be. Smoke rose in gray puffs from the rear of the burned-out hulk. It was a depressing sight. She'd always been a fan of inner-city living. She didn't view it as any more dangerous than any other part of the seven-county metro area. But if a bomb really had demolished that car, she might as well be living in Belfast.

Shaking off a sense of foreboding, she turned as Nathan brought the dessert tray into the room. He'd built a fire in the fireplace and she could see a decanter of brandy sitting next to a plate of fruit and cake. At least this part of the meal would be relaxing.

"Come sit down," he said, giving the fire a good stoke.

The night had turned chilly. She was glad for the added warmth.

After dimming the lights, he joined her on the couch. He poured them each a brandy, then handed her one of the snifters. "If you'd like me to warm it for you . . ."

"No, this is fine."

He smiled. "Help yourself." He nodded to the dessert tray. "I thought something light might be best. The cake is called *torta di limone e ricotta*. It's one of my favorites. Just a hint of ground almonds and lemon." Grabbing a couple of strawberries, he turned his attention to the fire.

As Sophie watched him, she sensed that something was on his mind. When she'd first arrived at the apartment, he'd been putting the finishing touches on their salads. She'd left him to his work and wandered around briefly, peeking into rooms and deciding that the renovators had done a wonderful job of restoring and updating. When she'd returned to the kitchen, Nathan had been standing at the sink, staring at an empty glass. She'd stood in the doorway and watched him for almost a minute. He'd never moved. He hadn't even blinked. It was probably arrogant, even silly, to think they still had the kind of bond that would allow him to confide in her. If he refused to talk to his uncle, a man with whom he'd always been close, why would he talk to a woman he barely knew anymore? But if something was wrong, if he was in trouble, mentally, emotionally, financially, legally, she wanted to know about it. It struck her that sharing confidences at a time like this might be unwise. Even so, she couldn't help herself. She had to know he was all right.

"Nathan?"

"Uhm?"

"Is something wrong?"

He hesitated. "Where did that come from? Do I look like something's wrong?"

"I don't know. You just seem sort of down. I noticed it the other day, too. When we were at New Fonteney."

Keeping his eyes on the fire, he said, "Mom's not going to buy the property. Paul talked her out of it."

She didn't believe for a minute that this was the source of his moodiness, but she also knew it must have upset him. "I'm sorry."

He shrugged. "Even Kenny thought it was a good investment. I just don't get it."

"Maybe Minnesota holds too many bad memories for her. She lost her husband here."

He looked over at her, obviously thinking about what she'd said, then turned back toward the fire. "I don't want to talk about my troubles tonight, Soph. I wanted this to be fun. A great meal. A lively conversation with . . . my . . . with you." His smile was sad. "I don't even know what to call you anymore."

"Friend?"

He shook his head. "That doesn't work, at least not for me." He turned and touched her hair gently, stroked it for a moment, then shifted his attention back to the burning logs.

"You said something the other day, Nathan. I was hoping you could explain it to me."

"Uh, now you're quoting me to myself. I always hate that. I'm notoriously abstruse."

It pleased her to think that she could still draw him out of his darker moods. "You said something about your life being a frustrated system."

He nodded grudgingly.

"You said you couldn't be close to your family, be happy, and have a conscience all at the same time. You could have any two, but not all three."

"Did I say that?"

"You did."

"Then it must be true." He leaned back and smiled at her. "Why are we discussing some idle comment I made days ago? Half the time I don't make sense, even to myself. I want to hear what you've been doing for the last twenty-five years. What you've learned about life and love and God and . . . and the significance of lime sherbet in American culture. What's it like to have a son, Soph? And, hey, we only talked briefly about your parents. You said they were on a round-the-world tour. I'd like to hear all about it. Does your dad still smoke those awful cigars? And your mother, does she still make those wonderful lemon meringue pies? God, I used to fantasize about them. Your parents always liked me, you know. Thought I was great husband material."

"You're changing the subject."

"The subject was boring."

"You and your frustrations aren't boring to me, Nathan."

"Careful," he said, taking her hand and drawing it to his lips. "I thought we'd decided on a course of action, or nonaction, as the case may be. You'd better not get too close or act too concerned. You might get burned."

"Don't be ridiculous. Friends can show concern."

He finished his brandy in one neat gulp, then set the glass down and eased over next to her, laying his arm across the back of the couch. "There. That's more friendly. Your term."

"You're hopeless." She sat up straight, taking a swallow of brandy. It was a struggle to be close to him and not let him know how much his physical presence affected her. She felt her face flush, though in the firelight she doubted he could see it.

They sat silently for several minutes, listening to the birch logs crackle and snap. She remembered now that as a young woman she'd often felt left out of his life, cut off from his innermost thoughts. She recalled writing in her diary once that she felt as if she'd been banging on the door to his soul for months hoping to be let in. It was a door that never opened. Funny, but all those melodramatic teenage maundering thoughts still seemed to apply.

There were so many subjects Nathan wouldn't talk about. For instance, his childhood. She assumed it was because he'd been hurt, although she had no idea what the details were. It was odd, too, because when she first got to know him, his family was like something out of a Fifties' TV show. Constance always looked perfect. Always wore a dress. Always had her hair styled at a beauty shop each week. She was often in the kitchen cooking something wonderful. Wayne was less overtly friendly but nice to her in his own way. He made lots of money and cooked hamburgers and steaks on the grill in the backyard. Emily was a tomboy. Full of high spirits. A good student, but also very pretty and active socially. Uncle Arthur had come to live with them just a month before she left for college. He seemed tired a lot, but with the exception of Nathan, Sophie had liked him the best. Indeed, the entire family had welcomed her with open arms. All except for Paul, that is. He was a freak of the first order, but it was the Seventies and he was a teenager. While Paul had never interested her, Nathan had consumed her.

Looking back on it now, part of the fascination for her had probably come from the fact that he'd been such a mystery. He'd been an intricate puzzle just waiting for her to figure out, not that she ever had. But she had fallen in love with him nonetheless. Maybe, after all these years, the essential mystery of Nathan Buckridge still drew her in—and demanded an answer.

Of course she wanted to tell him what had happened to her after she left the Church of the Firstborn. He deserved to know that he'd been right. She had been a fool to join such a crazy organization, and devote her whole life to serving a god some man had created in his own image. The church had been a sham, a cult, a power play by a sexually repressed Puritan who preferred control over everything else.

She also wanted to explain how devastated she'd been when her ex-husband had been granted sole custody of her son. It was the only time in her life that she'd ever truly considered suicide. She understood depression from the inside out, the feeling that you were at the bottom of a well and couldn't get out no matter how hard you tried. Sometimes she'd sit in a chair for hours, never moving, not even turning her head. Movement had required too much energy and thought. And thought was the enemy. She had protected herself by tuning the world out, but at the same time she had been sinking deeper into that awful pit. If that's how Nathan felt, she wanted to help him. But first he had to answer her question. "Come on, Nathan. Answer me."

"Refresh my memory again. I'm getting older, Sophie. My brain cells don't dance quite as well as they used to."

"The frustrated system."

"Oh. Right."

She could feel him begin to play with the short wisps of hair around her neck. He was crossing a line. They had a deal. But she wanted a response to her question before she pulled away.

"Well, I guess you deserve an answer. I'm sure I would have talked more about it the other day, but we got interrupted by the storm. And then later by a kiss."

She closed her eyes, trying to concentrate, but all she could focus on was the touch of his hand. This wasn't fair.

"Okay. I've got three elements that I've determined are essential to my world. One is being close to my family. Two is being happy with my life, content with my decisions. And the third is having a conscience, personal integrity."

"I don't understand why you can't have all three."

"Trust me, Sophie. I can't."

"So which one do you give up?"

The tips of his fingers moved to the soft skin on the inside of her neck. "Well, I guess I've always put my family first. That's a given. So the other two vie for dominance. Sometimes happiness wins, sometimes conscience does. Lately, it's my conscience that's been taking the worst beating."

"But you don't seem happy, Nathan."

He held her eyes. "No, I don't. Funny. Something isn't working anymore. My carefully constructed system is spinning out of control." He brushed his fingers across her upper back, but the movement quickly turned into a caress. "It reminds me of a poem I read last night. Do you still read poetry?"

She nodded.

"I was looking through a favorite volume of Yeats, and these lines struck me." He paused for a moment, then recited: " 'I know that I shall meet my fate/Somewhere among the clouds above;/Those that I fight I do not hate,/Those that I guard I do not love'."

"And what does that mean to you?"

"Everything," he replied simply. "It encapsulates my whole life."

She didn't understand.

"You make me happy, Sophie. That's all you need to know. Just seeing you again has given me hope. I've known for quite a while that my life had to change, but I needed some sort of catalyst. I don't know what I'm going to do exactly, but it can't be more of the same. The life I've been leading is eating me alive. In a few more years, there won't be anything left to salvage."

"Nathan, what a thing to say."

"It's true. And you're so beautiful."

She looked down. "I think you've changed the subject again."

"No, the subject has always been you." He drew her to him. "I love you, Sophie. I wish I could tell you everything that's going on in my life. Maybe I can one day soon. But for now you've got to trust me."

"Why wouldn't I?" She pulled away. "What's the problem, Nathan? Be straight with me."

He ran a hand over his beard, then folded his hands in his lap. "Okay, I'll give you this much. Remember I told you about Marie Damontraville?"

"The woman writing the biography of your mother."

He nodded. "I don't know this for a fact, but I believe she's on the verge of making some wild accusations. None of it's true, but once ugly rumors get started, they take on a life of their own."

"What sort of accusations?"

"I can't tell you that. Not now. But the story will break one of these days, probably sooner rather than later. I just don't want you to be confused by it. If you've got questions then, come to me. I'll tell you the truth. I don't care what the rest of the world thinks, but I do care what you think. I don't want you hurt by the fallout from this. I have no idea whether or not she plans to include our relationship in the book, but don't be surprised. I suppose I should stay away from you until all this blows over, but I can't. I won't. Not when I've just found you again."

He crushed her against him, kissing her with the same passion she remembered from her youth. "Just be with me for a little while. Then decide."

Kissing her again, he began to unbutton her blouse.

For Sophie, the moment became a blur of emotion and sensation. As his hands caressed her skin, she felt a rush of pleasure so intense, she almost stopped breathing. She wanted him as much as he wanted her. If she was going to stop him, it was now or never.

21

Sophie returned home around midnight. Ethel was asleep on her pillow in the bedroom, but Bram wasn't back yet. Grateful for a few minutes alone, she switched on the light in the bathroom, took off her clothes, and stepped into the shower. She stood in the water and the steam and tried to empty her mind of all emotion, but the clarity she was searching for escaped her. It was late and she was completely worn out. Perhaps tomorrow she'd be able to put what had happened tonight into some kind of perspective. And yet she was almost afraid to think about tomorrow. What would she see when she looked at herself in the mirror?

After drying off, she slipped into her pajamas and climbed onto the bed, sitting cross-legged in the middle of it.

In her effort not to think about Nathan this week, she'd thought of little else. Surely she could get a grip on her emotions now. The worst had finally happened. One way or the other, she had to deal with the aftermath.

Before she bumped into Nathan last Saturday, she hadn't thought about him in years. Now she needed to get back to that place of comfortable detachment. What was he really but a phantom, a ghost from her past, the projection of a silly, adolescent girl? After tonight, though, she couldn't deny his hold on her, a hold that was no longer just a memory.

Nathan Buckridge was deeply troubled. And sensing his vulnerability only intensified Sophie's feelings for him. If only he'd open up to her, tell her what was really bothering him. Arthur had been right about his nephew's depression. But Sophie felt certain that it was his life, not the chemicals in his brain, that had betrayed him.

"You look upset."

The sound of Bram's voice startled her. When she looked up, he was standing in the doorway. What was he reading in her face? What had she done to indicate that something was wrong?

"Bad night?" he asked.

"How long have you been standing there?"

"A few minutes. You look like you just lost your best friend."

Her expression softened. "You're my best friend."

"Well, then, you can stop worrying." He kicked off his loafers, removed his coat, and crawled onto the bed next to her. "Are you okay?"

"I am now that you're home."

A guilty look crossed his face. "Were you worried because I was late? God, I'm sorry, Soph. I should have called."

She slipped her arm through his, trying not to look guilty herself. "I knew you'd be home sooner or later. I suppose Jerry's pretty excited about his engagement."

"Jerry? Yeah."

"You didn't drink and drive, did you?"

"We ended up at a bar just up the street. I was close enough so I could walk home."

"Hey, what's on your shirt? It looks like soot. Dirt."

He tried to brush it off. "Terrible, isn't it? We've got to find a better laundry." Easing his arms around her waist, he held her tight. "Soph?" he said after a couple of seconds. "You've got to promise me something."

It felt so good to have his arms around her. "What, honey?"

"You've got to promise me that you won't go near Nathan Buckridge again."

She tried desperately not to react. "Why would you ask that?"

He drew back, looking at her with an intensity that almost frightened her. "He's bad news. *Very* bad news. You've got to trust me on this one. I can't explain any more right now."

"But, honey, he's staying at the hotel. If I run into him, I can't ignore him."

"Sure you can. If he says anything, just tell him you're nearsighted. Comes with age."

"Bram?"

"Okay, okay. But don't be alone with him. Make sure other people are always around."

"You make it sound like you think he's dangerous."

"He'll be leaving soon, right?"

"I assume so."

"It can't be soon enough for me." After a few more seconds, he looked down at his hands. "You know, Soph, I love our life. Not everyone would appreciate living in a hotel, I suppose, but . . . it suits us. It's sort of like . . . living on an elegant ocean liner."

"You were thinking, perhaps, the *Titanic*?"

"Right era, dear, wrong ship."

She was relieved at the change in subject. "But I'd say we're definitely the Nick and Nora Charles type."

"Again, right era but wrong actor."

She smiled. "Have I told you recently how great you look in a tuxedo?"

"Actually, I think you compared me to a penguin."

"I take it all back."

"Good." He kissed her softly. "No, this place is perfect for us. We may not have a vine-covered cottage with the picket fence outside, but we've got two wonderful restaurants right on the premises, an exercise room we may ignore to our hearts' content, and room service if we're too tired to go out."

"Don't forget the formal garden between the two wings, suitable for starlit walks. And the fact that our mutt is treated like a queen by the staff and the guests."

They leaned back against the pillows, considering their good fortune.

"The best part," said Bram, resting an arm over his head, "is that I get to live with you."

"That's the best part for me, too," she said, laying her head on his shoulder.

"Soph?"

"Hmm?"

"You, ah . . . you don't have any plans to see Nathan again, do you?"

"No. Let's not talk about him any more tonight, okay?"

"You probably think I'm just being the jealous-husband type." He began to play with the gold bracelet on her wrist. "I mean, I've got no reason to be jealous of him, do I? I'm still your one and only."

"You're my husband," she said, her eyes filling with tears. Her emotions were so close to the surface tonight. "I love you so much."

"I love you, too," he said, folding her in his arms. "Sophie, you're shivering."

"I'm fine now that you're home."

"You really were worried about me, weren't you? I feel like such a heel."

"Just hold me."

"Why don't I clean up a little first?"

"No." She held him tight. "You're fine just the way you are."

They settled back more comfortably against the pillows.

"God, I love being alone with you," he whispered, stroking her hair. "I'm the luckiest guy in the world."

Sophie closed her eyes. There was nothing she could say.

22

It was a little tricky, sneaking out of the Maxfield on Thursday morning with two of Marie's suitcases and her laptop computer without Sophie or anyone in the Buckridge family seeing him, but Bram managed the feat with his usual aplomb. At nine-thirty sharp he stood in front of Marie's door at the Ardmore and knocked. He had a key, of course, but he felt it wouldn't be right to just charge in.

The door opened almost immediately. "Ah," said Marie, smiling at him through her cigarette smoke. She was still wearing the white terry-cloth robe. The remains of her breakfast rested on a cart just inside the door. "If it isn't Mr. Smith."

She was making jokes and he was about to drop a suitcase on his foot. "This stuff is heavy, Marie. May I come in?"

"Have I ever denied you anything?"

He shot her a pained look as he lugged it all inside, piling it next to a mahogany desk. "I see your sense of humor survived the evening."

"Everything but my pride."

He turned to face her. "You know why I couldn't stay. I explained before I left."

"Right. You don't find me attractive."

Bram thought her pout, even in jest, was a little tedious. "You're very attractive. I'm just not in the market for an attractive woman right now. I'm married, and I happen to love my wife."

" 'Tell me the old, old story . . . of Jesus and His glory.' " She crushed out her cigarette, then started to walk into the bedroom.

Bram caught her by the shoulders and turned her around. "Listen to me for a minute. You said last night that you wanted something more in your life. That you envied people who lived in vine-covered cottages with white picket fences. Well, that's where I live, Marie. Not literally, but in my heart, that's what it feels like. I don't mean to hurt you, but I already have what you're looking for. You're one hell of a sexy woman, I won't deny that, and I wish you the best of luck finding a guy to share your life, but it won't be me. Even the best relationships are fragile. If you care about me at all, you wouldn't want to mess with mine."

"So now I'm a home wrecker."

"No, of course not. But if I'd let you seduce me last night, I'd be the home wrecker, and I could never live with myself if I hurt Sophie that way, if I made a fool out of her by sleeping around behind her back."

She stared at him for a moment, then gave him a hug. "Why are all the good men taken?"

"They aren't. You'll see."

Drawing back, she turned her face away from him and walked over to check on the suitcases. "I hope you brought the right clothes."

"Everything that was on the list. If it wasn't on the list, it's still back at the Maxfield."

She eyed him for a moment, examining him from head to foot. "God, but I love the way you dress. Yesterday it was tweed. Today it's a gorgeous cashmere blazer. You wear clothes, Baldric, the way some men wear their muscles."

"Thanks. I think."

"Did you bring my journal?"

"Under the red sweater." He waited with the bad news until she'd finished her search. When she looked up and saw the expression on his face, she said, "What? Something's wrong."

He handed her a sheet of typing paper. "It was on the floor of your room back at the Maxfield, pushed under the door."

Unfolding it, she read out loud: " 'Message received? You

could have been in that car, Marie. Leave town and stop your research. This is your last warning.' Hmm," she said, running her fingers through her long black hair. "Brief and sufficiently ominous."

"Call the police."

"No. Not yet." She opened her laptop, set it on the desk, then plugged it into the wall. "Maybe in a day or two, but I have to be free to complete my work first."

"I thought I was driving you to the airport this morning. Before I left last night, you made reservations to fly back to New York."

"I canceled them. I'm staying here."

She was so frustrating. "But it's not safe!"

"Nobody knows where I am. And nobody knows what I'll do next."

"Have you set up another interview?"

She nodded. "Laurie Lippert. She was a housekeeper, worked for the Buckridges from '72 to '74. She may have been in the house the night Wayne died. If so, she's the only one other than Constance and her brother who knows what really happened that night. I'm meeting with her at noon."

"Where?"

"Elk River."

"Oh, just . . . perfect."

"Now what are you sputtering about?"

"If you'd made it for this morning, I could have gone with you. My program starts at one."

"What a shame. I guess I'll just have to muddle through on my own."

"Why are you being so obstinate?"

"It's part of my womanly charm." She patted him under the chin, then lit another cigarette. "But I do need your help, my love. My car is parked in the Maxfield's lot, but for obvious reasons I can't use it. I need a second rental car, preferably in your name. Anything you can get me fast."

"Actually, it just so happens that I have a friend who works for Avis."

"You're a godsend, Baldric." She picked up the receiver and handed it to him.

"First you have to do something for me."

She narrowed her eyes. "Like what?"

"I want Sophie to read the interviews you gave me. It's important that she know the kind of man Nathan Buckridge really is."

"No. Absolutely not."

"Why?"

"What if she reads the material and goes directly to Nathan with it? It would be like handing Constance and her lawyers everything I've learned on a silver platter. They could destroy the evidence, buy people off, threaten them. No. I mean it, Baldric. That information is for your eyes only."

"But what if she promises she won't show it or even talk about it to Nathan?"

"You may trust your wife, but I don't. And I think you're being willfully blind if you don't realize she's still emotionally attached to that man."

He stiffened. "You're wrong."

"Maybe. For your sake, I hope so. But I can't chance it."

Bram could understand her fears, but he also thought she was punishing him for not sleeping with her last night. The fact was, Nathan was a potentially dangerous man. The only way Bram could prove it to Sophie was to let her read the interviews. Marie might not like it, but it was his decision to make.

Sitting down at the desk, he tapped in his friend's number at Avis.

23

"Come in," called Sophie, hearing a knock on her office door.

Instead of staying upstairs in the apartment to spend the morning brooding, after breakfast she'd come down to her office to work on the article she'd promised Yale McGraw, the one on George Gildemeister's career at the paper. Late yesterday afternoon the research assistant had finally come through with the information she'd requested. It had been faxed to the hotel and handed to her just before she left to have dinner with Nathan.

"Here's that box you asked for," said a young bellman, entering and setting it next to her desk. "And your car keys." He dropped them into her hand.

"Thanks a lot, Elvis. You saved my poor back a lot of stress." She'd ridden down in the service elevator with him. When she mentioned that she was on her way to the parking garage across the street to retrieve a heavy box, he suggested that he take care of it for her. Elvis was a bit of an apple polisher, but that was all right with her.

"Anything else I can do for you before I go?"

"Can't think of a thing."

He bent down close to her ear and lowered his voice. "There's a guy milling around outside your door, Ms. Greenway. I think he wants to talk to you, but he seems kind of unsure of himself."

"On your way out, ask him to come in."

"Will do."

A few moments later Nathan entered the room.

Sophie remembered what Bram had said to her last night,

but she had to see Nathan alone. Besides, she didn't believe
he posed any threat to her—at least not the kind Bram was
suggesting.

Nathan took a few seconds to get the lay of the land, eyeing
the richly paneled walls, the oil paintings, and the broad windows that overlooked the formal garden. Finally, turning his
full attention on Sophie, he said, "I didn't know if I should
bother you this early." He seemed uncomfortable, as if the
awkwardness of the occasion—the morning after the night
before—had confused his arms and legs.

They both had to answer the same questions today. Who
were they to each other now? Had something fundamental
changed between them? Or had nothing changed at all? By the
expression on Nathan's face, she could see that he expected
the worst, that her mood would be one of anger, shame, contempt, or just plain coldness. Perhaps he thought she wanted
nothing more than to forget last night had ever happened. And
yet a glimmer of hope remained in his eyes, too.

"Do you hate me, Sophie?"

"No," she said softly, "I don't hate you. But I'm not so sure
how I feel about myself."

"Did you tell your husband?"

"God, no!"

"Are you going to?"

"Nathan, listen to me. What happened last night . . . we
can't take it back, but—"

"I don't want to take it back."

"No," she agreed. "I'm not sure I do either. But it doesn't
change the fact that I'm married. And I love my husband. If I
told Bram that we'd slept together, it would hurt him terribly. I
don't want that."

"But you love me, too."

Something in his eyes told her she needed to tread carefully. "I care about you, Nathan. And I'm concerned for you. I
want to help you in any way I can."

"You already have." His serious expression changed instantly to one of excitement. "And because of you"—he
moved restlessly to the windows—"I've made a decision. It

represents a major turning point in my life. I'm going to have such an incredible surprise for you tonight, it'll knock your socks off. Next to finding a woman like you to love, it's probably the smartest move I've ever made."

"Nathan, you're not listening to me."

"Sure I am. I know it's complicated, but we'll work it out." He held up his hand. "But no hints about the secret, Soph. It's not official, so don't try to wheedle it out of me. When I get back to the hotel later today, we're going to celebrate. We'll both be walking on air."

Sophie had never seen him so wired, so unable to concentrate on anything but his own thoughts. "Nathan, I won't be able to see you tonight. Bram and I have a dinner date with some friends."

Bending down to give her a quick kiss, he said, "Wish me luck?"

She wondered if he'd even heard her. "Of course I do."

He kissed her again. "Later, babe." He was out the door so fast, she didn't even try to say goodbye.

Tossing her pen on the desktop, Sophie felt as if a whirlwind had just left her office, a storm that had blown some ominous clouds directly over her head. For the first time since she'd run into him last Saturday afternoon, it occurred to her that she had one hell of a nasty problem on her hands. His exuberance was so extreme that he was not only missing her cues but also her direct statements. Surely he could see how painful the situation was for her. She was hardly in the mood to celebrate, no matter what his good news might be.

Feeling at a complete loss, and more than a little concerned about when and where he might pop up next, Sophie returned to the feature story on George Gildemeister. She could easily spend all day worrying, but right now she didn't have the time. Besides, it would only make her more tense than she already was. In the middle of the night, she'd made a firm decision not to tell Bram what had happened. All she could do was pray that he never found out. Until she'd talked to Nathan a few minutes ago, she felt certain she could trust him to keep their secret, but now that he was bouncing off the walls in his excitement about God knows what, she wasn't sure of anything. Did he really think life was that simple, that making love was the same as a lifetime commitment?

Sophie struggled to remain focused. She finally finished the article around one o'clock. After calling up to the Fountain Grill to ask for a corned beef on rye and a side of cole slaw to be sent down to her, she faxed the final draft to Yale McGraw, explaining that if he wanted any editorial changes, she'd be at the Maxfield all afternoon.

She ate lunch alone at her desk going over hotel business. By two, she was ready to tackle George's box of files. If her personal life ever got back to normal, she was really going to enjoy the change of pace, moving between hotel matters and her new job as restaurant reviewer for the *Times Register*. Bram had been so right last night. She loved her life: the hotel, the chance to work with her son. And Bram, as always, was at the heart of everything. It was beyond her how she could have endangered something so precious. She wasn't the first human to make the same mistake and she wouldn't be the last, but it was the first time she'd ever cheated on her husband and it made her feel sick inside. Why did she see everything so clearly this morning, when all week she'd been walking around in a fog of memories? Highly seductive memories. She just *had* to push it, had to play with fire. It was a quality she'd recognized in herself many times before, and it usually got her into trouble, but this time the trouble could end her marriage.

Tackling the box with a fury born of self-loathing, she grabbed a handful of files and began going through them. Unfortunately, George hadn't had much of a system. The label might read, "New restaurants opening in May," but inside the file there'd be one of his many seed catalogs or a receipt from a grocery store. Most of what she found ended up in the trash.

During the next couple of hours, she was interrupted almost constantly by phone calls. Yale faxed her shortly after four with changes he wanted in the article. She glanced briefly at his comments, then returned to the box. She was making progress and didn't want to quit until she was done.

As she was paging through a bunch of George's most recent reviews, she found a fax that caught her attention.

> *From: Office 404*
> *To: GG*
> *Page: 1 of 1*
> *George: You're on the right track with the*
> *acid humor, but crank the whole piece up a*
> *few more notches. Make your opinion hurt.*
> *If you want the money, we want action.*

It was unsigned. When Sophie glanced at the top of the page, she saw that it said:

> *May 3   B.C.A.   Fax No. 203-994-9320   Pg. 1*

The B.C.A. part sounded familiar. As she thought about it, she remembered that Nathan had used the same initials on Saturday afternoon. Buckridge Culinary Academy. But what would someone in New Haven, Connecticut, want with a restaurant reviewer in Minnesota? Maybe there was another B.C.A.

First she called the operator and requested the area code for New Haven. Sure enough, it was 203, same as the one on the fax. She then called directory assistance and asked for the B.C.A. in New Haven. There was nothing like that in the computer directory, but the operator suggested it might stand for the Buckridge Culinary Academy, "an important school around these parts." It seemed highly unlikely that there was another B.C.A. in New Haven. So if George did get a fax from someone at the academy, who had sent it and why? Again she could be wrong, but the message sounded like editorial feedback, as if someone was instructing him to make one of his reviews even harsher. It also implied that George was getting paid to write a negative review. The next question was, What restaurant review appeared in the paper shortly after May 3?

Without checking Sophie thought she knew the answer,

but she had to be sure. Logging on to the Internet, she typed in the address for the paper's website. Sure enough, George's highly critical review of the Belmont appeared on May 7. Last Friday. It was also the same day the Buckridge family had checked into the Maxfield. Two nights later George was murdered, and Nathan was seen coming out of his apartment. There were simply too many coincidences for it not to be connected. But what did that say about Nathan? Had *he* sent George the fax? And if so, did he stab the poor man in the back on Sunday night and then leave him to die?

There were so many unanswered questions, Sophie's mind was a jumble of thoughts and emotions.

Before she could make sense of anything else, she had to find out what "Office 404" meant. And she had to find out now.

Glancing at her watch, she saw that it was nearly four-thirty. Maybe Nathan was back. Then again perhaps it would be smarter to talk to someone else first. Emily or Arthur might be able to give her the information she needed. That way, Nathan wouldn't have to know she'd discovered the fax . . . just in case. It upset her terribly to think he might be involved in something so foul. She wondered if George's first review of the Belmont had been bought and paid for, too. If so, then clearly someone at the academy wanted to put Harry Hongisto and the Belmont out of business. Paying a critic to destroy a restaurant was just about the sleaziest thing she'd ever heard. Not that all restaurant reviews or reviewers carried the same weight, but George had been the top man in town. People had listened to him, respected his opinion. He might not have been able to single-handedly kill a restaurant, but he could have certainly pounded a few nails in its coffin, especially if it was already in trouble.

Sophie marched straight to the elevators and rode up to the tenth floor. She'd decided to speak to Arthur first. As he was the least involved party, she hoped he wouldn't ask a lot of questions. She was about to knock when she heard shouts and then a chorus of angry voices coming from the suite. A second later the door flew open and Nathan burst out. He rushed past her without even acknowledging her presence.

An instant later Arthur exploded out of the doorway,

red-faced and out of breath. "Nathan, come back here!" he shouted. "Please! We've got to talk." He glanced back into the room, where Paul was reading the riot act to Constance. Arthur seemed torn, as if he didn't know what to do next. Turning to Sophie, he said, "I can't talk now."

"But what's wrong?"

Before he could answer, Emily and Kenny pushed past them into the hall. Tears mottled Emily's face and her eyes were badly swollen. Kenny's arm was around her shoulders. Together they walked silently toward their room. Inside the suite, Paul continued to shout at his mother. She was crying, too, begging for him to listen to her. The scene was utter pandemonium.

"If there's anything I can do to help . . ." said Sophie, trying to catch what Paul was saying. She heard the name *Damontraville* and then the word *ruined*, both uttered at shattering decibels.

Arthur closed the door, then took a hold of Sophie's arm. "Maybe there is something you can do. Go find Nathan. Get him to come back. Connie and I have to talk to him. It's absolutely imperative."

"Sure," she said, still hesitating.

"Go! Now!" He looked desperate.

She turned and hurried to the elevator. Nathan must have gone either up to his room or down to the lobby. Betting on the lobby, she charged through the fire door into the stairwell and descended the steps as fast as she could. Waiting for an elevator in even the best hotels could take all day.

When she reached the main floor, she spotted Nathan all the way across the lobby. Before she could shout for him to stop, he'd disappeared out the front doors. She raced to catch up with him. Just as she made it to the street in front of the Maxfield, she saw him climb into a yellow cab.

As it pulled into traffic, she waved to the next taxi in line, a red and white, jumping up and down in her urgency to get it moving. "Follow that car," she said to the driver as soon as she was safely inside.

"Excuse me?" he said, turning around to stare at her.

"That yellow cab. Up there." She pointed. "Come on! I don't want to lose them!"

There was a hint of disbelief in his eyes.

"Let's go. Move it!"

He blinked a couple of times, then said, "You betcha, lady. Whatever you say." He set the meter and they were off.

Sophie was glad that she'd dressed casually today. In the back pocket of her jeans was one of Bram's old billfolds. That meant she had money and credit cards with her. If she'd had to race to her office to get her purse, she would have lost precious time.

They were now in hot pursuit of the yellow cab, heading east on I-94. Sophie couldn't imagine what had happened in Constance's suite to upset everyone so. "Do you think the driver of that yellow taxi knows he's being followed?"

The driver tipped his cap back. "I doubt it. You know, ma'am, don't take this the wrong way, but I've been in this business for over thirty years and I've never had anybody tell me to follow a car before." He glanced at her in the rearview mirror. "You some sort of private eye?"

"Afraid not."

"A jilted lover maybe?"

"Just a concerned friend."

He nodded. "We don't want to tip them off that we're on their tail, so we'll just cruise along back here for a while."

"Good idea."

Half an hour later the yellow cab took the 95 cutoff through Bayport, heading straight for Stillwater. By now, Sophie had a good idea of where they were going. "When we come to country road 74, turn right."

"What's our destination?"

"Have you ever heard of New Fonteney?"

"The Cistercian monks? Sure, everyone around here's heard of them. But I read the place was up for sale."

"It is." She watched out the front window, trying to judge how much farther they had to go. "There's a back entrance to the monastery. Slow down and let the other cab get there first."

They took the last few bends in the road at a leisurely pace.

Sophie wished she had a sweater. The late afternoon had turned cool, and this close to the river there would be a breeze.

"Hey, you guessed it," said the cab driver. "Thar she blows."

The yellow cab had pulled off the road into the small clearing by the south gate, the same place where she and Nathan had parked on Monday.

"Pull up behind it."

The driver brought the car to a slow stop but left the motor running.

"Stay here," she said, wasting no time climbing out of the backseat. "I don't know how long this will take, but I want you to drive me back to St. Paul." She pulled the billfold out of her back pocket and handed him two twenties.

"No prob."

Pushing her hands deep into the pockets of her jeans, she approached the yellow cab, her anxiety growing with each step. "Hi there," she said to the driver, seeing that Nathan was nowhere around. "Where's your passenger?"

The man took a bite of his sandwich, sizing her up. "Gone."

"Gone where?"

He nodded to the gate. "Inside the monastery."

"Is he coming back? Are you waiting for him?"

He popped some potato chips into his mouth. "Nah, I'm taking my dinner break. It's a pretty spot. Thought I'd take advantage of it."

"That's nice," she said, glancing worriedly toward the entrance.

"Hey, you a friend of his?"

"I am, yes."

"He's in pretty bad shape."

"Really? Did he say anything?"

"Nah, but a couple times I looked back and saw him crying. Say, since you're here, why don't you take that crap he left." He nodded to the backseat. "I'd have to turn it in to the office, file a bunch of papers, and I got no time for that."

When she opened the door, she found a manila envelope. "Okay. Thanks."

"Don't mention it." He went back to his sandwich.

Sophie slipped a few of the typed pages out and studied them. They seemed to be part of an interview. Walking back to the red and white, she tossed it inside. "Remember, don't leave."

"I'm not going anywhere," said the driver. "But this is going to cost you a bundle."

She set off down the trail, realizing she had no idea where Nathan might be. If she shouted his name, would he hide from her or would he be glad to see her? Deciding not to take any chances, she followed the path through the woods to the main hall. As soon as she emerged into a clearing, she could see a light coming from inside the low, vine-covered building. She watched for a moment, hoping to locate him, but finally grew impatient and started down the hill.

The wind off the river ruffled her short blonde hair as she sprinted toward the hall. The fresh air felt good after being cooped up in an office all day, especially since it was that golden time of evening when all the greens and blues deepened and sunshine covered the world in honey.

Approaching the side entrance, she suddenly grew cautious. In the courtyard outside the main hall, she could hear someone retching. All her instincts told her to run to Nathan and help him. And yet how could she when she didn't even know what was wrong?

She waited until the retching stopped, then crept to the edge of the building and peered around. Nathan, sitting on a long wooden bench, was in the process of opening a bottle of champagne. The scene made no sense. Why would a man who'd spent the last few minutes in physical and emotional agony be opening a bottle of bubbly? She watched silently from the shadows as he popped the cork, took a swig, rinsed the wine around in his mouth, and then spit it out. Tipping the bottle back, he drank a good half of it before he stopped and set it down on the ground. He looked terrible. His clothes were wrinkled. His eyes were all puffy and red.

Moving away from the building, she called his name.

He didn't look up. "Go away," he said in a low, thick voice.

"It's Sophie."

"I know who it is." He took another swallow. "I want to be alone."

"But are you all right?"

He dropped his head in his hands. "I can't talk to you right now. Go home. Your husband's waiting for you."

She wasn't about to let him chase her off that easily. "Your uncle wants you to come back to the Maxfield. He says he needs to talk to you. So does your mother."

He laughed, but it was a bitter sound. "There's nothing to talk about."

She walked a few paces closer. "What happened? You look . . . awful."

He looked up, watching her with his dark eyes. Ignoring her question, he finished the last of the champagne and tossed the bottle away. Then he leaned back, grabbed another from behind the bench, and began to peel off the foil. "I don't want to be rude, Sophie. So just go away, okay?"

"Don't you think you'd better slow down? Champagne can hit you like a ton of bricks."

"I've already been hit with a ton of bricks. Notice, I'm still standing. Well, sitting, if you want to get technical, but I can stand."

"At the rate you're going, not for long. Nathan, what's wrong? Why won't you talk to me?"

He pressed a hand against one eye. "Just go. Please."

He looked as if he might start crying again. "We used to be able to talk about anything."

"The operative words are 'used to.' Times change. I've changed. I haven't wanted to admit it, but so have you. Go on, Soph. Get away from me while you still can. I'm poison. My whole family is poison."

"Why would you say such a thing?"

He stood and shouted, "Leave it alone, damn it! Get the hell out of here!"

The anger in his voice shocked her. Backing up, she said, "I won't leave until I know you're all right. That you won't do anything foolish."

"God, Sophie. Don't you know me better than that? I'm not going to hurt myself. I like living way too much. That's part of the problem."

"I wish you'd talk to me. Maybe you'd even share some of that champagne."

He looked down at the bottle in his hand. "That was the idea," he whispered.

"Excuse me?" She hadn't quite heard him.

"I promise I'll talk to you tomorrow. But right now I've got to be alone." He stared at her a moment longer, then turned and carried the bottle into the main hall, shutting the door behind him.

When Sophie finally returned to the cab, she found the driver leaning against the front fender, smoking a cigarette.

"Did you find him?" he asked.

She nodded. "Let's go."

He took one last puff, then dropped the cigarette on the ground and crushed it with the heel of his boot.

Sophie climbed into the rear seat and tipped her head back, closing her eyes. If Nathan wouldn't talk to her, it seemed unlikely that anyone else in the Buckridge family would either. Something terrible had happened in Constance's suite. She'd never seen Nathan so upset.

Remembering the manila envelope, she opened it and drew out its contents. As the driver pulled back onto the highway, she glanced at the heading on the first page: INTERVIEW: LAURIE LIPPERT, ELK RIVER, MINNESOTA, THURSDAY MAY 13. That was today. Maybe this would shed some light on the current Buckridge family chaos. She settled back in the seat and began to read.

* * *

Journal Note

INTERVIEW: LAURIE LIPPERT, ELK RIVER, MINNESOTA, THURSDAY, MAY 13

M: *Thanks for allowing me to come to your home.*

Lippert: *Believe me, it's my pleasure. I've been wondering if anyone would ever show up to ask me about Connie Buckridge.*

M: *Let's start at the beginning. You began working for the Buckridges when?*

Lippert: *In the summer of '72. I'd just graduated from high school and needed a summer job. After a few weeks, I realized that I really liked housekeeping. It made sense to me. I'd had an office job between my junior and senior years and I hated it. I'd come in and sit down at my desk in the morning, shuffle some papers around, do a little typing, talk on the phone, and then it would be five and I'd leave. I mean, what's all that about? Boring as hell, too. But cleaning a house felt like I was accomplishing something concrete. I could live at home, save my money, and I didn't have to punch a time clock. I could wear whatever clothes I felt like wearing that day, and if I was ten minutes late or had a doctor's appointment, nobody made a big deal out of it. Connie wasn't much of a stickler for rules. I liked that. As long as I got the job done, and done well, she was happy. Really, the only thing she insisted on was that I was out of the house by dinnertime. Otherwise, I could pretty much come and go as I pleased.*

M: *Just out of curiosity, what time was dinner?*

Lippert: *I normally tried to leave by five. Sometimes it got to be a little later. But six-thirty was the cut-off. Evenings were family time. Connie didn't want any staff around, not even the part-time cook.*

M: *You never stayed past six-thirty?*

Lippert: *Oh, well, if there was something coming up, like a dinner party that weekend, I'd occasionally have to work late.*

M: *How often did Constance give dinner parties?*

Lippert: *A few times a month. And then spring and fall cleaning was another heavy work period. But I got paid a bonus at the end of it, so it was never a problem.*

M: *What did you think of the Buckridges?*

Lippert: *I really thought Nathan was handsome and fun. He was always nice to me. He had a girlfriend, so I knew I didn't have a chance with him, but we still talked a lot. He liked to talk, and so did I. Sometimes he'd sit in the room I was cleaning. Or if I was outside shaking rugs, he'd help me.*

M: *What about the others?*

Lippert: *Will I be quoted?*

M: *Not without your permission. As I told you on the phone, if I decide to use any of this interview in my book, I'll need to get your authorization. But I'm hoping that everything you tell me today will be on the record. Otherwise, it won't be of much use.*

Lippert: *(Hesitates) Okay, I get it. I'll go on record, what the hell. Paul was a self-consumed jerk. And extremely sloppy. Connie picked up after him. I picked up after him. Even Emily picked up after him every now and then, and she was no paragon of neatness herself. He pretty much ignored me, thought I was the "hired help" and usually treated me like I was too stupid to understand basic English. It bothered me a little, but then people like him are dinosaurs in my book. By the time I'd quit working at the Buckridge home, I'd made big plans for my future. I was going to have my own housecleaning business, with lots of employees. And I was going to make a ton of money. I haven't made a ton yet, but I'm doing pretty well for someone with a limited IQ.*

M: *Yes, Paul sounds like a real winner. But what about the others in the family?*

Lippert: *Emily was nice enough. She was pretty social, so she wasn't around much. Connie was a great boss. If she didn't like the way I did something, she'd tell me straight out. She didn't make me feel like a naughty child either. Some women are awful that way. They hint. They never actually come out and say what they want, so you're never sure you're doing it*

right. And then they have the nerve to treat you like a "bad girl" for not being able to read their minds. It's ridiculous.
M: *What about Wayne and Arthur?*
Lippert: *Wayne was pretty quiet. He wasn't around much during the day, so I never really talked to him. He was always pleasant, but then . . . I don't know . . . he seemed sort of distracted. I think he really loved Connie and felt bad that he was in such terrible shape physically. There were always lots of pastries and cookies around the house, and I guess that's what he ate. I know Connie was worried about his health. Nathan told me he had a heart problem. Oh, and then Arthur. (Pauses; face turns serious) I can't leave him out. We had morning coffee together occasionally. I liked him, I guess. It's hard to remember now. He was very thin when he first arrived. Nathan told me he was some sort of CIA operative in Saigon. He'd been captured by the Vietcong and tortured. I thought it was all very tragic and heroic. He never would talk about it, so I finally stopped asking him questions. He was interested in philosophy and psychology, so we'd discuss that sometimes. I guess . . . I thought he was a little odd. I figured everyone else thought so, too, but nobody ever commented on it.*
M: *Odd in what way?*
Lippert: *I don't know. I could never put my finger on it. He just didn't react normally sometimes. And he was on a lot of different medications. I saw them when I cleaned his room.*
M: *Do you remember the names of the medications?*
Lippert: *(Shakes her head) Sorry.*
M: *Where was his room in relation to the rest of the house?*
Lippert: *All the bedrooms were on the second floor. Connie had her office on the first, off the living room, and next to it was the den. That's where Arthur stayed. I got the impression that Connie wanted to keep an eye on him during the day. He slept a lot, particularly at first. As he got stronger, he started going out, like to the library or to a movie.*
M: *Did Connie ever go with him?*
Lippert: *If she had time. She was pretty busy with her TV show. I think most days he was on his own.*

M: *I understand that you were working at the house on the day Wayne Buckridge died.*

Lippert: *That's right. (Grows excited)*

M: *What time did you leave that day?*

Lippert: *Everything had gone wrong that afternoon. I don't remember all the details now, but I was supposed to have the good silverware polished and put away before I left. I didn't get started on it until almost five. I worked quietly in the kitchen until I heard Wayne drive up. He usually parked in the driveway and then he'd come into the house through the kitchen door.*

M: *What time was that?*

Lippert: *Around six. I remember because he was home early and it was unusual. Normally, he never got home until after seven. He said he was feeling awful—very tired—and was going up to his room to bed.*

M: *Was that unusual?*

Lippert: *Well, he complained of being tired a lot. But he always worked a full day.*

M: *Who else was home that night?*

Lippert: *Connie and Arthur. The kids were all away. Nathan was out of town, I think. And Paul was at one of his high school football games. Emily was probably at a friend's. I don't remember exactly.*

M: *What happened next?*

Lippert: *(Hesitates) Look, Ms. Damontraville, I was there, so I know what I'm talking about, okay? I'm not trying to hurt anyone.*

M: *No, of course not.*

Lippert: *I assume you've already heard Connie's story about what happened that night.*

M: *I've been told that when Wayne felt the heart attack coming on, he must have called out for her, but he was upstairs in their bedroom and she was downstairs in her office. She said she had music playing so she didn't hear him shout. She didn't even know he'd come home.*

Lippert: *None of that is true. (Hesitates again) When the*

police and the paramedics came, I'd already gone, so they never heard anything but what Connie told them. I'm positive she didn't know I was in the kitchen. I'm sure she assumed I'd already left. So, to this day, she has no idea that someone else witnessed what happened. At the time, I just didn't want to get involved, especially since Connie was such a well-known person in town. I also didn't want to be part of a scandal. Besides, I was a kid, twenty years old. I wasn't sure people would believe me.

M: *Just tell me what happened. Take your time. I want this to be as accurate as possible.*

Lippert: *Oh, it'll be accurate. I'll never forget that night. (Clears her throat) Like I said, Wayne came home a little after six. The kitchen was in the back of the house. You had to go through the pantry into the dining room to get anywhere else. That's what Wayne did. First he grabbed himself a beer, then he loosened his tie and set his coat and briefcase on the kitchen table. I assumed he wanted to go say hi to Connie before he headed upstairs. I was done with polishing the silverware by then, so as I finished putting it away, I heard the first scream. I raced into the pantry and hid behind the door, opening it just a crack so that I could see out. There was another scream and a few moments later Wayne staggered into the hall between the dining room and the living room. His face was bright red, and the look of total revulsion on his face was one I'll never forget, not until the day I die. He just kept repeating, "Oh, my God. Oh, my God!" After a few seconds, he rushed back into the living room. I screwed up my courage and followed. I knew he wasn't well, and I was afraid his heart would give out from all the excitement. As I crept partway around the living room arch, I saw him standing in the doorway of Arthur's bedroom about fifteen feet away. He said something like "This is disgusting! He's your brother, for God's sake!" As he backed up, I saw that Connie was in Arthur's bed. She was naked, covered partially by a sheet. Arthur was naked, too, standing next to the bed, looking almost as white as the sheet covering Connie. It was horrible. Revolting. Wayne kept shaking his head. Then he said some-*

thing like "How could you do this, Arthur? I took you in. Gave you a place to live. She's your own sister, for chrissake!" Arthur just stared at him. He tried to explain. Said something like "You'll never understand us." His voice was extremely cold. He and Wayne argued some more. By this time, Wayne was positively furious. He threw a vase at Arthur, but Arthur ducked at the last moment and it smashed into the wall behind him. Connie shouted for Wayne to stop. She said something like, "Can't you understand? We've been apart so long. It just happened." That's when Wayne said, "I want you out of here, both of you. Now!" Connie got up out of bed. The sheet fell to the floor. God, I was so embarrassed I could have died, but I couldn't leave. I had to know what was going to happen. Wayne and Connie stared at each other. Finally Connie said she refused to leave. It was her house, too. She'd bought and paid for it every time she'd let Wayne put his hands on her. Wayne was really shocked by that. He said, "But you love me." "I never loved you," she said. How could she love a man like him? That's when Wayne sort of stumbled backward against the couch. He looked dazed, like he didn't know what to do next. Eventually, he just walked out of the room and went upstairs. Connie and Arthur stood there like statues. They didn't even look human. Neither moved. I couldn't move either. It was like we were all waiting for something to happen. Finally it did. From upstairs, Wayne shouted, "Connie, my medicine! Help me." Connie looked at Arthur. I think she was about to go when he put his hand on her arm. He ordered her to stay put. I knew there was a good chance Wayne would die if he didn't get his meds, but I was afraid for my own life if I let those two weirdos know I was still in the house and that I'd seen and heard everything. So I stood very still. Wayne called again. Connie and Arthur sat down on the bed. Wayne called one last time. I heard this muted thump and then everything was quiet. Connie started to cry. Arthur put his arm around her, but he never tried to console her. I think she said something like "He's dead." And then Arthur said, "I hope so."

M: *What happened next?*

Lippert: *I don't know. I tiptoed back to the kitchen, shut off all the lights, and left by the back door. Instead of walking around the side of the house, crossing the driveway, and leaving through the front yard, I climbed over the fence into the next yard and left through their front yard. I didn't want Connie or Arthur to see me.*

M: *And you're positive they never realized you saw and heard all this?*

Lippert: *Connie would have said something to me if she'd known. She would have acted differently. When I came back the next day, it was like none of it had happened. She'd made up this story about how Wayne died and everyone believed her. I worked for her another month, then said I had to quit. That last month was agony. I cleaned the house for the get-together after the funeral. I saw how devastated the kids were, and I knew that Connie and Arthur had to lie constantly to keep the truth a secret. It was more than I could take. I never wanted to see anyone in that family again. Everything I've told you is the God's honest truth, Ms. Damontraville. I'd swear to it on a stack of Bibles.*

M: *That's not necessary, Laurie. I believe you. You've been a huge help. Please, just one word of caution. Don't tell anyone about this interview. Researching a book is a very sensitive time for both me and those I talk to. I'd like you to keep this under your hat until the book comes out. If anyone in the Buckridge family contacts you—*

Lippert: *Will they?*

M: *I doubt it, but you never know. The best thing to do is to just refuse to talk to them. Make that clear and unequivocal.*

Lippert: *If I have to, I'd lie. I really want to see the truth finally get told, especially after keeping it inside me all these years. But I don't want to deal with Connie Buckridge. I'm still a little afraid of her.*

M: *I understand. Again, many thanks.*

End of E-mail to Pluto

* * *

A few personal comments for my journal.

It was awful—truly horrible—spending even one night without my laptop and my journal. I drank enough brandy to put myself into a coma, but the gash on my ear still hurt, pretty much all night. Normally, if I can't sleep, I get up and work. All I had to help me while away the hours was the TV and my wounded pride. This morning, however, at least the cut felt better. I changed the bandage before Bram arrived. I didn't want to have him fuss over it—or me. After last night, I didn't want him that close ever again. All a woman can do is try, I guess, and that's what I did. I think he's making a big mistake. I wouldn't be at all surprised to find that Sophie and Nathan are having an affair—or will be in the near future. But he'll have to deal with that on his own. Once someone says no, I'm gone.

One more comment. I know that Bram may be upset when he finds that I've left the Ardmore Suites, but I can't chance remaining in St. Paul any longer. When I first arrived in Minnesota, I wanted to stay at the Maxfield so that I could watch the Buckridges up close. But now that my cover is blown, and my life has been threatened, I have to get away. Perhaps I should have left sooner, but the fact that I'd hired a bodyguard lulled me into a false sense of safety. If I'd had any real idea of how dangerous Constance Buckridge would turn out to be, I would have done many things differently. But hindsight doesn't help me now, or more important, it doesn't help Rafferty. I feel terrible—and partially responsible—for what happened, and I intend to see that whoever planted that car bomb pays a price.

I may stay in Elk River tonight or find something in Minneapolis. Bram helped me when I needed him most, and I'll be forever grateful. But for now I have to disappear, and that means from him as well. I left him a note. When he comes by the Ardmore later tonight to check on me, he'll receive it. I hope he isn't too angry. Why should I care, right? I shouldn't, damn it all, but I do. Lucky me. Thirty-seven years old and carrying a torch for a married man who happens to love his wife. Pathetic.

24

Sophie tossed and turned all night. For some reason, Bram was sleeping almost as badly as she was. He'd been in a foul mood ever since he'd walked in the door, late for their dinner date with two old friends from Sophie's days at *Squires Magazine*. He didn't seem to be directing his ill humor at her, so she figured it was probably a work-related problem and he'd talk about it when he was ready.

Sophie had arrived home from New Fonteney shortly after six. She went straight up to Arthur and Constance's suite to tell Arthur that she'd found Nathan and he was okay. After reading the interview with Laurie Lippert, she finally understood what had caused that highly charged family scene. It was a startling revelation, one that no doubt rocked the family to its very foundations, but she wasn't sure she believed it.

Perhaps this Lippert woman had a grudge against Constance or maybe she just saw the opportunity to get her name in print—in a big way. Sure, she sounded sincere. It all sounded plausible, but that didn't mean it was the truth. Then again if it was accurate, if Constance had slept with her brother, it was just the kind of dirt Marie Damontraville was looking for. And that meant it wouldn't be long before the story was published for all the world to see. Sophie thought it would be best, however, not to let Arthur know, at least for now, that she'd read the interview.

Arthur thanked her profusely for finding Nathan. He said again how worried he was about him. When Sophie asked where Constance was, he nodded toward one of the bedrooms but offered nothing more. He was obviously in no mood for a chat. Before she left, he asked for directions to the monastery. She assumed he intended to drive out to talk to Nathan. She didn't mention how drunk Nathan was likely to be because she didn't think he should be alone tonight. Arthur might be the last person on earth Nathan wanted to see, but perhaps, in some convoluted way, he was the best person for the job.

Sophie still wanted to talk to Emily about the Buckridge Culinary Academy, specifically office 404, but after what the poor woman had just gone through, it wasn't the right time. Paul was another possible source of information, but he'd never been all that friendly to her, and he, too, had just suffered a major emotional blow. Her questions would have to wait. Not that she would put them on hold for long. A man's life was at stake. She thought about going to the police and telling them what she knew, but since her information implicated Nathan, she wanted to wait until she knew more. She didn't want circumstantial evidence to convict another innocent man.

After dinner, she and Bram walked back to the hotel and turned in early. Bram didn't feel much like talking. He'd been his usual charming self at the restaurant, but once they were alone, Sophie sensed his fatigue. And because she had so much on her mind, engaging in their normal banter would have been a struggle. She was actually grateful for Bram's pensive mood.

When the alarm finally went off at seven A.M., Bram stayed in bed while Sophie showered. As he was getting dressed, she prepared a light breakfast of whole-wheat toast, fresh melon, and yogurt. Whatever problems he'd had on his mind last night were still on his mind this morning. Over breakfast she made a few tentative stabs at getting him to talk about it, but he changed the subject each time. Before he left for the station, they stood at the front door and kissed goodbye.

"Everything's okay, isn't it?" she asked. She couldn't let him go without reassurance that he hadn't found out about her and Nathan. It was hard to accept that for the rest of her married life, a sword would be hanging over her head—a sword she'd hung herself. "Have I done something to upset you?"

"God, no," he said, kissing her again and then holding her tight. "It's not you. It's a friend. I think this person may be in some serious trouble and I don't know how to help."

"I'm sorry to hear that," she said, feeling herself relax in his arms. "Is it a close friend?"

"Sort of," he said after a few seconds. "I guess I care more than I thought I did."

"You'll think of something."

"I hope so." He backed up. "Say, Soph? Have you found out yet when the Buckridges are leaving town?"

She was instantly on guard again. "No."

"Could you?"

"I could try. Why?"

He paused for a moment, then continued. "There's something important I want you to read tonight. And don't give me any excuses about having to work late."

"Is it about Nathan?"

"It's about his whole family."

"Come on, Bram. I can't wait until tonight."

"I'm taping an interview with Governor Ventura in less than an hour. I can't stay. But remember your promise to stay away from Nathan."

Sophie wasn't sure she'd ever made such a promise, but she didn't want him to worry. "I'll be careful."

"Good. That whole family is a disaster, Sophie. Stay away from all of them."

She scrutinized his face. "Why would you say something like that?"

"I'll let you see the proof tonight." He gave her one last peck on the cheek, then hurried down the hall to the elevators.

As she cleaned up the breakfast dishes, she wondered what information he could possibly have on Constance Buckridge and her family and where he'd found it. If he'd somehow gotten ahold of a copy of the Lippert interview, well, sure, it made some awful accusations about Constance and her brother, but they posed no danger to Sophie. And what could he have on

Nathan other than his general antipathy toward one of Sophie's ex-boyfriends?

Pouring herself another cup of coffee, she took it into the living room. She was about to sit down on the couch when she heard a knock at the door. She immediately thought of Nathan. Although she had mixed feelings about seeing him this morning, she still hoped it would be him. When she answered the door, she was surprised to find Constance standing in the hallway.

"Are you alone?" she asked, smiling at Sophie with that same open yet mischievous look millions of TV viewers had come to know and love.

"My husband just left," she said, holding the door open. "Come on in." Surely Bram had to be wrong. Constance might be many things, but she wasn't dangerous. At one point in her life, Sophie had thought of Constance as her future mother-in-law. They'd even been fairly close. Of course, all that had ended when she broke it off with Nathan.

As Constance entered, her eyes fell on Ethel, who was snoozing on her pillow under the dining room table. "So that really is your dog," she said, crouching down to get a better look.

"Afraid so."

"I've seen her downstairs on her pillow in the lobby. She makes an unforgettable hotel mascot."

Ethel's eyes opened slightly, sensing that she was being talked about.

"She's old," said Sophie, "but young in spirit."

"She's not a terribly active animal."

"No. She's always been far more cerebral, if you know what I mean. Guarding tennis balls and examining bugs represent the limit of her athletic accomplishments."

Ethel yawned, smacked her jaws a couple of times, then closed her eyes.

"I guess I'm not very interesting," said Constance.

"Oh, don't take her apathy personally. She's apathetic about most everything."

"Except tennis balls and bugs."

"And cookies. She has standards."

Constance watched her a few more seconds, then stood up, straightening her belted sweater and wool slacks. "We've hardly had a chance to talk since you came to Kitchen Central with Nathan last weekend. I thought it was about time I remedied that. Did I come at a bad moment?"

"No, not at all." She led the way into the living room. After everything that had happened yesterday, Constance looked none the worse for wear. Sophie figured her reasons for dropping by extended beyond mere sociability, so her natural curiosity kicked into high gear. "Can I get you something to drink? Some coffee?"

Constance patted her stomach as she sat down on the couch. "No thanks. I just finished breakfast and I'm stuffed. Both Arthur and I have really been enjoying the Fountain Grill."

"It's a great café," agreed Sophie, sitting down opposite her. It felt funny talking so casually after what she'd just learned. Perhaps, somewhere in the back of her mind, she did believe Laurie Lippert. At the very least, the woman's accusations colored the way she looked at Constance now. "So what's it like being back in Minnesota after all these years?"

"It's been profitable in terms of the book tour. I've done almost a dozen interviews, four bookstores, several radio shows, and a couple TV shows. Can you believe that this is the first time I've spent any real time here since I moved out east?"

"Nathan mentioned that. I assume Minnesota holds some bad memories for you."

Constance turned her attention to a tall white vase of bright yellow daffodils sitting in the center of the coffee table, then glanced admiringly around the room. "Yes, a few. Nobody really wanted to start the tour here except for Nathan."

"Because of New Fonteney?"

She nodded. "It just wasn't the right spot for us. I know he's disappointed, but Paul pretty much runs the culinary academy and he was against it."

"Perhaps Nathan could be in charge of this branch?"

"You know, when we first started up the school, I wanted

Nathan to run it, but he turned me down flat. I suppose, in the long run, Paul was the better choice. He's a lot like his father, a natural at business. Nathan is more artistic and more introspective. Perhaps that's why I love him so much. Oh, he does some guest lectures occasionally. He's quite a brilliant chef, you know. I'd love him to do more teaching, but he seems to need his freedom right now. That's why he likes running around the country making sure the restaurants we own are up to snuff. Kenneth Merlin, my son-in-law, handles most of the business details, but Nathan is in charge of the culinary integrity at each site, and that's every bit as vital to me as the financial bottom line."

Sophie nodded, sipping her coffee. Everything Constance said was interesting, but she wished that she'd get to the point. "You look well. Stardom must agree with you."

Her smoothness faltered. "Celebrity has its ups and downs. Speaking of which, I, ah . . . I understand you came to the door yesterday during a family meeting."

"I guess I showed up at a rather bad time."

"Oh, don't apologize. You had no way of knowing. You see, Sophie, I won't bore you with the details, but an extremely vicious woman picked yesterday to slander me in the worst possible way. Unfortunately, she passed her lies on to my children. You saw the result. They were so totally unhinged, they just exploded. They wouldn't even give me a chance to explain."

"I'm sorry. That must have been a terrible position to be in." Sophie tried to keep her comments sympathetic. Actually, she was surprised that Constance would talk to her about it.

Pulling a small throw pillow in front of her, Constance continued. "There's a woman, her name is Marie Damontraville. She's writing a biography of yours truly. Unauthorized, of course. She's been doing research in town all week. And lucky me, she happens to be staying right here."

"Damontraville?" said Sophie. "I don't remember that name on the guest register."

"That's because she uses an alias, which should give you some indication of the sort of person she is."

"What name did she register under?"

"Lela Dexter."

Sophie's eyes opened wide.

"Do you know her?"

Taking a moment to let it sink in, she said, "No, but my husband does."

"Well, tell him to keep away. She's a black widow spider, Sophie. A wretched, pathetic woman who feeds on other people's tragedies. Her books are notorious for being sleazy tell-alls, pure tabloid journalism."

"Didn't she do one last year on Elton John?"

"Yes, and I'm amazed he hasn't sued. Yesterday she supposedly interviewed a woman who worked for me back in the early Seventies. Somehow, she managed to slip copies of the interview under my children's doors here at the hotel. Well, of course they were shocked at what this onetime employee said. I was shocked, too. We called an immediate family meeting, but it disintegrated into a shouting match."

"I heard that part."

"I'm sure the entire floor heard it. You know how much my family loves to argue, Sophie. You've been there for some of our finer moments. Nobody ever agrees on anything, and I'm used to that. But to get blindsided by this woman and not even have the chance to defend myself—well, needless to say, I spent a sleepless night. Arthur and I met with the children again this morning and tried to get them to listen to reason. I mean, for all I know, the entire interview was made up by Ms. Damontraville. If she did talk to that ex-employee, what she got was the result of a long-standing grudge, a vendetta that's been smoldering inside that woman's head for years."

"What grudge?"

"I fired her for stealing, Sophie. It was right after Wayne died. Even before he died, we'd both noticed some things were missing: a pair of twenty-four-carat gold cuff links from his dresser drawer, an antique pearl-handled letter opener from my office, and about five hundred dollars in cash from a small metal box we kept in one of the closets. I mean, I couldn't believe it was happening. I liked Laurie. I trusted her. But one morning, just two days after Wayne's funeral, I caught her going through my jewelry box. She'd already pocketed one of my favorite rings. I guess she figured I was too grief-stricken to notice what was happening. Well, I fired her on the spot, but she begged me to keep her on for another two weeks. She said she hadn't saved any money, and if her parents found out what she'd done, they'd kick her out of the house and she'd have no money and no place to live. I guess I'm a sucker for a sob story, so I let her stay until the end of the month. I checked her pockets and backpack every night before she left. On her final day, she took me aside and said she'd given it some thought and she wanted me to know that she planned to get even with me one day. Nobody messed up her life like I had and got away with it. I should have turned her over to the police right then and there. I regret now that I didn't."

"So you're saying the entire interview was a lie?"

"Absolutely. Arthur made an impassioned plea to everyone this morning. He denied *everything* the woman said about us. I mean, what she accused us of was totally insane! Thank God, they all listened to reason. As Arthur said, we can't let someone as morally bankrupt as Marie Damontraville destroy everything we've all worked so hard to build. Kenny stood immediately and backed him up. Of course, Kenny's primary concern is that his children receive their rightful inheritance. Same with Emily. And I want that, too. Nobody knows the kind of blood and sweat I've put into my career except me. And nobody, especially not some lowlife like Damontraville, is going to take it away from me with a bunch of unsubstantiated rumors."

"Did Nathan attend the meeting this morning?"

"Of course. Arthur drove out to New Fonteney last night and brought him home."

Sophie was relieved.

"I understand you found him for us. That was another reason I wanted to come up here this morning. I wanted to thank you."

"I was worried about him, too."

"I know. I couldn't be more pleased that you're back in his life again. I haven't seen him so happy in years." She uncrossed her legs and sat forward a little. "Listen, perhaps this is none of my business, but did Nathan say anything to you last night about the interview?"

"Nothing," replied Sophie. Here was another reason Constance had come. She wanted to find out what Sophie knew.

"Good. That's good. The less people who know about it, the better."

"What will you do if Marie Damontraville makes the information public?"

"We'll sue. Essentially, it all comes down to one embittered employee's word against mine and Arthur's. There are no other witnesses. That's the point I made at our meeting this morning. On the one hand you have Laurie Lippert, a thief, a woman who's carried a grudge all of her adult life. Damontraville simply put the gun in her hand. On the other side of the equation, you have an eminent clinical psychologist, a man who has helped thousands of people over the years with his books and his approach to personal therapy. And finally you have me, a national figure. My life is an open book, Sophie. My honesty is unquestioned. I don't think I'm being overly confident to believe a judge would take our word over hers. But we're still hoping we can do something to prevent the book from ever being published. Kenny is an excellent lawyer. And when it comes to the family business, he takes his job very seriously."

"I'm glad everyone's calmed down," said Sophie. "It's hard to live with a lot of family strife."

"Especially when it's so unnecessary."

Sophie had to reread the interview. She wasn't as confident as Constance was that if it came to a trial, it would be resolved that easily. Laurie Lippert's account was credible and compelling. Even if it didn't turn out to be true, all it would take was one person to sniff out the story and print it in a newspaper or a magazine. It would be like lobbing a hand grenade inside the Buckridge food tent. Sophie was certain that what had motivated Constance's children to keep silent on the matter wasn't just their belief in her ultimate innocence but rather their own sense of self-preservation.

Sophie had always known that Constance was a complex woman and that her reasons for acting the way she did were rarely ever simple. That's why she wondered if Constance hadn't appeared on her doorstep this morning for another reason as well.

Perhaps she thought that Nathan would eventually talk to Sophie about the interview. Before it happened she wanted to make her pitch that it was all a lie. Interestingly, she had explained *why* it had happened, but not *what* had happened. In essence, she'd programmed Sophie to adopt a certain position without revealing any of the details. If Sophie hadn't already read the interview, she might have taken Constance and Arthur's side out of . . . what? Loyalty? A sense of shared history? Lack of any real, concrete information? Or perhaps mere nostalgia? She'd known and liked these people in the past. How could they have changed that much? Whatever the case, Constance undoubtedly hoped to buy herself some insurance where Nathan was concerned by making sure Sophie *felt* she understood the real story, even though, cleverly, she'd never said what it was. And *that* little maneuver had created more doubt in Sophie's mind than anything Laurie Lippert had said.

Now that she'd gotten what she'd come for, Constance rose from the couch. "Well, I guess I'd better let you get some work done. You're a busy woman these days, I hear. I've taken up enough of your time with my problems."

But Sophie wasn't done yet. "How long will you be in town?"

"We're leaving on Sunday. Arthur and I, and then Emily and Kenny, will all go on to St. Louis. Paul flies back to New Haven. The academy is starting its summer semester next week, so he has to be there. And Nathan . . ." She paused, looking uncertain. "I'm not sure what his plans are. He told me this morning that he may stay on a while longer in Minnesota. I assume you have something to do with that."

"We definitely have some talking to do."

"Be kind to my son," said Constance, laying a hand lightly on Sophie's arm. "If for some reason you've decided you don't want to be with him, break it to him gently. He's been a lost soul for the past few years. We used to be so close when he was a boy. I would have done anything to make him happy. I still would."

"I know he loves you."

"And he loves you, too. Funny how the people we love can disappoint us the most. That's not meant as a criticism, Sophie. Or if it is, it's a criticism we both share. Nathan has always been my pride and joy, the heart and soul of my life. I just wish he'd confide in me the way he used to. I can't stand to see him in pain." She stopped when she got to the door, then turned around. "You have a son, don't you?"

"I do."

"He's how old?"

"Twenty-two."

"It's not easy being a mother, whether they're five or fifty. Sometimes what you do to make things better only makes things worse."

"I know."

"But we can't stop trying." Constance gazed at Sophie a moment longer, then suddenly gave her a hug. "Maybe it's not in the cards, but I hope you know how much I would have loved for you to become my daughter-in-law. When Nathan brought you home, I told him, 'That's the one. Don't let her get away.' "

"I had no idea—"

"You're a fine woman, Sophie. You're smart. Determined. And exceedingly kind. Sure, we all make mistakes, but you and Nathan would have been an unbeatable team. I hope you won't take my comments as some sort of undue pressure. They're really just the ramblings of an old woman who unfortunately understands regret all too well."

"You're not old, Constance. But you're right about it not being in the cards for Nathan and me. I'm sorry."

"I'm sorry, too. More sorry than you'll ever know."

25

"Don't push me, Kenny. Maybe you can go to St. Louis with her, but I can't. I can't even stand to look at her! Sleeping with her brother. It's disgusting!"

Sophie was standing outside the door to Emily and Kenny's suite. The Maxfield's walls were thick, but not thick enough to muffle the sound of shouting. She wasn't surprised to find that not everyone in Constance's close-knit family had believed her story.

"Calm down," Kenny demanded, though his own voice sounded anything but calm. "Can't you at least give your mother the benefit of the doubt?"

"No! And you wouldn't either if she'd let your father die in agony. Good God, she didn't even lift a finger to help him!"

"If you believe that Laurie Lippert's story, yes. But I don't. And I think it's outrageous that you'd take a total stranger's word over your mother's."

"That's because you don't know what I know."

"Meaning what?" He sounded annoyed.

"She never loved my father."

"Here we go again."

"She didn't! That's why he was so depressed all the time. Dad did everything he could to make her happy. He took her on tons of trips, paid for her millions of cooking lessons, ate all the crap she served him without ever complaining that it was too rich or too sweet or just too freaking *much*. And where did it get him? He died a hundred pounds overweight and alone."

"Are you saying she tried to feed him to death?"

"Don't patronize me."

"Emily, be reasonable."

"You think you know everything because you're older than me? Or is it because you're one of the county's preeminent scum-sucking bottom feeders?"

"Why do you always insult my profession when we get into an argument? If it weren't for me, sweetie, your mother's business would already be in ruins."

"Look, all I'm saying is, my mother broke my father's spirit. And she did it deliberately. I was only a kid, but I knew the score. I tried to be there for him when he was down, but all he ever wanted was her. Sometimes he seemed almost desperate."

"You're exaggerating. All families have problems. Mine sure did. Did I ever tell you about my cousin Arnold?"

"I don't want to hear about your goddamn cousin again! Maybe I'm not as hard-assed as you are. Or maybe I'm too sensitive. But you weren't there. I was! I saw the desperation in my father's eyes when he'd kiss her goodbye in the morning. It was still there when he got home at night. He was like a little boy begging for affection. Oh, I'm not suggesting that Mom wasn't pleasant. She was always pleasant. Except for Paul, everyone in the whole freaking family was pleasant."

"Is that bad?"

"It's stifling! Dad may have been packing away the food, but he was literally starving to death. Eventually, all he had were his pies and cakes. Do you know how that made me feel? I needed him. Paul needed him. But all he wanted was *her*."

"You really hate your mother, don't you?"

"Yes! I thought I'd put the anger behind me, but this trip's brought it all back in living color."

"I'm sorry you came. I never should have suggested it. I just thought . . . I mean, I wanted to see where you were born, where you grew up. I hoped it would bring us closer together. Believe it or not, I do love you, Emily."

"You mean you love my mother's money."

"Sure!" he shouted. "So what if I do? But is it so impossible to believe I care about you, too? About our children and what we could give them if we only hang in there? I'm not like your brothers. I'm not a driven jock like Paul, and I'm certainly not handsome and noble like Nathan. I'm just an average guy—albeit an exceedingly smart lawyer—who played some angles once and won. Along the way I happened to fall in love with the fairy princess, the one I was planning to swindle."

" 'The Fairy Princess and the Swindler'. Refresh my memory. Was that by Hans Christian Andersen or Tom Wolfe?"

"I'm not the Prince Charming type, right?"

"You said it. I didn't."

"You know, Emily, sometimes you remind me of your mother. You accuse her of being an ice queen. The next time you speak to your mirror, take a good look at yourself."

There was silence inside the suite. Sophie leaned her head closer to the door.

After a few seconds, Kenny said, "I just wish I knew who slipped that interview under our door. I suppose it was Damontraville."

Again no response.

Finally, Kenny called, "Get back in here. We're not finished."

"I am!" came Emily's muted shout.

Sophie assumed that she'd left the room. It might not be good form to eavesdrop on other people's conversations, but in this case Sophie couldn't help herself. She'd been there during the last two years before Wayne died. She'd eaten at their table, laughed at their jokes. And all the while she'd had absolutely no idea that these emotional undercurrents even existed.

After another full minute of silence, Sophie decided to knock. If the argument wasn't over, they could resume it after she left.

Kenny answered the door. Removing a cigarette from his mouth, he said, "Sophie, hi."

"Morning. I was hoping to talk to Emily for a few minutes."

He glanced over his shoulder. "She's in the bedroom packing. I'm sure she'd love some company. She's clearly tired of mine." He stepped back, taking another drag on the cigarette, then stubbed it out in an ashtray. "Actually, I was just on my way out, so you ladies can gab to your hearts' content."

"Don't leave on my account."

"I wouldn't. Constance has a book signing in St. Cloud this afternoon and I'm driving her up."

"You've got a beautiful day."

"Lucky us," he said, feeling in his pocket for his car keys. "Emily," he called, "you've got a guest. Try not to draw blood. She's just an innocent bystander." Nodding to Sophie, he closed the door on his way out.

Emily emerged from the bedroom folding a sweater. "Hey, what a nice surprise."

Sophie tried not to stare. Since the last time she'd seen Emily, her long golden hair had been transformed into a jumble of different-colored dreadlocks. Orange. Purple. Red. Green. She'd wound a wide paisley scarf around her head and the dreadlocks exploded out the back. "What did you do to your hair?"

She touched one of the braids. "I got bored. Do you like it?"

"It's . . . dramatic."

"Yeah. I needed a new look. My kids won't even recognize me."

"Did you go to a salon?"

"There's a fabulous one just up the street. I mean, when Mom's off doing one of her interviews, what am I supposed to do? I'm not that interested in photographing downtown St. Paul. Kenny's always busy with tour details. Paul's been nothing but a grump. And Nathan's never around. Anyway," she said, sitting down in the living room and motioning for Sophie to do the same. "What can I do for you?"

"I was hoping to get some information."

"About what?"

Sophie perched on the arm of a club chair. "I don't know if you're aware of this, but I have a twenty-two-year-old son."

"Yeah, Nathan mentioned him. Rudy, right?"

"That's right. He just graduated from the University of Minnesota. During his senior year, he had a part-time job in our hotel kitchen and discovered that he really likes working with food. I thought I should ask one of you about the Buckridge Culinary Academy."

"Paul could give you much more information."

"I knocked on his door," she lied. "Nobody's home."

Tapping a finger against her cheek, Emily said, "Oh, that's right. He did say he had some business out of the hotel today."

"I'd just like to get a general feel for the place."

"Well, hmm. What can I tell you?" She thought for a moment. "It's on the semester system. One fall and one spring, and then a shorter summer session. Oh, and it's expensive."

"I assumed as much."

"But it's worth it. The grounds are beautiful. And the facilities are state-of-the-art."

"How many new students do you accept each year?"

"Around twenty-five. Rudy would have to go through a fairly rigorous selection process."

"So you don't just take anybody who walks in the door and hands you a check."

"Hardly. Paul says that to become a chef, even to go through chef's training, a person has to be really committed. I don't get it myself. That's why you should talk to him. I mean, they work those poor idiots like they're on some sort of prison ship. While you're at the academy you eat, breathe, and sleep food. It would drive me crazy. But the students—the ones who don't wash out—seem to love it. Rudy would live in New Haven and commute to the campus. There aren't any dorms."

"Why's that?"

"If a student doesn't make it to class in bad weather—a blizzard, a monsoon, a killer tornado—he's not going to make it to his restaurant after he graduates, and that's unthinkable. Chefs *get* there, according to Paul. They're passionate about their work. And that's what we train, the men and women who will be the future leaders in the culinary community. We aren't interested in training food-service workers. That's for someone else to do, like vo-techs."

"Does Constance do much lecturing?"

Emily placed the folded sweater on the coffee table. "Maybe once or twice a year. Nathan does special demos every now and then. He's a wonderful teacher. When it comes to food, he's got this amazingly creative mind. He's probably more talented than anyone else in the family. I don't count, by the way. I think the stork delivered me to the wrong address. Give me a cheese and pickle sandwich and some carrot sticks and I'm in heaven."

Sophie laughed. "Yeah, you were never much of a foodie. But, tell me now, is Paul in charge of the school, day to day?"

"That's right. He's got this amazing office on the top floor of the administration building. Pretty snazzy digs for my grubby brother. But then I guess he's not so grubby anymore."

"How about Nathan?"

"He's not there enough to need his own office."

"And your mother?"

"Oh, sure, she has one, but it's just because of who she is. She's not around much either. Usually, if Nathan or Kenny—or even if I—need a place to work when we're there, that's the office we all use."

"Then if I wanted to send a note to Nathan at the academy, I'd send it to that office?"

"A love note?"

"None of your business, Emily."

She grinned. "It's room 404, Buckridge Culinary Academy, New Haven, Connecticut. You'll have to get the zip from someone else. Oh, and if you'd like to fax him, Mom's office has its own private number. I know Kenny uses it all the time for academy business. It came in pretty handy for me, too, when I was working on Mom's new cookbook."

Sophie held up her hand. "Faxes are too public."

"Too public for what?" Another grin.

Sophie was thrilled. She'd easily found the information she'd come looking for. The hard part would be figuring out who'd used the fax in Constance's office to send a message to George Gildemeister.

Noticing that one of Kenny's cigarettes was still burning in the ashtray, Emily got up and crushed it out. "God, I hate those things."

"I thought you smoked."

"I do, but those things stink." She scrunched up her nose in distaste. "I like good old-fashioned menthol weeds. Nathan prefers Marlboros. God, you'd think he was a marine or something. And before Paul quit, he'd smoke anything that didn't crawl away fast enough. Sticks. Pencils. Chalk. An occasional asparagus spear."

"It's wonderful that he was able to stop."

"Well, he's stop*ping*. Mom thinks he's got a will of iron, but I've seen him fall off the wagon a few times when he thought nobody was watching. We're all supposed to be smoke free by the end of the year. Like that's going to happen. You'd have to saw off Arthur's hands to get him to quit. It's the family curse."

"I guess we're all cursed with something."

"God, look at the time," said Emily. "I've got a lunch date in less than an hour and look at me. I've got to shower and dress."

"And that's my cue to leave." Sophie got up off the arm of the chair.

"Maybe you'll be coming out to New Haven to visit Nathan one of these days," said Emily, walking her to the door.

"I don't know."

"Well, I'll keep my fingers crossed. Not that I envy you getting involved with the Buckridges again. What is it they say? This isn't a family; it's a life sentence."

Sophie smiled. So did Emily. But they both knew she wasn't joking.

Journal Note

Friday afternoon

As I type, I'm sitting in my car on Penn Avenue in south Minneapolis.

A major surprise in my E-mail this morning. A note from Pluto. It seems he's figured out that I'm no longer staying at the Maxfield. That means, of course, that he's been watching my room. Not that I didn't assume it already.

But that wasn't the surprise. He said he wanted to meet with me in person. I thought I might get a rise out of him after I sent off the Laurie Lippert interview yesterday, but I never expected this. I almost couldn't believe it. And then, when I realized he was serious, I had to think about it long and hard before I responded. I was simply too curious not to go, but I also thought it might be a trick of some kind, or at the very least I knew some risk was involved. I needed to minimize my vulnerability. That meant the place where we agreed to meet had to be public, with lots of people around.

It didn't seem logical to me that Pluto was the same person who'd threatened my life—and taken Rafferty's—but the fact that he was connected in some way with the Buckridge family gave me pause. He still refused to identify himself. I assumed his reticence was based on his own fears, whatever that might mean. He suggested a park near downtown Minneapolis, one that's very open and always has lots of people in it. He said he knew what I looked like and he'd find me. I suppose we could have used Rice Park in St. Paul, but it's too close to the Maxfield. Someone might have spotted us. So I replied to his E-mail and agreed to his terms. We'd rendezvous at Loring Park at noon. Turns out it wasn't far from where I stayed last night.

As soon as I sent off my answer, I got to wondering. Which Buckridge would I finally meet face-to-face? Who hated Constance enough to want to see her reputation trashed in what would undoubtedly become a New York Times *bestseller? I went through all the names. Paul. Nathan. Emily. Arthur.*

Kenneth. *Actually, last night, I even began to toy with the idea that Constance herself was Pluto. It would certainly appeal to her more Machiavellian instincts.*

What if, in a sense, Constance had hired me—without paying a dime—to make sure her past was buried so deep that no one would ever find the truth, no matter how hard they tried? Taking that theory a step further, if I continue to pass information on to Pluto, I might be ensuring that Slice and Dice *will never be published. Before it went to press, I'm sure my sources would have all been bought off, threatened, or even worse. And so, as of last night, I'd made the decision to cut Pluto out of the loop. He'd been as helpful as he was probably ever going to be, and I had to put the book first.*

And then I got the E-mail this morning, which was a total curveball. By now, Pluto probably knows me pretty well. And that means he knew I couldn't turn down the opportunity to meet my "Deep Throat" face-to-face.

So shortly before noon I hooked up my lapel mike, the one I use when my subject is uncooperative and won't allow me to record the interview. It's probably illegal in this state to record someone's voice without his or her knowledge, but I always do it, just for my own protection. The special tape recorder consists of a cordless mike inside a gold pin I wear on the lapel of my blazer. The recorder itself remains in my purse.

At noon, I was seated on a bench a few yards from a small bridge, where I passed the time by feeding the remains of my lunch to a couple of unusually friendly squirrels. The park itself is fairly flat. Right in the center is a small lake—man-made, I'm told, but lovely nonetheless. People were sitting on the grass eating lunch. Some men were playing horseshoes on a dirt range. The tennis courts were full. Across the street from the park is the Guthrie Theater, the Walker Art Center, and the Minneapolis Sculpture Gardens. Up the street is the Basilica of St. Mary's. So Pluto had kept his word. He did pick a spot that was highly public, with lots of foot traffic.

As I waited, hiding behind my sunglasses, I checked out everyone that approached. By twelve-fifteen I began to wonder if I was going to be stood up. Then, strolling over the bridge carrying a briefcase, Pluto appeared. Was I surprised when I finally saw who it was?

Not really.

The truth is, if I'd had to bet, I would have placed my money on Paul Buckridge. He had the most tenuous connection to Constance. He wasn't related by blood. When his real mother died all those years ago, he may have resented the fact that Constance became his "new mom." Then yesterday he found out that Constance had allowed his father to die without so much as lifting a finger to help. And after reading the interviews I'd sent him, he had to have some questions about Constance's role in his mother's death. Perhaps he'd had those questions even before I began my research. I was about to find out.

INTERVIEW: PAUL BUCKRIDGE, LORING PARK, FRIDAY, MAY 14TH

M: *I thought you weren't going to make it.*

Paul: *I was delayed at the hotel. My mother's on the warpath about you, Ms. Damontraville. She wants you stopped. You were smart to leave the Maxfield when you did.*

M: *I didn't have a choice. Your mother had some thug blow up my bodyguard and his car. I could have been killed—and Rafferty was.*

Paul: *But you're okay. I was horrified when I heard the news, but as long as you remain undercover, you'll stay that way.*

M: *It's no way to live.*

Paul: *It'll be over soon. Once Connie realizes she can't win, that she'll be exposed one way or the other, she'll back off.*

M: *From your lips to God's ears.*

Paul: *I'm right. You'll see.*

M: *You haven't told her anything specific, have you? You've kept all our communications a secret?*

Paul: *I want you to be free to do your work. That's why I'm here. I've got something for you. (Opens briefcase and removes some papers) You asked for my mother's medical records. Here they are. I've also included all her insurance reports. I've had these copies for some time, even before I came back to Minnesota. You can see that my mother was sick from May of '63 through December. She died on the sixteenth. Just to refresh your memory, Connie Jadek took over as cook in June '63.*

M: *So you suspect your mother's death wasn't natural?*

Paul: *I think she was poisoned.*

M: *By Constance?*

Paul: *(Nods) I can't prove it, but I think she was after my father from the day she began working for us. The only way she could get him to marry her, which was what she was after, was to get rid of my mother.*

M: *You really believe she's that ruthless?*

Paul: *Without a doubt. I mean, she let my father die after she got what she wanted, right? Laurie Lippert said exactly that.*

M: *She married your father for his money?*

Paul: *Sure, and his position in the community. She used him. He loved her—God knows why—and he bent over backward to give her everything her heart desired. When he wasn't needed any longer, when he stood between her and her endless appetites, she as good as killed him with her own two hands. She's sick and perverted, and evil to the core. Look at what she was willing to do to you to stop your book from being published! Yes, Ms. Damontraville, I think Connie Jadek is capable of anything.*

M: *So what did she use to poison your mother?*

Paul: *It's right there in your interview with Phil Rapson. Antifreeze.*

M: *You mean the antifreeze Nathan took from the garage?*

Paul: *(Nods)*

M: *But Nathan said that it was Wayne who asked him to get it for him.*

Paul: *Isn't it obvious? Nathan lied. My father didn't even know what Phil was talking about when he asked about that leak in the car's radiator. There never was a leak in my father's radiator. Nathan got the antifreeze for his mother.*

M: *You think Nathan was in on it?*

Paul: *(Shakes his head) He was a poor dupe, just like my father.*

M: *I'm curious. What do you think of Nathan?*

Paul: *I like the guy. I mean, we never agree on anything, not even the time of day, but that's okay. He's a decent, hard-working person, and an extraordinarily talented chef. I respect that. I just wish he weren't related to Connie. If she'd been out of the picture, I think we could have been really good friends. He's always felt such loyalty to her that I could never completely trust him. She inspires loyalty in some people, I guess, but she'll never get it from me. I see right through her act. So does my sister. We've never been able to put any pressure on Nathan because we both knew he'd always take her side, and neither Emily nor I want to lose him. He'll never be a Buckridge, like Emily and me, but after all these years he's family.*

M: *What about Arthur Jadek?*

Paul: *Yeah, what about him? He's a pervert, just like his sister. He tried to be a father figure to us after Dad died, but I didn't buy it. I resented him, almost as much as I resented Connie for trying to replace my mother.*

M: *Do you think he and Constance continued their sexual relationship?*

Paul: *It wouldn't surprise me. Then again a couple years after Dad died, Arthur went away to get his doctorate. He was gone for several years. And then he lived in Chicago for a while, where he did postdoctoral work at Northwestern. He finally settled down in Boston. Became a professor of clinical psychology at Boston College. He wrote a few books during that period. Since we were in New Haven by then, he and Connie got together quite often. And he was always around at Thanksgiving and Christmas. He'd take his summer vacations with us. So I suppose if they were sexually involved, they must have gone for long periods apart. Maybe it was just that one time. I don't know and frankly I don't care. I hate them both for what they've done to my family. I wish we'd never heard of Arthur and Connie Jadek.*

M: *Tell me, Paul. Why did you contact me several months back with that tantalizing offer to help me dig up dirt on Constance Buckridge? What precipitated it? And why the anonymity and the name Pluto?*

Paul: *(Holds up his hand) That's a lot of questions. I was hoping to make this a short meeting.*

M: *But you can't leave without giving me some answers. Please. It's important to me, especially if you want me to risk my safety by continuing my research.*

Paul: *(Thinks about it for a few moments) Well, I guess, in the back of my mind, I'd always felt there was something odd about my mother's death. I was only a kid at the time—four when she died—but I had eyes and ears, and things didn't feel right to me. People were sneaking around. Doing a lot of whispering.*

M: *What people?*

Paul: *I don't remember. I just remember that people stopped talking when I came into a room. Maybe it was my dad. Or maybe it was Connie. But I was left with the impression that the adults around me knew something I didn't. And since my mother had just died, I assumed it had to do with her. You realize, of course, that the big scandal I thought you'd uncover was the fact that Mom had been poisoned. The other stuff you've found came as a complete shock. But we still don't have the answer to my mother's death, and we can't give up until we do. I hired some private investigators a couple years ago, but they never got anywhere. All it did was make me more frustrated—and more determined.*

M: *But was it just a childhood feeling you were going on? That's all? There has been nothing else that led you to the conclusion that your mother had been poisoned?*

Paul: *This may sound sort of silly, but the fact is, a few years back, a neighbor of mine came rushing over to my house one* day. His dog was sick and he needed to get him to the vet right away, but his wife had the car. They had a second car, a beater, but it wasn't working. He'd been puttering around with it in the garage for days, trying to figure out why it wouldn't start. Anyway, he wanted me to drive him. When I saw the dog, I was shocked. I mean, I'd known him since he was a pup. He was a cute little guy, about fifteen pounds. Curly brown hair. He was always bright and frisky, ready to play at the drop of a hat, but that day he seemed disoriented, almost drunk. He was dizzy. Very unsteady on his feet, and at the same time lethargic. By the time we pulled into the parking lot of the pet clinic, he'd begun to vomit. He was obviously in pain. We got him into the examination room right away and the vet checked him over, but it was too late. He died on the examination table. That's when the vet started asking a bunch of questions. Did my neighbor have any open bottles of antifreeze around? Sure, he said. He'd been working on his car in the garage. He'd drained the old antifreeze into a pan so that he could work on the radiator. The vet said that the dog had probably ingested some of it. Apparently tons of dogs and cats die every year because of antifreeze poisoning. It tastes good, kind of sweet, and given any chance at all, they'll go for it. It doesn't take much to kill a dog, and even less to kill a cat. Needless to say, my neighbor was devastated. He said he didn't know how he was going to explain it to his wife and kids. If he'd only known, he would never have been so careless. We stayed and talked a few more minutes, and then the neighbor went into the back room, where they got the dog ready to take home. He wanted to bury him in the backyard. Anyway, the vet and I were in the examination room by ourselves for a few minutes. I mentioned, jokingly, that it seemed like the dog had had the same general symptoms my mother did before she died. He said, Oh, humans are easily poisoned by antifreeze, too. Every now and then he'd read a case about it in the paper. It was hard to trace, because it mimicked so many other health problems. I told him my mother had been ill for *about seven months before she died. She'd gone to a lot of doctors and had a bunch of tests run, but nobody had ever been able to help her, or even figure out what was wrong. Every guy had a theory, but none of them matched. I told him that I thought my father had finally given up in frustration and decided she was a hypochondriac. She did have those tendencies, I guess. That's when the vet asked what her specific symptoms were. I thought about it for a minute, then said that she had been very tired all the time. She'd slept a lot. She had frequent bouts of vomiting and abdominal pain. I remember that vividly. She'd lost a lot of weight. Also, she'd been dizzy, had major trouble with her balance, and that's why she had eventually stopped driving. And then she'd always complained of headaches and back pain, especially when I wanted her to play with me. I think my father mentioned once that she had unusually low blood pressure. And right before she died, she'd had some vision problems. I recall that because I used to have to sit very close to her when I'd go into her room. Otherwise she couldn't see me. The vet listened to all of it, then said that it was really hard to diagnose something like that years after the fact, but that everything I'd told him was consistent with antifreeze—he called it ethylene glycol—poisoning in humans. I left that veterinary office with my head spinning. Surely my mother hadn't been poisoned. It was unthinkable. But the more I thought about it, the more it made sense. That's when I sent for the medical and insurance records. I did my own research and it sure looked to me like a definite possibility. I even considered having my mother's body exhumed, but I knew I'd have a fight on my hands with the rest of the family if I didn't have more proof. The private investigators were a bust, so—*

M: *You found me.*

Paul: *(Smiles) I was at a bookstore one afternoon, browsing, and there was the book you'd just done on Elton John. You were exactly what I needed. I don't mind telling you that I have no qualms about destroying Constance Buckridge, Ms. Damontraville. I'd survive the scandal just fine. So would the academy. And so would Emily. Beyond that, let the chips fall where they may. When I read that interview with Rapson, the part where he mentions Nathan sneaking into the garage for a gallon jug of antifreeze, well, right then and there I knew we had her. I mean, it just made me more positive than ever that Connie poisoned my mother. One serendipitous element to this whole poisoning thing is, my mother liked to drink. And the worse she felt, the more depressed she got, the more she drank. Turns out that the antidote to antifreeze is alcohol. If you know someone has inadvertently drunk some ethylene glycol and you get them to an emergency room, that's one of the treatments. Because Mom was drinking fairly heavily at the time of the attempted poisoning, the alcohol interfered with the breakdown of the antifreeze. See, the booze competes for the same metabolizing enzyme as the antifreeze. And since plain alcohol wins, the antifreeze is excreted unmetabolized by the kidneys. That's why it took her so long to die.*

M: *How ghastly!*

Paul: *It's appalling. But right now it's only a theory. You've got to help me prove it's true.*

M: *I'll do my very best, Paul. You already know that. (Long pause) But you didn't answer one question. Why did you pick the name Pluto?*

Paul: *I thought you would have guessed. That was the name of my neighbor's dog. I just thought it had a certain symmetry to it. Pluto led me to the truth about my mother. And Pluto was going to be your guide, too.*

M: *And the reason you wanted to remain anonymous?*

Paul: *I didn't know if I could trust you. Now I realize I can. Only problem is, we haven't got much time. My mother's going to mount a campaign against this book that will tie your publisher up in legal knots for years. Kenny Merlin will see to it. You need to get the information, then get back to New York, or wherever the hell you do your work, and write. We'll get the press in this country so worked up about it, nothing will be able to stop the book from coming out. It's simple freedom of speech. Not even my mother can abridge that. (Hands over the records)*

M: *I'll have a physician go over them, just to make sure we're on the right track.*

Paul: *Fine. Remember, don't contact me in person. Use my E-mail address, or my cell phone. (writes down number.)*

M: *When are you leaving?*

Paul: *Sunday morning. Try to nail something down before then, okay? It's important we keep the momentum going. The idea that she'll finally be exposed for what she really is, well, it's driving her crazy and I've got a ringside seat. (Grins from ear to ear) Did I promise you a great story or what?*

M: *You did, indeed.*

Paul: *You'll make a small fortune on this one.*

M: *And what do you get out of it?*

Paul: *(Another smile) Revenge. That's what this is all about. Connie Jadek's head on a plate, her total destruction. But somehow, now that I'm this close, it hardly seems enough for what she did to my mother and father.*

26

"You've got to find her!" demanded Constance. She was pacing in front of the windows in her suite, feeling as if the life she'd taken for granted was about to be snatched away from her. Arthur had gone downstairs to buy some cigarettes for both of them. This wasn't the time to kick the habit.

"Just . . . take a pill or something," snapped Kenny. "Pour yourself a drink. But calm down." He sat casually on the couch, obviously annoyed by Constance's anxious mood. "You've been acting like this all day. The people at that bookstore in St. Cloud must have thought you were on something."

"If your reputation was on the line, you'd want that Damontraville woman found, too!"

"It's not just your reputation that's hanging in the balance,
Constance, it's my livelihood. It affects me, my wife, and my
children. I never should have tied my star to a sinking ship.
Gee," he said, looking mildly shocked, "I think I just mixed
my metaphors."

"How can you take this so lightly?" By now, her heart was
pounding. Maybe she did need a drink.

"I'm hardly taking the situation lightly. You've made it perfectly clear how important this is, how desperate you are. I'm
handling it, Constance. Have I ever failed you before?"

She shook her head.

"And I won't now. I've got three of the top private investigators in the Midwest out looking for Damontraville even as
we speak."

"Hire ten. Twenty. I don't care what it takes, we've got to
find her and stop her." She fell into a resentful silence. Finally, walking over to the wet bar and removing a bottle of
vodka from the freezer, she said, "What if she releases what
she knows to the press?"

"She won't. It would steal her thunder. She's saving it all
for the book she's writing."

"God, I hope that's true. At least it would give us some
time."

He raised a cynical eyebrow. "You know, Constance, I'm
only human. I'd like to know why I'm busting my ass to keep
yours above water. Maybe you should tell me all your secrets
before they're discovered and put on display for the whole
world to see."

"Don't be ridiculous. I've got nothing to hide."

He sighed heavily, clearly out of patience with her. Grabbing a handful of cashews from a container on the coffee
table, he popped a couple into his mouth, then glared at her as
he chewed.

Constance decided to pour herself that drink. After downing
several swallows, she noticed that he looked tired, his face
drawn with fatigue. This hadn't been easy on any of them.

"Don't tell me you actually believe what that ex-employee of mine said? Arthur and I could never do anything so loathsome. And as far as Wayne's death goes—"

He held up his hand. "Save it for the cameras."

"But it's important that you believe me."

"Why?"

"Because you're family."

"Funny. Paul seems to think that if your last name isn't Buckridge, you're not quite human. You may have been married to *the man*, Constance, but you're every bit as suspect as I am."

"That's not true."

"Wake up, woman. Paul despises you. What he found out yesterday only added fuel to his fire."

She carried her drink to a chair and sat down. She knew Kenny might be right, but she'd never permitted herself to dwell on it. She'd been too busy with her career to worry about Paul and his childhood resentments. In a way, she supposed he was just another casualty in the mess she'd made of her life. Not that she'd done it all by herself. The great Wayne Buckridge bore as much responsibility for the mess as she did.

Hearing a knock at the door, she said, "Will you get that? Arthur probably forgot his key again."

"I'm not the butler."

"Oh, forgive me. I wouldn't want you to put an inadvertent crease in your suit by doing some physical labor." He was such a prima donna. "I'll get it myself."

"No," he said, rising from the couch. "I have to leave anyway. I've got to drive Emily to the airport."

She cocked her head. "The airport? Why?"

"She's going home."

"But we're all supposed to fly to St. Louis on Sunday."

"She changed her mind."

"Without telling me?" When he opened the door, Constance saw Nathan standing outside.

"Another Buckridge in name only. Come on in, bro. Join the party."

Constance drained the last of the vodka from her glass, then stood. She felt unreasonably happy to see him, even though she feared he'd come to give her more bad news. Perhaps he was leaving, too. Her greatest fear was that everyone would leave her in the end. She breathed in deeply to calm herself.

"I'd like to talk to my mother alone," Nathan said coldly, standing just inside the door.

"No problem." Kenny smiled. "I was just on my way out." Looking back at Constance, he said, "I'll be in touch the minute I hear anything."

"Good." She paused, then added, "When are you and Emily leaving?"

He checked his watch. "In about an hour."

"Tell her I want to talk to her first."

"I'll give her the message. I can't promise anything."

As the door closed, Nathan asked, "Is Arthur here?"

"He's down in the lobby."

He nodded. Walking around for a few seconds as if he was searching for a place to sit but couldn't find a surface that suited him, he finally lowered himself into the chair next to his mother.

"I'm so glad to see you," she said, trying to steady her voice as she resumed her own seat. "I was hoping you'd come with us to the bookstore in St. Cloud."

"I couldn't. I, ah . . . had some business to take care of. Actually, I've got something to tell you. It's important."

"What is it?"

He cleared his throat. "I'm buying New Fonteney. As of this afternoon, I'm giving you notice that I intend to quit my job as the national manager of the B.C.A. restaurants."

Her eyes widened. "But, Nathan? I don't understand."

"I'm going to live at the old monastery, Mom. I'm moving back to Minnesota for good. I've put down a substantial down payment, and I plan to get a bank loan for the rest. I intend to turn the place into a restaurant or a cooking school. I haven't decided which, but I've got plenty of money in the bank to live on until I do. Whatever I decide, with my credentials, it shouldn't be a problem."

"Is this because of Sophie?"

"Partly. I signed the purchase agreement yesterday and I was hoping to give her the good news last night. But when that interview dropped on us out of the blue, I couldn't." He scratched the side of his beard, then looked away. "I hope I can convince her to leave her husband and marry me someday, but whether she does or not, I'm putting down roots here. I've had enough traveling to last me the rest of my life."

"But I thought you liked to travel."

"Traveling's okay, I guess, but I've been running away from my life, Mom, or, more specifically, from my lack of a life. This may be my last chance to create something of my own."

Constance gripped her hands together in her lap. "But a bank loan. You don't need to do that. You can borrow the money from me."

"No." His voice was sharp. "This has to be something I do on my own. If it fails, I'm the only one to blame. I'm sick of working with other people, letting them call the shots, make the decisions I should be making."

"You mean Kenny?"

"Kenny. Paul. You. New Fonteney is going to be mine. I love it out there. It's the paradise I thought I'd never find."

Constance suddenly felt frightened. "Are you leaving me because of what that awful woman said in that interview?"

"Mom, listen to me. I made the decision to buy the monastery before any of that came up. And I'm not leaving you. I'm just changing jobs."

They both knew it wasn't that simple. "Then you believe what I said this morning? It was all a lie, you know. I would never sleep with my brother! And Wayne, his heart gave out. There was nothing I could do."

His gaze dropped to the carpet. "You'd better prepare yourself for the worst, Mom. If you can't stop Marie Damontraville's book, you're going to have to figure out how to handle it in the media. You can deny it, of course, but there's still going to be fallout. How bad it will be is anyone's guess."

"I'll sue!"

"If you do, other information could come out. Do you understand what I'm saying?" He fixed her with his intense brown eyes. "You have to be careful. Maybe Damontraville found out about Pepper Buckridge, or maybe she didn't. Until we have all the facts, we have to play it cool."

Constance felt a thump of alarm in her chest. "God," she whispered, "do you realize what it could mean if the police find out? There's no statute of limitations on murder."

Nathan squeezed her hand reassuringly. "Trust me. I've still got a few cards up my sleeve."

"But if she finds out, how can we stop her? Kenny's got men out all over the city trying to locate her. And even if we do find her, what if we can't scare her off or buy her off?"

"I'll take care of it," said Nathan. "I've always protected you and I won't stop now. I plan to be away from the hotel tonight, but I don't want you to worry. I've got something I need to do."

"What?"

"Just cross your fingers and wish me luck."

"Nathan, if anything ever happened to you—"

"Nothing's going to happen to me. But do me a favor. Tell the rest of the family that I'm calling a meeting for seven tomorrow night. By then I should have a solution to this whole mess. I want everyone to come out to New Fonteney."

"Why not meet here? It would be much easier."

"No. It has to be New Fonteney. *My* turf."

"Can't you give me some idea of what this is about?"

He rose from his chair. "Tomorrow, Mom. Think good thoughts, okay? With any luck, this will be over soon."

27

"What a story," said Sophie, tossing the last of the interviews on the dining room table. She'd been reading for almost forty-five minutes, trying hard to distinguish fact from opinion. "But I still don't get it. Marie Damontraville just *gave* these to you?"

Bram was sitting across from her, nursing his after-dinner iced tea. "She needed someone she could talk to. An unbiased ear."

"So she picks you? Someone who's almost a total stranger?"

"What can I say? I've got a face women trust."

Sophie did a double take. "That's not exactly the way I'd describe your effect on women. The night I saw you together I got the distinct impression that Ms. Damontraville was giving you the eye."

"The evil eye?"

"No, dear. She was flirting. And," she said, pausing for effect, "she looked distinctly predatory. Like a hawk zooming in on a mouse."

"How flattering."

"Just an observation."

He shrugged indifferently. "We merely bumped into each other one night. She realized she'd been on my radio show a few years back. We got to talking. She was really shaken up after she got that threatening note pushed under her door. Then Kenneth Merlin shows up to bribe her off the story. She was alone in town, Soph. I got drawn into the whole mess simply because I'm a good listener. And that's the truth. I will say that when she finally came clean and told me she was working on a biography of Constance Buckridge, she caught my interest immediately. I mean, if it turns out this ex-boyfriend of yours comes from a long line of serial killers or psychopaths, I wanted to know about it."

"Please," Sophie muttered, leaning back in her chair. She wondered if she'd made a mistake by starting out the evening with the announcement that, on May 7, George Gilde-meister had received a fax from someone at the Buckridge Culinary Academy instructing him to make his review—his second critique of the Belmont—even more vitriolic than it already was.

When Bram heard the news, he was appalled.

Sophie added that one could easily infer from the situation that George had sent a draft to Constance or one of her inner circle in order to obtain approval. Why? Very simple. Money had been offered in exchange for a scathing review. Sophie and Bram both agreed that it was disgusting. They also agreed that there was no reason why it shouldn't have worked—unless, as Sophie pointed out, George suddenly came down with an attack of guilty conscience.

After reading all the interviews, Sophie was itching to know what had gone on in that family all those years ago and what impact it had on the present.

"It's not impossible that Nathan's behind it all," said Bram, using his deep, authoritative radio voice.

"Is that your opinion or Walter Cronkite's?"

He folded his arms over his chest. "Nathan could have been the one who murdered Gildemeister." Nodding toward the interviews, he added, "He also could have poisoned Pepper Buckridge. After all, he took the antifreeze from the garage. We have an eyewitness to attest to that."

"Bram, he was only nine years old."

"So?"

"Behavior like that would make him a total sociopath."

"And precocious, too. Look, somebody in that family planted a bomb in Sean Rafferty's car, and it wasn't Nathan's dear old mama. I doubt Constance knows all that much about internal combustion engines. And now I find out that Nathan was in Gildemeister's apartment the night he died—and that he might be part of a plot to sink the Belmont so that the Buckridges can add a new gourmet bistro to the growing list of academy-run restaurants. Maybe he's behind everything, Sophie. He's certainly in a pivotal position."

She shook her head. "I can't accept it."

"Why not? Because you're still in love with him?"

Now he'd gone too far. "Don't turn this into something it isn't, Bram. I'm not in love with Nathan. It's just . . . I know him better than you do. He's a good man. A gentle man. He could never murder anyone."

"Most people who commit murder don't have two horns and a tail. They look just like you and me. And they do what they do, not because they're evil or sick, but because their backs are to the wall and they see no other way out."

She knew he had a point. That's when she recalled what Nathan had said to her on Wednesday night. He'd warned her not to get too close to him because she might get burned. She'd taken it as a veiled comment on the sexually charged nature of their relationship. But after what she had found out today, she wondered if he hadn't been talking about something else. Perhaps he'd been referring once again to his "frustrated system." In light of what she now knew, the comment took on an ominous portent. What if he had jettisoned his conscience, his sense of right and wrong? "Look, Bram, Nathan came clean about being at George's apartment that night. He even told me why he was there."

"Which could all be a lie. If he'd murdered the man, he's hardly going to tell you the truth, especially if he's trying to wheedle his way back into your life."

"That's not going to happen and he knows it."

"For all I know, Sophie, he already has."

She closed her eyes. This was a nightmare. Bram couldn't know what had happened, yet he sensed something was different. But it *wasn't* different. She'd slept with Nathan, but it would never happen again. "Please, sweetheart, just drop it. You're making way too much of something that was over a long time ago."

After a couple of tense seconds, his expression softened. "I'm sorry. I'm not trying to upset you. It's just . . . when I think of you spending time with that jerk, I get a little crazy. I never thought of myself as the jealous type, but I guess maybe I am."

She reached across the table and took his hand. "I love you. You've got nothing to be jealous of. Nathan and I are just friends, and not even that. We hardly know each other anymore. But there's still a connection. I can't explain it. And he's in trouble. I can't just turn my back on the man."

"My wife. Father confessor, psychologist, and social worker all rolled into one."

She smiled, glad that he'd let her off the hook—for now. "Help me think this through, okay?"

"Should I make us a pitcher of martinis first?"

"Do you think it would help our thought processes?"

"No, but it might put me in a better mood."

She patted his hand. "Why don't we save it for a reward? We'll enjoy it so much more when we're done."

"If you say so, dear."

"Don't grit your teeth, darling. It'll wear them out. And don't be angry."

"I'm not angry. I'm thirsty."

Still sputtering at each other, they adjourned to the living room. Bram sat down on the couch and patted the spot next to him. Once Sophie was seated, they put their feet up on the footstool and Bram entwined his arm around hers.

"There, now we're at least more comfortable."

"Don't drift off on me, buster. We've got some heavy analyzing to do. Okay, we have two different threads we need to follow. One present tense, one past."

"Let's take the past first." He sat up a little. "Marie Damontraville has uncovered some intriguing facts about Constance Buckridge and her family, starting with Arthur Jadek's sudden disappearance in the late Fifties and his equally sudden reappearance in 1973. Also, we have a brief sexual liaison between sister and brother and the accusation that both Constance and Arthur sat by and let Wayne Buckridge die when they had it in their power to get him the medicine that might have fore-stalled his death."

"Well put."

"By the way, if the D.A. thinks that last part could be proved beyond a reasonable doubt, it might qualify as 'depraved in-difference.' They could both be indicted for murder."

Sophie had no idea. "But it can't be proved."

"Not yet, but give Marie some time. Now, as harmful as these interviews would be if they made it into a book or a magazine article, you're right. It's still Constance's word against Laurie Lippert's as to whether the worst of the accusa-tions are true. You mentioned to me earlier that Constance has already made a plausible case for why this ex-employee might lie. Since there were no other witnesses—at least none that we know of—Constance and Arthur have deniability on their side. My point is, I think it's possible that Marie hasn't unearthed the worst of Constance's secrets yet. If that's the case, she's not safe as long as she's working on that wretched book."

"You're referring to Pepper Buckridge's death?"

"Exactly. To keep a potential poisoning under wraps, Con-stance, or someone in her family, resorted to murder. Whether or not Nathan is responsible for Raffety's death, I'll bet he knows who is, and that makes him legally culpable, no matter how much you want to deny it."

Sophie tipped her head back and closed her eyes. "This is such a disaster," she said, a hollow feeling growing in the pit of her stomach. Pulling herself together she added, "I won't defend him, but I don't think we should convict him without knowing all the facts."

Bram conceded the point with a shrug.

"Okay, now it's my turn," said Sophie. "I'll continue on with the present."

"Gildemeister's death."

"I want to run through all the new information I've gathered."

"I'd be happier if I was sipping a martini."

"I'd be happier if we were sitting on a beach in Bermuda, but we're not. Now Harry was arrested for George's murder because he admits he was in George's apartment that night, and he had a motive. He'd also threatened George in a note he hand-delivered to the paper, as well as in various other letters discovered at his house. But Harry swears that when he left George's apartment that night, George was still alive. He further suggests that George was waiting for someone else to arrive, which meant he more or less shooed Harry out."

"And we know that other person was Nathan," said Bram, "because a woman across the hall saw him. Did you ever tell Nathan about her?"

"Actually, I did. But Nathan swears that when he got to George's apartment, the door was open and George was already dead."

"How convenient."

She held up her hand for quiet. "Ada Pearson, George's neighbor, said that Harry got there about six-thirty. She heard an argument a little while later. Then she went to the kitchen to eat her dinner. During dessert, she heard more arguing. Then it was quiet for about half an hour, so she looked outside to see what was going on just as Nathan left the apartment. If Nathan had arrived after Harry left—say, seven-fifteen or seven-thirty—and another argument ensued during Ada's dessert, let's say Nathan did murder him. If so, why did he stick around for another half hour? I saw him leave at eight."

"Maybe he was looking for something," said Bram. "That fax you found?"

She hadn't thought of that. "I suppose it's possible. But it's equally possible that what he said was true. Someone else may have arrived while Ada was eating dinner. That person had the second argument with George. The murder wasn't premeditated. Whoever did it just picked up whatever was handy, in this case a knife, and stabbed George in the back. Then he took off. Nathan arrives about half an hour later, sees George's body, and hightails it out of there so fast he doesn't even close the door."

"But, Sophie, you're forgetting something. Nathan's job is to oversee all the B.C.A. restaurants. I'm sure part of his responsibility was to scout out locations for new acquisitions—

restaurants with significant potential but currently in trouble: situations they could manipulate to their financial advantage. That fits the Belmont to a T. Who knows? Maybe Nathan does this all the time. How many restaurants did you say the academy owned?"

"Nine."

"I'll bet more than one of them was damaged by a bad review before it sold out to the Buckridges. But the fly in the ointment this time was that, like you said, George's conscience must have gotten the better of him. After all, he'd just seen Harry. They'd argued. Maybe Harry said something that hit a nerve, made George feel guilty about what he'd done. When Nathan arrived to pay him off, let's say George refused the money, although I doubt that would have gotten him killed. Suppose he also said he was going to admit publicly what he'd done and tell who'd put him up to it. Nathan couldn't allow that. It could have ruined everything. They'd be sued by so many people, they could have lost millions, not to mention the negative media fallout. Constance and everyone associated with her would have been vilified. So he does the only thing he can. He picks up the first weapon he sees and takes care of the problem."

"But maybe it wasn't Nathan," insisted Sophie. "There had been enough time for someone else—Kenny, Paul, even Constance—to arrive, take care of George, and leave before Nathan showed up."

"You know," said Bram, scratching his head, "how come nobody ever mentions Arthur in any of this?"

"Because he's not really part of the family business."

"But maybe he is. He's retired, right? Maybe he's taken more of an interest in Constance's affairs in the last few years."

Sophie had never really thought of that.

"But back to Nathan for a second. When he told you he wanted to talk to George about New Fonteney, he was lying. It doesn't make any sense. What could George do for him? If Nathan wanted someone to help him market a new cooking school, he would have gone to a marketing agency. I'm sure the Buckridges already employ several. One of them would do market research. I'm sure that's all standard operating procedure."

Sophie had to admit, Nathan's story had seemed a bit thin. "Maybe he did lie, but that doesn't mean he killed George."

"It had to be one of the Buckridges," said Bram. "Who else would know to make Harry the patsy? Harry had a serious grudge going against George, but not everyone would immediately think of that. The man was set up. It's so damn obvious!" Turning to look at her, he added, "It's time we take what we have to the police. We've got Ada Pearson's testimony. The fax sent to George from the academy. The fact that he'd been bought off to write negative reviews. I'd say it's an open and shut case. Let the police figure out the particulars."

"But it's *not* enough, sweetheart. It's still just circumstantial evidence. The cops could make a case against Nathan and they could be wrong all over again. I couldn't live with myself if I had anything to do with making that happen."

In complete frustration, Bram flung his arms in the air. "I give up."

"Just give me one more day, okay? One more chance to talk to Nathan."

He shook his head. "You're not safe talking to him alone. I should be with you."

"But he won't talk if you're there, Bram. You've got to be reasonable. Besides, he'd never hurt me. I'm certain of it. If I don't get him to open up about George's murder tomorrow, then I agree, we take what we know to the police."

Bram was about to respond when the phone rang. "I'll get it," he said, grabbing the cordless off the end table. "Hello?" He paused. "Hey, Harry. We were just talking about you. What's up?" He listened for a moment, then said, "Slow down and speak up. I can hardly hear you." After nearly a minute, he put his hand over the receiver and said, "He sounds upset, Soph. Says the police are after him again. They think he's some sort of new menace."

"Why?"

"He won't say over the phone. But he's scared. And he's got

some crazy notion that you promised to help him clear his name."

She gave a weak smile.

"Well? What do I tell him? He wants to talk to us right away."

"Here?"

"No, over at the Belmont."

"It's closed."

"We're supposed to knock twice on the loading-dock door and wait. He'll let us in."

"Tell him we're on our way."

28

Harry held a finger to his lips. He was carrying a candle, lighting their way through the dark kitchen. "I've got more candles burning back in the bar. Nothing you can see from the street, so we should be safe."

Even in the darkness, Sophie could see that Bram's reaction was the same as hers. Harry seemed overly paranoid. The pressure of his upcoming murder trial was getting to him.

The interior of the restaurant was silent and almost cold. For Sophie, the silence only heightened the sense of emptiness and despair. Restaurants were like theatres, full of the music and chaos of life, but for the Belmont the curtain had come down for the last time. No wonder a heavy melancholy suffused the air surrounding her. She wondered if Bram felt it. She knew Harry did.

"Why are we whispering?" asked Bram. "Nobody's here but us, right?"

Harry stopped abruptly and turned around. "You weren't followed, were you? I told you to take precautions!"

"No," said Sophie, reassuring him with her most soothing voice. "We weren't followed."

He stared at her a moment, then continued on through the dining room and into the bar. "Have a seat," he said, nodding to the red vinyl–covered stools. Ducking under the counter, he popped up on the other side. "Can I fix you two something to drink?" He tossed a white cotton rag over his shoulder, then cupped his hands together expectantly.

"What are you having?" asked Bram.

"A Stinger. My third of the evening, and not my last."

"Do you have any hazelnuts?"

"Of course I've got hazelnuts," said Harry, looking annoyed.

"Drink whatever you want," said Sophie. "I'll be the designated driver."

"Make it a stinger then," said Bram, pleased with the arrangement.

"I'll just have a ginger ale," said Sophie. She really didn't want anything, but she could tell that Harry needed to make a show of hospitality. After all, he'd been in the hospitality business for more than thirty years. The Belmont might be officially closed, but it was still his.

"Coming right up." The normality of preparing drinks provided him with a momentary calm. He worked quickly, his hands knowing instinctively where to find every ingredient. He'd already set the bar up with ice and some twists of lemon. The beer pulls probably weren't working, but all the liquor bottles were still in place. After setting the paper napkins and glasses in front of them, he lifted a bowl of the Belmont's traditional party mix up on the counter. "Enjoy," he said, though his usual smile was absent. Then, saluting them with his glass, he took a hefty sip of his own drink. "That's better. Now we can get down to business."

"What happened?" asked Sophie, glad that the formalities were over.

Harry considered the question. Wiping the countertop

with the towel, he shook his head. "The D.A. wants to revoke my bail."

"What!" Sophie was shocked. "Why?"

"Seems there's a woman over at Gildemeister's apartment building who says she saw me enter his place. She even heard our argument."

"Really?" Sophie shot Bram a look that warned him not to reveal the fact that they already knew about the woman. His slight nod told her he understood.

"So?" said Bram, chewing on some peanuts. "She saw you enter his apartment. You already admitted as much. What's the big deal?"

"The big deal is, she's been getting threatening phone calls. Apparently, some investigator from the prosecutor's office nosed around the building one last time, just to make sure they had their facts straight. They don't want any surprises during the trial. Anyway, this woman—her name is Ada Pearson—said she'd seen me go into George's apartment, but when she found out she might have to testify in court, she clammed up. Refused to say another word, except that for the last two days she's been receiving scary phone calls. They started on Thursday around noon. She said she was terrified to go anywhere now, even to the laundry room. She demanded that the investigator leave, but before he did, he got the impression that she might know something more, except that she was too frightened to talk."

"This Ada Pearson, she has no idea who called her?" asked Bram.

"Just that it was a man. He said if she didn't keep quiet, she wouldn't live to see her next birthday."

"How awful," said Sophie.

"Yeah, and what's worse is, the police subpoenaed her phone records. The threatening calls were all made from a pay phone at a gas station just around the corner from my house. They think I made the calls. I mean, how could I do it? I didn't even know the woman existed!"

"That's why they want to revoke your bail?" asked Sophie.

"You got it. The police came to my house this afternoon.

Luckily, I was out running some errands. My neighbor told me about it when I got home. There was a message on my answering machine from my lawyer telling me what was up. What could I do? I couldn't stay there and just let them come get me. I *can't* go back to that jail cell."

"So you came here," said Bram.

"I'm gonna sleep here tonight and tomorrow night and for as long as it takes."

"You realize the police may come here looking for you."

"God, what am I gonna do?" he rasped, leaning his elbows on the bar and rubbing his temples with the tips of his fingers. "Someone's trying to frame me. Why can't they see that? If I was gonna call this woman and make threats, I certainly wouldn't do it from a phone that was a stone's throw away from my front door. The police must figure I've got the IQ of a . . . a prune pit!"

"Calm down, Harry," said Sophie. "Remember your blood pressure."

"Screw my blood pressure." He finished his drink in two neat swallows.

As he made himself another, Sophie watched him, the wheels turning inside her mind. "Tell me something," she said finally, playing with the straw in her ginger ale. "Has anyone offered to buy your restaurant?"

"Sure," he said, not looking up. "But how's that gonna help me now?"

"Who made the offer?" asked Bram.

"A guy named Merlin. Kenneth Merlin. He works for Constance Buckridge, the famous TV chef. She runs a culinary school out east. From what he said, the school owns a bunch of restaurants around the country. They staff them with their graduates."

"And they want to buy the Belmont," said Sophie.

He nodded. Setting his drink on the bar, he added, "Merlin made me a decent offer. I mean, it's nothing like what I might have gotten once upon a time, even a year ago. But under the circumstances I thought it was reasonable."

"Did you accept?" asked Bram.

"I told him I'd think about it. I would have taken the offer, too, except that I was arrested. Thankfully, Merlin gave me a number where he could be reached. I've called him a couple of times, left some messages, but he hasn't gotten back to me yet. I wish he would. I need the money to pay for my defense." He picked up his drink.

"Harry, slow down with the booze," said Sophie. "You shouldn't be drinking so much, especially now."

"What else have I got? My wife's dead. My business is in shambles. And I'm going to jail for a murder I didn't commit. I'd say I deserve a few good pops." He downed half the glass.

"Not at the expense of your health. Look," said Sophie, "you can't stay here. There's nowhere to sleep."

"The floor looks pretty damn good to a guy facing a jail cell."

She couldn't let an old man sleep on the floor. Her father would have a fit if he found out she'd left Harry to fend for himself in his time of need. "You're coming back to the Maxfield with us. You can call your lawyer in the morning, but for tonight you're sleeping in a decent bed. Have you had dinner?"

"I'm a hopeless cook. I always ate at the restaurant." His words were beginning to slur.

Sophie pushed the drink away from him. "Come on. No arguments."

Offering her a grateful smile, he ducked back under the bar. "You're the best, Sophie. I'm gonna tell your father what a good girl he raised just as soon as he gets home from his trip."

"You do that."

Together, Bram and Sophie helped him out to their car.

Once he was belted into the backseat, Bram shut the door. Speaking softly, he asked, "When did you tell Nathan about Ada Pearson, that she'd seen him coming out of George's apartment?"

"Wednesday afternoon."

"And the threatening calls started on Thursday."

"I know what you're thinking."

"He made those calls, Sophie. And he did it in a way that pointed the finger at Harry. He's a cold-blooded killer, and he wants an innocent man to take the fall for him. What other conclusion can you draw?"

She thrashed around in her mind for something to say, some reason why Nathan might not be guilty. "He could have told someone else about it. Paul. Constance. Kenny. Maybe one of them made the calls."

Bram took ahold of Sophie's arm. "Why do you refuse to face the obvious?"

"Because it's not obvious to me."

Totally out of patience with her, he got into the car on the passenger's side and slammed the door. "Let's go."

He was angry and Sophie was helpless to do anything about it, at least for tonight. She wasn't the kind of woman who cried easily, but she could feel tears welling up in her eyes. She had to talk to Nathan tomorrow, and then, no matter what the outcome, she and Bram would go to the police with what they knew. If they didn't, Harry would be convicted of a murder he didn't commit. As much as she wanted to give Nathan the benefit of the doubt, she couldn't allow Harry to be falsely convicted.

Journal Note

Friday, Midnight
Red Wing, Minnesota

Late this afternoon I was forced to check into a fourth hotel, again without so much as a toothbrush or a stitch of clean clothes to my name. After I got back from an afternoon interview, I found two nasty-looking thugs milling around in front of my hotel room door. They were packing guns under their expensive suits and looked like they weren't going to leave anytime soon. Thank God they didn't see me. I was standing behind a group of people on a crowded elevator and was about to edge my way to the front when the doors opened. I spied them immediately, so I bent my head down and hid behind a tall man until we reached the next floor. Feeling as if I'd just had a near-death experience, I got off and rushed to the stairway, making a hasty exit. I left everything behind, except for what I had with me—the clothes on my back, my purse, and my laptop computer. I headed east on Interstate 94, then south on Highway 61, and finally ended up at the St. James Hotel in Red Wing. It's about an hour south of the Twin Cities. I don't know how Constance found me, but I'm not taking any more chances. I bought a blonde wig and I'm wearing it for the duration of my stay in Minnesota, which won't be long. I leave tomorrow.

After the interview I conducted this afternoon with Beverly Custerson, Constance's best friend during the late Fifties and early Sixties, there's no reason for me to stay any longer. The mystery surrounding Pepper Buckridge's death, and the dynamics of much of the Buckridge family history since that time, will never be fully cleared up, at least not by anyone outside the family. The whole situation was more convoluted than I ever thought. Pepper was indeed poisoned. But more on that later.

I called my editor, Noel Maslin, from my hotel room around six and explained the situation. He totally concurred with all my decisions, said I should leave at once. I told him that I would put a copy of all the interviews and my personal comments in the mail to him before dinner. I also asked him to send someone to the Maxfield Plaza in St. Paul and the Hyatt Regency in Minneapolis to pay my hotel bills and retrieve my clothing and personal effects. I have no intention of doing it myself, but I want everything sent back to my apartment in New York as soon as possible.

I'm convinced now that my original concept of Slice and Dice *as a biography of Constance Buckridge will no longer work. What I've been able to uncover is definitely explosive. However, I believe that Constance would never allow it to be*

*published as a straight biography, even an unauthorized one.
So what I have in mind is something more along the lines of a
personal memoir, what happened to me while I was working
on the book. That way I get to include how I was initially
pulled into the situation by a "Deep Throat" named Pluto
and my eventual meeting with Paul in the park. I can also include the death threats, Kenneth Merlin's attempt to buy
me off, Rafferty's death from a car bomb, my running from
hotel to hotel, the revelations in the interviews, the history of
the Jadek and Buckridge families, and finally my dalliance
with the handsome Bram Baldric. (I may change that part
just a bit.)*

As far as I'm concerned, this new take on Slice and Dice
*absolutely screams major motion picture. I see the book
now as something along the lines of* All the President's Men.
*A blockbuster full of intrigue, sexual corruption, suspense,
good guys and bad guys, twists and turns, romance, and
eventually even murder. Writing the story this way will allow
a much more suspenseful examination of the subject through
my real-life experiences. It's still going to be a bestseller—my
editor was more excited than I've ever heard him before—but
the gloves will be off because the subject of the book will be
me, not Constance.*

*I told Noel that I want to knock out a first draft in a month.
I'm flying to London tomorrow. I have a flat in Chelsea that I
use when I need to get away. Without any interruptions, I
know I can produce something significant in that period of
time. Noel promised that he'd set the wheels in motion to rush
the book into print. I also explained that, before I leave the
country, I intend to put in motion a plan to protect myself
from Constance and all her hired henchmen. She may track
me to London, but this will tie her hands. She won't be able to
touch me. It's something she'd never expect, but by tomorrow
morning she's going to realize I mean business. Noel agreed.
It's perfect, and it will only heighten interest in the forthcoming book.*

*I just have one more appointment to make before I get on
that plane tomorrow. It's risky, but I'm going to be on my*

guard. My only regret is that I won't have a chance to say goodbye to Bram. He helped me more than he'll ever know. Perhaps we'll meet again one day. It's a thought I choose to hold on to.

Now on to the interview with Beverly Custerson.

After I finished my discussion with Paul at Loring Park, I called to get my voice mail at the Maxfield. I was hoping to hear from Phillip Rapson. It was the only number he had for me, and I've been waiting for his call. Thankfully, he was a man of his word. He'd left a message saying that Constance's best friend, one Beverly Custerson, was still living in town. She and Tom, her husband, had divorced many years ago. Phillip gave me her number and I, of course, called immediately. It turns out that she lives just a few blocks from the Lyme House, the restaurant where I'd met with Oscar Boland last Saturday night. Since I knew the area and wouldn't need to consult a map, I asked if I could come over right away. She said to give her an hour. So I drove to the location in south Minneapolis and sat in my car typing up the transcription from the interview with Paul.

Finally, at two-thirty, Beverly met me at the door of her home, a modest colonial on Penn Avenue. She was a small woman, dressed in dark slacks and a red cotton blouse. Her gray hair was clipped short. She seemed friendly, but her general demeanor was somewhat dour. (She reminded me of my aunt May, though without my aunt's penchant for vodka and lemon. May was never without a glass in her hand.) After introducing me to her two cats, Beverly ushered me into a study off the living room. She'd already prepared some coffee and was so insistent that I try one of her homemade bars that I finally gave up and ate one just to keep her happy. (If I'm going to waste calories, it wouldn't be on a Pumpkin Raisin Delight.)

INTERVIEW: BEVERLY CUSTERSON, MINNEAPOLIS, FRIDAY, MAY 14

M: *When did you first meet Constance Buckridge?*

Beverly: *Back then I knew her as Connie Jadek. She didn't marry Wayne Buckridge until, oh, let me see, about '64. We first met in '54 when she came to live with her brother, Arthur. My husband and I had just married the year before. We were both in our early twenties, struggling to make ends meet. You know how it is. But Connie, she was a really sad case back then. Sixteen and pregnant by some boyfriend back home in Wisconsin. Her parents kicked her out as soon as they found out about the baby. Connie and the boyfriend tried to live together for about a month, but it didn't work. He took off and left her to deal with the pregnancy alone. She had no other choice but to come to Minneapolis. Arthur was a good four or five years older, just finishing his degree at the U. He was a nice young man, lived across the hall from us. Quiet but friendly. The intellectual type, if you know what I mean. We all lived in an apartment building on 31st and Aldrich. The Peoria, old but nice, across from a park. You could tell that sister and brother were close, but the pregnancy was a surprise—and a little hard to take—even for Arthur. Somehow he managed to pay for little Nathan's birth. Connie didn't have a dime. Arthur was working nearly full-time and going to school, so Connie was a complication he didn't need, but he was a good-hearted guy. Family was important to him. I always respected him for that.*

M: *I understand that you and Connie became best friends.*

Beverly: *Yes, we were as close as sisters for over ten years. But shortly after she married Wayne Buckridge, Tom, my husband, was transferred to Thief River Falls up near the Canadian border. After living in a big city all my life, it felt like moving to Siberia, but we managed. I was never happy there, but I stayed until our divorce in '87. I kept in contact with Connie for a while by letter and occasionally by phone, but time and distance have a way of changing relationships. And then, once Connie started doing her TV show, she didn't even have time to write anymore. We just drifted apart. All we've done for the last twenty-five years is exchange Christmas cards. But I will say this. After such a bad start, she's certainly made a success of her life. I'm proud of her. She was always . . . I'm not sure how to say this. She did things her own way, no matter what other people thought. Sometimes she made up her own rules, but she was never cruel or mean. She had a big heart.*

M: *You were considerably older than Connie. What drew you together?*

Beverly: *Well, several months after she moved into Arthur's apartment, I found out I was pregnant with my first child. The fact that we were both expecting at the same time created an instant bond. Once Connie realized that Arthur would take care of her, she couldn't have been happier. She really wanted the baby. I think her childhood had been pretty rocky. She didn't talk about it much, but I could tell there hadn't been a lot of love. She thought Nathan would bring something she'd missed to her life. And I really believe he did.*

M: *You said that Connie and Arthur were close. Did anything about their relationship seem odd?*

Beverly: *(Hesitates) No, not really. What exactly do you mean?*

M: *You tell me.*

Beverly: *Well, they fought some. But that's only natural.*

M: *Over what?*

Beverly: *Money, mostly. They lived in an efficiency apartment. That couldn't have been easy. Connie got a part-time job as a checkout girl at a grocery a few weeks after she arrived, but she had to quit in her eighth month. All that standing was making her feet swell. Her doctor said she needed to keep them up as much as possible. But, really, most of the time they both seemed pretty content. Arthur graduated in the spring of '54 and was immediately offered a terrific job at a big company in town. That was right before Nathan was born, so money problems eased a bit. They even moved into a one-bedroom in July. Nathan was one month old. I gave birth to Janet in August and we had a big party when I got home from the hospital. Even back then Connie loved to cook.*

M: *Were Arthur and Connie affectionate with each other?*

Beverly: *I suppose. But Arthur was a reticent kind of man, not physically demonstrative. When I'd hug him, he always seemed kind of stiff. Not that there's anything wrong with that.*

M: *I understand that Arthur disappeared from Connie's life in the late Fifties.*

Beverly: *(Shakes her head) It was a terribly traumatic time for Connie. Something just seemed to snap inside Arthur. He lost his sense of balance. Sometimes he'd be incredibly talkative but say the oddest things, and at other times he wouldn't talk at all. After a while we started seeing him less and less. Connie tried to cover, but I know he wasn't coming home at night. And then when he was fired from his position at General Mills, she was beside herself with worry. Arthur was her only means of support. She had a toddler to care for, and now her brother wasn't around to provide for them. Not to mention the fact that she was scared to death about the state of Arthur's mental health. When he disappeared, she nearly had a breakdown herself trying to find him. But she never did. Not until years later.*

M: *Connie told her family—her children, her husband—and the house staff that Arthur had been a secret agent for the government and that's why he couldn't talk about where he'd been or what he'd done for the last fifteen years. Did you know she'd lied about that?*

Beverly: *(Smiles) Sure, I knew. She wrote me all about it. She had to make up some kind of cover story. She didn't think Wayne would tolerate her brother's presence if he knew he'd had mental problems. After she married Wayne, she had plenty of money to hire people to look for Arthur. Finally, in '73, someone found him. Connie checked her brother into a hospital right away. The doctors put him on some drugs, even tried some experimental vitamin therapies, and slowly he seemed to come out of his fog. Connie's love and devotion was a big part of that. I know she would have done just about anything to help him recover. After all, she owed him so much. And, off the record, I think she felt a little guilty, like maybe if she hadn't created so much stress in his life, he might never have gotten sick in the first place.*

M: *After Arthur disappeared, did Connie date?*

Beverly: *Never. She didn't have time.*

M: *How did she survive financially?*

Beverly: *Well, after she accepted that Arthur was gone for good, she had a series of part-time jobs. I tried to help her out by baby-sitting Nathan. With the money Arthur had saved in the bank, she was okay for about a year. But eventually she didn't have enough to pay for rent and food and clothes and medicine. She was desperate. I couldn't just stand by and watch. That's when I talked to Tom. I insisted that she move in with us. Tom was hesitant at first, but he eventually gave in. We had a two-bedroom and it worked out okay.*

M: *What year was that?*

Beverly: *Let's see. I was pregnant with our second child, so that would make it the winter of '59. She lived with us until she went to work for Wayne and Pepper Buckridge about a year and a half later. She paid us what she could, which was never much, but she did most of the cooking and cleaning, and even some baby-sitting for me. She had part-time jobs during the day, but when Nathan was sick or I couldn't take care of him after school, she'd have to come home. When that happened too often, she'd get sacked. It wasn't an easy time for single mothers. There wasn't the kind of help there is today.*

M: *Did she like working for the Buckridges?*

Beverly: *Yes, I think she did. She especially appreciated the fact that she and Nathan lived on the premises, and when her son got home from school, she was there. Nathan was seven when they moved in. A really nice kid. Connie didn't mind the hard work. You have to understand, she always had this unshakable sense that she was going to make something of herself one day. I don't think she knew what that meant exactly, but she believed she'd have money, so much that she'd never have to worry about it again. I think the fame part came as a surprise. Don't ask me where she got the notion, but it would come up every now and then. I know it kept her going during the worst times. The hardest part about living with the Buckridges was the way Nathan was treated. Pepper Buckridge let him play with her son at first, but then she changed her mind. Nathan was forbidden to be in the main part of the house. After school, he could play outside at a park or go next door and play with the little girl who lived there. I believe her name was Andrea. They were almost the same age and really hit it off. I think she was his only real friend for many years, until she moved away. But if he was in the house, he had to be up in the room he shared with his mother. Connie didn't have the money to buy a TV, but she did get him a radio. But, honestly, it wasn't just the fact that he couldn't feed the sunfish off the dock, or play on the beach in front of the house, or watch the TV in the family room, or play with Paul; it was the fact that he was treated like a second-class citizen that really got to Connie. I imagine it got to Nathan, too. He was always an exceptionally bright child.*

M: *So, Constance must have hated Pepper Buckridge.*

Beverly: *Hate might be too strong a word, but yes, something like that.*

M: *Nathan, too?*

Beverly: *I never heard him say a word against Pepper, but I'm sure her rules hurt.*

M: *What did Constance think of Wayne Buckridge?*

Beverly: *At first I think she liked him. He seemed so serious to her that she'd joke with him, not often but every now and then. Eventually he started to respond. He even joked back. Connie thought they were developing a friendship. (Seems hesitant)*

M: *But later?*

Beverly: *Well, after she'd worked there about a year, Wayne made a couple of passes at her. She rejected them, of course, but he didn't stop.*

M: *How do you know all this?*

Beverly: *Oh, Connie and I got together every Thursday. It was her day off. We'd have lunch or go for a walk. Sometimes she'd come over to the house. Tom and I'd bought a small rambler in Richfield by then. Or we'd go shopping. But we al-*

*ways had these long conversations. Connie needed someone
to confide in, someone she could trust, especially after Wayne
started pressuring her to have sex with him.*

M: *Are you saying that Connie had no interest in him at all?*

Beverly: *Lord, no. He was a good fifteen years older. I mean,
she liked him okay, but the idea of having sex with him repulsed her.*

M: *Really? Other people I've talked to have said that it was
the other way around. Connie tried to seduce Wayne.*

Beverly: *That's absolute hogwash. Believe me, I know. I was
even there once when Wayne came home. It was after Connie
had taken the job as their cook. We were in the kitchen talking
and Wayne walked in the back door. He nodded to me, made
no effort to introduce himself, and then, in my presence, he
came up behind Connie and pinched her in the ... well,
lower regions. I was appalled. So was Connie, though she
just moved away. But she blushed a deep red and tried to ignore it. She told me later that she was terrified that she'd lose
her job if she didn't put out, so to speak. Come to think of it,
here's an even more telling situation I witnessed. Once, when
she was over at my house for lunch, we looked out the front
window and there was Wayne sitting in his car, staring at the
front door. That's when Connie admitted to me that he'd been
following her around town for months. I mean, the man was
obsessed, and that's the truth. Connie wanted nothing to do
with him. As an employee, she had to be friendly, and like
most women she second-guessed herself. She wondered if
she'd done something to give him the wrong impression, the
idea that she was "interested." But the fact was, she wasn't,
and yet she had to deal with him every day and be pleasant.
As I said, she liked him, okay, even felt a little sorry for
him. He and his wife kept separate bedrooms. He ate most of
his meals alone in the dining room. Little Paul was almost always asleep by the time he got home from work. From what
Connie said, Pepper was a total hypochondriac. Or so
everyone thought.*

M: *Are you suggesting that wasn't true?*

Beverly: *(Hesitates again)* I'm not sure how much I should say. *(Puts a hand over her mouth)*

M: *About what?*

Beverly: *(Seems uncomfortable)* I wouldn't want this to appear in a book. You have to understand, it all happened so long ago. Connie's obviously made peace with what happened. I don't have the right to open up old wounds.

M: *Perhaps they're not so old. Would it surprise you to learn that Paul Buckridge believes his mother was poisoned? He's thinking of having her body exhumed.*

Beverly: *(Appears shocked)* But he mustn't do that.

M: *Why not? It may be the only way to prove how she really died.*

Beverly: *He should leave well enough alone!*

M: *But if Connie actually poisoned her, if Pepper was murdered, he deserves—*

Beverly: *Connie? Excuse me, but what are you saying? Connie had nothing to do with Pepper's death. It was Wayne Buckridge who poisoned his wife. He'd been feeding her small amounts of antifreeze for months. I told you, he was obsessed with Connie. He wanted her at any cost, so he slipped the poison into Pepper's Coke. She had a lot of stomach problems and liked to drink things that were fizzy. Little did she know that the fizzy liquid was causing the stomach problems, the weight loss—and eventually would kill her.*

M: *Did Connie know about the poisoning before the fact?*

Beverly: *She had no idea. She just thought Pepper was sick and getting sicker. After Pepper died, Wayne came to her and asked her to marry him. She refused, of course. That's when he told her what he'd done. And he said that if she refused to marry him, he'd go to the police and tell them that Connie had poisoned Pepper. After all, she was the cook. She had daily access to all of Pepper's food and drink. Wayne said it wouldn't be hard to make the police believe that Connie had been after him all along. Maybe he'd even admit to sleeping with her once or twice. He'd be full of remorse for his part in his wife's death. But when he rejected Connie's ever-growing sexual demands, how could he know she'd resort to poison to*

get rid of Pepper? Well, as you can imagine, Connie was horrified. It all sounded so plausible that she felt sure Wayne
could make the accusation stick. After all, to the outside
world, all she had going for her were her looks. It would seem
natural that she'd use them to better her station in life. She
came over to my house the same night he proposed. I'd never
seen her in such a panic. First she told me what Wayne had
done and then she said she'd go to jail if she didn't agree to be
his new wife. She begged me to tell her what to do. What could
I say? Wayne had all the cards. If she didn't agree to his
terms, she'd end up in prison. Nathan would go to a foster
home. Their lives would be ruined. After she calmed down a
little, she mentioned that Wayne had insisted that it would be
good for Nathan to finally have a real family. Connie couldn't
give him much—she had no money and never would—but
Wayne could give him the world. The best schools. Music
lessons. Summer camps. After they were married, he promised to make Nathan his legal son. He told her he loved her
like he'd never loved anyone else in his entire life, that he
didn't want to go on living without her. When she got home
later that night, she found him sitting on the back porch. He
asked her again to marry him. Had he been so wrong to think
she cared for him just a little? She asked him to give her a day
to decide. She talked to Nathan about it. He was nine or ten at
the time. I don't know what he said exactly, but the next day
Connie told Wayne she'd marry him, but that she wouldn't do
it right away. There had to be a decent waiting period after
Pepper's death. She didn't want people to get the wrong idea.
She asked for two years. He agreed to one. And exactly one
year to the day after Pepper died they were married.

M: *You believe this story?*

Beverly: *It wasn't a story, it was the truth.*

M: *But you only heard Connie's side of it. Wayne's might have
been very different.*

Beverly: *Are you suggesting she lied? That Wayne didn't
poison his wife?*

M: *All I'm saying is that there's no independent verification.*

There were no other witnesses to what was said or done. It's Connie's word against Wayne's.

Beverly: *Exactly. That's just the way he set it up.*

M: *But Connie could have set it up, too. Did you ever talk to Wayne Buckridge personally, ask him if any of this was true?*

Beverly: *Heavens, no. After I learned what he'd done, I was afraid to open my mouth in the man's presence.*

M: *Then what you know is simply what Connie wanted you to know.*

Beverly: *It wasn't like that! She wasn't lying!*

M: *At this point, Beverly, an unbiased party would be hardpressed to prove what happened. Constance is still alive to tell her tale, but unfortunately, dead men are notoriously silent.*

29

When Bram arrived at the church on Saturday afternoon, a long line of cars was just leaving for the cemetery. Pulling in behind a rusted Bronco, he followed the funeral procession until it reached the iron gates of Lakewood. It was a cool, windy day, the kind of spring weather that made a person glad to be alive, especially in the face of a death that seemed both senseless and unnecessary. Bram hadn't really known Sean Rafferty, but he felt it was important to pay his last respects. He was also hoping that Marie might be somewhere in the crowd. He knew it was a long shot. If she was still in Minnesota, she would be keeping a low profile. Attending the funeral of her murdered bodyguard probably wasn't smart. Even so, Bram felt there was a chance she might come.

After Marie had left the Ardmore Suites, Bram realized that finding her would be difficult, if not impossible. The note she'd left behind simply said thanks for the help and have a good life. It wasn't enough. Bram had to know she was all right, and he wanted to see her one last time.

He parked his car on 36th Street and, without waiting for the stoplight to turn green, hurried into the cemetery. By the time he reached section 17, the graveside ceremony was already underway. Either Rafferty had a lot of friends or his family was large. People stood ten and twelve deep around the casket as the minister intoned a prayer. Bram stayed in the background and surveyed the mourners. Marie didn't appear to be among them.

Feeling oddly let down, he waited until the minister was done and people started to walk back to their cars, then climbed a hill behind the burial site for a better look at the crowd. As he reached the top, he noticed a woman sitting on a gravestone about thirty yards away. She was wearing oversize dark glasses and a tan raincoat, the collar pulled up around her neck. The lower part of her chin was also covered. Her hair was blonde and short, and she looked to be a good thirty pounds heavier than Marie, but something about the woman made him hesitate.

Returning his attention to the mourners, Bram spied a man stepping slowly away from the crowd. Once he was halfway up the hill, the man stood still and watched the group disperse. As the wind blew his suit coat against his body, Bram noticed a slight bulge under his left arm. What was a guy who was packing a concealed weapon doing at Rafferty's funeral? Glancing back at the woman on the headstone, he made a quick decision.

"A sad day, isn't it?" he called, moving quickly down the hill toward what he now assumed was one of Constance Buckridge's hired thugs.

The man looked around but didn't respond.

As Bram got closer, he put his arm around the fellow's shoulders. "I'm . . . Mortimer Brewster. Sean's uncle from

Vermont. I can't believe he's gone. A real special guy, huh? How'd you know him?"

The man seemed uncomfortable with Bram's arm across his back and tried to move away, but Bram held on tight and began walking him down the hill and away from the woman on the headstone.

When he finally spoke, the thug's voice was almost sweet. Coming from such a potentially menacing hulk, it seemed incongruous, almost comical. "We met . . . at a party."

"Yeah, Sean loved to party down. Did you know his favorite drink was root beer?"

The guy was trapped. He had to at least pretend he'd come for the funeral. "No, I didn't."

"Yup. Ever since he was a kid. Root beer, root beer, root beer."

"Fascinating."

"It is, isn't it?" The crowd was thinning. "Say, I didn't catch your name."

"It's . . . Smith."

"Isn't it just."

"What?"

"Such a tragedy. And to think Sean left a wife and six kids behind."

The man peered sideways at him. "I thought he wasn't married."

"Well he wasn't until last week. He married a woman with six kids. Can you believe it?"

"I guess his uncle would know."

"Which way's your car?"

He pointed to a blue Firebird parked along one of the cemetery's gravel roads.

Bram headed straight for it. "What a coincidence. My car's right over there, too. I suppose you're coming back to the church for the late lunch. Some of us burly men types should get back there and make sure they've got all the chairs set up. It's the least we can do for Sean."

"Lunch?"

"Sure. Everyone will be there. I'll introduce you around.

You'll adore his mother. She's a stitch. Although she probably won't be in top form today. Normally, when I introduce people to her, she'd still be telling them jokes an hour later."

Smith swallowed hard. He wasn't an Einstein, for which Bram was duly grateful.

As they approached the Firebird, Bram let go of his shoulders. Smith turned quickly to survey what was left of the crowd. "Say, Mortimer—"

"You can call me Mort."

"Right. Mort. You seem to know your way around this group. Have you seen a woman—about thirty-five? Long dark hair? Delicate features? Pretty? I was hoping to hook up with her today. We're old friends."

"Nope, sorry. Haven't seen anyone like that."

Smith continued to look around the cemetery, but after a few more moments, he gave up. "Well, time to hit the bricks."

"Sure, I understand." Bram resumed his sad demeanor. "You know, I'm the kind of man who believes Sean is looking down on us right about now and smiling. Maybe he's even laughing his head off." He socked the thug on the arm. "It's been a pleasure meeting you, Mr. Smith. See you back at the church."

"Sure. Whatever." After getting into his car and starting the engine, the man drove off.

Once the Firebird was out of sight, Bram dashed back up the hill. As he reached the top, he looked toward the headstone, but the woman was gone. "Damn," he muttered, pushing his hands into his pockets and kicking a rock out of his way. Maybe it hadn't been Marie after all. Donning a disguise would have been logical, but if she'd spotted him—and he felt certain she had—she would have stuck around.

He was about to give up and head back to his car when he saw the same blonde woman hiding behind the trunk of a large elm, motioning him over. Hurrying toward her, he saw that she was all light pink lipstick and blonde bangs, sort of Dusty Springfield meets Petula Clark. Even so, he was sure it was her. "Marie?" he said, stopping a few yards from the tree.

"Lower your voice and come with me," she whispered. She

led the way through the gravestones, down the other side of
the hill and across a gravel road to where a Buick Riviera was
parked. "Get in," she said, slipping into the driver's seat.

Once Bram was seated on the passenger's side with the
doors and windows locked, Marie sighed with relief. "How
did you recognize me?"

"Are you suggesting you look different?"

"Come on, Baldric. Be nice. It's been a rough week."

He smirked at her. "The dark eyebrows were a big clue."

Her eyes shot upward. "Oh."

"The truth is, I had a hunch you'd be here today. That's
mainly why I came." He continued to smirk, realizing how
good it was to see her again. "What have you got on under
that raincoat?"

"Four sweaters."

"Good thing it's a cool day."

"Cool? I'm dressed for an ice floe in the North Atlantic.
What do you think of the wig?"

"It's definitely you."

She laughed. "God, it's good to see you again. I've missed
you."

Bram wondered if he'd missed her, too. He hadn't thought
about it that way, but maybe he had. "I'm just glad to see
you're all right. I thought maybe you'd left Minnesota by
now."

"I'm leaving today. My flight's at three." Glancing down at
the straining buttons on her raincoat, she added, "I'm going
to keep wearing the disguise for the duration. My vanity will
just have to suffer."

"Are you heading back to New York?"

"No, I'll be out of the country for a while."

"Working on the book?"

She nodded. "Thanks for taking care of that private
investigator."

"Is that what he was?"

"I assume so. He glanced my way a couple of times during
the funeral ceremony back at the church, but I guess the dis-

guise must have worked. Constance is trying to track me down. Two of her muscle men almost nailed me last night at the Hyatt Regency in Minneapolis. Thankfully, I saw them in time to get away."

"You sound like you've been having lots of fun since you dumped me on Wednesday."

Now she looked annoyed. "I didn't dump you. The last thing you needed was to get more involved in this mess. I care what happens to you, Bram. I don't want you to get hurt."

"But if you get hurt, that's okay."

"No, of course not. But this is my job. You're just an innocent bystander."

He held her eyes. "Yup, that's me, the last of the innocent bystanders."

As if on cue, they both turned to look out the front window. The silence inside the car grew awkward.

Finally Marie said, "I bought myself an insurance policy last night. Constance won't be able to touch me after today, not without the entire world knowing she was behind my broken knees or my sudden demise. Since the spotlight will be aimed straight at her, I'm betting she'll back off."

He glanced over. "What did you do?" When she didn't respond, he said, "Why do you look like the proverbial cat that just swallowed the proverbial canary?"

She grinned. "The managing editor at the *American Inquisitor* is a good buddy of mine."

"You talked to a tabloid?"

"If you buy today's issue, you'll see that Constance and I made the front cover. Beauty and the Beast." She laughed.

"But what did you tell them?"

"A little of this, a little of that. Enough to tantalize their readership and create a ready audience for my book when it comes out. And I made it very clear that I feared for my life, that while on the story my bodyguard had been murdered in a car bombing. I said that my information was explosive, and that if anything untoward or violent happened to me, the police would know where to look."

Bram had to give her credit. It was a brilliant stroke. "Actually, Marie, there may be another secret in the Buckridge closet. My wife's uncovered evidence that one of the Buckridges murdered George Gildemeister, a food critic at the *Times Register*."

She sobered suddenly. "I've been following that story in the paper. But the police think some restaurant owner did it."

"Don't quote me, but I'm pretty certain Nathan Buckridge will be arrested in the next day or two. He was at George's apartment the night he died, and he lied to my wife about why he was there. Sophie discovered some information that proves one of Constance's inner circle was paying George to write a negative review."

"Of the Belmont?"

"You're a quick study. Sophie's theory is that George got cold feet at the last minute. That he threatened to blow the whistle on the Buckridges' game."

"But why would they want to shut down a restaurant?"

"Because they wanted to buy it. The Buckridge Culinary Academy currently owns nine restaurants around the country. I'm sure they're always on the lookout for a place with a great location and reputation, but one that's currently in trouble. With a nasty shove from the local food guru, the restaurant falters and finally closes. Then they rush in and buy it for a song, and nobody's the wiser."

Now Marie looked positively entranced. "Will you keep me informed about this? It's very important. I need all the details."

"Sure, I suppose. You'll have to give me an address where I can reach you."

She pulled out a card and wrote the address on the back.

"London," he said, looking up at her.

"It's a lovely flat in Chelsea. You're welcome to join me, you know. Anytime."

"You know I can't do that."

"Of course. What was I thinking?" Hesitantly, she touched his hand. "I just wish we'd met years ago."

"It wouldn't have made any difference. You wouldn't have been willing to settle down with a boring old radio guy."

She lowered her eyes. "How did you get to know me so well in such a short time? You're right. I love what I do. It's the most exciting job in the world. I'm never going to be in one place very long, and that's what makes me such a bad relationship risk. You're well rid of me."

He stared at her. Finally he said, "I guess this is goodbye then."

"I hate goodbyes. Don't make this awkward, Bram. Just wish me well and go. You know I wish you the same."

But he couldn't leave. Not yet. Holding her hand to his lips, he said, "It's been quite a ride."

"It has," she agreed.

"Maybe when you come through town on your next book tour you'll let me interview you again."

"If you're lucky."

He smiled. "Stay safe, okay?"

"I will."

He stared at her a moment longer, his feelings more mixed than he would have ever thought possible. "You're a strong woman."

"I am," she said, tenderly touching his cheek. "If I weren't, I'd stick around and fight for you until I won, and then I'd make the rest of your life miserable. Count your blessings, Baldric."

After a few more seconds, he said, "Goodbye and good luck." Opening the door, he got out, leaned down to take one last look at her, then set off up the road. When he knew she couldn't see him any longer, he bent down and rested his hands on his knees, feeling for all the world as if someone had just whacked him in the stomach with a baseball bat.

30

Sophie couldn't believe her luck. She'd finally found it, the clue that would identify the real murderer of George Gildemeister. If she hadn't decided to finish looking through the box George had given her, she never would have discovered it. But now that she had, she had to follow it to the finish, even if it led straight to Nathan. It was such a small matter, she could easily understand why the killer had overlooked it. By the time the deed was done, he'd probably forgotten he'd even left it behind.

After Bram left for the funeral, Sophie had come down to her office to get in a few hours of work. She'd tried to reach Nathan all morning, leaving notes in his mailbox and on his voice mail. She'd even gone up to his suite and slipped a note under his door. So far, he hadn't responded. Perhaps that was a blessing in disguise. When she finally did talk to him, she hoped she would no longer be in the dark.

Once she'd finished going through George's files and the box was empty, she discovered that in the bottom, much to her surprise, a cigarette butt remained. Under other circumstances she might have overlooked it, but since George was so antismoking—he never allowed anyone to smoke in his presence—she had to wonder where it had come from. She picked it up and looked at it. It was a little longer than a normal butt, as if someone had put it out before it was finished. The filter tip was tan and had a gold rim near the bottom. Below the band was a tiny picture of a clock with two men on either side. She had no idea what brand it was. Then it hit her how the butt had come to be in the box.

This was how she envisioned it. Sophie'd called George at four last Sunday and said she'd stop by around eight. Sometime after her call, he must have dumped the last of his files in the cardboard box and placed it outside his door. Then, at six-thirty, Harry came by unexpectedly. George buzzed him up and offered him a glass of wine just to prove he was magnanimous and forgiving, that he had no hard feelings even after the vicious letter Harry had sent to the paper. For the next few minutes Harry vented his anger. George listened and eventually hustled Harry out the door. Harry had mentioned that he'd had the distinct impression that George had been expecting an important visitor.

Somewhere between the time Harry left and the time Sophie arrived, George had another visitor, possibly two. If Nathan was telling the truth, if he'd walked in and found George already dead, then the person who came directly after Harry but before Nathan must be George's murderer. The timing would have been tight, but it was possible. Sophie believed it was one of the Buckridges, someone who'd come to pay George off for the negative review. But the question was, which Buckridge? She figured that whoever arrived after Harry had been smoking a cigarette. Since all of the Buckridges were hooked, the assumption wasn't a stretch. George probably demanded that he, or she, put it out before entering the apartment. The visitor probably crushed it out, made sure it was cold, then tossed it in the nearest trash—the box sitting next to George's door.

The visitor then entered. They talked. George must have done something upsetting. There was another argument, the second one the neighbors heard that night. And finally the visitor murdered George.

Sophie didn't believe that George's death had been premeditated. The murder weapon had been snatched from the counter simply because it was there, within easy reach. If someone had intended to murder George, it seemed unlikely that he or she would do it at George's apartment where neighbors might notice the comings and goings of visitors. Not that the murderer hadn't improvised brilliantly by taking the

murder weapon with him or her and then planting it in
Harry's neighbor's garbage can. Harry was the perfect patsy.
He had motive, opportunity—and the knife was the means. If
Sophie could find out which Buckridge smoked the brand of
cigarette she'd found in George's file box, and if her theory
held, it seemed to follow that *that* person was guilty of a
homicide.

Emily had mentioned that she liked the menthol variety.
Nathan smoked Marlboros. The rest of the family . . . who
knew? But she was about to find out.

Making a quick call to the weekend housekeeping manager, Frances Lester, Sophie explained the situation. She
asked if the rooms on the tenth floor of the north wing had
been cleaned yet. Luck was with her. Frances said that the
maids were currently on eleven. That's when Sophie asked
Frances to personally go up to rooms 1004, 1027, and 1031.
She instructed her to place whatever cigarette debris she
found in separate plastic bags, label each bag with its room
number, and then bring all of them down to her office.

While she was waiting for Frances to collect the evidence,
she called a local tobacconist and described the cigarette in
George's file box. The man recognized it at once. He identi-
fied the brand as Nat Sherman on Fifth Avenue in New York.
A pricey smoke with a classy pedigree, not one he sold to
every Tom, Dick, or Harry—his words. She was thrilled with
the news and immensely relieved, because it meant she could
scratch Nathan off the list.

For the next half hour she tried to keep busy. She was about
to call the Fountain Grill for a late lunch when it occurred to
her that there was one person in this whole mess she hadn't
talked to yet. She couldn't help but wonder if David Polchow,
the chef who'd quit in a huff and walked out of the Belmont,
might not be connected to the Buckridges in some way. Specifically, it seemed inconceivable to Sophie that a man with
his culinary credentials could allow a pâté that tasted like
wallpaper paste to be served to his customers unless he was
doing it for a reason. If the Buckridges could pay off a reviewer, why not a chef?

If she recalled correctly, Harry'd said that Polchow lived in an apartment near Riverplace. She found the number in the Minneapolis phone directory and placed the call. As the phone was ringing, she considered the best way to approach him. Tell him the truth up front? Question him a bit first? She didn't have much time to think about it because he answered on the third ring.

"Hello?" came the high, slightly nasal voice.

"Is this David Polchow?"

"Speaking."

"This is Sophie Greenway. We met the other night at the Belmont. I'm the new reviewer for the *Times Register*."

"Yes, Ms. Greenway, I remember you." He sounded friendly enough, certainly not the furious chef she'd met a little more than a week ago.

"Do you have a moment to talk?"

"What's this about?"

"The Belmont."

Silence. "It closed."

"Yes, I know. I'm wondering if you were aware that Constance Buckridge was interested in buying it."

"If that's true, then good for Hongisto. I'm sure he'll get a fair price."

Sophie had no such assurance. "Did you know the Buckridges paid George Gildemeister to write a negative review of the restaurant?"

More silence. "That's nonsense. Where'd you hear such a ridiculous story?"

"I have a fax, Mr. Polchow. It was sent from the Buckridge Culinary Academy to George Gildemeister, dated this past May third. In it George was directed to make his forthcoming review even more critical. If he failed to do so, he wouldn't get paid. His review of the Belmont appeared on the seventh."

"What do you want me to say? If it's true, I knew nothing about it."

"I understand you and Paul Buckridge are pretty good friends." She knew this was a stretch, but she'd seen them together in the Maxfield's lobby just the other night.

"So?"

"Were you working for him, too? Was he paying you to lower the quality of the Belmont's food?"

"That's absurd! Slanderous! You print something like that and I'll sue!" His voice rose a good octave. "I'm a chef, Ms. Greenway. Food is my life. If I serve substandard fare, I'm the one who gets the black eye."

"Not if the job only lasts a couple of months, and the restaurant is already considered a hopeless case."

"I resent your implication!"

"I don't care what you resent, but you'd better keep listening. See, I also have proof that someone in the Buckridge family murdered George Gildemeister to keep him from blowing the whistle on their little scam. If George had made a clean breast of things, the Buckridges would have been in serious legal trouble, not to mention what it would have done to their reputation. If you're mixed up with them, Mr. Polchow, you could easily be considered an accomplice to murder." She didn't know if that was true, but it sounded good.

"I don't believe this!" His voice had taken on the same hysterical edge she'd heard that Friday night. The only difference was, this time it wasn't an act.

"I have a theory you might be interested in. I believe that the Buckridge family has done it before, paid a reviewer to write a negative review. Then they'd simply wait for the restaurant to go belly-up. I suppose that sometimes it worked, sometimes it didn't. But when it did, Kenneth Merlin would sweep in and make a low but reasonable offer to buy the place, and the owner would take it because his business was all but ruined. Do you know anything about that, Mr. Polchow?"

"I certainly do not."

"Because if you did, and you cooperated with the police, they might overlook the fact that you accepted a bribe and that you were part of a scheme to defraud the owner of a legitimate business, a scheme that led to a murder."

"You've got to believe me. I had nothing to do with Gildemeister's death! I've never even met the man. Honestly, until this minute I thought Harry did it. That's what all the papers say." He sounded desperate.

"*Do* you know if the Buckridges have pulled this stunt before?"

More silence. "Look, Ms. Greenway, if I could get information, details, do you really believe the police would go easy on me?"

"Did you accept a bribe?"

Hesitantly he said, "I don't have to answer that."

"You're right. You don't." She waited, allowing her silence to do what her words couldn't.

Finally he said, "If I did take a bribe, it wasn't much."

"Who gave you the money?"

"Look, I was just doing a buddy a favor. I didn't think it was a big deal because the Belmont was already in so much trouble. It was just a matter of time before it folded. I simply gave it a nudge. And, believe me, I knew nothing about a murder. I never would have signed on for anything like that."

She figured that was all she was going to get—for now. "Could you dig up some specifics about other acquisitions by later today?"

"Why so fast?"

"I intend to take what I know to the police tomorrow morning. If you were to come with me and had that information in your hand, you'd be in a better position to bargain."

"You sound like you figured this out all by yourself."

"I did."

"You're smart, Ms. Greenway. I take it that you're the only one who knows the truth? You haven't talked to the police or confided in someone else?"

She lied. "That's right, but after tomorrow your window of opportunity will be closed. You haven't got much time."

More hesitation. "I'd want a lawyer present."

"Of course."

He thought about it some more. "Give me until tonight. I'll find out everything I can and then I'll call you. Is it a deal?

Please, Ms. Greenway. I never realized this had gotten so out of hand."

Sophie gave him her number. "Be smart, Mr. Polchow. Keep this to yourself."

"Oh, absolutely. I'll call you by ten. I promise."

As soon as Sophie hung up, Frances knocked on her door. She poked her head inside and said, "Can I come in?"

The moment of truth had arrived.

"Did you find anything?" asked Sophie, erupting out of her chair. She was so anxious to look at the evidence that she all but grabbed the plastic bags out of Frances's hand.

"Jeez," said Frances, patting her orange hair into place. "Those people up there must all be on the verge of dropping dead of lung cancer. I've never seen so much cigarette trash."

The bags had been clearly labeled according to room. "Thanks," said Sophie. "You did a great job."

"Made me feel like a secret agent." Frances snapped her gum.

Sophie checked Constance's room first. A couple of the butts matched the Nat Sherman, but the majority were Virginia Slims and dark cigarillos. The next suite was Paul and Nathan's. Again most of the cigarettes were either Marlboro or Carleton Lights. There were two or three Nat Shermans, but clearly the person smoking them had been a visitor, not an occupant of the suite. Finally she picked up the bag from Kenny and Emily's room. A few of the cigarettes were menthols, Emily's brand, but the overwhelming number were Nat Shermans. Sophie had finally found her man. Unless she was badly mistaken, Kenneth Merlin had been George's mystery visitor last Sunday night, the man who'd murdered him and then tried to frame Harry. It made sense. Considering that Kenny took care of the business side of Constance's affairs, it was logical that he ultimately made the decision to end another man's life to protect the future of the business.

"This is perfect," said Sophie. "Just what I needed." She'd already bagged the cigarette she'd found in George's cardboard box. It would all go to the police tomorrow.

Thanking Frances again and then sending her on her way,

Sophie punched in the number to Constance's suite. She was through waiting for Nathan to call.

Arthur answered the phone.

"Hi, this is Sophie."

"Hey, good to hear from you. I hope we get a chance to see you one more time before we leave tomorrow."

"I hope so, too," said Sophie. "What time is your flight?"

"Four-twenty."

That gave her a little more leeway. "Listen, I've been looking for Nathan all day, but we haven't connected. I really need to talk to him. I don't suppose you know where he can be reached?"

Arthur sighed. "Well, let's see. We've planned a family meeting at New Fonteney for seven tonight. My guess is, he's already there. He had phone service hooked up yesterday, but I don't have the number. Constance copied it somewhere, but she's not here at the moment. She went downstairs to pick up a fax. If you wanted to drive out around six, I'm sure you'd find him. He's in the process of moving into the visitor's cabin. Do you know where that is?"

"Visitor's cabin? I thought you'd passed on buying the place."

"We did. But then Nathan turned around and bought it himself. I assumed he'd told you. The closing was on Friday."

"This is the first I've heard of it."

"Well, it seems he's quitting the job he's been doing for his mother and moving out there. He wants to open a restaurant or his own cooking school. Personally, I think it's a fine idea."

"I do, too."

"And since he'll be staying in the area, you two can see each other more often."

That wasn't such a fine idea. "He's not doing this just because of me, is he?"

"You'll have to ask him."

She intended to. "Thanks for the info. I owe you one."

"If I hear from him, I'll let him know you're on your way out."

"Thanks, Arthur. You're a doll."

Once she'd hung up, she glanced at the clock. It was getting close to five. If she left now, she'd easily make it by six. But first she had to leave a note for Bram.

Retrieving a piece of hotel stationery from her top desk drawer, she wrote:

> *Honey, I'm off to New Fonteney to talk to Nathan. I found some evidence today that proves he had nothing to do with George's death. Turns out it was Kenny. I'll explain more later. I should be back at the Maxfield by eight. Keep the home fires burning. Let's have a quiet dinner when I get back. We've got lots to talk about.*
>
> > *Hugs and kisses,*
> > *Me*

She folded the note and slipped it into an envelope, wrote his name on the front, then grabbed her car keys and purse and hurried out to the lobby. After dropping the message off at the concierge desk, she headed for the front door. She couldn't wait to talk to Nathan. She knew now why he'd been so depressed for the last couple of years and then so excited on Thursday morning. He also knew what Kenny had been up to, but to remain on good terms with his family, Nathan had buried his sense of right and wrong. It wasn't a fair trade. She needed Nathan to tell her the full story behind George's death. Until he made a complete break with the damaging parts of his past, he'd never be truly free. He deserved a life on his own terms. After tonight she prayed that's what he'd find.

31

Constance sat on the bed in her suite and stared at the fax she'd received a few minutes ago. Tears flowed freely down her cheeks, not because she was sad but because she was so deeply touched. This honor was the culmination of nearly thirty years of perseverance and hard work. Her secretary back in New Haven had faxed a copy of the letter to the Maxfield, knowing Constance would want to see it right away.

> *Dear Ms. Buckridge:*
> *It is my great pleasure to inform you that you have been chosen by the Escoffier Society of America as this year's recipient of the Auguste Escoffier Lifetime Achievement Award. Each year the society singles out an individual for the excellence of his or her work within the American culinary community. Past recipients have included a panorama of the finest culinary talent in the nation. The award ceremonies will be held at the Dorothy Chandler Pavilion in Los Angeles in late July. The night before the award is given, you are invited to be the honored guest speaker at the International Culinary Guild's annual banquet.*

Constance looked up when she heard Arthur calling her name, quickly followed by a knock on the door. He stuck his head inside. "I think you'd better come out here."

She didn't like the tone of his voice. "Why?"

"Kenny's stopped by. He's got something you need to see right away."

What now? she thought to herself, angry that she couldn't

have one moment of peace to savor her triumph. Rising from the bed, she draped a white cotton sweater around her shoulders, tying the arms across the front of her blouse, then walked quickly out to the living room.

Kenny and Arthur were standing together at the bar reading a newspaper.

"What is it?" she asked, growing more tentative when she noticed the anxious look on Kenny's face.

"I think you should sit down," said Arthur.

"Just tell me."

Kenny walked over and handed her the paper. "Look at this first."

Constance winced when she saw that the front page contained a picture of herself and Arthur, with a headline that read "Bon Appétit? Famous Cooking Diva and Eminent Brother Linked in Sex Scandal." For a moment she felt dizzy, as if she might faint. Both men were instantly at her side, helping her to the couch.

"What are we going to do?" she gasped.

Arthur snatched the paper away from her. "You don't need to read the article. It's nothing but lies."

"We have to sue!"

"I'm on it," said Kenny. "I've already made several calls to the *American Inquisitor*. I've talked to the publisher and the managing editor. I told them we wanted a retraction or they'd have a major lawsuit on their hands."

"How did they respond?" asked Arthur.

"They felt they had sufficient proof to back up their report and they were going to sit tight. We could sue if we wanted to, but they're standing by their story. Of course, they wouldn't reveal their source, but we already know who's behind it."

"Damontraville?" whispered Constance. "But I thought you said she'd sit on what she'd found. Why give it away when you can write a book and make millions?"

"She's running scared," said Kenny. "The inside article makes that clear. The whole thing is nothing but a veiled message to us. If she gets hurt in any way, the police will come knocking on our door. We've been put on notice."

"Oh, God," said Constance, dropping her head in her hands.

"Our perceived overreaction to the book probably forced her to make this alteration in her plans. I just wish I knew what other surprises she's got waiting in the wings."

Arthur sat down next to Constance, pulling her close to him. "It's going to be okay," he said, stroking her hair.

"How can you say that? In a matter of days the whole world will think of us as depraved. Perverted. I can't bear it. How can I ever show my face in public again?" She couldn't hold back any longer. Her tears gushed forth in a torrent.

"You mean more to me than anyone else in this world," he said simply, his voice gentle. "You always have. We've done nothing wrong. We've just tried to protect our privacy."

"But at what cost?" Her lower lip trembled violently.

An instant later someone began banging on the door. When Kenny went to answer it, he found Paul standing outside, his face flushed with anger.

"I'm so sorry, Paul." Constance sniffed, the sight of him starting a new round of tears. She scraped at her cheeks, trying hard to hide the devastation she felt inside. "Kenny . . . he's already talked to the paper about the article. We're demanding a retraction."

Paul stayed next to the door, glancing from face to face. "What paper? What article?"

"The one in the *American Inquisitor*," she replied, taking the tissue Arthur offered her.

Kenny handed it to him.

Paul stared at the front page a moment, then hurled it across the room. "You're a walking disaster," he snarled, glaring at Constance. "And you're going to take this entire family down with you!"

Kenny elbowed him in the ribs. "Before you throw your tantrum, could I borrow your cell phone? I left mine in my room and I've got to make a couple of important calls."

Without taking his eyes off Constance, Paul ripped the phone out of his pocket and handed it over. "Look at this," he demanded, flinging a folder toward her that he'd brought with him. "It's an interview with an old buddy of yours. Beverly Custerson. Ring any bells?"

Arthur kept his arm around Constance's shoulders. "What about her?"

"If you're wondering who sicced Damontraville on this family, I did. And I'm damn proud of it. I want the whole world to know what a crime against nature you are!"

"Paul!" she cried. His hate was as palpable as his physical presence.

Arthur leaped to his feet. "Don't talk to your mother like that."

"Who the hell are *you*? You're as twisted as she is. Constance Jadek's *not* my mother. Pepper Buckridge was my mother. And she'd be alive today if that woman hadn't poisoned her!" He pointed an accusing finger at Constance.

She was so shocked, it took a moment before she could speak. "Who . . . who told you that?"

"Not your buddy Beverly Custerson, that's for damn sure. She says you explained to her how my father poisoned my mother so he could marry you." He laughed, but it sounded more like a cry of outrage. "What kind of an idiot do you take me for? You primed that woman with a false story so that if any of this ever came out, someone would back up your little fiction to the police."

"Paul, you've got to listen to me. I don't know what's in this interview, but I didn't poison your mother. I swear it."

"I don't believe you! I've already contacted a lawyer. I want my mother's body exhumed. Once we establish that she was poisoned, I'm going to make sure you're arrested for murder!"

"That's enough," said Arthur. "Nathan was right. We need to meet to discuss all of this, but we can't do it here. We need privacy. Are you still planning to drive out to New Fonteney?"

Paul gave them both a hard look. "I wouldn't miss it for the world."

"Good. Then we'll see you there."

Constance could tell by the look on Paul's face that he

didn't like being dismissed, which was just what Arthur had done. She felt her own outrage so keenly that she was glad Arthur had taken over. If he hadn't, she might have said something she would have regretted later. Or maybe that had been her problem all her life. She'd been too worried about other people's feelings. Perhaps she should just tell the truth and let the chips fall where they may. The way she'd chosen to live was nobody's business but her own, and yet now that the tabloids were about to offer her up on a silver platter to be ripped apart by that great American two-headed dragon—an insatiable public and a prurience-driven media—she might as well come clean. Whether or not her children ever spoke to her again, there were some important truths they had to hear.

Kenny had retired to Arthur's bedroom to make his phone calls. When he finally returned to the living room, everyone was gone. Checking his watch, he saw that he had about forty-five minutes to make it out to New Fonteney. Nathan might have his reasons for calling the meeting, but Kenny had reasons of his own for wanting to be there.

After his conversation with David Polchow earlier in the day, he'd come to the conclusion that there was only one way to extricate himself from the walking disaster that was the Buckridge family. He'd just spoken with Nathan, filling him in on what Sophie had discovered. If she was allowed to go to the police with what she knew, the jig would be up. While they were talking, Sophie had shown up at Nathan's door. It was perfect. Kenny had ordered him to keep her there, emphasizing that Nathan needed to impress on her the ramifications of what she was about to do. At all costs, she had to be talked out of going to the police. He told Nathan to use whatever emotional leverage he had left. Unfortunately, Nathan hung up before Kenny got a real sense of how far he was willing to go.

The fact was, the only people Kenny really cared about in this whole mess, other than himself, were Emily and his children. He had to protect them, had to make sure that none of this touched them in any way. It was simple human survival, the most basic of all motivations. But it was pure luck that that tabloid article had appeared today. It played right into his hands.

As he was about to leave Constance's suite, Paul's cell phone rang. Clicking it on, Kenny said, "Hello?"

"Don't talk" came a female voice. "It's Marie. I've only got a few seconds before I board my plane. I just received an incredible E-mail and I had to pass it on to you right away."

"Okay," he replied, realizing that she thought he was Paul. He listened as she repeated the information, then said she'd be in touch.

Kenny shut off the phone and slipped it into his pocket. Well, wasn't that just the kicker? After everything he'd done to preserve Constance's good name, and now to find out it was all for nothing. The Buckridge family was in for one hell of a surprise tonight, compliments of Marie Damontraville.

32

"How about a glass of wine?" asked Nathan, laying the final birch log in the fireplace, then striking a match and setting the kindling ablaze.

Sophie was standing at a picture window overlooking the St. Croix. The monks had built the visitor's cabin directly behind the dining hall, allowing it an unobstructed view of the river valley as it sloped gently toward the water. The interior was simple but comfortable. The walls were the same rough-hewn wood used in the other buildings, and the furnishings were either new or made in the monks' workshop. Nathan had placed a small bouquet of lilies of the valley in the center of a long, narrow dining table. The scent filled the cabin with springtime.

"Wine would be nice," said Sophie, turning to face him. He was wearing one of the monk's robes. With his beard and his unruly black hair, he looked the part of a medieval friar. He'd explained that he found the robes amazingly comfortable and was glad a few had been left behind.

Sophie had driven to the old monastery for a specific reason, but she wanted to ease into the discussion, not hit Nathan over the head with what she knew the second she walked in the door. She planned to be long gone by the time the family meeting started. She had no desire to run into Kenny Merlin. But she figured she had a good half hour before she had to leave. "Arthur tells me you've bought New Fonteney."

He smiled. "I wanted to tell you right away, but the last couple of days have been pretty crazy." He glanced up at a small wine rack in the kitchen, twisting the bottles around so that he could read the labels more clearly. "What would you say about trying a Shiraz port? Someone gave me a bottle, told me it was a monster."

Sophie didn't doubt it. A Shiraz was nothing if not screaming fruit. Still, it sounded fun. "Sure, why not?"

"I can't vouch for it," he added, making a clean slice through the covering just under the rim, "so it will be a trial run for both of us." After he'd poured two glasses, he came into the living room holding them up and asking, "Where do you want to sit? I think it's a little cold on the deck. I've noticed that it's a lot chillier out here at night than it is in the city."

"Let's sit by the fire," said Sophie. She would have preferred to go for a walk, have the conversation out in the open air, but the fire looked inviting and so did the wine. There was a kind of unadorned peacefulness about the cabin that appealed to her. It must have appealed to Nathan, too, because he seemed completely at ease.

After tossing a couple of overstuffed pillows on the floor, Nathan sat down, waiting for Sophie to join him. When she did, he handed her a glass, then closed his eyes, breathed in the bouquet, and took a sip. "Yikes!" he said, his eyes popping right back open. "It's about what I expected."

Sophie tasted it next. "It's definitely one of the most flamboyant ports I've ever tasted."

"Flamboyant, huh? Ever the diplomat. It will serve you well in your new part-time profession."

There it was. Her opening. "Nathan . . ." She set the glass down, then drew her knees up to her chest. "The truth is, I came out here tonight because I . . . I needed to talk to you."

"I assumed you weren't here in your capacity as welcome wagon hostess." He smiled, then sobered, gazing at her thoughtfully before looking into the fire. "It's about George Gildemeister."

She wondered if she'd said or done something to give herself away. Keeping her eyes straight ahead, she said, "I know your family bribed him to write that negative review of the Belmont. I found a fax in some of George's papers. It's pretty damning."

"Why am I not surprised? You always did like a good mystery. You can't stand being in the dark."

"That's one of the reasons I was so drawn to you."

"Gee, and here I thought it was my boyish charm—and the profound nature of my soul."

"That, too."

He shook his head. "I wish, just this once, that you'd left well enough alone."

"I couldn't, Nathan. A friend of mine will go to prison if I don't do something to help him." She paused, trying to get a fix on what he was thinking. Was he actually going to let an innocent man take the rap when he had the power to stop it? "I want you to tell me what happened the night George died. You were there. So was Kenny. I have evidence to prove that, too."

"Have you talked to the police?"

"Not yet."

He leaned back against one of the pillows. "You realize, of course, that if you tell them what you know, it will ruin my family."

"If I don't tell, a friend will be convicted of a murder he didn't commit. I don't want to hurt you, Nathan, but I don't see how I can sit on this much longer."

"No," he said, pinching the bridge of his nose. "It's all my fault. I didn't realize I was doing it, but I've put you in the middle. Now I've got to get you out."

"What does that mean?"

He gave her a long look, then said, "Part of what I told you was true. When I got to George's apartment that night, he was already dead. Kenny and I were supposed to meet with him at seven-thirty to pay him off. I was late. Kenny was early. Not that it mattered because he found George dead, too. See, he told me that as he was getting out of his car, he saw Harry coming out of the building. Kenny knew who he was because the first night we got into town he'd driven over to the Belmont to check the place out. I mean, I knew I didn't murder George. And Kenny said he hadn't either. It just seemed logical to both of us that Harry must have done it. I felt terribly guilty for the part we'd played in George's death, but what could I do? And then when the police arrested Harry, I just prayed that they wouldn't find out who else had been there that night. But after what you told me in the park, I knew that a woman had seen me coming out of the apartment. I told Kenny I was afraid the police might pick me up for questioning. For obvious reasons, we didn't want that to happen. See, Kenny had already made a bid to buy the restaurant. If someone put two and two together, we would have had some pretty fast explaining to do. Anyway, Kenny said he'd take care of it."

"He did," said Sophie, her expression hardening. "He made a bunch of threatening phone calls to the woman, said she wouldn't live to see her next birthday if she didn't keep her mouth shut. She's so terrified she won't even leave her apartment."

"God, I had no idea." He hung his head.

"That's not all. Kenny made the calls from a pay phone just around the corner from Harry's house. That means the police think Harry did it. They want to revoke his bail and toss him back in jail. He's an old man, Nathan. He can't stand much more of this."

"I know. And I'm sorry. But you have to understand, until yesterday I thought he really was guilty. Now I know he's not. Kenny lied to me."

He seemed to be in such distress that Sophie gave him a moment before asking, "How did you find out?"

"This is such a nightmare. I'm not sure I'm ever going to wake up." Taking a deep breath, he continued. "Yesterday I was leaving the hotel when I bumped into him in the lobby. He was about to drive Emily to the airport and he was waiting for her to come downstairs. Knowing Emily, I realized it could take a while, so I told him I needed a word. He tried to put me off, but I wouldn't let him. We moved over to an empty corner and I told him about my suspicions. Something you said last Wednesday afternoon in the park kept eating at me."

"And that was?"

"You said George's neighbors had heard *two* separate arguments the night he died. I wondered about that. You don't know Kenny, but I do. He's a liar by nature, and a man with zero scruples. So I confronted him. I told him what I'd learned and then I asked him point-blank if he'd murdered George. He denied it, so I pressed harder. And I kept pressing until he told me the truth.

"According to Kenny, George was in meltdown mode that night. He'd just talked to Harry and something Harry said really got to him. George was feeling intensely guilty for what he'd done. When Kenny took out the money to pay him, he refused it, said he'd decided to come clean. He was going to call the paper in the morning and make a full confession. Well, Kenny couldn't allow that. He tried to talk him out of it. He used every argument he could think of, but nothing got through. He even offered George ten times the money we usually pay. He knew he couldn't just leave when George was in that state of mind. If the press got wind of what we were up to, all hell would break loose. I'm sure that deep in his soul, assuming he has one, Kenny sees himself as our savior. George had to be stopped, so he stopped him. And, he was quick to point out, since I'd been there too, who could say what had really gone on? After all, the woman across the hall ID'd *me*, not him. And even if the cops were able to somehow prove he'd done it, I'd go to jail as a coconspirator unless I went to the police right then, which he knew I wouldn't. He had me by the throat."

"So you did nothing."

He nodded. It was a simple gesture, and yet she could see the desperation in his eyes. "I had an important meeting in Duluth last night. It wasn't something I could put off. So yes, I left. But I haven't thought about anything else since Kenny told me what really happened. And, I admit, I'm scared to death of going to jail. I'm a coward, Sophie. I'm on the brink of finally getting my life together, and everything will be blown to bits if I do what's right." He turned his face away and stared once again into the fire.

"I'm sorry, Nathan."

After a long moment he said, "Yeah. Me, too." His voice was barely audible. "I was incredibly stupid to get involved in this."

"Sounds like you've done it before. Bribed a restaurant critic, I mean."

He picked up his wineglass. "A couple times. Kenny handled it. Kenny handles everything. I found the properties, then he moved in and did all the dirty work. But nobody'd ever turned on us before. When I talked to him yesterday, I could see he was genuinely frightened. My mother has no idea what we've been up to."

"Does Paul know?"

"Actually, he was the one who came up with the idea. It must have been about four years ago. It was a joke really. He threw it out one night after a few too many beers. We all laughed, talked about how much we loathed food critics. But Kenny wouldn't let it drop. He saw right away that the idea had potential. We'd just paid through the nose to buy a restaurant in Seattle, and Kenny thought this might be a way to create a more favorable bottom line. Paul and I both pretty much stayed out of it. The Buckridge boys keep their hands clean, Soph. Kenny took it from there. He's good at what he does. But sometimes, he doesn't have the best judgment. He goes too far."

"Like the car bomb, the one that killed Sean Rafferty."

Nathan drew his arms close around his body, as if he felt a chill. "Yes, like Rafferty. I suspected Kenny might be behind it. He confirmed it yesterday. His excuse was that Mom had ordered him to do whatever it took to stop Marie Damontraville. He felt he had carte blanche to take any action he deemed necessary."

"Why do you keep this guy around?"

Nathan's look was sharp. "Isn't it obvious? He's got the backbone the rest of us lack. I could have stopped this restaurant crap from happening, but I didn't. Neither did Paul. It was good for business, which thrilled Mom to no end. And Paul was amassing a stable of restaurants that fit right in with his long-term goals. I may travel around the country making sure everything is running smoothly, but it's Paul's kingdom I'm managing. He made sure his name went on all the deeds, along with my mother's."

"Not yours?"

"The truth is, I simply don't care. Paul's ego is on the line when it comes to the academy and the academy-sponsored restaurants, but it's never really meant that much to me. All that's ever really mattered to me is my mother." He took a sip of wine, then set the glass on the table behind him. "Since I've come back to Minnesota, it's like . . . like I've gone to visit a graveyard where my past is buried but all the corpses are up and walking around. Why don't they have the decency to stay in the ground, Sophie? The past doesn't belong in the present."

She wasn't entirely certain what he was talking about now, but the subject seemed to have changed. "No," she said, touching his hand lightly. "It doesn't."

His gaze swung back to her. "I wasn't talking about *you*."

"But I'm the past, too, Nathan. And that's where I should stay."

"No!"

"What are you going to do about Kenny? About George's murder?"

"I don't know." He pressed the tips of his fingers against his mouth.

She felt immensely sorry for him. And she also felt a little sorry for herself, too. If Nathan didn't come clean and make a full confession to the police, it would force her hand. She'd be put into the position of becoming the whistle-blower. "You have to tell the truth."

"I know. But the problem is, if Marie Damontraville writes her book, my mother's already in deep trouble, even if it all turns out to be lies, innuendo, and misunderstandings. But if her sons and her son-in-law are mixed up in a homicide, she'll have no chance at all. She'll be crucified in the media, and Kenny and I will be crucified in court."

Sophie turned at the sound of a car pulling up outside.

"God, what time is it?" asked Nathan. "I don't have my watch on."

Sophie checked hers. "It's quarter to seven. Somebody's early."

He shot to his feet. "You've got to get out of here."

Her thoughts exactly.

Picking up her purse, Nathan tossed it to her. "Come on," he ordered.

She grabbed her coat and followed him through the living room, down a long hall to the back door.

"Damn," he said, looking outside.

Sophie could see that his mother's car had just pulled up next to Paul's.

"This way," he said, racing back through the living room to the front door.

Just as he opened it, Kenny came bounding up the steps two at a time. Something about the phoniness of his thin-lipped smile made Sophie's skin crawl.

"Hey, Kenny," she said, slipping into her coat. "Nice to see you." Turning back to Nathan, she said, "Maybe you could call me in the morning."

"Sure thing."

Kenny shot Nathan a cautionary look. "If you stayed, Sophie, we could all go out to dinner later. My treat. I hear there's a wonderful restaurant in Stillwater. The Lowell Inn?"

"Sounds fun." She tried to keep her voice light. "But I'm afraid I'll have to take a rain check. I'm expected back at the Maxfield."

He leaned casually against the railing, then pulled a gun out of his coat pocket. "Get inside."

The horror on Sophie's face matched Nathan's.

"For God's sake, Kenny, put that away."

"Sorry, bro. No can do." Pressing the gun to Sophie's back, he said, "Move."

Sophie had no choice. She followed Nathan back into the cabin.

33

The rest of the family was just entering through the back door, walking slowly down the long hallway toward the living room, when Kenny whispered, "Somebody's got to be in control of this meeting, so I elected me. Keep your mouth shut about the .38 and nobody will get hurt."

Sophie didn't believe him, but there was little she could do about it now.

Nodding for Sophie and Nathan to sit on the couch, Kenny dipped the hand holding the gun back into his coat pocket and stood next to the fireplace. "Looks like we're all here," he said with unnecessary cheerfulness as Constance and Arthur perched on a wooden bench, their backs to the kitchen, and Paul threw himself sullenly into an overstuffed chair.

"Sophie was just leaving," said Kenny, "but I invited her to stay. She may be part of the family soon, if Nathan has his way." His eyebrows danced.

Sophie tried to smile through her fear but figured it was unconvincing. Not that anyone seemed to notice. Each member of the family looked so preoccupied, she felt her presence had barely registered.

"You'd better see this," said Arthur, tossing the tabloid newspaper to Nathan.

Nathan winced when he saw the front page. "God, this is terrible!"

Sophie swallowed hard as she read the lurid headline. It was the disaster Nathan had been fearing.

"We have Paul to thank for our current problems," continued Arthur, his words clipped. "He's the one who convinced Marie Damontraville to target Constance."

"Is that true?" asked Nathan.

"Don't blame me!" said Paul, exploding out of his chair. Then fixing Arthur with a contemptuous stare, he added, "You don't speak for me or my motives, so just shut up."

"Come on," pleaded Nathan, "let's keep this civil."

"Fuck civil! I told everyone else, so I might as well tell you. I'm going to have my mother's body exhumed. I want an autopsy done. She was poisoned."

"I know," said Nathan softly.

Paul's eyes narrowed. "Of course you know. You probably helped your mother do it."

"My mother didn't poison Pepper Buckridge."

"Right," Paul said, an angry crimson spreading over his cheeks. "Constance Buckridge is the personification of womanhood. She's too pure and noble to harbor emotions like hate and greed. Come on, Nathan, don't you realize she lied to you just like she lied to everyone else? She fed some friend of hers a line of bull about my dad wanting my mother out of the way so that he could marry her—the maid, for chrissake. It's ludicrous."

Arthur handed Nathan a file folder. "This is Damontraville's most recent interview—again, compliments of Paul.

She talked to a woman named Beverly Custerson. Both Constance and I knew her back in the Fifties, before I got sick."

"You mean before you lost all your fucking marbles," said Paul, his voice brimming with disdain. "That whole secret agent story. How pathetic can you get? If I hadn't been a kid, I would have seen right through it. And you wonder why I have a hard time believing anything you or Constance say."

Sophie knew she didn't belong here. It was hard to watch a family, people she'd once loved, disintegrate right before her eyes.

"We told you that story," said Constance evenly, "because I was afraid your father wouldn't let Arthur come live with us if he knew the truth. Arthur needed constant care after he got out of the hospital."

"Right. And we all know what kind of care you chose to give."

"That's enough," snapped Arthur.

"Oh, I don't think it's nearly enough," bellowed Paul. "What's it like to sleep with your sister, Art? Did it start then, or were you sleeping with her back in the Fifties, too?"

"My personal life is none of your business," Arthur replied firmly, attempting to retain some shred of dignity. And yet, with all the eyes in the room centered directly on him, it was a losing battle. "You don't have a clue what it was like for me."

Paul bent over him. "You wanna give us the details?"

Arthur glanced at Constance, then looked away. "No."

"Oh, come on," Paul taunted. "I'd like to know. For instance, what was it like listening to my dad call for help when you knew he was dying? Did you enjoy it? Did it make you feel powerful, like you'd taken his wife away from him right under his nose? You disgust me, you know that? What kind of a man are you?"

"Stop it!" demanded Constance, standing up and meeting Paul's eyes. "I was the one who refused to help your father. Your source was wrong. Arthur wanted to go to him, but I was the one who held him back. Wayne deserved to die for what he did."

"Right. He loved you. He gave you a good life. He bought

you everything you ever wanted. He took you all over the world so that you could indulge your little hobbies. He really deserved to die for *that*."

"He took my life from me," said Constance, "just as surely as he took your mother's from her. And then he informed me that he'd turn me over to the police unless I married him."

"That's a lie!"

"It's the truth," said Nathan. His voice expressed no anger, just weariness. "I was there. I heard it all."

Paul turned to look at him. "Don't do this, Nathan. Don't lie to protect her. She's not worth it."

"I'm not lying. Your father poisoned your mother. He used antifreeze. He even sent me out to the garage one evening to fetch it for him. He said he needed it for the radiator in his car. I believed him. But *he* was the liar, Paul. I was in the house the day he issued that threat to my mother. Pepper hadn't even been dead twenty-four hours. Wayne Buckridge was a bastard, a sick man. Maybe my mother shouldn't have let him die, but I understand why she did it. He used your mother's death and my mother's love for me to force her into a loveless marriage."

"Take that back!" Paul thrust a fist in Nathan's face.

"I can't. It's the truth. And if you don't believe me, there was another witness to what your father said to my mother that day."

"You're making it up as you go along. You're just as pathetic as she is."

"Remember Andrea Shaw, Paul? The girl who lived next door? She was a couple years older than me, but we played together all the time. She was with me that afternoon. We were in the pantry. We'd just come in from outside, so nobody knew we were there. Your father and my mother were talking in the kitchen. We heard it all. Andrea wanted to tell her parents, but I stopped her. I was glad I did, because later Mom made us both promise to keep what we'd heard a secret. Andrea and I talked about it a few times after that, but we finally made a pact never to discuss it again. I went to visit her last night, Paul. She lives in Duluth now. While I was there, she typed out a short statement. It's in my briefcase over on the desk if you'd care to look at it. It confirms what I just told you."

Paul glanced at the briefcase but made no move toward it. "I don't believe you," he said after a few seconds, though his voice had lost some of its conviction.

"Go ahead and have Pepper Buckridge exhumed," said Constance, sitting back down next to Arthur. "If you force the issue, you'll only succeed in proving to the world what kind of monster your father really was."

Paul whirled around to look at her. In a voice full of loathing, he said, "I wish to God this family had never heard of Arthur or Connie Jadek."

Kenny had been silent throughout the entire argument, but now Sophie watched him as he moved away from the mantel. He cleared his voice, then said, "Something truly amazing happened to me about an hour ago. I was just leaving the Maxfield to drive out here when I got a call on Paul's cell phone."

Paul felt his pocket. "*You* got a call?"

"Well, it was for you, of course, but I took the message. It was from Marie Damontraville. Seems she was about to get on a plane but had just received a fascinating piece of information from one of her field researchers. She wanted to pass it on."

"She must have thought you were me," said Paul, looking indignant.

"Guess so." Kenny seemed to be enjoying himself. He paused. Then looking around as if he was about to make a momentous announcement, he said, "Connie Jadek died in Libertyville, Wisconsin, when she was five years old."

Constance gasped.

"Say that again," said Paul.

"You all heard me. And that leads to my next question." Fixing his eyes firmly on Constance, Kenny said, "Who the hell are *you*?"

* * *

Bram returned to the Maxfield after spending the afternoon working in his office at WTWN. He was tired and wanted nothing more than to mix himself a dry martini and sit out on his balcony with his feet up on a footstool. Mosquito-free evenings were springtime events in Minnesota. They didn't last long. He knew that Sophie had probably talked to Nathan today, and he wanted to hear all about it, but first he needed a mental-health moment. Saying goodbye to Marie earlier in the day hadn't exactly been the highlight of his week. Even though she'd told him not to worry, he was still concerned for her safety, and he would continue to be for a long time to come.

Before going upstairs he checked Sophie's office, the place she'd normally be on a Saturday afternoon, but he found it empty. Her cell phone was right where it shouldn't be, in its battery charger. If she'd left the hotel, it meant he couldn't reach her. Feeling thwarted, he headed toward the elevators, but before he reached the side hallway, one of the bellboys trotted up with a note Sophie had left for him at the concierge desk.

Thanking the young man, Bram opened the envelope and took out a piece of hotel stationery. He read through it quickly, happy at least to know where his wife was, but unhappy about her destination. He was hoping she'd be able to meet with Nathan at the Maxfield. Safety in numbers, that sort of thing.

As he stuffed the note in his coat pocket, he looked up and saw Harry coming out of the kiosk. "Damn," he muttered to himself, hurrying toward him. Didn't he realize he was a wanted man? Sophie had ordered him to stay in his room.

"Evening, Harry," Bram said, clapping him on the shoulder, then taking him by the arm and leading him toward the back stairs. They could walk up two flights and catch the elevator on three. Fewer prying eyes. "Didn't you see the paper this morning?"

"Of course I saw it," said Harry, yanking his arm away.

"The police are officially looking for you. You shouldn't be wandering around the lobby."

"I got bored," he grumbled. "I needed some fresh air. A few snacks. And some reading material. Don't worry, I was careful."

Since Harry was carrying neither, Bram had to ask. "This isn't the first time you've come down here today, is it?"

"The third. Let me tell you, that little store of yours was really jumpin' around three. That tabloid newspaper was selling like hotcakes. And hey, someone told me Constance Buckridge and her family are staying at the Maxfield. Have been all week. I didn't believe them, but then I saw the whole group march out of here, and let me tell you, nobody was in a good mood."

"What time was that?"

"An hour ago, maybe."

Now Bram was worried. As he glanced toward the front doors, two uniformed policemen entered the lobby.

"Listen to me, pal. You've got to get out of here."

Looking around, Harry said, "Oops. The fuzz." He ducked his head.

"We don't want to attract any attention, so play it cool."

It wasn't far to the back stairway. As soon as the door closed behind them, Bram told Harry to stick close. He led the way down to the basement, then out into another hallway. At the far end, they got on the service elevator, which took them back to the main floor. Since it put them right next to the rear exit, Bram unlocked the door with his key and pushed through. Finally they were out on the street.

"Listen," said Bram, drawing Harry close. "I want you to wait in the alley. Stand in the shadows until I come to pick you up."

"Where are we going?"

"You said you were bored, right?"

"Yeah."

"We're going to visit a monastery."

Harry blinked twice. "I'm not very religious."

Bram didn't care what Sophie said about Nathan's innocence. He didn't like the idea of her being alone with him out in the middle of nowhere. Not that he knew where New

Fonteney was, but he'd get directions on the way. Harry would just have to come along for the ride.

Kenny had dropped his bomb and the explosion had been suitably deafening. Sophie wanted to say something to erase the stunned look on Nathan's face, but that was up to his mother now.

As the silence settled around them, Constance sat next to Arthur, looking deeply shaken. Everyone was waiting for her to respond to Kenny's question, but so far she hadn't. Finally, after standing and straightening her dress, she said, "My name is Betty Kovak, or at least it was when I was growing up in the Forties back in Madison, Wisconsin. My father was a professor at the University of Wisconsin and my mother was a housewife. My father and mother were also alcoholics. My childhood was miserable, full of fights and abuse, and very little love. In 1953, when I was fifteen, I took a job at a local café. I worked afternoons and weekends, anything to get out of the house. I met a boy, fell in love, and got pregnant, all within the space of six months. When my parents found out about the pregnancy, they threw me out of the house. I had no choice but to go to where my boyfriend was and beg him to take me in."

Constance looked tenderly at Arthur, then sat down and took hold of his hand. "This wonderful man sitting next to me isn't my brother. But I took his name long before I had any right to it. I lied to him about my age. He thought I was seventeen when we met. When he found out I was pregnant and barely sixteen, he was scared. I don't know what the laws are now, but back then he could have gone to jail for statutory rape. He was a junior that year at the University of Minnesota, well on his way to a fine career and a good life. But it all would have ended if the authorities had found out. Mostly, though, we were afraid of my dad. If he discovered where I'd gone and who the father of my child was, he would have hurt Arthur, maybe even killed him. Certainly he would have turned him over to the police. My father's temper had ruled my life ever since I was a small child. So when I got to Minneapolis and one of my boyfriend's neighbors, a woman named Beverly Custerson, asked me who I was, I said I was Arthur's sister, come to live with him because I was pregnant and desperate. It was a lie, of course, but Arthur and I felt it was a necessary charade. That way, my father could never find me.

"I knew that Arthur's sister, Connie, had died as a young child. We figured out later that we could get a copy of her birth certificate and use it to help me get a driver's license. And then I used the driver's license and the birth certificate to help us get a marriage license when I turned eighteen." She looked around the room, waiting for reactions, but encountered only incredulous stares. So she continued. "We were married in the spring of 1956. But then Arthur got sick. I didn't understand mental illness back then. I just knew he wasn't the person I'd fallen in love with. Nathan, you were barely five when Arthur left for good. I thought my world had ended. In many ways, it had. I struggled for almost two years to keep us off the streets, and I managed, with the help of friends, to do just that. I took any job I could get. I never stopped looking for Arthur, but by the time I took the position as maid at the Buckridge household, I was twenty-three years old. No longer a girl. The time Arthur and I had spent together felt like a dream.

"After I married Wayne, we settled into our life at the house. I already loved Paul like my own son. I felt sorry that he'd lost his mother and tried to make up for it, but it wasn't easy. I hired private investigators to find Arthur, but by the time I gave birth to Emily in '66, I was sure he was dead. Still, I always had someone out there looking. In 1973, the miracle happened. Arthur was discovered living in a flophouse on Lake Street. But, as I quickly discovered, he was still very ill. He was so thin and he didn't recognize me.

"Funny. I always thought that his homecoming would be so different. He'd be completely over his sickness, he'd know me and I'd rush into his arms. Life isn't like that, I guess. But slowly, as his strength came back and the drugs they put him on took effect, he came back to himself—and to me. I'd never been so happy. Our love was as vibrant and alive as it had been all those years ago. For Arthur, time had stopped. He'd aged fourteen years since I'd last seen him, but I was still the only woman he'd ever loved. For me, however, time hadn't stopped. I'd married another man, a man I hated. I knew the marriage wasn't legally valid because Arthur hadn't been gone seven years when Wayne and I were wed. I was still legally married to Arthur. When I thought of what Wayne had done to me, it gave me a great deal of satisfaction knowing I could drop that on him at any time.

"And yet, before Arthur returned, I'd made a kind of peace with my life. That all changed in the blink of an eye in 1973. The problem was, if I told Wayne the truth, Emily would have been hurt terribly. She would have become the child of an un-married couple. I knew she'd be devastated. The only family she'd ever known would have been ripped apart. But if I didn't tell the truth, I denied Nathan his real father. Either way, somebody lost.

"I'm ashamed to say that my answer was finally deter-mined by money. Arthur needed drugs, expensive drugs. And he needed therapy. Returning from the brink of madness is a long and expensive journey. If I told Wayne the truth, my ac-cess to that money would have been cut off. I wanted Arthur to have the best. It seemed ironic that Wayne would end up paying for it, but that irony also appealed to me. After Arthur moved into the house, he started thinking about going back to school. Again the issue was finances. He didn't have a penny, but I did. When Wayne died, the entire estate came to me.

"Arthur went back to get his master's at the University of Minnesota and later his Ph.D. at UCLA. And yes," she added, "I did sleep with my husband on the day Wayne found us to-gether. He shouldn't have been home that early, but he was. He was so angry, I never had a chance to tell him the truth. I wanted to that day. I would have risked everything just to see the look on his face, but he died before I could tell him. Maybe his medication would have helped him, maybe not. It's probably the single worst thing I've ever done in my life, and I don't regret it for a minute. His death set things right. I was finally free of him, and I had the resources to give my husband everything he needed to get well. My regrets lie solely with my children."

Arthur was silent throughout Constance's explanation. Now it was his turn to talk. "Nathan, you have no idea how many times I've wanted to tell you I was your father. I'm so proud of you. You've become such a fine man. Your mother and I were young and stupid, too young to see that the decisions we made would affect our lives—and yours—forever. But we loved each other and we loved you. We never tried to hurt anyone, we were just trying to survive. Every life is an odyssey. One never knows from one minute to the next what's going to happen. If you could just find it in your heart to forgive us. Ever since I came back into your life, I've tried to be there for you. If you could just tell me I haven't failed completely . . ."

Sophie could feel Nathan stir beside her. He'd been so still while his mother was talking, she'd almost forgotten he was there.

He eased slowly to the edge of the couch, leaned his elbows on his knees, and said, "You'll have to give me a little time. This is pretty . . . mind-bending."

"As much time as you want," said Arthur quickly, hopefully.

"As far as forgiveness goes," continued Nathan, "there's nothing to forgive. I know how devoted you've been to my mother all these years and she to you. And you've been a good friend to me. We were all caught in a web and we couldn't get free. I'm sorry you had to keep so much of your life a secret. I'm sad to say that I know what that's like."

"But no more secrets now," said Kenny, his voice once again oddly cheerful.

"This is disgusting," said Paul, glaring at everyone. "This touching little family scene makes me want to puke. Emily's going to be thrilled to find out she's illegitimate. You lost me a long time ago, Constance or Betty or whatever the hell your name is, but you'd better be prepared to lose your daughter now, too."

"We've got to call her," said Constance, her lower lip beginning to tremble. She grabbed Arthur's arm. "I don't want her to hear this from someone else. Where's your phone?" she asked, glancing over at Nathan.

"No phones," said Kenny.

Constance looked up at him, surprised.

"We've got another little matter we've got to discuss before this meeting's over. Constance, I doubt anyone's bothered to fill you in on our involvement with George Gildemeister and the Belmont, but perhaps one of your sons would like to do it now."

"Gildemeister?" repeated Arthur. "Isn't he the man who was just murdered by that restaurant owner?"

"Turns out," said Kenny, stepping directly in front of the fireplace, "that Mr. Hongisto, the restaurant owner, didn't do it. But one of us did."

Constance shot off the bench again. "What are you saying?"

"Sit down."

"Don't order me around."

"I said, sit down!" His voice had risen to a commanding shout.

Constance stared at him for a moment, then did as he asked. A look of panic suddenly crossed her face. "You mean, someone in this family—"

"That's right. It was Paul's idea. Bribe a food critic to pan a restaurant, then wait to see what happens. If it falters and looks as if it may close, the Buckridge boys zoom in and buy it at a huge discount. How do you think we managed to acquire all those ritzy restaurants at such great prices?"

Constance looked dumbfounded. "Nathan, is this true?"

"Nathan should know," said Kenny with a dry smile. "He's the one who took care of Gildemeister."

"That's a lie!" said Nathan.

"There's even an eyewitness," continued Kenny. "But he had to do it. Gildemeister was going to blow the whistle on our operation. We couldn't have that. I suppose when it comes right down to it, Nathan is a hero."

"You're slime, Merlin," said Nathan.

Sophie could tell he was barely restraining himself, but Nathen knew Kenny had a gun. That changed the balance of power.

"God, I had no idea," said Paul. "You're in some pretty deep shit, bro. We all are. I agree with Kenny. We have to deal with this right now."

Kenny ignored them both. "I've been thinking about this all day. Our world seems to be crashing down around our ears. Constance and her brother-husband have just been labeled sexual outlaws for all the world to see and judge. Turns out Paul and Emily's daddy was a murderer. Don't think that won't be emblazoned on the jacket of Marie Damontraville's book. And we have a more immediate issue in George Gildemeister and his recent demise. Any suggestions? Solutions?"

"You know what?" said Paul. "I've had it. My solution is to wash my hands of all of you." He was about to get up when Kenny pulled out his gun.

"I'm the one who's *had it* with this family. And I've decided there's only one way out."

Sophie's eyes opened wide. "What do you mean?" she asked, attempting not to stare at the barrel.

Holding the gun almost casually, Kenny continued. "Here's how I see it playing out. Paul Buckridge thinks Constance murdered his real mom. To help him discover the truth, he finds a woman who is known for writing tabloid-style investigative biographies of famous people. He promises her a great story. But when he finds out his father murdered his mother, it's too much for him. At almost the same moment, he sees his own career going down the drain when an article in a national magazine breaks the story that his stepmother is a sexual deviant. Since his career is inextricably tied to hers, he feels his life has been destroyed. All he can think of is revenge.

"He calls a family meeting in a remote area, an old monastery. When everyone gets there, he pulls out a gun and demands that one member of the family tie the others up." Looking directly at Paul, Kenny reached inside his coat and pulled out a roll of duct tape. "Here," he said, tossing it to him. "Do it."

"You want me to tie up my family?"

"Wrists behind their backs, ankles, and one piece of tape across each mouth. And do it tightly. I'm watching."

"What if I refuse?"

Slowly, Kenny leveled the .38 at Paul's chest. "You have to ask? But if you cooperate, I think we might be able to strike a deal."

"Meaning what?"

He paused. "You hate these people as much as I do. We'll make it look like a murder-suicide. Only in this scenario Nathan will be the one who goes crazy, not you. We'll have to tweak the motivation slightly, but it won't be a problem. What do you say? We'll take over the family business together. I could do it alone, I suppose, but I need someone like you. I'm not a chef. Besides, Emily loves you, and I love Emily. We can make it work. I know we can. Is it a deal?"

Paul looked from face to face. Finally, a smile tugged at the corners of his mouth. "I like it."

"Me, too. Now get busy."

As Paul began to unroll the tape, everyone in the room started talking at once.

"You'll never get away with it," said Nathan.

"Paul, you're not thinking clearly," cried Arthur. "Don't help him do this to us!"

"Let's just talk about it for another few minutes," said Constance, sounding desperate. "Surely we can come to some other conclusion!"

"I was supposed to be home an hour ago," pleaded Sophie. "My husband has called the police by now. And he knows where I am."

"Then we'd better hurry," said Kenny. "By the way, I'm so pleased you could join us this evening, Sophie. It saves me the trouble of having to track you down later."

In a matter of minutes everyone was bound and gagged.

"Now it's time for the gasoline," said Kenny, walking around and checking Paul's handiwork.

"What gasoline?" asked Paul, edging over to the fireplace.

"It's out in my car."

"You're going to burn the place down?"

"I know. It's such beautiful wood. But it's a sacrifice we have to make. And, lucky for everyone, it will go up in a matter of minutes."

"I'll go get it," offered Paul. "Toss me your keys." As Kenny reached into his pocket, Paul grabbed the fireplace poker and lunged at him.

Kenny stood his ground and shot Paul point-blank in the head. The fireplace poker dropped next to Kenny's shoe as Paul hit the floor with a thud.

Through her gag, Constance began to scream.

"This whole family is nothing but a bunch of fucking morons," muttered Kenny, slipping the gun back into his pocket and then dragging Paul out the front door by his feet.

34

On the way through Stillwater, Bram and Harry pulled into a gas station to get directions to New Fonteney. After starting the pump, Bram approached the service desk and cornered the first person he ran into, a young kid who looked about sixteen. "You ever heard of New Fonteney?" he asked.

The kid stopped and scratched the side of his arm. "They played in town last winter, I think. Rhythm and blues, right?"

"Right," said Bram, heading into the garage. This time he found a middle-aged man sitting on a stool, wiping the grime off a carburetor. "Excuse me," he said, then waited for the man to look up. "Do you know where New Fonteney is?"

"Sorry. Ask Dean. He's lived around here longer than me."

"Where would I find him?"

He shrugged. "Probably around back having his dinner."

Bram darted out of the garage door, sprinted past the rest rooms on the side of the station, and finally found a white-haired man sitting on a plastic lawn chair. He was halfway through a peanut butter and jelly sandwich. "Are you Dean?"

"Last I heard."

"The guy inside said you'd be able to give me directions to New Fonteney."

"That depends."

"On what?"

"On which entrance you're looking for."

"Isn't there a main entrance?"

"Sure, but it's not as scenic. If you park near the south gate, you approach it from the woods. Spectacular view of the river."

"I'm not into grandeur. I'm into speed."

"Your loss." He took a sip of Coke, then adjusted his glasses. "Take 95 out of town. When you come to County Road 74, turn right. It's about five miles from there. You can't miss the sign. Well, unless it's dark." He peered up at the sky. "It's getting on toward dusk. Might be a problem."

"What's the sign look like?"

"One of those metal types. White with black lettering. Not very big. Sometimes, if nobody's been around to cut down the brush, it can get buried."

"One more reason to love the great outdoors."

"Just remember it's about five miles after you turn onto 74." He took a bite of his sandwich, then chewed for a moment. "Or . . . is that 17?"

"We'll find it," said Bram, feeling that if he stayed a minute longer, he wouldn't even be able to find his own car.

Kenny dumped Paul's body in the grass outside the cabin. Yelling for everyone inside to stop their wailing, he rushed back to his car. After opening the trunk, he slipped on a pair of leather gloves, then removed two three-gallon plastic drums and set them on the ground. There was no reason to hurry. The monastery was private property. It wasn't as if people just wandered in and out. But Kenny knew he couldn't rest until he'd finished the job he'd come to do.

Picking up the gasoline drums, he headed back to the cabin. The first order of business was to drag Paul's body farther away from the door. Once he'd positioned him correctly— facedown, left arm pinned beneath him, right arm curved up toward his head—Kenny spent a few minutes wiping his gun clean of prints. Squeezing Paul's hand around the handle, he positioned the index finger on the trigger and fired, sending a bullet whizzing into the air over the roof. That set up the suicide part of the murder-suicide.

Next, he unscrewed the cap from a plastic drum and began to spread the gasoline around the base of the house. Since it was a wood-frame building, it would go up fast. He would tell the police that, yes, he'd come to the cabin for the family meeting but had left almost immediately, after Nathan had confessed to two murders, George Gildemeister's and Sean Rafferty's. He was sickened when he found out the truth. He knew from talking to Paul earlier that he was in a depressed, even desperate mood, but they'd always been such close friends. Perhaps that's why he'd let Kenny go when he had such a gruesome ending planned for everyone else. It made a good story, the friendship part adding just the right touch of pathos.

The light was fading fast, which was perfect in Kenny's estimation. He emptied the first drum on the side of the house that faced the river, then fetched the second. As he worked his way around the back, he found himself whistling for the first time in years. It wouldn't be long before all his problems would be over. Instead of being the object of loathing, he and Emily would be pitied by a compassionate nation. Perhaps he'd even call Marie Damontraville and offer her an exclusive interview. For a price, of course, most likely a cut of the royalties. But one thing was for sure. The Buckridge name, while sullied, would continue under Kenny's leadership to be a viable force in the American culinary community.

* * *

Out on the highway both Bram and Harry missed the sign that would have directed them into the main gate of the monastery. After they realized they'd gone too far, they backed into a dirt road overgrown with weeds and turned around. A few minutes later Bram spied several cars parked in a small clearing. He pulled off the road into a patch of scrub brush, then switched off the motor. He'd expected to find Nathan's and Sophie's cars, but there were three more, none of which he recognized. He assumed they belonged to Nathan's family, and that meant he wasn't sure what he was about to walk in on.

"Stay here," he said to Harry. "I'll be right back."

"Are you sure you don't need any help?"

Bram wasn't sure at all, but he'd rather keep Harry where he knew he wouldn't have to worry about him, especially if matters got ugly.

Heading up the path toward what looked like a chapel, he tried to make as little noise as possible. He had the element of surprise on his side and he didn't want to blow it. As he neared a low, vine-covered building, he thought he smelled gasoline. He glanced toward the river thinking that there might be a boat landing somewhere close, but the water was too far away—and the smell was too strong.

Panic seized him as he rounded the rear of the building and saw a man dumping gasoline around the base of a small cabin. Since nobody else was around, Bram knew it could only mean one thing.

With no time to plan, he rushed forward and dove at the man's feet, sending him sprawling. When a lighter flew past his head, Bram knew he'd arrived just in time. Another few seconds and the cabin would have gone up in flames—with Sophie inside. He didn't know that for a fact, but he *knew*.

Bram struggled with the man in the grass, trying to pin his shoulders. "Merlin!" he said finally, his hands groping to find his jaw, his neck. "Where's my wife?" he said, pressing hard, forcing his head back.

"Who the hell are you?" choked Kenny. Without waiting for an answer, he slammed a knee into Bram's stomach. Bram doubled over and Kenny slid out from under him. A second later something hard and heavy caught Bram in the stomach again. As he twisted onto his back, he saw that it was one of Kenny's size-ten wing tips. The blow left him gasping for air. Even so, he managed to grab Kenny's leg as he tried to stand and flipped him on his back. Bram's eyes raked around wildly, looking for a weapon. That's when he saw a stack of logs piled next to the cabin. He scrambled toward them. When he looked around, he saw that Kenny was heading straight for him, a steel crowbar held over his head. Bram had no idea where he'd found it, but as it sliced through the air in front of him, he ducked out of the way. Then he swung a log hard at Kenny's midsection—and connected.

Kenny grunted as he hit the grass face first. In a flash, Bram was on top of him. He tried to jam Kenny's arm behind his back, but the man was surprisingly strong. They rolled around, all arms and legs, slugging and struggling and swearing, until somehow they were both standing again. Bram took a couple of deep breaths to get his bearings, but Kenny had already grabbed for the log. He lunged at Bram so fast, all Bram could do was duck. This time, however, as he shot back up, Kenny connected with a vicious blow. Pain exploded inside Bram's head. Staggering backward, he fell against a bush, sinking into the branches. He didn't black out, but a thick fog enveloped him. He struggled not to fade, but the soft blackness at the edges of his mind seemed so inviting. When he finally opened his eyes, he saw that the building was ablaze.

"No!" he screamed, trying to extricate himself from the grasping branches.

"Jesus," snarled Kenny, turning around. "What the hell is your head made of?"

His head might be hard, but the rest of his body felt like jelly. He tried to get up, but before he made it very far, Kenny was standing over him with the crowbar.

"Feel a little like a fly trapped in honey, do you?" the lawyer asked. "Don't worry. You won't feel a thing in a minute." He raised the bar with both hands.

"Drop it!" came a deep voice from behind them.

Kenny whirled around just as Harry lifted a gun and

pointed it directly at his chest. The light was almost gone now, but the spreading fire lent an eerie glow to the scene.

"Mr. Hongisto," said Kenny, his expression turning flat. "What the hell are you doing here?"

"I'm with him." He nodded to Bram. "Put it down. Now!"

Kenny dropped the crowbar in the grass.

Bram tried once more to get up. This time he made it. Whipping off his tie, he bound Kenny's hands behind his back, then ordered him to sit down. As he dashed past Harry, he told the older man to keep Kenny covered. "Don't take your eyes off him, got that? Not until I come back."

"Will do."

Bursting into the cabin through the already open front door, Bram found the interior thick with smoke. He covered his mouth and nose with his hand, not that it helped much. He could make out the outlines of people seated around the room, all bound and gagged. He rushed to Sophie first, pulling the tape off her mouth.

She choked on the smoke, coughed deeply, then rasped, "Get a knife from the kitchen to cut us loose. Otherwise it's going to take forever."

Bram realized she was right. But he didn't have to go to the kitchen. He always carried a tiny pocketknife. It wasn't much, but it was enough. In a matter of seconds, he had her hands free and then her legs. "Get out of here," he ordered. "I'll take care of the rest." He could tell she didn't want to leave. "Don't make me carry you out. There isn't time! Crawl. There's more air near the floor. And call 911." He handed her his cell phone, hoping it hadn't been broken during the fight.

Reluctantly she did as he asked.

After she was safely outside, Bram turned his attention to Constance. She'd already passed out from the smoke, but Arthur, who was sitting next to her, was still conscious. Bram worked quickly to free them both, then helped Arthur drag her out the front door and down the steps, finally laying her on the grass.

"Where's Nathan?" shouted Sophie.

Suddenly from inside the cabin came the sound of cracking and then breaking wood. One of the ceiling joists crashed diagonally across the room as part of the roof collapsed inward.

Sophie screamed.

"You can't go back in there," shouted Arthur. "He's my son. Let me do it." Before anyone could stop him, he rushed back into the burning cabin.

Bram and Sophie knelt next to Constance, checking her vital signs. She had some burns on her right arm and shoulder. The wounds looked deep and painful. It was probably best that she was unconscious.

"Did you call 911?" asked Bram.

Sophie coughed. "They're coming."

"The smoke's so thick in there it's like the middle of the night." Bram coughed a few more times himself, trying to clear his lungs. "Maybe I should—"

"No." Sophie gripped his hand. "You stay put."

He could see not only the fear in her eyes but also the resolve.

An instant later Arthur appeared. He was on his hands and knees, struggling to drag Nathan out of the door by using the belt of his robe. Arthur looked as if he was about to collapse.

Bram and Sophie rushed to his side.

The steps were burning now, but they managed to get them both down to the grass without anyone's clothing catching on fire. Nathan was out cold, but he was breathing. Arthur was coughing so deeply he couldn't talk. His hands also looked like they were badly burned. But they were all alive.

Sophie grabbed Bram and held him tight. "You were my only hope. But I didn't think you'd come. When the fire started outside and we could see it climbing the walls, coming in through the windows . . ." She stopped and closed her eyes.

Bram brushed the soot off her cheeks, then crushed her in his arms. She was shivering. "I'll always come, sweetheart. I knew you needed me. I don't know how, but I did."

"Must be ESP," she whispered.

"Good karma."

"A true Zen connection."

He smiled, kissing her softly. "Or maybe it's just love."

35

On Sunday morning Sophie and Bram sat in the passenger lounge outside gate 31, waiting for Rudy and John's plane to land. After a night spent partly at the hospital and then later at the police station, they'd arrived late at the airport, hoping the plane hadn't arrived early. But when they checked the arrivals and departures screens as they came in the doors, they saw that flight 892 from St. Louis had a flashing DELAYED sign next to it.

"Now what?" asked Sophie, too exhausted to be worried but worried nonetheless.

"It's probably nothing," Bram assured her. "I got on a plane once in Detroit. We couldn't leave because the food hadn't been delivered yet. We must have twiddled our thumbs for an hour before the plane was stocked and ready for takeoff."

Sophie wanted to believe the cause of the delay was something that simple, especially after what they'd been through last night. But the way her fortunes had been running, she had a feeling this was more of the same. "We better ask somebody what's going on."

After waiting in line for half an hour to talk to a TWA official, they were informed that Rudy and John's plane from Washington, D.C., had been late landing in St. Louis and that the connecting flight from St. Louis to Minneapolis/St. Paul International had experienced a mechanical problem just before takeoff. The woman suggested that if they moved to the gate, someone there would keep them updated about the status of the flight.

"Why can't they tell us whether or not the plane's taken off?" asked Sophie, peering into her paper coffee cup as if it contained something suspicious.

Bram shrugged. "Bureaucrats. They're everywhere. Under rocks. Hanging from trees."

They'd certainly run into their share of bureaucrats last night.

As soon as the police, the paramedics, and the fire department had arrived at the monastery, Kenny Merlin was taken into custody and everyone else was hustled to the nearest hospital. The medical examiner had been called to deal with Paul's body but didn't arrive until after they were gone. While they were waiting to get into the paramedic van, Sophie watched the firefighters hose down the burning cabin until it posed no danger to the other buildings.

The burns on Arthur's hands and Constance's shoulder and arm were serious and required further medical treatment. Nathan's hair had been singed, not life-threatening, but he'd swallowed so much smoke that the emergency-room doctor suggested he stay in the hospital overnight for observation. Bram and Sophie were released with nothing more than a few bumps and bruises but were told to take it easy for the next few days.

"I don't consider this taking it easy," said Sophie, drumming her fingers on the arm of the chair. She eyed a 747 as it rolled past the windows.

"It's only an hour or two by air from here to St. Louis," said Bram. "Once they finally get airborne, it won't take long."

"I wish that damn 'delayed' sign would stop flashing."

He glanced up at the screen, then shook his head. Slipping his arm around her shoulders, he squeezed her neck reassuringly. "You're exhausted."

She looked at him sideways, then smirked. "And you look like W. C. Fields."

"Thanks." He touched his swollen nose. "It was a lucky punch."

After being released from the hospital, Bram, Sophie, and Harry had all been driven to the police station in downtown St. Paul. Once they were seated in an interrogation room, Sophie told her story, everything from finding George's body last Sunday night to her final conversation with Nathan at New Fonteney. She also mentioned the evidence she'd discovered along the way. Perhaps it wasn't her place, but she said she was sure Kenny had been behind everything. The police seemed to agree.

Before the three of them left to go home, they were informed that Kenny would be arraigned in the morning, charged with two counts of first-degree murder, one count of second-degree murder, four counts of attempted murder, and one count of arson. There were some other charges pending, one having to do with the possession of an illegal firearm, but by the time the entire list had been read, Sophie's mind had shut down. All she knew was that Kenny would get what was coming to him, and Harry was a free man.

The only problem that still concerned her was Nathan. It was possible, even likely, that he would be charged as an accessory after the fact to George's murder.

"Do you think Nathan will end up in prison?" asked Sophie, sitting up straight and finishing the last of her cold coffee.

Bram didn't say anything for almost a minute. Finally he bent his head and replied, "I am a hopelessly flawed human being."

"Why do you say that?"

"Because, even after everything that's happened, I'm still jealous of Nathan Buckridge."

"Sweetheart—"

He held up his hand. "I should have told you this before we left the hotel, but I didn't. I talked to Al Lundquist this morning."

"And?"

"Seems Nathan has already hired himself a lawyer. She's negotiating to get all the charges against him dropped."

Sophie didn't understand. "Is that possible?"

"It's probably some sort of plea-bargain arrangement. In return for his testimony against Kenny, he'll be given full immunity. Or, at least, that's what they're asking for. Al thought he'd get it, which means he won't do any time. Nathan will be able to open his cooking school forty miles from the hotel and be a thorn in my side for the rest of my life."

"Honey, it's not going to be like that."

"He was your first love, Soph. That's something I can never be. I came along after Norman Abnormal. As I've said many times before, anyone would look good next to him." He sighed, then sat back in his chair. "The thing is, last night, when I wanted to go back into the cabin to help Arthur drag Nathan out, you said no. You wouldn't let me. It felt like you'd chosen me over him. That really meant something to me. But this morning that same niggling sense of doubt's still there."

She gazed up into his gentle green eyes. How could she tell him *she* was the deeply flawed human being? He'd picked up on her ambivalence and to tell him it hadn't been there would be to play with his sense of reality. She wouldn't do that. None of what she'd done had been fair. And yet he was right. If a choice had to be made, she *had* chosen him over Nathan last night, and she always would. "Sweetheart, listen to me. You may not have been my first love, but you're my last. That's what counts. You've got to know how much I love you."

Over the loudspeaker a woman's voice announced, "We have just been informed that flight 892 from St. Louis to Minneapolis/St. Paul has been diverted to O'Hare International in Chicago. We have no further information, but as updates become available, we'll pass them on to you."

Bram and Sophie were on their feet in a flash and heading toward the desk. So were forty other people.

"Can't you give us a reason?" demanded Bram.

A chorus of voices chimed in behind him.

"All I can tell you is that the plane experienced a mechanical problem shortly after takeoff," said the TWA official. "The pilot felt it was best to divert to a closer airport."

"What kind of mechanical problem?" asked a skinny, be-spectacled young man standing next to Sophie.

"I don't have the details," said the woman. "If you'll all take your seats, I promise I'll pass on any information I receive."

"Like hell she will," muttered Bram, storming back to his chair.

Sophie slowly followed, fighting off an intense feeling of anxiety. She'd been sleeping poorly all week and then last night she'd barely had three hours. She needed to keep re-minding herself of that fact as a way of explaining why she was reacting so emotionally. Under other circumstances, she would feel the same anxiety, but she wouldn't be on the verge of coming apart, as she was right now.

"Are you okay?" asked Bram.

As she sat down, she could tell he was watching her. "Fine," she said, afraid to say anything more.

"Can I get you another cup of coffee?"

"Sure. Decaf."

"Would you rather have a drink?"

"I'd rather have my son on the ground."

"We'll hear something soon."

She watched him walk over to the coffee kiosk.

Half an hour later they were still waiting. They'd barely spoken. Words seemed to make it worse, as if discussing the situation made all the terrifying possibilities more real.

Around noon Sophie got up and stood by the windows. Every few minutes a plane would land or take off. It all looked so effortless. Why couldn't Rudy's flight be like that? As she turned around to take another look at the arrivals screen, she noticed that the DELAYED sign next to the St. Louis flight had been replaced by a flashing ARRIVED sign. Others had noticed the change, too. Some were pointing. Some had already approached the desk. The same woman's voice came over the loudspeaker again. "Flight 892 from St. Louis has just landed. Passengers will be deplaning through gate 31 on the red concourse. For those of you waiting for this flight, we thank you for your patience and hope that TWA may serve you again soon."

For the first time since she'd entered the airport, Sophie relaxed.

"What do you suppose happened?" asked Bram, coming up behind her. He cupped his hands around her shoulders and kissed the top of her head.

They watched a 737 slowly pull up to the gate. "I don't know," said Sophie, crossing her hands over her chest to place them on his, "but we're about to find out."

Everything happened quickly after that. In a matter of minutes people were getting off, walking up the long ramp toward their friends and family. Sophie and Bram waited for their first glimpse of Rudy and John. Finally two familiar heads bobbed up the ramp. In an instant Rudy was in Sophie's arms. She felt as if she never wanted to let him go.

Bram hugged John. Then they exchanged partners.

"God, you're both so tan," said Sophie, standing back, unable to take her eyes off her son. "You look wonderful. Even more handsome than when you left."

Rudy, who had a naturally ruddy complexion, blushed an even deeper red. "Come on, Mom. Don't start."

"We thought the flight had been diverted to Chicago," said Bram as they began their long trek up the concourse to the baggage area.

"Some light kept coming on in the cabin," said Rudy, switching his carry-on bag to his other hand. "They told us it meant there was excessive heat in the belly of the plane."

"They didn't tell us that right away," said John, picking up the story. "The head flight attendant only told us about the warning light. But when the pilot finally explained what was going on, he said we were diverting to Chicago. But then the light went off, so they thought it was just a wiring problem. They told us we were in the clear and would be landing in Minneapolis as planned."

Rudy nodded. "About half an hour ago the light came back on again and this time they couldn't get it to go off. I think they were pretty worried. The flight attendants were buzzing around, but nobody was saying much."

Sophie could feel her knees growing weak.

"You okay, Mom?" asked Rudy, glancing over at her.

"Fine." She smiled. She really *was* fine now that he was home.

"But we landed okay," continued John. "I don't mind telling you, I was holding my breath for the last twenty minutes."

"But that's over and done with now and we're back," said Rudy, giving Sophie an unexpected kiss on her cheek. "So what have you two been up to while we were away?"

He clearly wanted to change the subject. That was okay with her. "Oh, not much," she answered.

"Well, now that we're home, we'll liven things up." He elbowed John in the ribs. "You guys are too staid, too calm. You need to get out of your rut, create some adventure in your lives."

"Is that what we need?" asked Sophie.

"Absolutely. Live dangerously. It keeps the juices flowing."

Smiling up at Bram, Sophie said, "We'll work on it."

Pan-Roasted Chicken in Garlic, White Wine, and Fresh Rosemary

3 tablespoons butter
3 tablespoons olive oil
4 cloves garlic, peeled but left whole
1 medium frying chicken, quartered, washed, and patted dry
A small bunch of fresh rosemary, cut into one-inch pieces (You can use 1/2 teaspoon dried rosemary, but the taste is very different)
Salt and freshly ground pepper to taste
3/4 cup dry white wine

After heating the butter and oil in a deep skillet on medium heat, add the garlic, then the chicken quarters, skin side down. When the chicken is browned, turn the pieces over and add the rosemary. Be careful that the garlic doesn't burn and turn black. If this happens, take it out. But if it remains golden, leave it in. Turn the heat down if the cooking oil starts to spatter.

Once the chicken is well browned on both sides, add a sprinkling of salt, several grinds of pepper, and the wine. The wine should bubble for 2 to 3 minutes, then lower the heat until it's just at a simmer. Cover the pan and cook slowly until the chicken is done. (A 2 1/2 pound chicken should take about 35 minutes.) Turn the chicken several times while cooking. If the cooking liquid seems to be drying up, add a couple of tablespoons of water and shake the pan to distribute.

When the chicken is done, remove it to a warm platter. Remove the garlic from the pan, as well as all but 3 tablespoons of the liquid. With the heat on high, add 2 or 3 tablespoons of water to the pan, scraping up the browned bits until you have a flavorful sauce. Adjust seasoning; pour over the chicken.

Torta di limone e ricotta

6 tablespoons soft butter
³⁄₄ cup granulated sugar
¹⁄₃ cup ricotta
3 eggs, separated
1 ¹⁄₂ cups flour
4 tablespoons fresh lemon juice
Grated zest of one lemon
1 ¹⁄₂ teaspoons baking powder
¹⁄₃ cup almonds (skinless; ground to a fine powder in a blender)
Powdered sugar for dusting

Preheat the oven to 350 degrees. Grease a 9-inch spring-form pan, then line the bottom with parchment paper. Grease the paper and dust with flour.

Cream the butter and sugar together, then beat in the ricotta. Next, beat in the egg yolks one at a time. Add 3 tablespoons of the flour, the lemon juice, and the zest. Sift the rest of the flour and the baking powder together and add to the mixture, beating only long enough to incorporate. Stir in the ground almonds.

Beat the egg whites until they form stiff peaks. Fold them carefully into the batter. Turn the mixture into the pan. Bake for 45 minutes, or until a toothpick inserted in the center of the pan comes out clean. Allow the torta to cool for 10 minutes before turning out onto a rack to cool. Dust the cake with a generous amount of powdered sugar before serving.

About the Author

Ellen Hart's other Sophie Greenway novels include *This Little Piggy Went to Murder*, *For Every Evil*, *The Oldest Sin*, and *Murder in the Air*. She is also the author of the Jane Lawless mysteries: *Hallowed Murder*, *Vital Lies*, *Stage Fright*, *A Killing Cure*, *A Small Sacrifice*, and *Faint Praise*. A two-time winner of the Minnesota Book Award for Best Mystery/Detective Fiction, Ms. Hart is a gourmet cook and former chef. She lives in Minneapolis.

The author's E-mail address is ellenhart@earthlink.net.

In Conversation . . .

ELLEN HART
AND SOPHIE GREENWAY

I rarely socialize with my characters when I'm not working with them on a story. My free time between books is usually spent pursuing my many hobbies—mountain climbing, hanggliding, hot air ballooning, race car driving and of course, my favorite, bungie jumping off the Hennepin Avenue Bridge.

After I was assigned this interview, I called Sophie at the Maxfield Plaza in St. Paul, hoping to talk to her the next day. Her secretary put me off, saying that Ms. Greenway had a busy schedule and wouldn't be able to fit me in until the following week. Needless to say, I was perturbed. After all, I was the one who'd discovered her. Ten years ago I spotted her playing the bit part of a brainless sexpot in an old Mickey Spillane novel. I knew she had potential even then. She hasn't always been the easiest person to work with, but then talent, I've found, has its thorns.

The following Monday afternoon, I entered through the heavy glass front doors of the Maxfield Plaza and walked quickly to Sophie's office. Since the last time I'd been at the hotel, new wool carpeting had been installed—replacing the oriental rugs I'd used in the first five books. I wasn't pleased. I was also surprised to see Ethel, the dog I'd given to Sophie and Bram for their second book together, lurching around the lobby, growling at the guests as she sniffed handbags and luggage in search of food. Clearly, matters were getting out of hand.

Just as I was about to knock on Sophie's door, a woman suddenly emerged. I had to move fast to prevent her from running me down. I'd seen her before, but couldn't place the face. She eyed me with thinly veiled contempt, then proceeded to the reception desk.

Sophie's smile was sufficiently welcoming as I entered, but

I knew something was up. Since I was still a little disoriented from my near collision, I lowered myself a bit awkwardly into a chair on the other side of her desk. I straightened my skirt, then took out my notebook. And that's when it occurred to me who the mystery woman was.

SOPHIE: I'm so glad you could make it today, Ellen. What's it been? Five, six months since we last talked?

ELLEN: Let's dispense with the formalities, okay? Why was Patricia Cornwell here?

SOPHIE: Patricia Cornwell? You must be mistaken. That was my, ah . . . therapist.

ELLEN: Your therapist carries a gun under her blazer?

SOPHIE: She has a permit. Now, what did you want to talk to me about?

ELLEN: My editor at Ballantine wants me to interview you.

SOPHIE: You don't sound too thrilled about it.

ELLEN: I'm just a little miffed that you'd talk to Patricia Cornwell behind my back.

SOPHIE: Look . . . even if it was Ms. Cornwell, whatever we had to say to each other is none of your business. I mean that in the nicest possible way.

ELLEN: Sure.

SOPHIE: So . . . this meeting isn't about a new book then?

ELLEN: No, but since I'm here, I should tell you that we've got another one coming up this summer.

SOPHIE: Hmmm. Summertime. When exactly? I hadn't penciled that in.

ELLEN: We start the story conferences in July.

SOPHIE: Actually I may have a conflict. (*Excuses herself to answer her intercom*) Yes? . . .

SECRETARY: Ms. Greenway, you have a call from Mr. Leonard on line one. He's calling long distance—from LA.

SOPHIE: Tell him I'll return his call in a few minutes.

ELLEN: Mr. Leonard? Elmore Leonard?

SOPHIE: No, Ellen. Bob Leonard, my dentist.

ELLEN: Your dentist lives in California?

SOPHIE: It's a global economy now, dear. You really need to get out more—away from your computer and off those mountain tops.

ELLEN: Say, why the new look? The Joan Crawford eyebrows? And all the heavy red lipstick? That isn't you.

SOPHIE: All actresses like to stretch. I'm . . . still . . . evolving, shall we say.

ELLEN: Where's Bram, by the way?

SOPHIE: He's having lunch with . . . friends.

ELLEN: You make that sound pregnant with meaning.

SOPHIE: Well, some of your mystery writing pals around the Twin Cities have really been wining and dining him lately. After our success with *Murder in the Air*, he's become quite the hot property. Authors are always looking for good talent, you know.

ELLEN: What authors? I demand to know.

SOPHIE: Oh, R.D. Zimmerman. M.D. Lake. Kent Krueger. All the usual Minnesota suspects.

ELLEN: What ingratitude! I've made you and Bram into the Nick and Nora of the new millennium! And this is how you treat me? Did I ever tell you the story of where I found Bram?

SOPHIE: I've heard this a million times—

ELLEN: Doing a bad Cary Grant imitation in an old Bette Davis biography.

SOPHIE: He's come a long way since then. Actually . . . he's even been talking to P.D. James recently.

ELLEN: Why?

SOPHIE: He does a wonderful English accent, you know.

ELLEN: I get it now. My characters are preparing to jump ship! This is mutiny!

SOPHIE: He's even been contacted by Anne Rice.

ELLEN: He's going to become a vampire?

SOPHIE: A mummy.

ELLEN: But we're under contract for one more book! You can't just leave me high and dry.

SOPHIE: We won't. We're nothing if not professional. But after that . . . I think you better contact my agent.

ELLEN: When did you get an agent?

SOPHIE: After I had dinner with Mary Higgins Clark in New York last week. She recommended one.

ELLEN: Who?

SOPHIE: Atticus Finch.

ELLEN: The lawyer in *To Kill a Mockingbird*?

SOPHIE: He's branching out. He's been stuck in that small Southern town far too long. You get moldy after a while. I'm not kidding. Anyway, why don't you have your people call my people and set up the dates for the story conference on the new book.

ELLEN: I don't believe this. I made you what you are today.

SOPHIE: You could have made me a little thinner and a little younger. But would you ask my advice?

ELLEN: You're a character.

SOPHIE: And your point would be?

ELLEN: You can eat anything you want in my books and you don't gain weight.

SOPHIE: Unlike you.

ELLEN: This interview is over.

SOPHIE: Don't go away mad. But do close the door on your way out.

ELLEN: Wait until my editor hears about all this.

SOPHIE: You mean Joe Blades? Last I heard, he was negotiating a juicy part in a Jackie Collins novel—one of her infamous love epics, I'm told.

ELLEN: I need a drink.

If you enjoyed
SLICE AND DICE, savor all of
the Sophie Greenway mysteries
by ELLEN HART

THIS LITTLE PIGGY WENT TO MURDER

FOR EVERY EVIL

THE OLDEST SIN

MURDER IN THE AIR

SLICE AND DICE